PRAISE FOR AUTHOR REKTOK ROSS

Rektok Ross offers "readers genuinely diverse characters, each of whom continues to grow throughout the narrative... Brace for impact readers, [Ross] holds little back."

—*Kirkus Reviews*

Rektok Ross has "inborn talent for the kind of narrative driven storytelling that makes for a compulsive page turning read from cover to cover... Unreservedly recommended..."

—*Midwest Book Review*

"If you like action, suspense, and the horror real life can sometimes dish out, you can't go wrong... Rektok Ross delivers!"

—*Reader Views*

"[Ross] does a great job of making you care for [her] characters, keeps you guessing, and [gives] lots of chills."

—*Double the Books*

"Ross crafts relatable, multi-dimensional characters and weaves together her signature recipe of thrills, chills, romance, and social commentary."

—*Temple of Geek*

Rektok Ross is "an exciting addition to the YA scene."

—Evelyn Skye, *New York Times* best-selling author of *The Crown's Game*

"Ross' thrillers are fast-paced and feature capable women in the lead. There's nothing to not like!"

—*Popverse*

PRAISE FOR SKI WEEKEND

*Winner of the WILLA Literary Awards, San Francisco Book Festival Awards, National Indie Excellence Awards, Next Generation Indie Book Awards, Independent Press Awards, Reader Views Literary Awards, CIBA Dante Rossetti Book Awards, Readers' Favorite Book Awards, American Fiction Awards, IAN Book of the Year Awards, and Firebird Awards!

Named a Best Book of the Year by Cosmopolitan, Entertainment Weekly, Yahoo!Life, Parade, Brit + Co., Book Riot, J-14, The Strand, She Reads, and more!

"This is a suspenseful book that had me thoroughly hooked from page one… The emotional journey of *Ski Weekend* is relentless…"

—*Readers' Favorite*

"Rektok Ross delivers an absolute dynamic story packed with goofy teens, heart-stopping moments, romantic tension, and one adorable pup in this adrenaline-filled survival story."

—*BooknBrunch*

"Rektok Ross thrills readers with an electrifying winter tale that will have you wondering if that snow-filled adventure you've been planning is worth risking your life!"

—*Key Biscayne Magazine*

"A pacey thriller with moments of great tenderness—and spine-chilling horror."

—Lauren Kate, *New York Times* best-selling author of *Fallen*

"A nail-biter with some surprising moments. Recommended for high school and YA collections."

—*School Library Journal*

"Hand this to students who like thrillers and books about survival!"
—*Youth Services Book Review*

"Constantly twisting and emotionally relentless, *Ski Weekend* is a story of survival, friendship, and family… Alternately heartbreaking and hopeful—a chilling, thrilling read."
—Laurie Elizabeth Flynn, bestselling author of *The Girls Are All So Nice Here*

"This book will send so many chills up your spine, you'll feel like you're alongside the snowbound characters. The only time I don't recommend reading this book is right before bed. You won't be able to sleep, and you won't want to."
—Jeff Zentner, award-winning author of *Rayne & Delilah's Midnight Matinee*

"All the intensity and thrills of *The Hunger Games* packed into one car over a snowy weekend. Secrets, lies, strong characters, and twists will keep readers turning pages. If you've ever wondered how far you would go to survive, you need to read this book."
—Eileen Cook, author of *You Owe Me a Murder*

"Ripped from the headlines, *Ski Weekend* is so real you'll be shivering with the characters, fighting the elements, and asking yourself—what would you be willing to do to survive? Forget Netflix and chill. Binge this book."
—Sorboni Banerjee, Emmy Award–winning journalist and author of *Red as Blood*

"Ross weaves a stirring tale where each of her characters wrestle with choices that could result in life or death—some survive, and some don't."
—Paul Greci, award-winning author of *Surviving Bear Island* and *The Wild Lands*

SALEM'S
FALL

ALSO BY REKTOK ROSS

Writing as Rektok Ross:

DARK SEASONS THRILLER SERIES

Ski Weekend

Summer Rental

Spring Harvest

Salem's Fall

STANDALONE TITLES

The Pop Star and the Devil

*

Writing as L.G. Ross:

Prodigal

NEVER MISS A RELEASE.

Get exclusive giveaways, review copies, and enter to win free gifts and more. Subscribe to my newsletter:

www.RektokRoss.com

SALEM'S FALL

A THRILLER

REKTOK ROSS

Ic13 Books

Copyright © 2025 Rektok Ross
All rights reserved.

No part of this book may be reproduced in any form or by any electronic or mechanical means, including information storage and retrieval systems, without prior written permission from the publisher.

This is a work of fiction. Names, characters, businesses, places, events, and incidents are either the products of the author's imagination or used in a fictitious manner. Any resemblance to actual persons, living or dead, or actual events is purely coincidental and not intended by the author.

Published by Ic13 Books

Wilmington, Delaware, USA, 19808

www.Ic13Books.com
Ic13 Books name and the Ic13 Books logo are trademarks of Ic13 Books or its affiliates.

Published 2025

Printed in the United States of America

Print ISBN: 978-0-9882568-9-7
E-ISBN: 978-0-9882568-8-0

Library of Congress Control Number: 2025910995

Cover design by Dane Low and team
Interior design by Robert Harrison

For those who fell for the monster—and learned how to bite back.

Double, double toil and trouble; Fire burn, and caldron bubble.

—William Shakespeare, *Macbeth*

Be careful hunting witches. The darkness doesn't know the difference.

—From *Blood and Bone: New England's Hidden Histories of Magic, Mysteries, and the Occult*

CHAPTER 1

Boston, Massachusetts
October 1 (Four Weeks Until Halloween)

The whooshing of the heater kicks on, startling me as it echoes through the empty halls of Whitehall & Rowe. I'm all alone and still getting accustomed to the solitude. The law firm is usually bustling with the energy of a high-octane circus, but tonight, it feels more like a tomb. Almost everyone else is crammed into a hotel conference room downtown, across from the courthouse, prepping for Monday's big trial. Normally, I'd be right there with them, mainlining Starbucks and helping the partners prepare their openings, but instead, I'm here in my tiny office, working on a total snoozefest research memo. This is my punishment for failure.

I glance up at the glowing computer screen, my frustration simmering as I angrily peck away at the keyboard.

Top of my class at Harvard Law.

Summa cum laude.

Editor of the *Law Review*.

And yet, here I am, writing a ridiculous memo a first-year law student could handle, sidelined from the real work because I missed some stupid forensic report on my last case. There was no real harm done, but one misstep was all it took to go from rising star to the firm's black sheep. Now I'm stuck in junior associate purgatory while one of the biggest white-collar criminal trials of the year is about to start. Charles Brandt, CFO of juggernaut energy company Harborline Energy Corp., is accused of securities fraud. The case made all the papers. Brandt could go away for the rest of his life if he's found guilty—and my firm is defending him.

Of course we are.

Everyone knows we're the best criminal defense firm in Boston.

Woodsen is only here because of her looks.

I shake my head, shoving aside the memory of Mark Sharma's petty insults. Mark is such an asshole. He'd been a complete dick when I'd screwed up a few weeks ago, telling anyone who'd listen that I didn't belong here. Mark is just a bitter senior associate at the firm who's been gunning for my failure ever since I turned him down for drinks a few months ago.

I've dealt with guys like him my whole life. Because of the way I look, people are always quick to judge me. Underestimate me. I've heard it all before: The professors thought I was pretty—that must be why I got good grades. The faculty advisor had a crush on me—that must be why I got the best internships. I slept with hiring partners—that must be how I got my job at the most coveted criminal defense firm in the state.

Of course, none of it was accurate, and it all ignored the real truth: I was smart and worked my ass off. I kept my head down. I didn't party or drink or do drugs. And I was willing to do whatever it took to succeed, *except* sleep my way to the top.

Still, all they saw was blonde hair and big boobs.

Whatever. Screw 'em.

I pull my focus back to the computer screen, the lines of text blurring as my vision narrows. No, I refuse to be that girl, the one who fades into the background and accepts her fate. I have too much to prove. If they want a research memo, I'm going to write them the best goddamn research memo this firm has ever seen.

Lucky hops onto my work desk, his sleek black fur catching the fluorescent light. It's ironic, having a black cat and living just miles away from Salem's Fall, a town famous around the world for its witch trials. Growing up in New England, I'd always heard black cats were supposed to be bad luck, but Lucky's become family ever since I found him in an alley eight years ago. The only family I really have around anymore besides my little sister Madison and my Aunt Aggie.

My cat stretches out, yawning like he's had the hardest day of all, when he's pretty much done nothing but gotten two delicious meals, oodles of treats, and countless naps.

"Tough life, kiddo," I say, chuckling as I scratch behind his ears. "Don't know how you do it."

Lucky purrs in response, unfazed. Technically, we aren't supposed to have pets in the office, but since this is going to be another brutally late night for me—and no one else is here anyway—I figure some rules are meant to be broken.

My phone buzzes on the table, and I groan as I see my little sister's name flashing on the screen.

"Hey, sis! Guess where I am?"

Madison's voice is too bright, too bubbly. Loud music pumping in the background tells me all I need to know.

She's drunk.

"Maddie, you better not be calling me from a bar."

"C'mon, James. It's Friday night!"

"And midterms are coming up." I pinch the bridge of my nose. "You should be in the library—studying!"

She giggles into the phone. "Well… I *am* with David, the hot guy from my study group I told you about. Doesn't that count?"

"No." I rub my temples, one finger poised over the red "End" button. "Mads, I gotta get this memo done. Go home—please!"

"Aww, don't be like that. This is your fault anyway." I can practically hear her pouting into the phone. "We were supposed to go to dinner tonight, remember? And you flaked. *Again.*"

"Hey, someone's gotta pay rent and keep the pantry stocked with your organic gluten-free mac 'n' cheese and overpriced protein bars," I fire back.

"Ha ha, very funny." She huffs. "C'mon, Jamie. You always do this. You're always blowing me off for some stupid work thing—"

"Hanging up now—"

"Fine, whatever. Can you Venmo me drink money at least?" Her voice turns pleading, and I can picture her standing inside some too-crowded bar, swaying in her high heels and some cute new dress she probably charged to my credit card without asking. "We want to get another round."

"You promised you'd stay in and study tonight," I say, trying to sound stern, though a part of me wishes I could trade places with her.

God, I'd love to be out. Dancing. Drinking. Forgetting all about this damn job for a few hours. But unlike Maddie—a college junior with a decent fake ID and no real responsibilities—I don't have that luxury. I never have, not even when I was her age. I'd always been too busy working side jobs and hustling, taking care of her.

"Just one more drink, I promise! He's soooo cute. You'd really like him—"

"Madison—"

"Come on, help a sister out," she says. "Remember, you're the one that taught me not to let guys buy my drinks at the bar. So really, I'm just doing what you told me…"

I sigh. I'm supposed to be the hotshot lawyer, but, even wasted, my little sister can negotiate circles around me. If only she'd apply those skills to her studies.

"*Strangers,*" I correct. "I told you not to let strangers buy your drinks. Let this David idiot buy you all the drinks he wants. He can probably afford it–unlike me." I glance at the clock. It's almost midnight, and I'm too tired to keep arguing. "I'll send enough for one more round. Then straight home, okay?"

"Thanks! Love youuuuuu!"

Madison hangs up, and I quickly pull up the app, sending her money. I lean back in my chair, wondering for a moment what it must be like to be Madison. How would it feel to be free of all responsibility and worry? My constant and draining sense of duty. My fear of failure. Ever since our mother died —and Dad went to prison for her murder—it's been my job to take care of Madison. She doesn't know the half of what it costs me, but if I don't take care of her, who will?

Lucky nudges me impatiently with his cold nose, hungry for a treat. I give him a few catnip crunchies from my bag, and after eating them, he closes his eyes and drifts off to sleep. Off in the distance, the firm's main phone line starts to ring over and over. Even the late-night receptionist has gone home by now.

I settle back at my desk, staring angrily at my memo again. I'm supposed to be summarizing the current state of the law for expungement of criminal records for minors, listing out all the procedures. Some senior partner's spoiled teenage daughter got caught shoplifting, and I need to help clear her record so she can get into an Ivy League school her daddy probably bought her way into. Not exactly the thrilling work I dreamed of during my law school days.

I skim through a few Westlaw articles online, my eyes darting between the text on the screen and my own half-written sentences. The assigning partner is expecting this on his desk tomorrow at 7 a.m., sharp. My fingers hover over the keyboard as I glance at the clock again. My deadline is looming, and I can't afford another screwup, even on something as dumb as this.

I type into the search bar the address to a somewhat controversial legal website my best friend from law school, Katherine "Katie" Tang, told me about. They have old memos and briefs on there. It's not something any self-respecting attorney would ordinarily use—sometimes the research is outdated. And relying on it too heavily? That's plagiarism.

Still, this is stupid busy work, and I could use a few hours of sleep tonight. Plus, someone's gotta get home and make sure my rascal of a sister makes it back at a decent hour.

For a moment, I contemplate sleep and Maddie versus a teeny, tiny little ethics flub. My moral compass quickly loses, and it's not even close. Just this once, right? It's not like anyone's going to know. It's just a minor expungement, erasing a stupid shoplifting case for an entitled brat. This isn't exactly life-or-death.

"Whatever it takes," I murmur, taking a deep breath and copying and pasting.

After that, all that's left is a spell check. I'm almost done with the memo when my desk phone rings, the sound jarring in the otherwise silent building.

"James Woodsen," I say, putting the call on speaker so I can keep typing.

"Where the hell is everyone?"

The booming voice on the other end is Quinn Kensington, one of the firm's most powerful partners.

I straighten in my seat, a jolt of adrenaline coursing through my system. At only thirty-one, Quinn Kensington is the youngest senior partner at the firm. He was just named a

"Top 40 Under 40 Attorney" in the entire metro area and is the only son of state Senator George Kensington. He's also movie-star handsome to boot.

Quinn is the partner responsible for hiring me, which is both a blessing and a curse. A blessing because being under Quinn's wing is the perfect place for any ambitious junior associate—unless said ambitious junior associate is also a pretty blonde, and then everyone assumes you were only hired because you must be sleeping with him. And I am very definitely *not*.

"They're all in prep for the Brandt trial," I answer. "Why? What's going on?"

"We've just been assigned a new high-profile murder case." He speaks fast, his words sharp.

"Okay... and?"

This is nothing new. We're Whitehall & Rowe. We get new high-profile murder cases every week.

"It's the Halloween Heiress Murder, Woodsen!" he snaps.

I suck in a deep breath.

"No way..."

The Halloween Heiress Murder is the murder case of the decade—maybe the century. It's been all over the news for the past year.

Vivienne Van Buren, a high-profile socialite, was found stabbed to death last Halloween. There was talk of dark cults and satanic panic. No one knew what was real and what wasn't. The murder itself was beyond bloody and gruesome, but that alone wasn't what made it so notorious. It was the fact that she was the fiancée of Damien Blackhollow—the gorgeous billionaire mogul whose family owns half of New England.

"Someone's finally been arrested?" I ask, trying to keep my voice steady. This is huge!

"Someone, yeah." Quinn makes a strange sound in the back of his throat. "You could definitely say that…"

A flash of disappointment hits me, and I sink low into my chair. I can't believe our firm has the Halloween Heiress Murder, and I'm going to be stuck writing damn memos for the foreseeable future.

"That's awesome, Quinn. Congrats."

"You're the only one in the office right now, Woodsen? Are you sure there's no one else?" he prods. "Anyone else?"

I groan, looking around the empty office. "Yeah, Quinn. I'm sure."

He sighs. "Okay, listen up. I need you to meet me at the criminal courthouse in five hours for the bail hearing." He pauses hesitantly. "Can you do that? No screwups this time."

I try not to feel insulted by his tone. Sure, I understand this is a huge case, and right now, my reputation is on the rocks, but posting bail is something a damn paralegal can do. Not that I have anything against paralegals, but, well, it's a bit of an ego knock.

"Yeah, Quinn. Of course I can do that." I take a deep breath. "But listen, I understand if you still don't trust me. I'm sure you can find someone else when the office opens in a few hours?"

"Can't wait!" he snaps. "We have to get the client out of there before the media gets hold of this. It's going to be a fucking shitshow once word gets out."

"I won't let you down again, Quinn," I say and hit send on my email, shooting off my expungement research memo. "I promise."

"I hope not. I'll send you the details."

"Okay, got it," I say, excitement curling in my belly as I grab my laptop and my dog-eared copy of the local court rules, and tuck Lucky into my tote bag. He mewls loudly, annoyed to be woken up from his beauty sleep. "Wait—Quinn, who is it? Who's the client?"

"Six a.m. on the dot," he says, ignoring my question. "Do *not* be late!"

The line goes dead, and I'm left staring at the phone, still in disbelief.

Holy shit.

The Halloween Heiress Murder. The case every criminal defense lawyer in the state wants, and it's landed right in my lap. I don't know whether to feel ecstatic or terrified. Maybe both. But one thing's for sure—I'm not writing any more memos this weekend. If things go well tomorrow, I'm about to be sitting front and center at the biggest murder case of the year.

CHAPTER 2

The early morning sky is still dull with the remnants of dawn as I approach the Boston Criminal Courthouse steps. My heart beats with exhilaration as I stare up at the massive building, an imposing fortress of glass and concrete that both intimidates and draws me in. It's a place where lives are literally remade or undone, and I can't help but feel excited by the sight before me.

At the top of the stairs stands Quinn, strikingly young and devastatingly handsome, the firm's golden boy and favorite son of New England's political elite. Tall and effortlessly charismatic, his face is all chiseled angles and controlled expression, commanding attention without a word. It's a face made for the cover of a magazine, though he prefers high-powered boardrooms and court hearings instead.

I first met Quinn when I was in my second year of law school, nervous but determined, as I walked into the interview room at Whitehall & Rowe. I'd expected to see some aging, uptight, gray-haired man, just like I'd met with at almost every other white-shoe law firm I'd interviewed at. Instead, I encountered this young hotshot in a sleek suit, not all that much older than me, but already carrying himself with a quiet, magnetic confidence. I felt starstruck, unprepared, like I'd walked onto a movie set instead of a law firm.

But then he smiled, warm and encouraging, and all my nerves settled.

We connected right away. He must have pulled for me behind the scenes because I got the summer associate job, and he's been a mentor and friend to me ever since.

"Woodsen," he greets me, his tone neutral, not unkind, but there's an edge that wasn't there weeks ago. I still feel horrible. I know I let down more than just myself when I screwed up our last case.

I'd been the junior associate on the team representing Allan Michelle, a prominent real estate broker accused of murdering his business partner. Buried in a stack of lab files was a forensic report I'd skimmed too quickly—a partial DNA match that helped our client and pointed to someone else. It wasn't the smoking gun, and someone else would've caught it eventually. Still, it was my job to catch it first.

I'd been exhausted, eager to move past the tedious document review, impatient to prove myself on a bigger stage. And in my rush, I got sloppy. Missed something I shouldn't have. It also didn't help that I wasn't trained to read lab reports—not exactly a skill they teach in law school.

Still, no excuses. It was a careless mistake, and it was mine.

Luckily, a senior paralegal flagged it and brought it to Quinn's attention. The case never truly went sideways, but the damage to my reputation? That was already done.

I've been climbing uphill ever since.

"Morning," I say to Quinn, feeling a bit jittery—not just because of him, though that's part of it. The guilt of disappointing him still lingers, but so does the weight of today. It's not every day I'm thrown into the deep end of one of the most high-profile murder cases Boston has ever seen.

Quinn's eyes flick over me, assessing, and I'm glad I took a few extra minutes to look presentable before running out the door. My blonde hair is tucked into a chic French braid and my makeup is tasteful. It's just enough to make my blue eyes pop and give my lips a soft pink hue, nothing overdone. I'd slipped into the nicest suit I owned: a pale pink tailored tweed that's feminine yet professional. It isn't designer, but the clean lines give it an expensive look. I know appearances are important to Quinn.

Plus, there's our mysterious client. Quinn still hasn't told me who it is.

"You look good," he says, that charming half-smile I'd been missing now on his face, and a warm satisfaction settles in my chest at his approval. "Let's go. The client is waiting for us inside."

I follow him through the courthouse double doors and down the hallway, the heavy atmosphere of the building pressing in on me. Marble floors. Dark wood paneling. The faint scent of coffee wafting through the halls. The early morning bustle is minimal, a few clerks moving through the corridors, some security guards and police, unaware of the storm brewing. It's unusually quiet, not just because of the hour, but because it's Saturday—court opened solely for this emergency hearing, a rare weekend exception. By the time the media gets wind of things, it'll be chaos in here.

We reach a small conference room just off the main hallway and take our seats. I glance up at the clock on the wall. The hearing is in two hours. Our client should arrive any minute, and I'm filled with anticipation as we wait.

"How do you feel?" Quinn asks me, his voice softening with a bit of concern. "You ready for this?"

"I'm fine," I say, trying to sound more confident than I feel. "Just nervous."

Quinn watches me for a moment longer, as if weighing my readiness. There's something else in his gaze—something more personal. It's always there, simmering beneath the surface, but never quite acknowledged. The tension between us has grown over time, but neither of us dares cross that line.

"You should be nervous, Woodsen," he says bluntly, his striking honey-colored eyes locking onto mine, their intensity unnerving. "The entire metroplex—hell, the entire state—is going to be watching us. This case could make or break your career and mine. Our client... he's tricky."

For the first time, his usual calm-as-a-cucumber demeanor betrays just a hint of tension as he adjusts his jacket. The way his fingers twirl around his designer Cartier cufflinks makes me realize that even the unshakeable Quinn Alexander Kensington can be rattled.

"Here, look for yourself," he says and hands me the case file. At the very top is a name that sends shivers down my spine.

I gasp.

"Our client is *Damien Blackhollow*?"

"Unfortunately." Quinn sighs, his jaw clenching before he continues, "I've known the man almost my whole life. There's no other way to say this—he's dangerous, James. Not just because of what he's been accused of, but because of who he is. He's got too much power and money. He's grown up his whole life believing he's untouchable, and perhaps he was. Until now." He swallows hard. "He isn't a good guy, and he plays by his own rules. He's not someone you let your guard down around. Got it?"

A prickle of unease creeps up my neck. Damien Blackhollow isn't just another client—he's the newly minted CEO of Blackhollow Industries, a multibillion-dollar empire dominating venture capital, private equity, and cutting-edge tech across New England. His family's legacy stretches back generations, built on cut-throat deals and ruthless precision. It had been big news when Damien had inherited it all after his father's untimely death a few years ago.

His father, Ian Blackhollow, was found floating face down in the indoor pool of their sprawling Nantucket summer estate, still dressed in his evening attire. The official ruling was accidental drowning, that he'd slipped near the water on his way to a dinner party, but there'd been hushed whispers and rumors that perhaps Damien had something to do with it in order to seize control of the company. Nothing ever came of it, though.

"You think he did it?" I ask in a hushed whisper.

Quinn shrugs. "I met with him briefly last night after the arrest. He claims to be innocent, but I guess we'll find out," he says, his eyes flicking up to the clock. "He should be here any minute. Stay sharp."

A moment later, in strolls Damien Blackhollow, as if he owns the place.

The man's presence is magnetic and unsettling, impossible to ignore. His midnight-black hair is styled back with a precision that feels almost surgical, exposing the sharp angles of cheekbones that could cut glass. His eyes are a piercing, nearly black shade, holding an intensity that borders on predatory, as if he's sizing up not just the room, but everyone in it. He's impeccably dressed despite the night spent in jail. Dark suit, perfectly tailored to his muscular frame, and a shiny Audemars Piguet watch glinting on his wrist. It's the kind of watch that costs more than most people's annual salary.

"Ah, Quinn, good to see you," he says smoothly, as if greeting a friend at a dinner party, his voice a rich baritone that rolls off him like silk. He takes the seat across from us and flicks his wrist, dismissing the two police guards at his sides. "And I see you've brought company."

His eyes lock on mine and it feels like the air shifts. There's something unnerving about the way he looks at me, a hint of amusement playing at the edges of his lips.

"This is James Woodsen," Quinn says with a curt nod in my direction. "She'll be assisting me today."

Damien's gaze continues to linger on me, a smirk forming. "James. Such a masculine name for a pretty girl."

I meet his gaze, determined not to let him rattle me. "It's unisex," I say drolly.

"Of course." His smirk widens, but there's something cold in his eyes. "Would you be a dear and grab me a coffee, James? It's been a long night, as you can imagine."

I suppress the twinge of annoyance that flares in my gut. Because of my age, looks, and gender, powerful men like this are always assuming I'm a secretary. Normally, I might say something to put the man in his place, but seeing as I'm already on thin ice, I decide not pissing off such an important client is the smart move.

"No problem." I go to stand, but Quinn puts a warm hand on my shoulder, pushing me down.

"James is my associate," he says. "Not your errand girl."

"Oh, I see." Damien exhales a quiet chuckle, the sound low and deliberate. "My apologies."

There's an unspoken tension in the room as the two men exchange looks. Whatever history exists between Quinn and Damien, it's clear they're not fond of each other.

"It's fine, Quinn. I don't mind," I say, trying to ease the tension. I turn to give Damien a forced smile. "I need a cup myself anyway."

"Let's begin, then, shall we? We don't have much time before the hearing," Quinn says, steering the conversation back to business as I walk over to the drink setup and grab three heaping mugs of coffee for everyone. "Let's go over the basics. What do you know about the state's case against you?"

Damien leans back in his chair, settling in. "Not a whole lot. They told me last night I've been charged with first-degree murder, as you know." His tone is casual, as if he's discussing the weather. "They didn't say much else."

I return with everyone's drinks and take my seat next to Quinn.

"Today is just the arraignment and bail hearing," Quinn explains as he studies the file and shuffles through paperwork, going over the arrest report. "The judge will inform us of the specific charges. We'll argue for bail. The District Attorney is going to push hard against it given the severity of the charges. Don Smith is a slimy shark, and he's going to fight for all he's worth on this case—you may have heard he's gunning for Attorney General? He's going to see you as his steppingstone to that, but we have some strong points in our favor."

Damien raises an eyebrow. "Such as?"

"You have no prior criminal record," Quinn says, reading from his hearing notes now. "You're a prominent businessman with strong ties to the community. We'll be able to argue that you're not a flight risk and pose no threat to the public."

"And do you think you'll win?"

Quinn's shoulders straighten, a cocky grin on his lips. "I've never lost a bail hearing, and I don't intend to start today."

Damien studies Quinn for a moment, his fingers tapping idly against the table, a slow, deliberate rhythm.

"You sound confident. I hope you're right," he says.

"I know Judge Matheson well," Quinn says. "She's tough but fair, and she's got a soft spot for me. I was on crew with her son at Princeton, and she's close with Dad."

"Ah, Senator Kensington. Hope your father is doing well these days." Damien glances at me again, the intensity of his gaze warms my skin, unwelcome and electric. "And you, James? How are you finding all of this? I imagine a violent murder trial is a bit… unsavory."

There's something in his voice, something taunting, challenging, like a cat playing with its meal.

"I enjoy felony cases very much, and I'm looking forward to being a part of your legal team. We'll do everything we can to make sure justice prevails." I choose my words carefully. It's against firm policy to promise him a win, but I want to sound confident too, like Quinn sounds.

Damien chuckles softly. "Oh, I imagine you will, James."

"We'll meet you in the courtroom, Blackhollow." Quinn stands and gives Damien a hard look. "I've got everything handled. Once we're in there, don't speak unless I tell you to."

"I'll be on my very best behavior. Don't worry," Damien says, giving Quinn a mock salute, but there's a sharpness behind his smile.

Quinn grabs the police guards who have been waiting patiently outside during our meeting, and we all head together to the courtroom to wait for the judge to arrive.

Quinn and I take our seats at the defense counsel table, Damien sitting between us. My shoulder is mere inches from his, and I can feel the heat radiating off him. His presence is electrifying, a magnetic pull that's impossible to ignore. I swallow, trying to keep my expression steady, but my pulse thrums in my ears, a mix of nerves.

My first major hearing.

My first go at being Quinn's second chair.

And, yes, the first time I've ever been this close to a man as powerful and intimidating as Damien Blackhollow.

The courtroom quickly begins to fill, and I realize with alarm that word of Damien's arrest has already spread like wildfire. Every pair of eyes scans the room, the energy palpable. People lean in, whispering in excitement, already building their own narratives.

A few moments later, the District Attorney strides in with his team, looking every bit the bulldog he's known to be. Don Smith is an older man with a balding head and a broad, thick frame that fills out his suit in a way that's more solid than polished. Despite his slightly rumpled appearance, there's an undeniable force about him—a kind of intimidating presence that suggests he's more than capable of tearing through any defense if given the chance.

Katie works for the DA's office, and I've heard horror stories about the man. She says he rides his team like Seabiscuit. Sure enough, a bunch of nervous-looking associates trail behind him in a neat line, carrying stacks of files and exchanging panicked looks and last-minute whispers.

Then the judge enters, small and slight, but commanding. Flanked by her clerk and the court reporter, she steps up to the bench, her presence immediately quieting the room. Her silver hair is pinned back meticulously, her black judicial robes lending her an air of authority and quiet power. Judge Ruth Matheson is known in legal circles for her sharp mind and her insistence on fairness. We're lucky to have her.

An almost electric stillness grips the room as the hearing begins. Damien stands beside us, his expression giving nothing away as Judge Matheson reads the charges. It all feels surreal as the judge describes in graphic detail the horrific and brutal slaying of Ms. Van Buren—the dozens of knife wounds, her blood covering the walls and floors of the bedroom.

I steal a glance at Damien, but his face remains impassive. He doesn't even flinch, doesn't react. I don't know how he can be so calm. My palms are damp, a sheen of sweat prickling at the back of my neck—and I'm just the attorney.

Then it's time to decide bail.

My fingers hover over the keyboard, taking notes, ready to access case law or pull up relevant precedent should the judge ask for it. The DA stands, his voice resonating through the packed courtroom.

"Your Honor, we're asking that bail be denied. Mr. Blackhollow is a billionaire with significant resources and poses a serious flight risk," he says. "He's accused of a heinous crime

—one that shows a clear and present danger to the community."

I glance at Quinn as he stands to argue. This is where the real battle begins.

Quinn clears his throat, his voice confident. "Your Honor, I'd like to direct the court's attention to *Commonwealth v. Hodge*, which reminds us that bail should be set with careful consideration of an accused's ties to the community and the presumption of innocence. Mr. Blackhollow has no prior criminal record, is a well-regarded businessman, and maintains deep roots here in Boston." He pauses, letting the weight of his words settle before continuing, "He's willing to surrender his passport and comply with any conditions the court deems necessary. There's no evidence to suggest he's a flight risk, nor does he pose any actual threat to public safety."

The DA scoffs. "Your Honor, with all due respect, I believe the brutality of this crime underscores the threat to the public," he says, his tone dripping with disdain. "Ms. Van Buren suffered twenty-seven stab wounds—her head almost *decapitated* from her body. This was the work of some unhinged madman—one who could turn dangerous again if left unchecked. The people of Massachusetts deserve protection."

"We strongly disagree, Your Honor," Quinn says, raising his voice. "*Commonwealth v. Muckle* is instructive here. The court in *Muckle* stressed that the conditions of release should account for the actual behavior of the defendant, rather than mere speculation as to what they could or could not do if bail were granted. In Mr. Blackhollow's case, any perceived risk can be fully mitigated through house arrest, electronic monitoring, and passport surrender."

The judge's gaze sweeps over both attorneys, her expression thoughtful as she weighs the arguments. The room holds its breath as the silence stretches, every eye fixed on the bench.

Finally, she speaks, her tone authoritative. "Mr. Blackhollow will be granted bail, set at two million dollars. He'll be placed under house arrest, subject to electronic monitoring, and is to surrender his passport and remain within the Commonwealth until trial."

"But Your Honor—"

The judge bangs her gavel. "We're adjourned," she says and gives the DA a dismissive, annoyed look.

Quinn offers a measured nod in my direction. It's a victory, but a small one.

Damien's face betrays nothing, no indication of relief or concern, as a deputy returns to collect him and take him to the holding room. "I expect regular updates from you," he says to Quinn, but his eyes linger on me. A smile, almost baiting, pulls at his lips. "And, James, I'm counting on you to keep him on his toes."

I nod back, not knowing the proper way to respond to that.

After Damien is escorted away, we head outside the courthouse and are immediately greeted by Mark Sharma—the jackass. My nemesis is out of breath, as if he'd sprinted over to catch us, his entire body vibrating with eagerness. The senior associate is dressed sharply in a pinstripe suit and a flashy, blindingly bright tie, his hair slicked back with too much product. Grudgingly, I have to admit that if not for his utterly odious personality, he'd probably be considered attractive by most people's standards.

"Sorry I'm late," he says, his eyes shifting from Quinn to me, lingering just a beat too long on my face. "We were up all night next door, getting ready for the Brandt trial on Monday. I got here as soon as I heard you needed help."

I barely suppress a groan. What a suck-up.

"Thanks for coming by so quickly," Quinn says. "We could use more hands on this. You think the trial team can spare your hours?"

"Absolutely."

"Good, because this is going to be massive. All hands on deck." Quinn gives us both a stern look. "I need you both back in my office early tomorrow morning to go over details. Mark, get us one of the lead trial paralegals and make sure we've got secretarial support." Without waiting for a response, he pulls out his phone and dials, already shifting into action. As he strides toward the parking lot, his voice is brisk, all business. "And, guys, be prepared for a long day."

As soon as Quinn is gone, Mark's eyes lock on mine with a mixture of condescension and disdain. I know exactly what's coming.

"Looks like I'll be playing babysitter," he sneers. "Hope you're up for this one, Woodsen. Wouldn't want another *'incident'*."

My stomach tightens, but I refuse to give this asshole the satisfaction of a reaction.

"I can handle it."

He chuckles, low and smug. "Based on your last fuck-up, I respectfully disagree. You should stick to research memos—you're not ready for this." He gives me a sleazy wink. "But hey, keep wearing those little pink suits and smiling pretty. Maybe Quinn won't notice you've got no idea what the hell you're doing."

Even if he's just trying to intimidate me, his warning has the intended effect. Uncertainty creeps in, wrapping around my resolve like a vise. I don't want to believe his words—don't want to give them power—but deep down, a quiet, insidious voice whispers:

What if he's right?

CHAPTER 3

Damien Blackhollow is released from jail and pays his eye-watering two-million-dollar bail the way most people order coffee—effortlessly.

It takes under an hour for his financial team to wire the money to the court. I can almost picture it: some fancy accountant transferring all that cash with a bored yawn, as if this is just another day for Damien. Meanwhile, here I am, stretching my paycheck so I can afford to take care of me and my sister, keeping a roof over our heads and putting three square meals on the table.

It wasn't always like this.

When we were growing up, our parents did all right when they were both working. Dad worked in IT for Blackhollow Industries, Mom an executive administrative assistant at the company. It may seem quite the coincidence that both my parents worked for Damien's family company, except that half the town is also employed there. Blackhollow Industries pays well too, but my parents were never good at saving. Dad burned through what little they had for his defense after he was accused of Mom's murder.

I was just sixteen when Mom was killed; Maddie twelve. After Dad's trial and conviction, we went to live with Mom's older sister, Aunt Aggie. Aunt Aggie did the best she could, but she was a single mom who barely had enough money for her own kids, much less two new mouths to feed. I got small jobs after school to help out as best I could, like babysitting and dog-walking, but it didn't make much of a dent in Aunt Aggie's bills. Even so, she insisted we stay with her, even after I turned eighteen and legally could be on my own.

I'm sure it was difficult, but Aunt Aggie was the best. Things got easier after high school. I could get higher paying part-time jobs while going to college and then law school. Waiting tables. Driving for Uber. I'd even sold my plasma a few times. Not so fun, but it paid pretty well. Suffice it to say, I couldn't at all relate to a man like Damien who could transfer millions in the blink of an eye.

The rest of my Saturday is consumed with coordinating to make sure Damien returns safely and comfortably to his posh mansion in wealthy Beacon Hill and is following all the rules of his release. There he'll remain under house arrest, but with the kind of sway he has and with Quinn's finagling, the judge has expanded "house" to loosely mean the entire state of Massachusetts.

Sure, Damien has to wear an ankle bracelet hidden beneath one of his custom-tailored thousand-plus-dollar suits and he surrendered his passport, but I get the feeling that if he wanted to leave the country, that won't stop him. The man has a fleet of private jets at his disposal. He can be halfway across the world before anyone notices.

Then I spend the evening memorizing the entire arrest file Quinn showed me at the courthouse and reading everything about the Halloween Heiress Murder I can find online. Quinn and Mark are taking the lead on drafting the outline for tomorrow's client meeting, but I try to be helpful, staying up late to put together additional questions for them to include.

By Sunday morning, I'm running on just a few hours' sleep—surviving on caffeine and pure adrenaline—as I step into the biggest conference room we have at Whitehall & Rowe. Affectionately dubbed the "War Room," the space is equipped with state-of-the-art technology: a massive, wall-to-wall digital screen dominates one side and discreet speakers and microphones are embedded in the ceiling. Soundproof glass walls ensure complete privacy. A sleek, polished oak table stretches the length of the room, and the gourmet coffee station in the corner is already stocked with the firm's best espresso beans. It's a room meant for high-stakes battles; every detail curated for success.

I'm almost thirty minutes early for our meeting, so I'm surprised to see everyone already in their seats at the conference room table. Quinn sits at the head of the table, tapping away on his iPad. Next to him is an empty chair, reserved for the client. On the other side of the empty chair is Mark, leaning back with an air of self-satisfaction. His overpowering cologne—a mix of heavy sandalwood and cheap synthetic musk—floats toward me as I approach, thick enough to choke on.

I notice with annoyance that the rest of the seats closest to the client's spot are also filled. Holly, Quinn's secretary, types away on her laptop as if her life depends on it, while Alex, our lead paralegal, sifts through stacks of documents. He's got a junior paralegal with him that I don't recognize.

They all look up as I take my seat—at the end of the table, the absolute furthest from the client. Great. Exactly where every ambitious attorney wants to be.

"Nice of you to join us," Quinn says, a flicker of displeasure on his handsome face.

"I thought we were starting at eight-thirty?" I ask, looking at the clock, confused.

"Eight-thirty?" Quinn repeats, like I'm speaking a different language. "We've all been here since six a.m., finalizing the outline for the client meeting. Blackhollow will be here any minute."

Mark makes a loud, patronizing clucking sound. "You really should check your email. I sent you the new time hours ago," he says with a smug expression on his face, looking far too pleased with himself.

I know immediately I've been set up. I check my inbox religiously. There was no email from Mark.

"Please try to be on time, James," Holly says, giving me a dirty look over the top of her laptop. "I know you're still new at this, but it's disrespectful to the rest of the team."

Holly hates me.

The woman is in her late thirties, with a messy, grown-out bob and sharp-winged eyeliner that emphasizes her permanent scowl. She's built sturdy and practical, like a workhorse, always wearing unflattering floral blouses that are a size too tight around her chest. And she's hopelessly in love with Quinn, not that he'd ever notice.

"Great advice, Holly," Mark says, condescension dripping from every word.

Alex, the paralegal, gives me a sympathetic nod. "It's fine. She's still learning."

As much as I want to lay into Mark—and Holly too—I bite my lip and pull out my laptop. I need to redeem myself with Quinn, but being a tattletale isn't the way to do it. I'm not sure anyone will believe me anyway. Mark, for all his dastardly machinations, has an excellent reputation at the firm and has been here far longer than me.

"I'm sorry," I mutter. "Must have missed it."

"Don't apologize," Quinn snaps. "A good attorney never apologizes. Just don't do it again. And Mark"—he turns to face the senior associate—"next time, send a text. You know emails can be missed in a time crunch."

Quinn subtly catches my eye, the corners of his lips tipping up, and I can tell he knows Mark is full of shit. But Quinn has to be careful. He can't be seen taking my side or playing favorites. Quinn is no idiot. He's heard the rumors about us as well, and I know he doesn't want to feed into them.

I look down, hiding my own smirk.

The door to the War Room opens right at 8:30 a.m., and the energy inside immediately shifts as Damien Blackhollow strolls in. He's perfectly dressed, of course, in another dark designer suit that looks like it was made just for him—which I'm sure it was.

He doesn't rush to sit but looks around the room with cold, calm arrogance. His presence creates a disturbance in the air. The man commands attention without even trying. It's like nothing I've ever been around before, and I've been around some heavy hitters. At Harvard, I was surrounded by brilliant, pretentious classmates and esteemed professors who thought they ran the world. Now, at the firm, we have power players dropping in daily—mayors, governors, even the occasional senator, like Quinn's father.

Damien's gaze lingers on me a fraction too long, a quiet intensity that makes my pulse stutter. Then he strides past Quinn, Mark, Holly, and even the paralegals before finally taking the empty seat beside me. Mark's expression tightens, and it's all I can do not to flip him the finger and gloat.

"Shall we begin?" Damien asks, his voice smooth.

Quinn nods, clearing his throat and glancing at his meeting outline on his iPad. As he dives in, I pull up my copy on my laptop, fingers flying over the keyboard as I take copious notes.

"We'd like to start by reviewing the charges and hearing your side of the story so we can build your defense," Quinn says. "I know we briefly went over attorney-client privilege at our first meeting at the county jail. You understand how that works, yes?"

"I say whatever I want. You keep your mouth shut." Damien grins. "That pretty much sum it up?"

Silence stretches for a beat. No reaction from Quinn—not a smirk, not a glare, nothing. Just the steady calm he wears like armor.

"We have your arrest file and some preliminary discovery from the prosecution," Quinn says, pointing to the stack of folders in front of him. "But it's incomplete. We'll work on getting more from the DA's office."

Damien leans back, exuding confidence. "What exactly do they think they have on me?"

"The prosecution is focusing heavily on the ritualistic elements of the crime." Quinn signals to Alex to begin distributing the crime scene photos to the team. Alex moves methodically, sliding each glossy image across the table. "I'm sorry, this will be graphic, but we have to get all the facts."

"I understand," Damien says.

"Your fiancée's body was found on the grounds of your Beacon Hill estate," Quinn says. "The reports state that her body was mutilated. Ms. Van Buren had multiple deep lacerations across her body, carved in such a way that investigators believe they were intentional symbols—symbols tied to occult rituals."

I shift uncomfortably in my seat as the photos make their way around the table and land in front of me. I've already read all the public details available, but the pictures from the DA's files are far more horrifying than any images my mind could conjure up.

That poor woman...

The crime scene is filled with symbols. Vivienne Van Buren's slaughtered body is marked from head to toe—intricate designs etched onto her skin—while the same ominous patterns stain the floor and walls, drawn in her fresh blood. The symbols are intricate, twisted, with no clear meaning. At least, not one that anyone can easily ascertain. Every amateur sleuth and true crime podcaster from Boston to the Berkshires who's been covering the case since last fall is convinced the symbols prove this isn't just a crime of passion or domestic dispute. They believe it points to something far darker.

"We'll have to be very careful with the media. They'll be ruthless," Mark says, leaning forward, almost eagerly. "They're going to milk the occult angle for all it's worth, especially with the murder taking place so close to Salem's Fall and Halloween right around the corner."

Damien doesn't flinch as he looks at the photos. He eyes the images of his dead, brutalized fiancée with the same level of interest someone might have scrolling through their Instagram feed.

"We'll need to address your alibi," Quinn says to Damien, pressing on. "The prosecution will argue for more than just a crime of passion due to the… *severe nature*… of the killing." He swallows hard. "They're going to try to prove premeditation. They'll say it takes time to make marks like that on a body. Lots of time to think while cutting. But if we can establish a clear timeline and alibi, we might be able to discredit their case."

Damien smiles, but there's nothing warm about it.

"My alibi is simple," he says. "I was at the All Hallows Gala, like I am every year. Blackhollow Industries is the biggest donor to the New England Historical and Cultural Heritage Museum. Vivienne got sick that night—bad case of stomach poisoning. She stayed in."

"That's good." Mark, the suck-up, nods along approvingly. "Very good."

Quinn, however, looks suspicious.

"I was there that night, Blackhollow," he says. "I don't

recall seeing you after the band came on around eight p.m., and the coroner is estimating the murder took place shortly before midnight."

"Gee, Quinn, I didn't realize you were keeping such close tabs on me," Damien says, lifting a dark brow.

Quinn ignores the jab. "Can anyone attest to your attendance at the Gala closer to the actual time of the murder?"

"Of course. I had company later that night." Damien's smile sharpens. "There was a woman. Blonde. Gorgeous. She was… enthusiastic."

I gasp, fingers pausing over my keyboard, unable to hold in my shock and disgust. "You were with another woman just hours before your fiancée's murder?"

Quinn shoots me a silencing look across the table. I freeze.

Shit.

I can tell I'm in trouble. I'm just a junior associate. I'm not supposed to speak much at these client meetings, and I'm definitely not supposed to chastise the client, but seriously? How gross can you get?

Damien shifts next to me and holds my stare, as if challenging. "It's not like I knew Vivienne was going to die that night."

"But… but you were going to be married?" I ask, unable to control the judgmental tone in my voice. I can't help it. I don't like cheaters.

"James—" Quinn says my name with a warning.

"It's okay. Nothing to worry about." Mark grins reassuringly at Damien. "We see cheating all the time. Our job isn't to make judgments," he says, trying to soften things, the sneaky weasel.

"I was *not* cheating." Damien flinches. It's the first time I see him show any real emotion. "Infidelity is unbecoming."

Quinn's brow furrows. "But then what—"

"Vivienne and I had already called it quits," Damien says. "She was planning to move out that weekend."

"And this woman at the party. What's her name so we can question her?" Quinn asks.

Damien shrugs. "I can't recall. It was a party. These things happen."

My stomach turns at Damien's lack of shame, his casual dismissal of whatever beautiful woman he'd spent the night with. How could he not remember her *name*? Is he that detached from reality? The more I learn about the cold man sitting beside me, the more I wonder what he's really capable of. I start to get the feeling he actually could be guilty of murder.

Maybe even worse things…

Mark, though, seems to find Damien's apathy inspirational. "Ah, the perks of being Damien Blackhollow, huh? Must be nice." He chuckles and raises his coffee cup like it's some kind of toast. It makes me want to punch him in his smug face.

Damien, to his credit, doesn't dignify Mark's comment with a response.

"The woman, whatever her name, won't help your case," Damien says, turning back to Quinn. "But I'm sure you'll manage. You are the best in the business, after all, aren't you?"

"We'll find another way," Quinn says, nodding along. "We can try requesting security footage from the party, if they still have it. It might capture those entering and leaving. If we can establish you were still there past midnight, it'll strengthen our timeline. The tighter the better."

"Good," Damien replies. "Spare no expense, but keep my involvement to a minimum. I do have a business to run."

"Of course. Wouldn't want to take up too much of your valuable time," Quinn replies smoothly, just a hint of irritation beneath his polished tone.

My gaze keeps going back to the murder scene photos on the table. Something about the symbols gnaws at me, an uneasy feeling that I can't shake. "These markings," I say, peering closer at the pictures. "They're not random. They must mean *something*, right? Do we know what?"

"James, let's stick to the order in the outline," Mark says with a frown, obnoxiously jabbing a finger at the document on his computer screen. "Quinn and I are leading this conversation for a reason." He turns to Damien with a tight smile. "I apologize. She's still quite green."

Damien's lips twitch. "Oh, is she?"

As much as I hate to admit it, I know Mark has a point. I'm out of line and there's a hierarchy here, but I want to prove myself to everyone, especially Quinn. I want them all to see that I've got a reason to be at this table too, and my gut is screaming there's something important about these symbols.

I swallow hard and decide, screw it. No guts, no glory, right?

"But it's exactly like you said, Mark," I say sweetly, ignoring Mark's jaw as it drops to the floor with indignation. "The media are going to push the occult angle because it's so sensational, and so, the prosecution will have to explore it too. We need to know if there's any connection between Damien and these symbols." I look right at Damien, steady and unflinching, searching his face for any reaction. "If there is, we should know about it now, before they find out."

I half expect Damien to brush me off like he's done with everyone else, but he meets my gaze with something that feels almost like respect.

"You're asking if I'm a witch?" His voice is low, almost teasing.

"No, of course not. Witches aren't real." I blush a bit. "But I think you know what I'm getting at. Does the prosecution have anything that can tie you to these symbols?"

For a moment, the room feels impossibly still. Then, with a dark chuckle, Damien replies, "Very good. I can see why Quinn keeps you around." He shakes his head. "No, nothing they'll be able to directly connect me to anyway. That's a dead end."

Quinn doesn't look convinced. He leans forward, resting his elbows on his knees.

"What about the missing engagement ring?" he asks, voice deceptively casual. "You wouldn't know the whereabouts of that, would you?"

My pulse kicks up a notch, and I lean in closer for Damien's answer. When Vivienne Van Buren was first murdered, the media made a big deal about her missing ring —a seven-carat canary diamond, reportedly worth over a million dollars. The initial speculation was that her death was the result of a botched robbery, that the killer had taken the ring and fled. But with no other signs of forced entry and nothing else missing from the home, that theory had always been weak at best.

Damien exhales, the barest hint of amusement flickering across his face. "Quinn," he drawls, "I could buy ten of those rings and then go shopping for a new yacht before lunch. What exactly would I gain from keeping it?"

"Fair point," Quinn says, watching Damien carefully. "Though I'm not sure the DA will see it that way. Obviously, with your arrest, it's clear they've decided to tank the robbery angle. They'll likely use the missing ring against you. They'll say you took it yourself, hoping to mislead the authorities, send them running around in circles."

Before Damien can respond further, Holly bolts up from her computer, her face pale.

"Quinn, you need to see this." Her voice shakes as she reads from her screen. "There's been a leak to the press. They're going nuts. They found the murder weapon. Some kind of knife, buried behind the new Blackhollow Industries building on Congress Street."

Quinn rushes to Holly's side, his eyes skimming over her laptop. "Did you know anything about this?" he asks, whirling on Damien.

"Of course not," Damien says, looking remarkably unbothered by this alarming turn of events. "I employ hundreds of people at that location. Could've been any of them."

"Shit." Quinn's eyes narrow at Damien as he reads the article out loud. "Says it's an *exceedingly rare* Black Obsidian Bloodstone Athame that was sold last year to one Mr. Damien Blackhollow for $120,000 at the New England Historical and Cultural Heritage Museum's annual fundraiser."

"So?" Damien shrugs. "I like to support the local arts."

Quinn's lips thin. "This is bad. Very, *very* bad."

"I don't see why," Damien says. "Anyone could've stolen my knife, used it to kill Vivienne, and then planted it at the new building to frame me."

"It has your fingerprints all over it," Quinn says.

My stomach drops as I pull up the article on my computer. It's all right there in black and white and none of it looks good for our case. Finding a murder weapon is bad enough, but one this rare and with physical evidence that ties directly to the suspect? That's going to be a major hurdle for us to overcome. This case is looking worse and worse by the minute.

"Does it now?" Damien asks, his voice soft but dangerous. "Oh well. I'm sure you'll figure it out, Quinn. That's why I hired you. Looks like things are about to get interesting."

CHAPTER 4

We're going to lose this case.

A highly uncommon murder weapon with a direct chain of custody tied to our client, plus his fingerprints are all over it. It's almost too easy for the prosecution… Either Damien is guilty as hell, or he's being framed by someone who knows exactly what they're doing. Either way, this case is already going to shit, and we've barely begun.

It's all I can think about as we finish up our initial prep meeting with Damien, and the feeling only gets worse after he leaves for the day to go back to house arrest and his palatial Boston estate. I should feel relief after he's gone. There's finally room to breathe in the War Room without him sucking up all the oxygen with his powerful presence. But instead, the unease lingers in my chest, twisting uncomfortably. There's something about this that feels all wrong.

It doesn't help that this case is also starting to seem just a bit too familiar. I usually try not to think about what happened to Mom—life is easier that way—but the eerie similarities between the two murders strike a chord I can't ignore.

Just like Damien's fiancée, my mother was found slain inside our house, the victim of a brutal knife attack. The authorities also found weird markings on her body and on the bedroom walls and floor nearby, some kind of runes or symbols, they said. And the murder weapon was also dumped far away from the house, right near my dad's office building. Yes, an office building also owned by Blackhollow Industries. Although that was the old building downtown, and not the new one on Congress Street, it's still quite the series of striking coincidences.

In contrast to Vivienne Van Buren's high-profile case, my mother's murder flew under the radar, probably because my family were a bunch of nobodies. The state prosecutor never even touched the occult angle in her murder. They didn't make much of anything, actually.

The State labeled it a tragic but run-of-the-mill domestic violence case. They never even tried to find any other suspects, even though my dad had no criminal history or record of violence, and my parents had a picture-perfect marriage right up until my mom's death. They'd been married almost twenty years, and I don't recall ever seeing them fight, not once. The only arguments they ever got into were about money and even those never lasted long.

Unfortunately, my dad didn't have the money or resources that Damien has, so they threw the book at him. He was tossed in prison without any real investigation or a fair trial. It's the reason I decided to become a lawyer—to ensure others like my dad get fair representation and real justice is served. This Whitehall & Rowe gig is just to gain experience and save up enough money so Maddie and I can live comfortably. The end goal is to have my own law firm one day or maybe even become a judge. Someone important with the power and resources to make a difference.

"Lunch is here!" Holly announces, bursting through the door with an armful of fishy-smelling plastic bags. She beams proudly, as if she's prepared a seven-course feast rather than simply placed a delivery order, and begins laying out sushi platters for everyone. "It's Quinn's favorite—Sushi Hero."

As she winks at her boss, my stomach churns. I feel queasy staring at the piles of crab, shrimp, and lobster rolls.

"Holly, don't you remember? Woodsen is allergic to shellfish," Quinn says and turns to me, looking apologetic as everyone else starts swarming the food.

"Oh, she is?" Holly's face is the picture of innocence even though she damn well knows this, nor is this the first or even the second time she's somehow "forgotten" my deathly allergy. "I'm so sorry, James," she says, voice dripping with fake sincerity.

"It's fine. I'm not really hungry," I say even as my stomach growls loudly in disagreement, making a liar out of me.

"You sure, hun?" Holly asks with a watery smile. "I can bring you some menus. You can order something for yourself, if you like."

This is not Holly being nice.

It's literally in Holly's job description to help attorneys order their lunch, along with booking travel and other administrative tasks so we don't spend our clients' time and money for things like this. She knows this. I know this. Everyone in the damn room knows this. But if I make it into a big deal, *I'm the one who's going to look like a petty brat.* This is a passive-aggressive bitch move at its finest. Annoyingly impressive, really.

"I'm sure," I say. "Thanks anyway."

"This looks amazing, Holls!" Mark grins happily as he loads up his plate with food and takes his seat again. "I still can't believe Blackhollow was dumb enough to leave the murder weapon at his own building. What a moron, huh?" he asks through a mouthful of sushi.

"That's the thing," Quinn says, tapping his chopsticks against the edge of the table, deep in thought. "Blackhollow is one of the most brilliant men I know. If he had killed her, there's no way he'd be careless enough for that." He shakes his head. "No, that little fuckup can't possibly be his, but it's designed to look like it is, so now we've got to deal with it. Plus, the alibi he gave us is far from solid. That's two strikes, right out of the gates, and we haven't even gotten into discovery yet."

"Not to mention the personality problems." I snort. "The guy doesn't even remember the woman he spent the night with while his poor fiancée was home getting butchered." I roll my eyes. "That's going to go over great with the female jurors."

I feel a twinge of disgust. It's clear how disposable people —especially women—are to this man.

"That's the least of our concerns," Mark says, waving a dismissive hand in my direction. "We've got way more pressing things here than worrying about a few silly women's sensibilities."

"Mark's right." Quinn sighs. "That's easy enough to fix with good coaching. But the evidence and lack of alibi… it's a real problem."

There's worry in his voice, and Quinn doesn't worry often. That's how I know this is bad.

"Couldn't we start by looking for security footage, like you suggested? Not just the Gala, but around Damien's house?" I ask. "He could have home security cameras. Or maybe there are nearby buildings with CCTV cameras that picked something up?"

"From a year ago?" Mark smirks. "Good luck with that."

"Sorry, Woodsen. Don't think so," Quinn says.

"The Gala idea you had, though, Quinn? That might work," Mark says. "I recall hearing about an investigation hold last year on the museum party footage. If we can get hold of those tapes, they could give us some clarity on Blackhollow's movements that night—or at least help disprove the prosecution's timeline."

"Excellent idea," Quinn says. "What else do we have?"

I want to say something and contribute, but it feels like every time I do, Mark just shoots me down. And Quinn, while much nicer about it, seems to keep agreeing with him. Mark has made it clear he thinks I'm out of my depth here, and I'm starting to wonder if he's right.

"There's the knife," Mark continues. "We should check security footage from the office building. See if we can catch who put it there."

"Yes, that's good," Quinn says. "I feel certain it won't be Blackhollow."

"Then we'll find someone who had it in for Blackhollow," Mark says, leaning forward, his tone gaining an edge of excitement. "Someone who stole the guy's fancy knife, got his fingerprints all over it, killed the fiancée, then left it on Blackhollow's company property where they knew it'd be found."

I groan out loud. "You sound like a silly *Criminal Minds* episode," I say, unable to keep silent any longer. This is getting absurd. "You really think a sane, rational jury is going to believe that?"

This case, it's a total mess. The deeper we dig, the more tangled it gets. There's no solid alibi, no witnesses to corroborate Damien's story, and now there's a weapon with his prints on it. Everything points to guilt.

"You know what, James?" Mark's voice drips with sarcasm. "I don't hear you coming up with any brilliant ideas. Or are you still a bit gun-shy after your last screwup?"

The comment lands like a punch, my face heating with shame and anger. I bite the inside of my cheek, forcing myself not to react. Not to let him see how deep it cuts.

"Yeah, that's what I thought." He turns to Quinn with a smug look. "Look, Quinn, this is a high-stakes case. We can't afford dead weight. Maybe we should look for another junior associate to staff on this?"

My pulse pounds in my ears as the room falls silent. The paralegals stop eating, stunned. Even Holly gasps at the outright rudeness.

"Knock it off, Mark," Quinn snaps, irritated.

"No, Quinn. He's right. Maybe I shouldn't be on this case," I say, closing my computer with a huff.

Quinn's eyes flick to mine, and for a moment, I see disappointment there. He's always supported me, always thought I had potential, even if he is still wary after my last failure. I can tell he wants to trust me, but he's cautious.

And he's smart to be.

"Now, we're getting somewhere." Mark grins at me like he's just won some kind of prize. "You're finally starting to make sense, Woodsen. This case is going to be tough, and we need people who can handle the pressure. You're not one of them."

His words sting, but in a way, they also confirm what I've been feeling all day. This case is a train wreck. Damien is not a good man, and I doubt he's an innocent one either. All the signs are there. And when we lose—because we *will* lose—it's going to reflect poorly on me.

I can't take a second failure. I'll be finished at this firm.

"Mark, that's enough!" Quinn barks, a flush rising to his cheeks. He exhales sharply, reining himself back in before turning to me. "Look, Woodsen. I'd love to have you on this. You're a hard worker, and you've got a sharp mind," he says, his voice quieter now, but even. "But I also get it—this case is a lot, especially for someone so new." He pauses, his gaze steady. "The choice is yours. Whatever you decide, I'll back you."

It's the out I need. The excuse to walk away from the nightmare this case is certain to become.

"I'd like to step aside," I say.

I pack up my things and head for the door while the others

resume the meeting. Voices hushed, heads together. No one skips a beat. It's like I was never even there.

Back at my apartment, Lucky greets me at the door. He brushes against my legs as he winds around me, purring softly. I give him a quick scratch behind the ears and toss my work bag onto the couch, feeling a strange mix of defeat and relief knowing I haven't tanked my career—*yet*. Though I guess I also haven't helped things much either.

It looks like it's back to research memos for me. No more court hearings. No more War Room. No more career-making cases. Just… mediocrity.

Later that night, I make dinner for Madison while she watches one of her silly reality TV shows on Bravo. I try to focus on the familiar motions of chopping vegetables and stirring sauces. My little sister is in a good mood, chattering away about her classes and the latest drama with her girlfriends. I nod in all the right places, but my mind keeps drifting back to the case I just walked away from.

Damien Blackhollow—the billion-dollar client with the biggest murder case in years. Though every instinct tells me I made the right decision leaving the trial team, it still feels a bit like swallowing glass, knowing what I might be missing out on. Cases like this don't just come around.

And if, by some miracle, we actually won? That would be like earning a fast pass to the top of the career ladder. One big win could cement my name, get me noticed by the partners, maybe even line up a promotion to senior associate way ahead of schedule. I'd have more control over my caseload, more respect from people—even assholes like Mark—and maybe I wouldn't feel this desperate need to prove myself all the time.

What if I made the wrong choice?

After we eat dinner and Madison goes to sleep, I lie down on the couch with the TV remote in hand. The news is already buzzing with the latest developments in the Halloween

Heiress Murder case. Damien's face flashes across the screen as they show clips of him from various high society events. The Boston Philharmonic Gala. The Kennedy Center Honors. The New England Aquarium's Blue Ball. The Met Gala.

I can't help but stare. Even if the man may be guilty as sin, there's no denying how impossibly good-looking he is. Even the female journalists who are supposed to be objectively reporting about a dangerous murder suspect are eating it up.

"Many don't believe Blackhollow could commit such a heinous crime. A man of his stature—so wealthy, so respected—it's sending shockwaves through the city," the pretty blonde evening news anchor says, her eyes gleaming. "The evidence looks bad, but his reputation remains strong. His legion of supporters remain firmly in his corner."

"That's right, Diana," the second female anchor adds. "Blackhollow is a pillar of the New England community, supporting local institutions like the Boston Children's Hospital and the New England Historical and Cultural Heritage Museum. His foundation funds countless scholarships and youth programs. And he's not too hard on the eyes either! Am I right?" She winks conspiratorially at her co-host. "Many believe this arrest is a political move, a ploy by DA Don Smith to gain traction as he kicks off his Attorney General campaign."

I turn off the TV. These women are seriously deluded, fooled by a pretty face and a big wallet.

My eyes start to close. I'm too tired to even get off the couch as sleep comes to me. Exhausted but also strangely at peace, knowing I've made the right decision. Guys like Damien—men with money, power, *and* looks—they can't be trusted. I learned that the hard way with my very recently ex-boyfriend, William Winthrop.

Fucking William.

I'd dated him for all three years of law school. William Winthrop III was a Harvard Law legacy; both his father and grandfather had gone there. He'd seemed like the perfect guy, the one I was certain was going to marry me—until I caught him in bed with one of my best friends. Men like William and Damien take what they want and leave destruction in their wake. Best to stay the hell away from the detonation.

Hours later, I wake to the sound of my phone buzzing on the floor. I squint at the screen.

It's Quinn.

"Woodsen!" His voice is clipped, urgent. "We need you in the office. Can you get here within the hour?"

"Huh?" I ask, my voice groggy as I wipe sleep from my eyes. "What's going on?"

"You're back on the case."

"Quinn, no!" I bolt up, suddenly wide awake. "I already told you. I'm not doing it."

"Sorry, but you don't have a choice. Neither of us do." Quinn sighs into the phone, resignation heavy in his voice.

"I—I don't understand."

"The firm's in full panic mode. As soon as he heard you were off the case, he snapped. He's threatening to pull his business and find another defense team," he says. There's a pause, then the faint sound of him exhaling sharply, like he's trying—and failing—to keep his frustration in check. "Blackhollow wants you back or he walks."

CHAPTER 5

October 12 (Three Weeks Until Halloween)

The next few days are packed with research and drafting motions and discovery requests for our case. Damien's trial is set for early April, which sounds far off, but actually isn't all that much time to prepare for a trial of this magnitude.

The media circus hasn't let up since Damien's high-profile arrest and bail hearing; it's only gotten worse. Every major newspaper in New England is covering the story, and Damien's name is plastered daily across every local news channel. Public fascination is at a fever pitch.

I still can't shake the nagging feeling that this whole thing is unraveling before we've even begun. Every night, I lie awake wondering if I made the wrong call agreeing to stay on—not that Quinn or the firm gave me much of a choice. Mark has been insufferable as well, of course. Every chance he gets to make me look dumb or incompetent, he takes. The guy lives to make me feel like I don't belong on the team.

Tuesday morning, he waits for me by my desk as I walk inside the office, smug and arrogant as ever. Before I can even set my tote bag down and grab my morning coffee, he's already on me.

"Got an exciting new assignment for you," he says with mock enthusiasm.

"Oh yeah? What is it?" I ask, already dreading the answer. No way this is going to be good for me. Not with that insufferably pleased look on his face.

"Quinn and I are going to meet with the DA tomorrow, so we're busy with more important matters. Here," he says as he hands me two enormous, bulging file folders. "Someone needs to track down the security tapes. You remember—the ones from the Museum Gala and the office building where they found the knife?"

"You really think we're going to find anything? We don't even know if they still have the tapes from the party," I say with a sneaking suspicion this is busy work, designed to keep me on some wild goose chase, far away from the real case work. "And as for the building, someone could've dumped that knife months ago, right? Even if they have security tapes, when would we even start looking?"

He pinches the bridge of his nose. "I don't have time to play Twenty Questions with you, Woodsen," he says, voice filled with annoyance, as if speaking to me is a personal burden. "Can you handle this without screwing it up, or should I call Holly? I'm sure even a secretary could manage something this simple."

I grit my teeth. "I'll take care of it."

"Good girl. Try not to make a mess this time."

As he walks away, I let out a groan of frustration. As if it isn't bad enough being on a case I'm almost certain we're going to lose, I have to be on it with this pompous asshole.

Still, if there's no other option and I'm stuck on this team, I'm determined to blow Quinn's mind with how good I am at whatever scraps Mark throws me. Blackhollow's, too—not that I care what he thinks.

Well, not much anyway.

I thumb through the files Mark has left for me, focusing on the task at hand. First up: the tapes from the museum's All Hallows Gala.

It doesn't take me long to find a phone number for the museum. Mark—or more likely one of the secretaries—pulled the entire directory. Mark has highlighted a few contacts for me that look promising. I start at the top with Sherri Baker, Executive Director. One thing I've learned, it's always best to go directly to the highest person in charge.

After a few rings, a bored-sounding woman picks up.

"Sherri Baker. How can I help you?"

"Hi, Sherri, this is James Woodsen with Whitehall & Rowe," I say in my most professional-sounding voice. "I'm working on a case, and we have reason to believe you may have evidence relevant to the matter. We need to obtain security footage from your All Hallows Gala that took place last Halloween."

There's a long pause, and I can practically hear the woman on the other end rolling her eyes.

"I'm sorry, but we don't just hand over security footage to anyone who asks."

"Yes, I understand, but it's part of an active criminal investigation," I explain, keeping my tone steady. "It's important that we—"

"Sorry," she interrupts, "but you'll need to go through the proper channels. Get a subpoena." She makes an annoyed huffing sound, and I hear papers shuffling in the background. "Now, if you'll excuse me. I've got the annual Gala coming up in less than three weeks and simply don't have time for this."

"But—"

The line goes dead.

I stare at my phone in disbelief.

Well, that was rude.

It's barely 9 a.m. and I'm already at my first dead end.

Good thing I don't give up easily. In a burst of ingenuity, I send out a quick text to my best friend Katie asking her to meet up. It's a long shot, but if it plays out like I hope it will, it might solve everything.

A few hours later, I head to the Sidebar downtown to grab drinks with Katie. Sidebar was one of our favorite hangouts when we were in law school. We had a lot of good times there, along with our other best friend, Jess Foster. Jess—the friend I no longer talk to after I caught her in bed with my scumbag ex-boyfriend, William.

The place is packed as I walk in, the noise and energy from the crowd filling the air. A few men catcall as I pass by, offering to buy me drinks. I ignore them, my eyes locked on my best friend, sitting at our usual table near the back of the bar.

Katherine Tang is striking as usual, even in her minimalist, effortless style: trim and athletic, dark brown hair pulled back into a practical ponytail, accentuating sharp cheekbones and piercing brown eyes. Tonight, she wears one of her signature plaid blazers over a sleek silk blouse, paired with fitted pants and Hermès leather loafers. Always polished yet understated. The kind of wealth that doesn't need to announce itself. A small pair of pearl stud earrings and her grandmother's antique gold Rolex watch, an heirloom from their Beijing diplomatic lineage, are her only accessories.

"Hey, bestie. Been way too long," I say and give her a big hug before grabbing the vodka soda she ordered for me. "Sorry I'm late. Quinn caught me just as I was leaving the office."

"Oh yeah?" Her brow lifts with a suggestive tilt. "Caught you *how*?"

"Ha ha. Not like that." I grin. "Just more work for our new case. He wants me to research a few new things for tomorrow morning."

"You're so lucky," she grumbles. "You get Brad Pitt's younger—and even hotter—lookalike for a partner, and I have Jabba the Hut at my office."

I laugh. "The DA isn't *that* bad."

"Oh yes, he is," she says. "If only Quinn was my boss, the things I'd do to him." She sighs dreamily. "It's really wasted on you, you know."

"Come on, Katie. He doesn't think of me like that."

"Oh, please." She snorts into her martini. "Quinn has it bad for you, and you know it. You're both just too damn stubborn to do anything about it."

After a few more minutes of drinking and catching up on the usual biggies—work, life, family stuff—Katie's demeanor shifts. She sips at her drink slowly and looks at me with a sincere, sympathetic smile.

"James, I just… I want you to know, I had no idea about Jess and William. I was shocked when I heard. If I had known, I would've done something—" She pauses, fidgeting with the stem of her martini glass. "You know that, right? You know I'm on your side?"

I reach out and squeeze her hand across the table.

"Yeah, of course I do, Katie. I know you'd never betray me like that." I smile, though it's tinged with bitterness. "Honestly, it's fine. William was… well, pathetic is the polite word for it. Clingy, spoiled, and way too possessive. He never could handle that my work mattered to me."

"Yeah, screw William. He's a man-child, and you're so much better off without him." She pauses and gives me a long, serious look. "But to be fair, you *do* tend to prioritize work over everyone else—even the people who really do matter. I mean, I've barely seen you in weeks," she says with a small shrug. "And… Maddie's been calling me. She's lonely, James. I know she seems all grown up, but she isn't. She still needs her big sister every now and then."

"I know. You're right." I look down, swirling the ice in my drink, a twinge of guilt creeping in. "Things have been so crazy at work, but I'll try to be better. Really, I will."

I give her a strained smile. It's a promise I want to keep, but we both know how it'll end. Work will always come first.

"So," I say, trying to sound casual. It's time to get to the real reason I asked Katie to meet me tonight. "Have you heard anything about the Damien Blackhollow case?"

She lets out a loud snort, thumping her hand on the wooden table. "You little sneak!" she says, swiping playfully at my shoulder. "I knew it!"

"Knew what?"

"I heard you were on that." She chuckles. "So that's why you dragged me here? I thought we were catching up, not working."

"We are, Katie!" I attempt to give her my most sincere smile. "I just thought you might have heard something. You know, since you work in the DA's office and all."

"I'm not on the Blackhollow case, James. It's way too high-profile for a first year." She sighs, leaning back in her chair. "But yeah, sure, I've heard bits and pieces. Everyone has. The entire office is buzzing about it."

She takes a long sip of her drink before her eyes flick over my shoulder, and she leans in closer.

"Okay, so not to sound like a complete degenerate, but... Damien Blackhollow?" She lets out a low whistle. "Jesus! That man is, like, objectively yumable. If he wasn't, you know, a big ol' lady killer." She scoots her chair in closer. "Tell me the truth, he's even sexier in person, isn't he? I bet he smells amazing too!"

I shake my head, laughing. "Oh my God, Katie. Get a hold of yourself, woman."

"I'm just saying he's smokin' hot!" She giggles. "I'd seriously let that man have his way with me, if you know what I mean. Well, everything but murder, of course. That seems excessive." She pushes her drink away and makes a sad little clucking sound in the back of her throat. "His poor, naive fiancée."

"He didn't do it," I blurt.

Even if I have my own sneaking suspicions, I'm certainly not going to let on to Katie what I really think about my client. She may be my best friend, but I never forget who signs her paychecks.

"Uh-huh." She props her chin on her hand, unimpressed. "You have to say that. You're his counsel." She swirls her straw around, thinking. "It's obvious to anyone with half a brain the guy did it. I mean, let's be real—someone that perfect has to have a flaw."

I roll my eyes. "That kind of twisted logic is not how our legal system works, and you know it."

"Maybe not, but it's how vibes work." She smirks before taking another sip of her drink. "I heard from some girls in Junior League that the guy is still planning to attend the All Hallows Gala in a few weeks. Can you believe that?" She scoffs, chewing on her lower lip. "Those crazy bitches are lining up for a chance to go out with a murderer."

"No way." I frown. "He wouldn't dare."

"Apparently, he hasn't missed it in, like, forever," she says. "Biggest donor, blah blah blah. But, like, read the room, dude."

"Obviously, we'll instruct him not to go."

Katie snorts into her drink. "Pfft. Good luck telling a man like that what to do."

I grab a few nuts from the dish on our table and chew thoughtfully.

"Speaking of the Gala—any idea if the DA has security tapes from last year's party? The night Blackhollow's fiancée was murdered?" I try to sound all nonchalant, and not at all like the desperate person I really am. "We're trying to get them, but the museum isn't exactly being cooperative."

Katie frowns. "You know I'm not supposed to give out information about an active case."

Ugh, I love her to death, but Katie is such a goody-goody sometimes. It really grates. To be fair, it's not her fault. She's rich, attractive, smart, and well connected; her life is pretty much a cake walk. I suppose it's easy to have black-and-white morality when you've never had to face any adversity.

"Oh, come on, Katie. Our offices talk all the time and share information. It's called discovery," I say. "It's not like you're giving me classified intel. I'm just asking if the tapes exist. That's all." I sigh and pop a few more peanuts into my mouth. "Besides, the law isn't a gotcha. Our jobs are to make sure the right person is behind bars and justice is served, right?"

She hesitates for a moment, then sighs, nodding her reluctant agreement. "See, this is why you got the top grade in Negotiations class. You've always been way too good at getting what you want."

I grin. "Thanks—I think?"

"Yeah, the tapes exist," she says. "I heard about some kind of investigation hold, but you'll have to subpoena the museum if you want access."

I groan, feeling my frustration rise. "That could take weeks. We don't have that kind of time."

"I'm really sorry, James," Katie says, giving me a sympathetic look. "I wish I could do more, but you're just going to have to go through the proper channels."

Screw proper channels.

Katie doesn't know it, but she's already given me everything I need. Now that I'm certain the museum tapes exist and they've already been given to the prosecution, I'm determined to get them for our side. Sure, I can obtain them legally through discovery, but that takes time. The sooner we get those tapes, the sooner we'll know what we're working with.

The next day at the office, I know exactly what to do. I take a deep breath and dial the museum's Executive Director's number again. This time, when she answers, I don't bother with pleasantries.

"Hi, it's James Woodsen again from Whitehall & Rowe—"

"Ms. Woodsen, as I told you yesterday, I don't have time for—"

"Do you have time for Damien Blackhollow, one of your biggest donors?"

She sputters into the phone, caught by surprise. "Well, yes, of course. But what does this have to do with Mr. Blackhollow?"

"Well, Sherri, I represent Mr. Blackhollow. He's aware that these tapes exist, and he asked me personally to contact you and ask for a copy ASAP."

This is a lie, of course.

Damien doesn't even know I'm calling this woman, but I think if he did know, he'd approve of my tactics doing whatever it takes. Something tells me that Damien and I have that in common.

"If you don't want to upset one of your most important patrons," I continue, "I suggest you release them to us right away."

Moments later, I'm confirming her address and arranging for our courier to pick up the tapes by lunchtime. I'm elated and can't wait to tell Quinn all about how I got the tapes—well maybe not *everything*, I might leave the tiny white lies out of it—but my initial excitement fades as soon as I start watching the videos.

At first glance, the footage shows exactly what I expected: party guests milling about the valet drive, talking, laughing, the usual. Damien arrives on schedule, right around 7 p.m., stepping out of his limo and looking especially dapper in a classic Tom Ford tuxedo. He's all by himself. No fiancée in sight. Then I see him leaving the Gala at 2 a.m., just like he said. That part is all good.

The problem is that his limo shows up a third time, right around 10 p.m. I can tell by the license plate that it's the same one. It's right around the time Damien would've had to leave the party to make it back to his house to commit the murder.

Unfortunately, I can't confirm who actually gets inside the limo. There's a weird blur on the screen right after the limo pulls up. The footage skips, almost like a glitch, and by the time it stabilizes again, the limo is gone.

That blur—it could be anyone. Even if it is Damien's own personal limo, his driver could be dropping off someone else at his order. A friend. Family member. Work associate.

But then I think back to something my Criminal Law professor once told us. When looking for clues in a case, if you hear hooves, think of horses—not unicorns. Sure, the blur could be all those things and any of those people, but the most obvious answer?

Damien Blackhollow.

CHAPTER 6

The low hum of the elevator echoes as I ride up to the newest and grandest Blackhollow Industries office building from the parking lot. The building is a marvel of modern architecture, designed by the renowned architect Jonathan Graines, with a price tag rumored to exceed half a billion dollars. Its sleek frame stretches high above the Boston skyline, a towering testament to the company's stature and Damien Blackhollow's unrelenting ambition.

In my hand is the thick file folder Mark gave me with the name and contact info for Alan Jefferson, the office manager of the building. Alan seemed like a nice enough man on the phone, and our call regarding my obtaining the security camera footage had gone smoothly, certainly more so than my back-and-forth with the museum yesterday.

Of course, that was to be expected. Alan worked for Damien, so he was more than eager to help out with anything his boss needed. We'd made an appointment to meet at his office on the twenty-first floor. I was hoping for a simple and straightforward hand-off and then planned to use the rest of the day to review the tapes.

The elevator doors slide open, and I step out into the expansive, ultra-modern lobby. Expensive abstract art, bold splashes of color against crisp white walls, pairs with sleek glass and steel lines to make the space feel more like a high-end luxury hotel than a corporate office. My heels click against the polished marble floor as I approach the security desk, clutching the folder and my tote bag.

That's when I see him.

Damien Blackhollow, in all his glory, leans casually against the desk. He's dressed in another designer suit, this one a dark cashmere blend that complements the color of his obsidian eyes. His expression is calm, amused.

"You're early," he says, a slow smile spreading across his face. "That's good. I like punctuality."

My pulse quickens. There's just something about this man that makes my skin go all prickly, like I'm standing too close to an open flame.

"Mr. Blackhollow? What are you doing here?"

He pushes off the desk and strolls toward me with that effortless grace of his. "Let's just say I like to keep an eye on things," he murmurs, his gaze never leaving mine. There's a weight to his words, a subtle hint that maybe he's not talking just about the case. "And no need for formalities. We're going to be working together for the long haul now. Please call me Damien."

"Okay, Damien." I swallow. "I'm just here to get some security tapes. I didn't realize you'd be involved. I got the feeling during our last meeting that you weren't all that interested in the day-to-day of your case."

"Is that so?" He raises a dark brow, and I realize my words might be seen as somewhat offensive.

"I'm sorry," I say, backpedaling. "I just meant—it seemed like you were busy with other important business matters and wanted us to handle as much as we could without bothering you."

"Oh, you're no bother." His smile widens. "It's just you

today, correct? Quinn and the rest of the Scooby Gang are elsewhere?"

"Yes, that's correct."

"Good."

My breath catches in my throat for a second. There's something in his tone, something warm and inviting, that momentarily throws me off balance.

"So, uh, what's the plan?" I ask, breaking eye contact and looking around the corner, wondering where Alan is. "Is your Operations Manager on the way?"

"I'm afraid Alan won't be joining. It's just us."

"Oh."

"I hope that's okay?" Damien's gaze flickers over me, a hint of amusement in his eyes. "Don't worry, I'll make sure you get whatever you need today."

He starts walking down the long hallway, gesturing for me to follow behind him. We step into another elevator that leads to the very top of the building and, moments later, the doors open directly into his office.

The space is breathtaking. The air is heavy with the faint scent of leather and cedar, grounding everything in quiet luxury. Rows of bookshelves line the walls, filled with old volumes—some in languages I can't quite identify. An enormous mahogany desk dominates the room, its surface nearly bare aside from a set of ledgers and a sleek fountain pen. Behind it, floor-to-ceiling windows reveal a sweeping view of Boston—sleek skyscrapers rising alongside historic buildings and the shimmering expanse of the Charles River winding through the city.

"I have to confess," I say, settling into an armchair in front of his desk as Damien moves to sit across from me. "I'm still a little confused how these tapes could exonerate you. I wanted to ask Alan about that. He mentioned on the phone that Blackhollow Industries first broke ground on this building over three years ago, but they only keep backup files for three months."

"Yes, that's correct."

"Right, so then the murder weapon could've been dumped here anytime in the past year. For all we know, it was disposed of months ago, and then we wouldn't see anything helpful on the tapes," I say. "This feels a little like an exercise in futility, if I'm being honest."

"How much did Alan tell you about this building?"

"Not much." I shrug. "I know it's newly opened, but construction has been ongoing for years."

"That's right." He nods along. "But this building and the surrounding area have only been accessible to the public for the last two weeks, after we finished primary construction. Before that, it was heavily guarded by armed security and a high-voltage electric fence," he explains. "My team takes security very seriously."

I frown, the implications sinking in. "So, you're saying the knife must've been planted recently… after the building opened?"

"Precisely," he says. "And whoever did it knows me—and my business—quite intimately."

Something in his tone makes me pause. I stare up at him curiously.

"You sound like you know who did this?"

"Just some ideas. Nothing concrete." He shrugs. "A man like me makes a lot of enemies."

"Have you and Quinn talked about this yet? About your *ideas*?" My heart races, a mixture of hope and excitement coursing through me. There's a possibility I could come back today not just with the tapes but with a list of suspects too. "If you know who did this, you have to tell us."

"Should," Damien corrects. "Should tell you, you mean. I don't *have* to do anything."

"You're right, I'm sorry." I chew my lip, knowing I need to play this just right. I'm good at getting what I want, but I'm not used to working with a man like Damien. "It's just that this could be huge for your defense…"

"Perhaps." Damien's expression closes off, the cool mask of indifference sliding back into place. "But it's not my job to find suspects to clear my name. It's yours."

I take a step closer, frustration and curiosity warring within me.

"We're your legal team—not miracle workers," I say. "Yes, it's our job to defend you to the best of our ability, but we can't do it without your help. If you know something, why wouldn't you—"

"Careful, James," he says, interrupting me. "I can see how much you want to contribute to this case. I'm not so self-involved to believe it's my wellbeing you're concerned with, per se, but I recognize ambition and drive when I see it. Good traits, to be sure, when kept in check. But don't let your overeagerness cause you to overstep."

I bite my lip again and remind myself I'm just the lowly junior associate on this case. He's right, I shouldn't be so bold with a client. I'm dangerously out of line.

"You're right. I apologize for my… overzealousness." I look down, shuffling my feet. "I just want to do a good job. I didn't mean to offend you."

"It's not me I'm concerned with," he says. "There are other forces at work here. Things in play you don't understand."

A chill runs through me despite the warmth of the building. There's a warning in his tone, but I'm not sure why.

"I can handle myself."

Damien's expression shifts, a glimmer of something dangerous crossing his features. "You may think that," he says, his gaze boring into mine with intensity, "but if you keep digging, you may not be prepared for the consequences."

"I know what I'm doing," I insist, lifting my chin. "I've dealt with cases like this before."

His smirk returns, slow and dark.

"You've never dealt with anyone like me, James," he says. "Trust me on that."

The words hang in the air between us, charged and potent, and for a moment, I forget to breathe. There's an intimacy in his tone that feels out of place, almost too personal for a conversation about evidence and security tapes.

I force myself to break from his gaze and look away. "I think I'd better get those tapes now," I say, standing. "I have a busy day ahead of me."

"I'm sure you do."

Damien leans forward, reaching into the sleek drawer beneath his desk and producing a slim black case containing the tapes. He hands them to me, his fingers brushing mine for the briefest moment, sending a chill up my arm. I clutch the tapes tightly, forcing my expression to stay neutral.

"Thank you."

"Be careful, James." His eyes hold a warning. "Whoever is framing me isn't going to take kindly to you poking around."

"Don't worry. I don't scare easily."

A glimmer of admiration flashes in his gaze. "I hope that's true."

Tapes in hand, I turn back toward the elevator, my heartbeat quickening with each step. I should feel good about what I've accomplished this morning, but a tight knot has formed in my stomach, refusing to unwind. I can't shake the feeling that I'm walking into a trap.

Or worse, that I'm already caught in it.

On the way home, I stop by the office to have IT load the

tapes to the server, so things are secure. This way, anyone on the team can remote access our firm's database online to cue up the files. After that, I head to my apartment to watch the security tapes on my laptop, sprawled out on my bed with Lucky curled up beside me. One thing about the firm, they work us to the bone, but they don't micromanage. As long as you're doing your job, most partners don't care where you're doing it from. That works well for me. I've got Madison and Lucky to take care of, and it's nice to be able to work from home on occasion and not always be shackled to my office chair.

As the tapes load, I think back to what Damien told me earlier, how the knife must have been planted within the last two weeks because the office building wasn't accessible before then. If this really wasn't Damien, and someone else is trying to frame him, why wait a whole year? Why now, right around the same time as his arrest?

I have a hunch that Damien's arrest and the murder weapon's sudden appearance are connected somehow. It's incredibly convenient that the murder weapon was found so soon after his arrest.

"What if they wanted to make sure the charges stuck after the arrest?" I ask out loud to Lucky. "What if the person who buried the knife tipped off the media? And the DA?"

It's a wild hunch, but not a crazy one.

I glance at Lucky, who is watching the screen as if he understands exactly what's going on. "What do you think, boy?" I ask, scratching behind his ears. "Should I start from the beginning or skip straight to after Damien was arrested?"

Lucky's ears twitch eagerly, and he taps the laptop's keyboard with his paw, starting the tapes on the day of Damien's arrest.

I chuckle. "Guess that's as good a place as any."

The footage plays, showing a busy building during the day. Employees coming and going. It's boring, monotonous... Nothing seems amiss. At evening time, the floodlights turn on, and I watch as security makes their rounds. Nothing interesting happens until the timestamp hits a few minutes before midnight. Suddenly, a dark figure sneaks into the frame.

My heart thumps in my chest.

Holy shit.

Can it really be this easy? Do I have the culprit right here on tape?

Judging by the height and build, it's definitely a man, but even with the floodlights on, it's still too dark to make out any discernible features. He gets closer to the camera, and just when I think I'm about to see his face, the screen flickers and the image distorts into a blur. A few more minutes pass until, just as quickly as it began, the blurriness clears. By then, the figure is long gone; it's as if they'd never even been there.

I can't believe it. It's just like the weird technical glitch with the Museum Gala tapes.

No, not just like.

It's *exactly* like those tapes.

My pulse quickens as I sit up, leaning in closer to the screen. Two tapes. Two locations. Two completely different servers. But both with the same strange distortions at critical times?

"What are the odds?" I ask, wondering aloud.

Lucky mewls next to me and tilts his head, as if to say, "Not good."

I shoot off a quick email to Quinn and the team, letting them know about my review of the tapes, and then rewind the video one more time. I squint at the screen, trying to focus harder, but the distortion makes it impossible to see anything useful. Frustration boils up inside me as I lean back against the headboard of my bed, rubbing my temples. The blurs on the tapes feel like a taunt, a deliberate attempt to cover up something important. But who would have the resources to pull off something like that?

And why?

My cell phone buzzes on the nightstand. I look over and see Quinn's name flashing on the screen, sending my pulse skittering. Quinn knows I'm working from home and rarely calls unless it's an emergency.

I groan, thinking back to my interactions with Damien this morning. While he doesn't seem like the type to complain, I *was* a bit rude to him. I hope this isn't going to be a lecture from Quinn on attorney-client relations—though I probably deserve one.

"Hi, Quinn." I answer, my voice edged with a bit of anxiety. "What's up?"

"James, are you sitting down?" His voice is softer than usual, heavy with a kind of seriousness I'm not used to hearing from him. Plus, I'm suddenly James—not Woodsen. Something is very wrong.

"Yeah… I'm sitting." My stomach tightens. "Why?"

There's a long pause. I hear his heavy breathing on the other end, as if he's trying to figure out how to say what's coming next.

"Quinn? You're kind of freaking me out?"

"It's… Mark." His voice cracks slightly. "He's dead."

The words land like a punch to the gut, knocking the air from my lungs.

"Dead?" I repeat, unable to process at first. "What do you mean?"

"There was an accident. He was hit by a car earlier today, crossing the street near his apartment…" He trails off, the weight of his words hanging in the silence.

For a moment, the world feels like it's tilting. I don't know what's up and what's down. I didn't even like Mark, it's true, but he was still a part of my life, still a constant presence at the firm. And now he's just… gone?

"James, I know this is sudden," Quinn says gently. "Why don't you take the day off tomorrow? Get some rest. And if you need anything, let me know, okay?"

"Okay." I swallow, my throat dry. I feel oddly detached, like I'm watching myself from a distance. "Thanks, Quinn. Um, talk to you later…"

I hang up and stare at the phone, my thoughts drifting in a haze.

Mark is dead.

I feel a strange emptiness, a dull ache somewhere in the back of my mind. A bit sad, yes, but more numbness than emotion, like my brain can't quite catch up to the reality of it.

Lucky nudges my hand with his nose, as if he knows exactly how I feel. I grab him close and snuggle into his soft fur for a moment, needing the warmth and connection of another living being.

A sudden ping from my laptop catches my attention. I turn, glancing at the screen, seeing a new email notification. The subject line reads simply: "YOU'VE BEEN WARNED."

What happens next almost seems to occur in slow motion. Lucky hisses softly, staring at the screen with those wide, yellow eyes, ears flattening as I click to open the email. It's a single image—a photo of what looks like a street, taken at dusk. The headlights of a car are caught in the frame, casting long shadows across the asphalt. In the corner of the picture is a crumpled, broken body. Blood and guts spew forth. Bones twisted at angles bones aren't supposed to twist. There's no mistaking things. It's Mark, lying motionless, dead on the ground.

Bile rises in my throat as I stare at the grisly image, my

heart hammering against my ribs. Someone was there. Someone took this picture and sent it to me. Someone wanted me to see this. Mark's death was no accident, like Quinn said.

No, this was deliberate.

And this email isn't just a warning—it's a threat.

CHAPTER 7

I lie awake, tossing and turning all night. I can't stop thinking about Mark's death and the cryptic, threatening email that followed. Can't shake the image of Mark lying crumpled on the street, dead. My bedroom feels too small, the air too thin, like the walls are closing in. I try to steady my breathing, fear echoing in my head.

Mark didn't just die. Someone killed him.

And I could be next.

Even when morning comes, the sunlight of a new day streaming through my bedroom window, I don't feel any better. Quinn told me to take the day off, but the last thing I want is to sit at home, alone, and let my anxiety and fear fester. Staying home all day would only mean facing the empty hours and filling them with what-ifs and unanswerable questions.

Instead, I feed Lucky and make breakfast for Madison, and then decide to make my way to the office where at least I can be surrounded by the mundane normalcy of files and paperwork. I'll feel safer within the high-rise walls of Whitehall & Rowe, where I can pretend, if only for a few hours, that things haven't fallen completely off course.

I step off the elevator and pass by Mark's office on the way to my own. The door is ajar, the light still on, as if waiting for his return. His workspace looks just as it did yesterday, when he was still alive. His "Legal Genius at Work" coffee mug still sits half-full, papers strewn across the surface in disarray. Whatever he was working on, now left unfinished. I feel a heaviness in my chest at the sight. Something about it seems painfully sad.

I pause as a folder on the corner of his desk catches my eye. "BLACKHOLLOW" is written on the top of the file in big blocky letters. I should probably keep walking, but something about the folder calls to me like a moth to a flame. I peek around the corner—his secretary, Penny, isn't in. Perhaps Quinn gave her the day off, too.

Before I can lose my nerve, I sneak inside Mark's office and beeline straight for his desk. Quickly, I sift through the folder and his files, the rustling of paper sounding too loud in the otherwise silent building. Part of me feels guilty, like I'm crossing a line that shouldn't be crossed, rummaging through a dead man's papers. Except... one could argue they aren't *really* Mark's papers. Technically, all attorney work product and client files belong to the client—or at the very least, the firm, since the case is still ongoing. Besides, these papers will ultimately make their way to Quinn's desk and then mine anyway.

As I read through the files, a pattern starts to emerge: articles printed from old archives about secret symbols and shadowy cults, notes on ritualistic practices and grisly sacrifices, and references to the dark history of nearby Salem's Fall —a place steeped in mysticism, infamous for the witch trials that took place there hundreds of years ago. Mark had clearly been delving deep into the occult aspects of the case, and the more I read, the more I realize this angle was something he took seriously. His notes are excellent, incredibly thorough. Mark was a shitty person, but I can't deny he was an excellent lawyer.

One symbol in particular catches my eye: a curved spiral with jagged lines radiating outward, intersecting with an inverted pentagram. Mark has drawn it multiple times throughout his notes. It's the same mark that was carved into Vivienne Van Buren's body and written in her blood on the walls and floors of the bedroom where she was found. On one of the pages, underneath the symbol, Mark has scribbled the words: "The Mark of the Veil – Blood Rite ritual – The Order of the Veil."

I step back, my pulse quickening.

The Mark of the Veil? Blood Rite?

What the hell is that?

"Woodsen? What are you doing?" Quinn asks, suddenly appearing in the hallway and startling me so badly I drop the folder. "I told you to take the day off."

"I know." I swallow hard, like a student in trouble with her favorite professor. "But my head wouldn't stop spinning. I needed a distraction."

He walks over to me, his hand settling on my shoulder, sending a wave of warmth through me. His expression is a mix of concern and exasperation, but underneath, there's something softer. "It's been a rough couple of hours," he says. "You need time to process."

"I'm fine," I say, though the lie rings hollow even to me. "I just need to—"

"No arguments," he says, cutting me off and grabbing my elbow. "Come on, you're getting out of here, at least for a few hours. I'm taking you to breakfast."

"Quinn, really, I'm fine—"

"You are *not* fine, no matter how many times you say it out loud. Let's go."

There's a finality in his tone that makes it impossible to refuse. Quinn Alexander Kensington is not the kind of man you say no to when he insists on something. I grab my coat and follow him out.

I'm surprised when Quinn walks past the bustling coffee shop near the office and stops instead in front of an expensive French pâtisserie tucked away in a quiet corner a few blocks away. It's the type of place with warm brick walls, soft lighting, and tables draped in crisp white linens. I've walked by it many times before and have always wanted to try it, but you need reservations months in advance. Plus, the prices on the menu are not for the faint of heart.

Quinn holds the door open for me, his hand brushing lightly against my back as I step inside. The maître d' greets him like an old friend and, despite the long line of people waiting to be seated, he escorts us into the dining room right away and finds a spot for us next to a beautiful, old-fashioned fireplace. Quinn helps me into my chair and takes the seat across from me, his long legs brushing against mine under the table.

The waiter approaches, a polished young man with a crisp white apron. Before I can say anything, Quinn holds up a hand. "Black coffee for the lady, no sugar. And I'll have an espresso." Then, as if an afterthought, he adds, "And please bring us a plate of your blackberry croissants. Thank you."

"Very good, sir." The waiter nods at Quinn. "I'll return shortly with your drinks and pastries," he says and leaves.

I blink at Quinn, surprised. "You remembered my coffee order?"

"Of course. You don't like things too sweet." He says it casually, but there's a flicker of satisfaction in his eyes. "But you'll want to make an exception for the croissants here. Trust me."

"This place is amazing. You're certainly full of surprises today," I say, trying to sound teasing, though I can feel the warmth creeping into my cheeks.

His eyes hold mine. "You have no idea."

The delicious smells of fresh baked goods and brewed coffee fill the air as our waiter returns moments later with our order. Quinn slides the steaming mug toward me, and the tension in my chest eases a little. The first sip is perfect, bold and rich, just the way I like it. I let the gentle heat seep into my palms as I reach for the plate of pastries he insisted on.

I take a bite and can't help moaning out loud. Quinn is absolutely right. Though I'm not usually a fan of sweets, my blackberry croissant tastes like heaven.

"Good?" he asks, chuckling softly.

"Oh my God! It's amazing."

Our eyes lock and the moment between us feels so nice, so easy, I almost forget all about the horror of last night.

"James, tell me, how are you holding up?" he asks, leaning back, watching me with a careful intensity. "You've been through a lot recently with Mark's death. And I know you still feel badly about the Michelle case and that forensic report… plus, you've got your hands full at home with Madison and Lucky." His voice softens, and I realize with a pang how much he's been paying attention to me—to my life, and not just the obvious work stuff.

I glance up, meeting his eyes. There's something tender and caring in them that makes it hard to breathe.

"I'm managing okay," I say slowly. "Things are better at home. Maddie's grades are up, though I still worry about her constantly. And Lucky's… well, Lucky. He's the best. Always around, especially when I need him the most. Almost like he knows."

Quinn's lips quirk into a small smile. "Smart cat."

"He is." I nod along. "Smarter than most people."

"And work?" he presses, leaning forward slightly. His hand rests just inches from mine. "How are you feeling about things?"

I let out a sigh. "It's just… you're right. I do still think about the Michelle case. And I don't want to let anyone down again. Not the firm." My throat tightens. "And definitely not you, Quinn."

His fingers brush against mine, just barely, but it's enough to send sparks dancing up my arm.

"You could never do anything to let me down."

For a moment, it feels like we're teetering on the edge of something—something more than just a professional relationship, something I'm not sure I'm ready for. But then he clears his throat, breaking the spell.

"Eat more," he says, nudging the plate of croissants toward me. "You'll feel better."

I take another pastry, more to appease him than anything else, but as I nibble on the flaky crust, I realize he's right. I do feel better. But it's not just the croissants—it's Quinn. The weight pressing on my chest eases a little more with each bite, the longer I'm here with him.

"Thanks," I say. "For this. For everything."

Quinn smiles, the kind of smile that feels like it's just for me.

"Anytime."

I take a deep breath, letting the sweetness of the moment seep in. Savoring it. But then something starts to shift deep down in my gut—resolve. I glance back up at Quinn, knowing he'll probably be annoyed that I can't just enjoy this time together and unwind, but I can't stop myself.

"I think I found something important in Mark's case files," I say, meeting his eyes. "He was researching the symbols found at the murder scene. Apparently, they're connected to something called the Order of the Veil. Seems like it's some rumored cult or shadow organization." My voice grows firmer as I speak, more confident. "According to his notes, there may be ties to a series of ritual murders in Salem's Fall—possibly dating back to the witch trials in the 1600s. It's vague, but definitely disturbing."

"Yes, I'm aware of Mark's research," he says. "He was on his way to Salem's Fall yesterday when he was killed. He was planning to meet with an occult expert there to discuss his findings."

I stare at him, stunned. "Why didn't you tell me about this?"

We're supposed to be a team, and teams are supposed to share everything. Does Quinn still not trust me? Even after all the hard work I've already put into this case?

It hurts, and not just because I feel excluded, but because of how much I care about Quinn and his approval. It matters to me probably more than it should.

"I was planning to. Mark was going to share with the whole team once he returned from the witness interview in Salem's Fall. And you were busy with the security tapes, remember?" He grins, a pleased look of approval on his face. "And doing a stellar job, by the way."

"They both had technical malfunctions. The tapes were worthless!"

"Not true," he says, shaking his head. "You did good work getting them so fast, and at least the Gala tapes give us a starting point on alibi. Even if we don't have a perfect timeline, the prosecution's copy will be blurred like ours is. They can't use the tapes as hard evidence against Blackhollow."

"Okay, well, who's going now?"

He puts down his espresso, confused. "Who's going where?"

"To Salem's Fall," I say, a bit impatiently. "Now that Mark is… um… well… someone still needs to go, right?"

He shakes his head. "After what happened to Mark, the firm has decided against it," he says. "It was a long shot anyway, and we have more important work to do here."

"You're just going to ignore a lead?"

"Salem's Fall is a dead end," Quinn says. "We have to focus on building Blackhollow's legal defense here, in Boston, not chasing after crazy conspiracy theories. If we start looking desperate, it could ruin the firm's reputation."

"Mark didn't think it was desperate," I say, feeling a surge of alarm rising in my chest. I don't know why, but I feel certain blowing off Salem's Fall is a mistake. "He's done a lot of research. It's at least worth checking out."

I look down at my coffee, mentally preparing myself because I know I need to tell Quinn about the threatening email from last night. It's important—critical, even—and not just to our case, but to Mark and his family as well. They deserve to know the truth about his death, that it was something more than just a tragic accident.

But the second Quinn learns about the email, everything will change. If Quinn knows, he's likely to pull me from the case. For my own protection, of course. It's a logical step for him to take, especially since I know how much he cares about me. I can't allow that to happen. I need to see this case through. I'm too invested now.

"Quinn, I—I need to tell you something," I say, my voice trembling. "I don't think Mark's death was an accident."

"What are you talking about?"

"After your call last night, I got an email. Someone sent me a photo of Mark's body; they were there, taking pictures." I shiver, disgust running through me. "It was *awful*, Quinn. Whoever killed Mark could be coming for me next. This isn't just about Damien. We have to find out who's behind this before someone else is hurt."

"*What?*" Quinn blanches, his expression shifting from shock to something harder. "Forward me the email." His voice is sharp now, urgent. "Right now."

I pull out my phone, hitting send.

Quinn reaches across the table, his grip firm around my wrist. "Why the hell didn't you tell me this sooner?" he asks, fingers tightening, his frustration bleeding through.

"I didn't want to worry you."

A tiny white lie. The truth is, I wasn't nearly as concerned with Quinn's feelings as I was about jeopardizing my place on the trial team.

Quinn exhales, dragging a hand through his hair. "Damn it, James. It's my job to protect you," he says, his voice rough. "I can't do that if you keep me in the dark."

"With all due respect, you're my partner—your job isn't to protect me, it's to work alongside me," I say. "Come on, Quinn. We both know I have to go to Salem's Fall."

"It's not just me or the firm." His gaze flickers with an emotion I can't quite place. Concern? Fear? Maybe even a hint of guilt. "The client doesn't want anyone else going either. He won't authorize any travel expenses."

My skin warms. I think I know what's going on. Damien obviously approved of travel when it involved Mark going to investigate. For whatever reason, he clearly doesn't want me going to Salem's Fall.

These damn men. Just who the hell do they think they are?

"Since when does Damien Blackhollow get to dictate how we conduct our defense?" I push my coffee and baked goods away with an annoyed shove. "It's our responsibility to advocate for our client, and that includes following *every* lead, no matter how strange. Damien hired us because we're the best. He needs to let us do our damn job," I say, crossing my arms over my chest. "And, frankly, if he doesn't like the way we do it, he should find another firm."

There's a long beat of silence as Quinn stares at me with a mix of both annoyance and admiration on his face.

"You're really something, you know that?" he asks. "I

never would've dreamed of talking to a senior partner like this."

I smile a bit sheepishly. "But that's why you hired me, isn't it? You'd hate having a 'yes man' on your team."

Affection flashes in his eyes, and I know I'm right. I am a handful, but I get the job done. Well, except for that terrible screwup on my last case, but that was a one-time thing, and I'm determined to make up for it.

"Okay, fine." Quinn exhales, a resigned look settling over his face. "You can go to Salem's Fall, but this is a quick trip. You find what you can and come back immediately," he says. "I'll deal with Blackhollow."

I jump up eagerly. Even though it's not exactly appropriate, and I'm not a hugger, I throw my arms around him.

"Thanks, Quinn! I won't let you down!"

He's so close, I can feel the heat between our bodies, the air between us charged with something unspoken. Quinn's eyes meet mine, holding me there, and for a moment, I see it—the concern for me, the protective instinct he's trying to disguise as professional caution.

My breath catches as he leans in further, just a fraction, his eyes dipping down to my lips before snapping back up again. Then, just as quickly, he pulls back, his jaw tightening. His voice drops lower, rougher.

"Be careful, James," he says. "I mean it."

CHAPTER 8

Lucky watches me on my bed with curious eyes as I pack my oversized suitcase. After I get the basics and my work supplies into my bag, I toss in a few extra outfits—far more than necessary. Quinn called this a quick trip to Salem's Fall, but I always like to be prepared.

My first real out-of-town work trip.

Excitement buzzes through me, though I know I should be wary too. If Mark was killed for getting too close to the truth, and that truth is in Salem's Fall, I'm walking straight into danger. And yet, all I can think about is cracking this case wide open. If I help Quinn win, the sky's the limit for me at Whitehall & Rowe.

As I zip the bulging suitcase shut, Lucky nudges his little nose against the leather handle. His yellow eyes flick up to me, curious with just a bit of concern.

"Don't worry, boy. You're coming with me," I say, tossing his favorite feather wand into my tote.

As if I'd ever leave Lucky behind. Maddie is far too unreliable to be trusted. She'd probably forget to feed my cat. She can barely remember to feed herself.

Plus, I hate being away from Lucky. He's been a constant source of love and comfort for me ever since I rescued him years ago. When I found him in the alley behind my high school a few weeks after Mom died, I'd been worried Aunt Aggie would make me take him to a shelter. But she'd been supportive of adopting the cat, reading that pets can do wonders for kids and grief. And she was right.

Lucky and I bonded right away. Back then, he was the only thing that got me through the nightmares as I dealt with the pain of Mom's death. It was uncanny, the way he adjusted to my moods, curling up beside me when I needed comfort, playful when I needed a distraction. Almost like he knew what I was thinking and needed even before I did.

Now, he trots after me as I roll my suitcase into the living room, his tail flicking like he already knows what's coming.

"You're going to love Salem's Fall," I joke, coaxing Lucky inside his cat carrier. "It's the perfect place for a black cat. You'll fit right in with all the other familiars."

"Okay, Sabrina the Teenage Witch." Maddie smirks from the couch, watching us. "You're such a weirdo, always talking to that cat like he understands you."

Lucky lets out an indignant little hiss, swiping his tail against the mesh of his carrier like he's insulted.

I shoot Maddie a smug smile. "See? He does."

She just snorts, shaking her head.

"Whatever."

"I should be back tomorrow, but the fridge is stocked," I tell her. "And I left a casserole for you too. It'll last you at least two meals, okay?"

"Gross." She makes a face. "I'll just order DoorDash."

"Eat the casserole, please. It's good for you. But here"—I grin, handing her two hundred dollars in cash—"for emergencies."

"Ohhh! Perfect!" She shoves the money in her pocket greedily. "I just saw the cutest new workout set for the gym."

"*Maddie*–"

"Thanks, Jamie." She gives me a kiss on the cheek. "Love you, big sis!"

I groan. She's incorrigible.

"Love you too. Be good, Mads," I say, heading for the front door. "Please study. And do *not* oversleep and miss any exams this week!"

"Of course!" she says with a big wink that is not at all reassuring. It makes me nervous to leave Maddie unchaperoned, especially during midterms, but I don't have much choice.

Though Salem's Fall is only a few miles from my Boston apartment, the drive takes almost an hour in traffic this time of year. People come from all over the world to the charming little New England town to celebrate fall and Halloween. Even the drive feels magical as the landscape changes from bustling streets to winding roads lined with ancient maple and elm trees. The leaves are already changing colors and starting to fall.

By the time I arrive, the sun hangs low in the sky, casting an orange glow over the narrow streets. It's only the first week of October, but the place is already a madhouse. Cars and people everywhere. Halloween decorations all around. Jack-o'-lanterns, witches' hats, and skeletons adorning doorsteps and porches. It's a town that feels caught between worlds with modern-day tourists weaving through streets steeped in history.

I head first to the Cauldron Cottage, the cute little bed and breakfast I found online. I'm lucky they had a last-minute cancellation. Getting housing here this time of year can be challenging. Most places are booked months, if not years, in advance. Not to mention finding a pet-friendly spot is never easy, but thankfully, the Cottage allows cats.

I check in and settle into my room, which is beyond adorable with all the Salem's Fall charm they promised online.

A pumpkin-orange flannel bedspread and a sign above the headboard that reads "Beware of Witches," which tries to look old and authentic, but I've already seen a dozen just like it while driving through town. A tiny black cauldron of silver-wrapped candies sits on the nightstand, a nice touch. Heavy purple curtains frame a window overlooking the cobblestone streets outside, while a wrought-iron candleholder casts flickering light, creating an inviting, almost eerie glow.

After unpacking, I settle Lucky with treats and water, then put Disney Junior on TV to keep him company. He lets out a low yowl in protest, clearly unimpressed as I head for the door, his eyes full of judgment.

"I'll be back soon. Keep your whiskers on," I tell him, slipping out for my interview.

I step out of the Cottage and head to the Wandering Raven, an occult gift shop, to meet Professor Hargrove—the expert Mark tracked down. As I walk along, an eerie thrill prickles my skin, raising the hairs on my arms. I haven't been to Salem's Fall since I was a kid, and it's still as delightfully peculiar as ever. Each storefront I pass is more eclectic than the last. Crystal balls, tarot cards, shelves of witchcraft books, and magical candles. There's an energy to this place, something old and charged that hums just beneath the surface, as if the town itself is watching, waiting.

I find the shop tucked away on a side street, its sign creaking in the wind. A bell jingles softly as I push the door open, the scent of old paper and incense surrounding me. All around are shelves packed with mysterious artifacts and rows and rows of books about magic and alchemy. At the counter is a college-aged girl, working the register. She nods like she's been expecting me and disappears into a back office to grab Professor Hargrove.

I browse the store while I wait. A dusty, leather-bound book resting on a wooden display catches my attention. *Blood and Bone: New England's Hidden Histories of Magic, Mysteries, and the Occult* is embossed in faded gold letters. My breath hitches as I scan the contents, spotting a drawing of the Mark of the Veil—the Blood Rite symbol—right away.

I can't believe it. What are the chances?

As I flip through the book, a familiar name leaps out at me—Blackhollow. My hand trembles on the page. It's the first direct reference to Damien's family that I've seen explicitly connected to the occult. There's no denying it now. Something strange is going on, and I'm right in the middle of it.

"You must be James Woodsen."

A voice startles me, and my jaw drops as I turn to find Mark's occult expert. Only, he's nothing like I imagined.

I was prepared for an old man with silver hair and a wizened face, but Professor Nicolas Hargrove is anything but. He's in his mid-thirties, with glossy chestnut locks that fall perfectly into place, a rugged jawline, and eyes that are the exact shade of polished emeralds. He wears a leather jacket over a casual button-down, making him look more rockstar than academic.

"Professor Hargrove?"

"Not what you were expecting?" His mouth curls into a half-smile as if aware he's caught me off guard.

"Honestly, I didn't know what to expect," I say, trying to maintain my professionalism. "But I certainly wasn't picturing an award-winning Occult Studies professor to look like… well, you."

He laughs, a low, rich sound that vibrates in the air. "I get that a lot," he says and extends a hand. "Nice to meet you." His grip is firm and warm, lingering a moment too long. He's so attractive, though, I don't exactly mind.

"Thanks for making the time, Professor. I appreciate it."

"The pleasure is all mine," he says. "And call me Nick. No need for formalities."

"Okay, great. Thanks… Nick." I grin. "As I explained on the phone, we represent Damien Blackhollow and are looking into some kind of secret society, or cult, I guess, called the Order of the Veil."

His gaze sweeps across the shop a bit warily.

"There's a quiet spot in the back where we can sit and talk more freely," he says and turns, gesturing for me to follow him to a small wooden table away from prying ears.

We sit down and he points to the book in my hand. "I see you've already found *Blood and Bone*. Excellent choice. May I?" He takes the book from me and flips it open to the chapter I was just looking at, pointing to the Blood Rite symbol. "This is what you came for, right? To learn more about its dark history?" I nod and lean in closer, reading over his shoulder. "Tell me, what do you know about the Veil so far?"

I glance up to find him watching me, a glimmer of excitement in his eyes.

"Just some things my associate found online." I pull out my laptop and begin to take notes. "I know it's some sort of organization with ties to the witch trials that took place here in the late 1600s, but I don't think Mark could find much else. It all seems very secretive."

He lifts a brow, a teasing grin on his face. "Well, I suppose that's the point with a secret society, hmmm?"

"Yeah, I guess you're right." I chuckle. "But that's why I'm here. Mark found your name and knew you were an expert on this occult stuff. He planned to interview you himself, but… well…" I glance down awkwardly. "You know the rest."

"I'm sorry about your coworker," he says, eyes filling with sympathy. "Were you two close?"

"Not really, but it was still quite a shock."

"I imagine it was." His gaze sharpens, his expression turning serious. "I've been studying occult practices my entire professional career, and I can tell you that the Order of the Veil is one of the most dangerous, ruthless groups of individuals I've ever come across." He plays with the corners of the book, almost nervously. "The Veil descends from an ancient secret society called the Order, which was created hundreds of years ago to address issues with supernatural entities existing in our world. At some point, the Order splintered into branches with different purposes. Some meant to protect humankind, others meant to control it." He pauses, looking at me. "I presume you've heard about what happened in that small farming town in the Pacific Northwest last year? Allium Valley?"

It takes me a moment and then I remember. It was all over the news. Last spring, a series of mass murders took place during a local music festival. Hundreds died. The town was shut off from civilization, blockaded by the killers so no one could escape. The authorities still hadn't figured out what happened or why, and the rumors were insane. Everything from a terrorist attack to supernatural monsters and aliens to devil worshippers.

"You mean the Garlic Groove Festival murders? Sure, who hasn't heard about that?" I ask. "The latest theory I heard was it was a bunch of farmers that got sick on bad garlic and went insane."

There's a long beat.

"That wasn't farmers…"

"No? What was it, then?"

"Vampire infestation."

I hold back my snort, my hands pausing over my keyboard. "You're messing with me, right? Vampires aren't real."

"The government and media won't tell you the truth, but that's exactly what it was," he says, stone-faced and serious. "One of the Order's factions—the Order of the Clove—is charged with protecting against vampires. I interviewed one of the surviving members, a young man named Ethan Park. He was in Allium Valley during the siege. It's all there in the research I emailed your colleague." He taps a finger thoughtfully against the table. "The Clove are the good guys, but the Veil is... different."

"Different how?" I ask, doing my best to hide my skepticism. Vampires?

Really?

It appears I may be dealing with a cuckoo conspiracy theorist, which I guess is unsurprising since conspiracies kind of go hand-in-hand with secret cults. I don't believe in the supernatural, but I'm already here, so I might as well see it through.

"The Veil was founded in the late 1600s during the Salem's Fall witch trials," he says, thumbing through the pages of the old book. "Unlike the Clove, which sought to protect humanity, the Veil embraced darkness, using ritual magic to harness supernatural power. I'm sure you know the basics of the witch trials. The hysteria that swept through the colonies, neighbors turning on each other, innocents imprisoned or executed."

He pauses, scratching his chin as he studies me. "But what you probably don't know is that some of the accused weren't so innocent. A small, elite group of townspeople—wealthy, powerful—were actual practitioners of ancient rites. Fearing for their own survival, they banded together, not just to protect themselves, but to ensure their influence would last. And over time, their ceremonies evolved into something else. Something... darker."

"What kind of ceremonies? You mean like a church service?"

"Not exactly." He smirks. "More like human sacrifices."

I gasp. "You're kidding, right?"

"Afraid not. They believed it allowed them to harness supernatural power."

This time, I can't resist rolling my eyes. A group that actually thinks they have magical powers? Like witches?

"But that's ridiculous."

"Is it?" he asks. "There are lots of things in this world we don't understand, but that doesn't mean they're not true."

I shrug, unconvinced, and point to the chapter in the book with Damien's family name. "Okay, what about the Blackhollows?" I ask. "Why are they mentioned here? What does Damien's family have to do with all this?"

"Why wouldn't they be mentioned?" He gives a dry chuckle, but there's a hard edge to it. "The Blackhollow family was one of the founding members of the Veil, after all."

I pause, cocking my head to the side. He looks deathly serious, but I'm having a hard time taking this all in.

"Are you really implying that the Blackhollow family—one of the most prominent, wealthiest families in all of New England—has been sacrificing people? For *power*?"

"Well, it's never been proven, but yes, those are the rumors, and I believe them." A muscle tightens in his jaw. "That family is... evil. And the murder you're investigating certainly fits the pattern of Veil rituals."

"Okay, even if I buy all of this—the Blackhollows founding this cult, or whatever, and the sacrifices—why would they keep performing these rituals now?" I frown, my mind racing. "The family is already rich and powerful. What's the point?"

"The point, James, is legacy. It takes a lot to get to the top, but even more to stay there." There's a pause and his gaze fixes on me. "You don't believe me, do you? You think I'm off my rocker?" He huffs, slumping down into his chair. "The Board of Trustees at New England University didn't believe me either. That's why I lost my teaching job. Or maybe they did believe, but the Blackhollow family is too powerful. They get rid of anyone who speaks up. Either they discredit you or much, much worse."

His eyes narrow and I catch a glimpse of something angry lurking just beneath his charming exterior. This isn't simply academic curiosity for him; it's personal.

"Listen, James, if you're going to keep digging, be careful," he warns. "Keep a low profile. They already know you're here. The Veil's reach is extensive. And your client, Damien Blackhollow? He may look pretty and respectable, but there's a deadly monster hidden under all that gloss. He's the worst of them. Trust me on that."

His words send a chill down my spine.

"Well... thanks for your time, Professor. This has been... eye-opening." Standing, I pull out my wallet. "I'd like to buy this book. How much?"

He smiles broadly, that magnetic charm flickering back on like a light. "It's yours. On the house," he says and escorts me to the front door. "And if you need anything else while you're in town, anything at all, I'd be more than happy to oblige."

I pause for a moment, considering his offer. Professor Cuckoo may have a few screws loose, but he's still cute enough for me to want to take him up on it—if I weren't so focused on my job.

Not to mention, my dance card is already uncomfortably full this week. There's Quinn and whatever the hell is brewing there, plus the unnerving pull I feel every time I'm in the same room as my murder-cult-member-slash-client Damien. The last thing I need is to add another wildly inappropriate contender to the mix—no matter how good-looking he is.

"Thanks, but I don't think I'll be in town for long."

"That's a shame." His face falls with disappointment. "Well, before you go, make sure you pay a visit to Strega's Hollow. The area was used during the witch trials, and it's become something of a memorial for the tourists. The Veil has strong ties to the place. You might find something interesting there."

I feel a strange mixture of relief and apprehension as I wave goodbye to the professor and head back down the winding streets. The wind picks up, scattering fallen leaves at my feet as the night air brings a crisp chill. I shiver, pulling my sweater tighter, and get the oddest sensation that someone is watching me.

Just as I turn the corner, I hear the sound of footsteps behind me. Too close. Too deliberate. I glance back and freeze as a figure emerges from the shadows, cloaked in darkness. It's not just the proximity that sends my pulse racing. It's the mask he wears.

Not some cheap Halloween mask typical for this time of year—this is something else. Ornate, imposing, silver-plated, polished to a mirror shine. Symbols etched into the metal. Eerily smooth. Expressionless. Hollow eye sockets, gaping like black voids.

Panic surges through my body as the figure lunges forward. Then there's a knife, glinting terrifyingly in the dim light. I twist away just in time to avoid the blade as it comes for me. Stumbling backward, I crash onto the pavement, breath knocked out of me, hands scraping against cold concrete. My heart jackhammers in my chest.

I need to run. I need to move. But my body won't listen. I lock up, frozen in pure, animal terror. A scream lodges in my throat as my attacker looms over me, shadow stretching long and monstrous beneath the streetlamp. The knife flashes again, rising high.

Everything else falls away—just the blade, the dark, and the gut-deep certainty I'm not getting out of this in one piece.

This isn't happening. This can't be happening...

Suddenly, a blur of movement barrels into the masked

figure. A stranger slams into my assailant, knocking the knife from his hand and delivering a series of powerful, efficient blows, driving him back. My attacker stumbles, clutching his ribs, then turns and flees into the night.

I'm still frozen on the pavement, chest heaving, shaking, as the figure turns toward me. I can't make out his face—the alley is too dark, shadows slicing across his features like a shield.

"Don't move," he says—quick and sharp, rough with adrenaline.

Something about that voice—

My breath catches.

I know that voice.

Strong, muscular arms slide under me, and I'm lifted gently—carefully—as if I might break. He cradles me like I'm something precious, one hand at my back, the other brushing damp hair from my face, fingers lingering for half a second too long on my cheek.

"Are you okay? Did he hurt you?"

I blink, stunned, my brain lagging. I try to speak, but nothing comes out.

"James," he breathes, raw with panic. "Say something. Please."

The shadows shift. A sliver of streetlight catches him just right, revealing his face at last—gorgeous, unmistakable, and seared into my memory. His gaze scans mine, his expression torn between fury and fear.

My jaw drops.

"Damien?"

CHAPTER 9

Salem's Fall, Massachusetts

Lucky purrs against my pillow, curled into a tight little ball at my head as the early morning light filters through the windows of my room at the Cottage. I lie in bed, my body aching from the events of the night before. I still can't believe I was attacked on the streets of Salem's Fall, which is both terrifying and shocking. But even more shocking? Being saved by Damien Blackhollow.

Why is he here?

How did he find me?

Lucky snuggles in closer, as if he knows I'm still a bit rattled. I reach up and scratch him behind the ears, feeling the comfort of his sleek, soft fur under the pads of my fingers. The light vibration of his purring relaxes me.

That is, until my phone blares with an incoming call.

"Woodsen!" Quinn barks, his voice sharp. "What the hell is going on?"

I wince, holding the phone away from my ear.

"Good morning to you too, Quinn," I say, sitting up in bed. I wipe the sleep from my eyes and squint at the screen. It's barely 7 a.m. "Everything okay?"

"Blackhollow called me last night. Said you were

attacked." Quinn's voice is strained, like he's been holding back his frustration all night. "What's wrong with you? I told you to be careful!"

I groan into the phone.

Fucking Damien.

Any gratitude I felt toward the man for the rescue last night vanishes. No doubt, Quinn is going to order me back home immediately, unless I can somehow talk my way out of it.

"It's fine. I've got it under control," I say, keeping my tone even. "It was nothing. Just a mugging. Damien showed up, and the guy ran off."

"*Just a mugging?* Are you insane?" he sputters. "You need to come back to Boston. Now, Woodsen."

"Listen, Quinn. I'm close to something here," I say, balling the bed sheets into my fists. "The meeting with Professor Hargrove went great last night. I've got some real leads now. Hargrove mentioned a place—Strega's Hollow—that might be connected to all of this. I need to check it out."

"Blackhollow said you could've *died* last night." Quinn's frustration is palpable, but I can hear the concern beneath it. "And now I've got him in my ear, telling me my junior associate is running around Salem's Fall, half-cocked, jeopardizing the case—and her own safety—while being targeted by God knows who."

"I'm not jeopardizing anything!" I snap. "You have to trust me, Quinn. Give me a little credit, please. I'm telling you, if I don't follow up on this lead, we could be missing something important."

He's silent for a beat, and I can tell he's trying to rein in his emotions.

"Fine," he says at last, his voice softening a bit. "Strega's Hollow and then home right after. No more unnecessary risks. Okay, Woodsen?"

"Sure," I say, crossing my fingers behind my back like a little kid, because something in my gut tells me this may be a lie.

I have no idea what I'll find at Strega's Hollow, but I have a feeling my work in Salem's Fall is far from done. There's something here, I just know it, and I don't think I'm going to find all the answers in just a few hours.

He sighs into the phone, and I can tell I'm not fooling him. Quinn knows me way too well. It's a problem.

"James—"

"I'll report back after Strega's Hollow." I rush to hang up before he can say anything else. "Gotta go. Lucky's whining for breakfast."

I drag myself out of bed, yawning as Lucky now waits expectantly by his food bowl. The cat is too smart for his own damn good. The dish clinks as I fill it, and he purrs, rubbing against my ankles before devouring his breakfast. Once he's settled, I turn to my own tasks, sifting through a flood of emails and drafting a case memo for Quinn, detailing everything I've uncovered in the last twenty-four hours. By the time I glance at the clock, it's nearly noon.

I hop into the shower, getting ready for my visit to Strega's Hollow. As the warm water pours down on me, my thoughts revert back to last night. After Damien appeared and took down the masked man with shocking ease, he helped me back to the Cottage without a word, just a steady hand at my back. He saw me safely inside, promised we'd talk in the morning, and then vanished again back into the dark. Hours later, I still can't seem to shake the image of him emerging from the shadows to save me—calm, controlled, and lethal.

How in the world was he able to get the upper hand on a dangerous thug? Unarmed, no less? He's tall and muscular, sure, but he's just a rich playboy businessman.

After I dry off and put my hair into a bun, I apply a bit of mascara and some gloss, and pick out a suit. It's a plum-colored wool skirt set, professional but cute, perfect for the cool autumn weather. I pair it with tights and my favorite chunky Mary Jane platform shoes. I'm overdressed for the day, but it never hurts to look professional. One thing I've learned—people are quick to dismiss someone who looks like me. Young. Blonde. Female. Dressing to be taken seriously doesn't always fix the problem, but it helps.

As I step into the Cottage lobby, I'm greeted by the scent of cinnamon and pumpkin spice. The place has a warm, lived-in charm. Dark wood paneling lining the walls. Worn leather couches and comfy-looking armchairs. Dried cornstalks and mini pumpkins set about as decorations. Tourists are everywhere, decked out in chunky sweaters and scarves, chatting excitedly about their plans for the day. Activities like ghost tours, tarot readings, and visiting witch memorials.

I stride over to the self-serve coffee bar and pour myself a steaming cup from the industrial-sized pot. There's a bottle of pumpkin spice syrup on the counter, but I pass, opting to keep my coffee strong and simple.

I take a long sip, letting the bitter taste warm me completely, and grab a freshly baked pumpkin muffin from the food tray nearby. With my coffee and pastry in hand, I feel ready to take on the world. But the moment I step outside the Cottage, I freeze.

Damien Blackhollow leans against the side of a sleek black Mercedes Maybach, arms folded across his chest. His eyes flick up to meet mine, a mischievous smirk playing on his lips like he's been waiting for me.

"Damien?" I take a step back, surprised. "What are you doing here?"

He straightens, his tall frame casting a shadow across the cobblestone street. "Making sure you don't get yourself killed."

"Are you following me?" I ask, my eyes narrowing.

"I don't keep stumbling upon you by chance, if that's what you're asking." He shrugs, unbothered by the accusation in my tone. "Quinn said you hadn't left town yet—despite my clear orders. I came to escort you back to Boston. It's not safe for you here."

My jaw drops, incredulous at his nerve.

"So you decided to *stalk* me?"

He chuckles softly. "Stalking is a bit of a stretch."

I cross my arms, stepping closer. "I assure you, Damien, I'm a grown woman and can handle myself just fine," I say. "I know you're the client, and I respect that, but you need to respect that I have a responsibility to do my job—the job you hired me for."

His expression hardens, morphing into something more serious.

"You think you know what you're dealing with, but you don't. You have no idea what's going on here," he says.

"Then tell me."

"Come with me back to Boston," he says and opens the car door, motioning me inside, "and perhaps I'll consider your request."

"You're impossible!" I shake my head, throwing my hands up in the air. "I'm trying the best I can to help you win this case. If you have information, why in the world wouldn't you share it with me? Unless—" I hesitate as a dark thought occurs to me. But no, I can't say that.

"Unless what?"

I know I should keep my mouth shut. Even if it feels like the lines between us are growing fuzzy, he's still the client. But I can tell by his expression that he's already guessed my thoughts.

"Unless it's something you don't want us to know…"

"Careful, James."

I can't help but feel like he's hiding something just beneath the surface.

"Why are you *really* here?" I ask.

He glances at me, one eyebrow raised. "I told you. I don't want to see you get hurt."

He sounds sincere, but something feels off. I have a sneaking suspicion it's not about my safety at all, but that he's worried about what I might uncover here in Salem's Fall. I'm certain Damien is keeping something from me—but what?

"I'm not some damsel in distress, and I don't need a bodyguard."

He exhales, shaking his head. "I would've thought last night—your little scare—would've sent you packing. It should've been enough for any sensible person with even a shred of self-preservation, at least."

"Some random mugger?" I frown. "Why would that make me leave town?"

His gaze flickers, lingering a second too long.

"Oh. Is that what it was?"

Something about the way he says it makes my stomach twist. I think back to last night, to the way the masked man had appeared out of nowhere. He hadn't tried to grab my purse or anything. Just lunged straight for me. That was strange for a mugging, sure, but what else could he have wanted from me?

I back away from Damien and his fancy car. "Listen, thanks for your chivalrous offer, but I'm staying. Besides, I have my own ride," I say. "I drove here with Lucky, and he's still sleeping."

Something tightens in his jaw. "Lucky? I wasn't aware you were… attached."

If I didn't know better, I would think Damien was jealous. I smile lightly. "He's my cat."

"Oh." His expression brightens. "I love cats."

"Really?" I raise a brow. "You don't seem like the type."

"Is that so? And what type do I seem like to you?"

Dark. Dangerous. Possibly murderous.

But, of course, I can't say any of that out loud to a client. Instead, I shrug and avoid his question.

"Thank you for your help last night and for checking on me today," I say, inching away from him. "But I'm afraid I must be on my way now."

"And where exactly are you going?" he asks, lips twitching.

"Strega's Hollow. I was told it might be important to your case."

His eyes narrow. "Strega's Hollow, you say? I'll go with you."

"That won't be necessary."

"I must insist," he says. "If I can't persuade you to go home, then I'm coming with you."

Annoyance flickers at me, but I have to tread carefully.

"It will be faster if I go alone. Clients don't usually accompany us on investigations," I say. "Besides, I don't want to bore you. This is just a kitschy little witch memorial. A tourist trap."

"Strega's Hollow is more dangerous than you realize."

I feel the hairs on my arms rise.

"Dangerous, how?"

"During the trials, it was a place where witches performed some of their most brutal rituals. That kind of... *activity*... leaves scars on the land."

"There were no witches." I scoff. "Just innocent people accused of crimes they didn't commit."

"Is that right?" His gaze sharpens, his voice dropping lower. "If you keep poking around Salem's Fall, digging into things you don't understand, bad things will happen." He reaches out, brushing a strand of hair away from my face, his touch lingering. "You need to be more careful. I wouldn't want anything to happen to you… not like what happened to poor Mark, your coworker." A slow, deliberate tongue click. "Pity."

My breath catches. "That was an accident."

Damien holds my gaze, studying me in a way that sends an uneasy pulse through me. "Was it?"

I try to keep my face impassive, but my mind is racing. Okay, yes, even though the official ruling from the authorities was a car accident, I still have my own doubts about the circumstances surrounding Mark's death. I've suspected something far more nefarious ever since the threatening email I received. But Damien wouldn't know about that, right? I certainly never said anything to him. I never said anything to anyone except—

"Quinn told you?" I stare at him, a bit annoyed.

"Of course, Quinn told me. He works for me. As do you, though you seem to keep forgetting that," he says, taking a step closer. "You want to go to Strega's Hollow today—fine. But you're not going alone."

"You may be my client, but you can't tell me what to do—"

"I can and I will," he cuts me off. "And if you want to keep working for me, you'd better learn to be a bit more *accommodating*."

He says it in a way that makes it crystal clear I don't have a choice. Not if I want to stay on the highest profile case of the decade with the firm's most important new client.

"Fine," I mutter, "but don't get in my way."

He smiles, a dangerous, magnetic smile that sends a jolt of electricity through me. "I'll do my very best."

CHAPTER 10

Outside the Cottage, Damien Blackhollow ushers me into the luxurious backseat of his chauffeured car. The leather interior smells faintly of money and privilege. As I slide into the seat, his driver, Bennett—a distinguished older gentleman with neatly combed salt-and-pepper hair and a meticulously kept uniform—tips his cap in my direction. Moments later, we're gliding down the road, Bennett steering with steady precision.

We arrive at Strega's Hollow just after one p.m. Bennett drives us up to the very front of the memorial, dropping us off at VIP parking. The place is buzzing with tourists. All around us are families, couples, and groups of teenagers flocking toward the entrance. The atmosphere is a weird mix of eerie and amusement park. Some are quiet and reverent, here to soak up the dark macabre history. Others laugh and take pictures with their phones, checking this off their list of spooky Halloween attractions.

Damien strolls along beside me, silent for once, as we walk the weathered path to the main gate. I steal a glance at him, his sharp jawline clenched. He looks disinterested, almost bored, but I can sense his tension. There's a subtle shift in the air around him, like he's trying too hard to appear unaffected.

Even in the daylight, there's an undeniable weight to this

place. A lingering feeling of history and foreboding. Something about it makes my hair stand a little on edge.

Finally, the main building comes into view. It's smaller than I expected. An old, stone structure that looks like it was carved out of the surrounding forest. Dark stones cracked and weathered. Ivy clinging to the walls. The roof is slanted, the shingles uneven, giving the place an almost hunched appearance, as if it's been sitting here for centuries.

As we pay our entrance fee and move inside the iron gates, I overhear a woman explaining to her young daughter that this is where "the bad witches were punished." The child's eyes grow wide with fear.

"Ridiculous." Damien snorts beside me as we're corralled into a small group and put into a waiting line. "It's like they're trying to make this place into some sort of haunted house attraction."

Before I can respond, our tour guide arrives. He's a tall, lanky man in his late sixties, with a shock of white hair and a frayed brown jacket that looks like it's seen better days. He carries a walking stick and his pale blue eyes sparkle with mischievous enthusiasm.

"Welcome, welcome!" His voice is loud and cheerful. "I'm Callahan, your guide today. I hope you're ready for some real Salem's Fall history. None of that watered-down stuff you get in the town square," he says, winking at the group and then ushering us all into the building.

Inside, it's dim and cramped, all creaking floorboards and rough-hewn beams. Shelves overflow with artifacts from the witch trials. Weathered apothecary bottles, Puritan relics, and even a few weapons like rusted blades and frayed nooses, each with a small plaque detailing its grim history.

Callahan launches into storytelling mode. "This place," he says, gesturing dramatically, "was once an execution spot for those accused of witchcraft. They say the energy here is unlike anywhere else in the world, charged by the very souls of all who perished here."

Damien scoffs next to me, but I ignore him, intrigued, as Callahan begins pointing at various objects inside the memorial. "Not everyone got a trial," Callahan continues. "Sometimes the townspeople would take it upon themselves to punish the accused. They were brought here and executed." He stops in front of a stone fireplace, its hearth large enough to hold a person. "Gather closer! Closer!" he calls out, his eyes sparkling in the muted light as tourists encircle him, cameras poised. "Legend has it that some witches were burned right here," he says, gesturing inside the fireplace.

An older woman next to me gasps, "How barbaric!"

Callahan continues, stopping next to a framed photo of a sad-looking woman named "The Marsh Witch," and tells us a particularly grisly story about how she was drowned in the marsh behind Strega's Hollow after being falsely accused of hexing the local minister.

"A convenient excuse to get rid of anyone they didn't like," Damien mutters behind me, his voice full of disdain, clearly uninterested in the tour's theatrics.

At one point, I catch him rolling his eyes as Callahan points out a rusty old witch's cauldron, telling us in a spooky voice that the cauldron is cursed and anyone who touches it will meet a tragic end. An older boy in our group shoves his younger brother toward the cauldron. The boy squeals, terrified, and misses touching its metal edges by mere inches.

"That's not really true, is it?" the boy asks Callahan, still shaking. "About the curse?"

"Yes, I believe it is. This whole place is cursed." Callahan pauses, savoring the tension. "You see, every couple of years, someone goes missing at Strega's Hollow. A worker restoring the site or a tourist who wandered a little too far off the path.

Police search, but they never find any bodies, no footprints, no signs of struggle. The Hollow just... swallows them up."

"They *disappear*?" I ask, my curiosity piqued. Damien looks at me sideways, as if warning me not to take this too seriously.

Callahan nods. "Never to be heard from again."

The group murmurs, and the mounting fear is palpable.

"People say this place is a thin spot. A place where the veil between the living and the dead—between good and evil—is especially fraught." Callahan inches toward the cauldron, though he takes care not to get too close. He lowers his voice. "You can feel it. Visitors here often report cold spots, whispers, strange sensations, invisible hands brushing against them."

I suppress a shiver. I don't know if it's just his words, but I swear the air around me has grown colder, the dampness clinging to my skin. I notice several others in our group, rubbing their arms, as if they're also feeling the temperature drop.

"Rubbish! I don't believe in that sort of nonsense," an older man scoffs, folding his arms across his chest.

Callahan smiles, a thin, knowing smile. "You don't have to believe, friend," he says. "But whether you do or don't, there's one rule you should always abide by: never come here after dark. That's when things get really... unsettling." He taps the floor with his walking stick. The sound seems to echo unnaturally, cutting through the air like a knife. "Shadows move where they shouldn't, and if you listen closely, you can hear voices—*whispers*—from the other side. Some say it's the spirits of the witches, crying out for justice. Others believe it's something far worse..." Callahan licks his lips, almost eagerly, and continues. "Okay, let's move on, shall we? I want to show you something truly special."

He leads us outside the building, circling the grounds and steering us toward the middle of the glade. In the center lies a large stone slab that looks positively ancient, its smooth surface cracked and weathered by time.

"Now here's where the stories get really interesting," Callahan says, gesturing at the stone. His voice drops to a low, conspiratorial tone, like he's about to share a secret. "This stone slab you see here, folks, has more history than any of the books or records will tell you. They say this slab was once used for human sacrifices."

Several people in our group shift uncomfortably. I hear Damien snicker beside me, a low, quiet snort escaping him. I glance over and give him a warning look, but he doesn't seem to care that he's being rude.

"What kind of sacrifices?" someone asks behind me.

"Legend has it there were real witches operating in Salem's Fall during the witch trials," Callahan explains. "These weren't the poor innocent townspeople accused, mind you. No, these were truly evil beings, using the panic of the time to hide their own dark agendas to gain power and make pacts with supernatural forces."

A couple of teenagers in the group laugh nervously.

"But that's just a made-up story, right?" A young woman in the back shivers, pulling her jacket tighter around her shoulders. "That's not true, is it?"

"Isn't it?" Callahan asks, his eyes narrowing. "Of course, there are naysayers. Modern historians dismiss it as lore created during the hysteria of the witch trials, and it's true there's little concrete evidence to support it." He grins wide, his eyes crinkling at the edges. "I suppose you all can decide for yourselves what you believe."

The tour concludes shortly after that and Damien grabs me by the elbow, steering me toward the exit. "What a sham," he says under his breath. "You ready to go?"

"I enjoyed it," I say, a bit annoyed by his dismissiveness. "I thought his stories were entertaining. It's part of the experience. Besides, if you think it's all a big joke, why are you here? You're the one who said this place is dangerous."

"Oh, the danger is very real—just not the tall tales that guy was spewing," he says.

I raise an eyebrow. "How so?"

He pauses, his eyes scanning the tree line. "Another time," he says. "Let's get out of here. This place has a way of getting to you if you stay too long." He points to the little gift store over by the main entrance. "Some light shopping before we leave?"

"I'm working, Damien." I snort. "I don't have time for shopping—"

"You'll like it," he says, grabbing me by the elbow and pulling me toward the store. "Trust me."

He steers me inside, and I'm immediately charmed by the place. The tiny shop is crammed with magical goodies, its shelves lined with beautiful, handmade trinkets. Things like crystals, spell books, and lucky talismans. It smells like freshly made chocolate and cinnamon, both of which they sell inside, along with homemade teas and candies.

Damien leads me over to the jewelry counter, where an array of colorful baubles glimmer beneath the glass. Small tags label each gemstone's purpose. Rose quartz for love. Amethyst for clarity. Garnet for strength. He barely glances at them, gesturing instead to a spectacular ring, sitting on a velvet cushion. It's simple yet elegant, with a sparkling diamond band and a large dark stone set in the center that seems to glow in the dim light.

"Beautiful, isn't it?" he asks, his gaze fixed on me, studying my reaction.

"It's gorgeous."

Without waiting for help, he reaches behind the counter and grabs the ring. He slides it onto my finger, and I feel a shock at the contact, a buzzing sort of energy flowing through me.

I clear my throat, unable to look away from the mesmerizing ring. "What's the stone called?"

"Black tourmaline. For protection," he says. "It's said to absorb negative energy, warding off harmful forces... or people." A faint smirk tugs at the corner of his mouth. "It also grants power to those who carry it. A solid choice."

I flip the price tag and gasp out loud.

"Ten thousand dollars! For a gift shop souvenir? Yeah, that's definitely not in the budget." I shake my head, flabbergasted, and hand the ring back to him, albeit a bit reluctantly. "Besides, like I said, I'm here for work, not shopping."

Damien keeps smirking, his eyes twinkling with amusement. "Of course."

As he puts the ring back behind the glass case, I have a hard time dragging my eyes away from the beautiful stone. It's so breathtaking. Maybe one day, I'll be able to afford things like that...

"Dinner?" he asks. "I know a great place in town."

I hesitate.

"As in... a working dinner?"

"Obviously," he says, though the teasing smile on his lips suggests otherwise. "If I were asking you on a date, you'd know it."

"Okay. Good," I say, almost a little disappointed. If I'm being honest, the idea of a date with Damien Blackhollow isn't the most offensive thing I've ever heard of. Not that I'd tell him that.

We swing by the Cottage first so I can check on Lucky and fire off a quick email update to Quinn. Damien's driver, Bennett, waits in the car while Damien follows me inside to the lobby. I assume he's just grabbing coffee or using the restroom as I rush to my room—but he follows me.

"Here, allow me," he says, taking the room key from me and unlocking my door with ease.

"Uh, what are you doing?" I scrunch my eyebrows. "I told you I need a few minutes."

He leans against the doorframe, one eyebrow raised, a playful grin on his lips. "I'm here to meet the infamous Lucky, of course."

"Lucky—my cat? Why on earth do you want to meet him?"

"Why wouldn't I?" Damien's tone is casual, but there's that glint in his eye, like he knows exactly how to get under my skin and is enjoying every second of it. "I'm curious about the male who gets so much of your precious time."

I pause, confused by this turn of events. Damien Blackhollow, billionaire venture capitalist and walking enigma, wants to meet *my cat*?

"Uh, well, I didn't know you were that into cats," I mumble, hedging. I'm not sure what I'm supposed to do here. This type of situation isn't exactly in the attorney-client relationships handbook.

"I'm into meeting things you care about," he says, his voice softening a touch. "Besides, from what I hear, this cat is very special."

That pulls a laugh out of me.

"You have no idea," I say, chuckling as I step into the room, tossing my bag onto the small desk near the window. "Fine, you can come in. But I'm going to warn you, Lucky doesn't like anyone, especially strangers. And he's *really* not into men."

Damien takes that as a challenge, grinning as he follows behind me. "Protective, I get it," he says. "I imagine that's how most men are with you."

My stomach does a little flip, and I mentally kick myself for how easily this man can get under my skin. I glance toward the bed, where Lucky is curled up, completely unfazed by the world around him. His sleek black body is stretched across my pillow like it's his world and the rest of us just live in it. Damien's grin widens as he approaches my bed, leaning down to get a closer look at Lucky.

"Hey, there," he says, his voice low and smooth, as if he's speaking to a person.

Lucky, to my complete shock, doesn't hiss or nip or show any sort of agitation. Instead of his usual death glare reserved for strangers, he actually lifts his head, yawning lazily before making his way over to Damien like they're long-lost friends.

I stand there, slack-jawed, watching as my fiercely territorial cat rubs his head against Damien's hand.

"You've got to be kidding me," I mutter.

Damien glances back at me, that smug expression firmly in place. "What was that you were saying about him not liking men?"

"I—I don't know." I cross my arms, trying to recover some semblance of dignity. "He hates everyone but me."

"Hm, guess I'm the exception," Damien says with a wink as he scratches behind Lucky's ears. Lucky—the traitor—is purring ecstatically, like he's known Damien his whole life.

I stare in disbelief, watching the bizarre lovefest between my cat and Damien.

"I don't get it. He's never like this," I say. "Ever."

"Maybe he senses something in me he likes."

I laugh. "Oh really? Like what?"

"Something good. Something... trustworthy." Damien's gaze holds mine, and for a moment, the air in the room feels thicker, heavier. My pulse quickens, but I shake it off, refusing to let whatever is building between us mess with my head. He's my client—*my client accused of murder*—I have to remember that.

"Or maybe he's just softening in his old age," I say lightly.

"Or you're bribing him somehow. Do you have catnip in your pockets?"

Damien chuckles. "I don't need to bribe cats, James. They just know like most women do—it's futile to resist me." He winks, but there's a hint of seriousness in his voice. I don't doubt he's telling the truth.

I look away, my eyes falling to the floor. "Lucky's just acting weird today. Don't let it go to your head."

My phone buzzes in my hand. A new email alert. I open my inbox and the subject line, in all caps, jumps out at me.

"STAY AWAY OR YOU'RE NEXT."

I gasp out loud, my heart pounding in my chest. Instantly, I feel Damien beside me, the air suddenly charged with tension.

"James? What is it?" he asks, his tone sharp. As he reads the email over my shoulder, his jaw tightens. "That's it. I'm taking you back to Boston."

But I don't care what he says, or that he's the one footing the bill. Not even the fear in his eyes gets to me. Real fear—for me. None of it matters. I'm just starting to crack the surface here in Salem's Fall.

No way I'm going back now.

CHAPTER 11

The restaurant Damien takes me to is beyond fancy. Far too fancy for a casual work dinner.

Dim lighting. Sleek white tablecloths. Crystal glasses gleaming under sparkling chandeliers. It smells like truffles and expensive leather. The snotty-looking maître d' was practically falling over himself when we walked in. I could tell without asking that Damien comes here often.

I stick out like a sore thumb. Even my pretty suit feels plain next to the designer-clad beautiful women around me. It makes me feel antsy sitting in a place where even breathing feels like it's costing money.

Damien watches me as if he can sense my discomfort. A faint smirk plays at the corner of his lips as he addresses the waiter. "We'll take a bottle of the Screaming Eagle Cabernet Sauvignon, and I'll have the filet. Rare," he says, his eyes never leaving mine as he orders. "She'll have the salmon with the beurre blanc on the side."

I raise an eyebrow. "Ordering for me now?"

He leans in, voice dropping. "You'll enjoy the salmon. It's fantastic."

"How do you know I didn't want the filet, like you?"

He gives me a look. "You don't eat red meat."

I swallow back my retort because he's somehow right

about me. I'm not sure how he knows, but it's true. I haven't touched red meat in years, not since my mother died. Something about knowing an animal was butchered—imagining the slaughter, the blood—became too much for me after her death.

"Well, maybe I was in the mood for something else." I look down at the menu again. "The mussels, for example. They sound great."

His smirk widens. "Perhaps next time."

I roll my eyes. The thing is, I really would rather have the salmon than the mussels, but it's infuriating how sure of himself he is. He walks into every situation like he belongs there, commanding attention, exuding power.

Even more annoying is the part of me that can't deny how attractive it is. I'm always the one taking care of everyone else. Maddie. Lucky. Even myself. But with Damien, it feels like for once I don't have to be in charge. He's taking care of me, even if it's in this obnoxiously domineering, overprotective way.

After the waiter leaves, Damien's expression turns serious. "I meant what I said before, back at your hotel. You need to leave Salem's Fall."

I snort into my fancy water goblet. "I'm not running away just because some nutjob sent a stupid email."

"This is the *second* threatening message you've gotten," he says. "Whoever sent them is watching you. And these people don't play around."

"It's just someone trying to mess with my head." I shrug, trying to play it cool even though I'll admit, the emails don't exactly give me the warm fuzzies.

"And if they try to mess with your life next? Or did you already forget how I had to save you last night? Not to mention your dead colleague, Mark." He exhales, almost nonchalantly. "Though if I'm being honest, that one doesn't seem like a great loss. I never did like the way he talked to you."

Unease prickles through me at the easy, almost casual way he dismisses Mark's murder. I've got no love lost for Mark either, but still, that doesn't mean he deserved to die.

"He wasn't *that* bad…"

"Forget Mark. He's inconsequential," Damien says, his gaze sharpening. "You, though? I might miss not having you around, pain in the ass though you might be." His voice drops lower, edged with more than a hint of concern. "When will you start taking these threats seriously?"

He's probably right. This is risky—even I know that—but admitting that to Damien feels like I'm losing some invisible battle between us.

"I'll be okay."

"And what about your sister Madison? What will she do if something happens to you?" he prods. "Think of her at least."

"I'm always thinking of Maddie," I snap. "What she needs is a roof over her head, college tuition, and dinner on the table. This job lets me give her that." I grab my glass and take a sip of the delicious but overpriced wine, leveling him with a look. "How do you know about Maddie anyway? Big mouth Quinn tell you that too?"

"She's all over your Instagram."

I almost spit out my drink. "Now you're stalking my social media?"

He rests an elbow on the table, fingers idly tracing the rim of his glass. "I simply eyeballed a few things. I like to be well-informed about the people who work for me."

"But my Instagram is private."

He grins. "Not for me."

I'm surprised and a bit flattered. Damien Blackhollow doesn't seem like the kind of man to spend time on social media sites. He certainly doesn't have any public profiles of his own. Okay, so maybe I've stalked him a bit too, but there was nothing there to see.

"Well, if you aren't going to be safer for Maddie, at least do it for Lucky." He studies me carefully for another moment. "How would the little guy take care of himself if something happened to you?"

"Lucky is fine."

"Hmmm, I suppose I could adopt him." His dark brow furrows as if he's seriously giving the idea consideration. "He did seem to take quite a liking to me, don't you think?"

"You're ridiculous," I say, a laugh slipping out despite myself. "Listen, I promise I'll be careful, but I can't go back yet. I'm getting closer to figuring this out. I need to see Professor Hargrove again tomorrow and ask him about what I learned at the Hollow—"

"Hargrove?" Damien's eyes flash and I feel the shift instantly. "Don't bother. I already told Quinn you're wasting your time with that quack."

"I disagree. Nick was really helpful yesterday," I say, surprised by the venom in Damien's voice. "I think he knows more than he lets on—about Strega's Hollow, and maybe even about the Veil. I believe he has knowledge and research that can help your case—"

"Not likely," he says, cutting me off. "Hargrove is obsessed with made-up stories and conjecture. Half of what he thinks he knows is pure fairytale, and the rest? All silly conspiracy theories he couldn't even prove back when he was still a real professor." He leans back, crossing his arms over his chest. "Trust me, Hargrove won't help. Your time will be much better spent elsewhere."

A small smile tugs at my lips.

"Like with you? At some extravagant, absurdly expensive dinner?"

He shrugs. "Perhaps."

"What's the matter? You don't like the idea of someone else helping me?" I tease.

His jaw tightens. "I don't like the idea of you wasting my billable hours on wild goose chases. You should focus on real leads."

"Oh yeah? What leads?" I scoff. "You haven't exactly been helpful."

Damien's lips twitch into a small, dangerous smile. He leans in closer, his voice soft but menacing. "You want my help? You want to know the truth about Strega's Hollow and the Veil?"

I stare at him, unsure where this is going. "Yes. I do."

"Then let's make a deal."

His eyes lock onto mine with a look that makes me feel like I'm hovering on the edge of something dangerous.

"What kind of deal?"

"Quid pro quo, Counselor," he says, his voice like silk, smooth and commanding. "You tell me something personal, and I'll tell you something about the Veil."

The air between us shifts, becoming heavier. This feels risky. Playing games with someone like Damien is a bad idea, but I need to know what he knows. If I'm going to figure out this case, then I need to understand the Veil.

"Okay, fine," I say as the waiter brings our food over. I take a small bite of the salmon and have to grudgingly admit that Damien is right. It's buttery and perfectly cooked, flaky and rich with flavor. "What do you want to know?"

"Tell me about your family. Tell me about your father."

The question catches me off guard, and my heart stutters in my chest.

"What about my father?"

"I've heard about his crime and the trial, but I want to know more. I want to hear it from you," he says, his voice cool and calculated. "You want to play in the shadows, James? You want to uncover dark truths? Well, you can't do that without letting some darkness in, yourself. So... tell me."

I hesitate, my fingers gripping the edge of the table. Why does Damien want to know about the worst thing that's ever happened to me? I rarely talk about my mother's murder.

"I don't see what that has to do with anything—"

"Absolute honesty or this conversation is over."

I suck in a breath, hating how easily this man can make me feel cornered, like there's no escape but to give in to him. But if I want to learn more about the Veil, there's no way out of this. So I do what I've always done—keep moving forward, no matter how much it hurts.

"My father was convicted of killing my mother," I say, my voice detached. I don't let myself feel the weight of the words. "Which you already know, I'm sure. It's not a secret. It was a very public trial. But before that, he was the perfect husband and dad. There was no warning at all that something was wrong. Then one night, when I was in high school... I came home and found him standing over her dead body."

Damien doesn't move. Doesn't say a word. He just watches me with that same intense gaze, waiting for me to continue.

"It wasn't the usual type of murder you see when spouses are involved. Not like domestic violence or a crime of passion." I swallow hard. "It was... ritualistic. Brutal. Bloody. There were strange symbols carved into her body... and in places around the bedroom. The police, my sister, they all believed he did it."

"But you don't?"

"He loved my mom more than anything. He wouldn't have hurt her," I say, shaking my head. "The trial was a total sham. The judge had his own agenda. His daughter had been beaten to death by her boyfriend, which is awful, but it also meant he thought my dad was guilty from the start. And Dad's lawyer was terrible. Completely incompetent."

"And that's why you went to law school? To right wrongs?"

I look up, stunned. It's bewildering, Damien's uncanny ability to see right to the heart of things. I don't understand how this man who hardly knows me seems to keep pegging me exactly right.

"It's not fair," I say, my fingers tightening around the stem of my wineglass, pressing hard enough that I half expect it to crack. "My mom's murderer is still out there, and if anyone in the criminal justice system had given a damn, things would've been very different for my family."

"I'm sorry. Truly," he says. "And now your dad is in prison?"

"For almost a decade now."

For a moment, silence lingers between us. Damien studies me, brows drawing together in thought.

"Interesting." He nods, like something is clicking into place. "I can see why you'd be drawn to my case."

I stare at him, feeling exposed, raw.

"Yes, there are some… similarities."

Vivienne deserves justice. My mother never got it. And if Damien is innocent, I want to save him—because I couldn't save my dad. But if he's not… then he belongs behind bars, like my mother's real killer should be.

"Well, I told you my secret," I say, swallowing hard. "Now it's your turn."

Damien cuts at his rare steak with precise, deliberate movements. "Very well," he says. "You want to know about the Veil? Let me tell you about my family."

His voice is low, almost hypnotic, as he shares the history of the Blackhollow family and how his ancestors joined the Veil during the witch trials in order to stay safe after watching their neighbors and friends being executed, burned at the stake.

He explains how the Veil operates in secret, even today,

with the primary goal being the founding families maintaining their power in New England. He says it all quite matter-of-factly, like the Veil is just another secret society of powerful people, like the Freemasons or the Skull and Bones at Yale University. I'm disappointed, but not surprised, when he leaves out all the nefarious stuff I'm most intrigued by—the occult ties and bloody rituals, the things Professor Hargrove spoke of.

Not that I thought he'd admit any of that to me.

He explains how his late father, Ian Blackhollow, and his late grandfather, Nathaniel Blackhollow, were both deeply involved as heads of the Veil. How the Veil has always been strongest with a Blackhollow heir at the helm, its influence rising and falling under their control. And then he tells me about his older half-brother, Lucien, the black sheep of the family.

"You should talk to him," he says, his tone casual but sharp. "Lucien can give you more answers than that nutjob professor."

"Your brother? How so?"

"Lucien was always closer to our father. He may have known things I wasn't privy to." He lets out a low, almost mocking laugh. "Closer to my fiancée too."

My breathing quickens. Is he implying what I think he's implying?

"Meaning?"

His eyes lock on mine, tellingly. "Exactly what you're thinking. Yes, they were having an affair."

Part of me feels for him. I despise cheaters and it can't be easy to discover your brother and fiancée are fooling around behind your back. But as his attorney, I have to note this is another bad fact that we'll have to deal with later on. Unfortunately, this also gives him a real motive for the killing.

"I'm sorry to hear that," I say. "I just ended a three-year relationship under similar circumstances."

"Well, you're better off without him, I'm sure." He gives me a sincere smile, almost admiring. "Anyone who'd cheat on you is a fool."

"Thank you," I say, warmth rising to my cheeks. Of course, I know William is an idiot, but it's nice to hear someone else say it, especially someone like Damien Blackhollow. "Your brother, where does he live?"

"Here. In Salem's Fall," he says and then pauses, thoughtful. "Come to think of it, he was also in Boston the night my fiancée was killed. You may want to ask him about that too."

"Will he meet with me?"

"Not willingly." He lifts a brow. "But, if you agree to forgo meeting with the professor tomorrow, I'll set it up for you."

"And you don't want me to talk to Nick again because…?"

Damien's smile is cold. "Because I don't trust him. Hargrove is playing his own game, and I don't want you caught in the middle."

"Okay." I nod along, reasoning that I can talk to his brother first, then circle back to the professor, if needed. "I'll talk to your brother instead."

I take a final sip of my wine, savoring the rich, velvety taste before setting my glass down and glancing at my watch. "It's getting late," I say, dabbing my napkin at my lips and pushing my plate away. "Can you drop me off at the Cottage? I want to change and head back to the Hollow."

Something about that sacrifice slab nags at me, like I missed something important earlier. And if the Veil still uses the Hollow, like our tour guide had hinted, then night would be the perfect time to catch them.

Damien stills. "Now?"

"Time is of the essence, don't you agree?" I raise a brow.

"And I can't think of a better time to investigate a creepy, possibly cursed location than at night."

He leans back in his chair, slow and deliberate, arms folding across his chest. "Tell me, James—do you ever listen to anyone?"

"Excuse me?"

"I've already warned you that place is dangerous and now you want to go back by yourself—*and at night*? Even that quack tour guide told you, don't come back after dark." His voice drops lower, mocking. "But no, you're going to march right in because you know better than everyone, right?"

"I'm a grown woman, Damien," I say, heat rising in my cheeks, my irritation flaring. "I can do whatever the hell I want."

"You shouldn't *want* to be a reckless idiot."

"Well, I guess I do." I huff and shove my chair back, the legs scraping against the floor. I toss my napkin onto the table and glare at him. "I'll get a taxi. Thanks for the lovely meal."

"Come now, James. Let's not ruin the night over this." He tilts his head, watching me carefully. Then, just as smoothly as he'd gotten under my skin, his demeanor shifts completely. His posture eases, his mouth curving into something almost... agreeable. "If you're that set on going, I'll take you myself."

I hesitate for half a second, thrown off by the sudden shift. My pulse is still hot with irritation, but something about his voice—low, smooth, coaxing—makes me hesitate.

"Really?"

His lips twitch like he's amused by my skepticism. "Yes, of course."

I try to decide if he's just saying this to pacify me or if he actually means it. I suppose he looks sincere. Or at least as sincere as Damien Blackhollow can look.

"Well… okay, then."

"Good." He nods, taking another sip of wine. "Why don't

you use the ladies' first before we go? Looks like it's going to be a long night."

Not a bad idea. The wine and water are already catching up with me, so I excuse myself to the bathroom. When I return to the table moments later, Damien looks up, apology etched in his features.

"I'm sorry for being an ass," he says. "I just don't want you walking into something you can't handle." He lifts his wineglass and gestures to me. "Truce?"

I nod, cheersing him, even though I probably shouldn't let him off the hook that easily. But when he looks at me like that—genuine, apologetic—it's hard to stay mad.

The wine slides down my throat, warm and rich. When I set my glass down empty, a satisfied smile tugs at his lips. He tosses his black American Express Centurion card on the table and signs for the bill.

As we step outside and head toward Damien's fancy car, a wave of drowsiness creeps over me, slow and heavy, like a weighted blanket settling over my shoulders. My legs feel unsteady, and I stumble for a moment before his hand finds the small of my back.

"You okay?"

I nod, though the movement feels sluggish.

"Seems you're a bit of a lightweight, hmm, Counselor?" he teases.

I sway again, and Damien steadies me with a firm but easy grip. "Guess I'm out of practice."

I rarely go out drinking anymore. I'm always in the office, always working.

Damien opens the passenger door and helps me into the backseat, sitting beside me while Bennett drives. Inside the car, the drowsiness deepens. I press my palms against the cool leather of the car door, trying to stay awake. My head lolls slightly before I catch myself, blinking hard.

What the hell?

I only had those two glasses of wine, didn't I? Or... was it three?

Damien watches me from across the seat, his gaze steady, almost assessing.

"Guess I should stick to one glass while on the job, huh?" I joke, my voice sluggish, thick.

"It was a long day. I'm sure you were already tired."

I am tired. So very, very tired. Like I want to go back to my room and sleep for days.

"The Hollow," I whisper, trying to push through the fog creeping in. "I need to get to the Hollow—" The yawn pulling from my chest interrupts my words.

"You're not seriously still planning on going tonight, are you?"

I open my mouth to argue, but suddenly, the thought of stumbling through the dark woods of the Hollow feels impossible.

"No." I slump further in my seat. My brain is melting into syrup. "Guess not."

By the time we pull up to the Cottage, my eyelids are so heavy, I can barely keep them open. Damien walks me inside, his hand pressed to my back as he guides me toward my room. His touch is gentler than I thought a man like him was capable of. As I turn to say goodbye, I find him standing far too close, his dark eyes locked onto mine.

"You're stalking me again," I mutter, half-joking, half-serious as I lean against my door for support. He takes the key from my shaky hands and helps me unlock it.

"Just making sure you're safe."

"Thanks, but I've got it from here," I say, lifting a brow. "And you can't keep following me back to my room. You're my client. It's not... proper."

"I'm not," he says, stepping back with a mock bow and

pointing to the room beside us. "I'm going to *my* room—next door."

I sway, gripping the edge of the doorway. "You… you booked the room next to mine?"

"Of course. If you insist on staying in town, at least this way, I can keep an eye on you."

He gives me a little wink, then turns and walks away, leaving me standing there, sleepy, hazy, and suddenly unsure of everything.

CHAPTER 12

I wake up feeling like I got hit by a truck. My head pounds, my mouth dry as sandpaper. I squeeze my eyes shut against the morning light filtering through the thin curtains, but even that feels like an effort.

God. How did I get so drunk?

I don't drink much anymore, and yeah, I was tired—but still. How embarrassing... Maybe it was the wine?

I've had plenty of red wine before, but never anything that expensive. Maybe my body just wasn't prepared for whatever outrageously overpriced vintage Damien had ordered.

I let out a groan and push myself upright, my limbs sluggish, as my gaze catches something unexpected on the other side of the bed. A small box sits on the nightstand.

That's odd.

I don't remember seeing it when I came in last night. Then again, I don't remember much of anything after dinner.

I frown, rubbing my temples as I push the covers off and reach for the box, opening it.

Inside is the ring I'd admired at Strega's Hollow, the breathtakingly beautiful one from the gift shop. The large black stone lies nestled in soft blue velvet, gleaming, dark and smooth, like polished night. I run a finger over the cool surface. I never said I wanted it, but Damien had noticed. A strange warmth flickers through me—half irritation, half something else entirely.

Next to the box is a note.

For work purposes, of course.
—D.B.

I roll my eyes.

Sure. Because every client gives his attorney expensive jewelry…

Though I know I shouldn't, I slide the ring onto my finger and smile as it twinkles and shines in the light. It fits perfectly.

Before meeting up with Damien, I throw together a quick outline for my witness interview with his brother, Lucien, and get myself ready. An hour later, Damien picks me up in his sleek black Mercedes to take me to Lucien. I'm still achy, my body slow to shake off the lingering haze from the wine last night. But Damien? He looks amazing. Fresh. Unbothered. Like the alcohol didn't touch him at all.

"Good morning, Miss Woodsen." Bennett, his driver, tips his cap with a polite smile as I step inside the car. "Would you like any refreshments before we go? Evian? Sparkling water, perhaps?"

I press my fingers to my temple. My head still feels like mush.

"I'm okay, Bennett," I say. "But, uh, thanks."

Damien slides into the backseat beside me, his gaze flicking over, assessing.

"And how are we doing this morning?"

"Still pretty crummy," I admit. I still don't understand what happened last night. My lips quirk into a self-effacing grin. "You didn't put something in my drink, did you?"

Damien exhales a dry, humorless huff. "Do I seem like a man who needs to drug his dinner dates?"

"No, of course not." I shake my head, chuckling. "I'm just joking."

Still... it is odd.

Damien flicks a glance at Bennett, who hands him a cold water bottle. Without missing a beat, Damien passes it to me. "Drink," he orders. "You seem to have lost some precious brain cells last evening. Rehydrate and let's hope they return."

I take the water from him hesitantly.

"I'm fine. Really."

"Relax, Counselor," he says, voice dripping with amusement. "I assure you it's not poisoned."

I roll my eyes, cracking the seal and taking a sip. "Ha ha. Very reassuring."

When I glance up again, Damien is watching me, gaze locked on my hand. "You're wearing it," he murmurs, his eyes gleaming with undisguised delight.

I glance down at the ring on my finger, twisting it. "Oh. Right." I clear my throat. "I brought it to give it back to you."

He smirks. "And yet there it is, still on your finger."

"So it is," I sigh, holding my hand up so the black stone catches the light. It's unprofessional and I *know* I'm supposed to return it, but I just don't think I can part with something so lovely.

"You deserve to have beautiful things, James. It looks good on you."

"You shouldn't go around giving your attorneys expensive jewelry, Damien. It's highly inappropriate," I huff, but I can't stop the small, traitorous smile that tugs at my lips.

We both know, appropriate or not, I'm going to keep the ring. It's a character flaw, but oh well.

"*Inappropriate?* I'm offended," Damien says dramatically,

resting an arm lazily across the back of my seat as the car pulls away from the Cottage. "Aren't you offended, Bennett?"

"Don't tease the lady, Mr. Blackhollow. Nice women like Miss Woodsen don't like that." Bennett gives me a big wink in the rearview mirror. "They like gentlemen."

"Oh, what do you know about women, Bennett?" Damien scoffs, but he's smiling at the older man, his affection clearly on display.

I stare out the window as we drive, my fingers playing with the soft, tailored seam of my lilac blazer. I'd taken extra care with my outfit this morning, knowing I was going to spend the day with Damien. Beneath the pretty blazer, I'm wearing a silky ivory blouse, its low-cut collar just a hint flirty, and high-waisted trousers that flatter my figure. The look strikes the right balance between polished and feminine.

The quaint streets of Salem's Fall pass by in a blur as we head toward the countryside. Vibrant buildings and cobbled roads quickly give way to rolling hills and towering trees, their leaves shifting to brilliant shades of yellow, orange, red, and gold.

"So where are we meeting your brother Lucien?" I ask, looking over at Damien.

"Blackthorn Manor."

"Oh? What's that?"

"My family's ancestral estate," he explains. "It's been ours since Salem's Fall was founded. Lucien lives in the old house just off the main grounds."

Ancestral estate? Main grounds? I have no idea what to expect, but wherever we're going, it sure sounds fancy.

Damien hasn't said much about his older half-brother, Lucien, but what little I've found online hasn't exactly been heartwarming. The brothers share the same father, but not the same mother. Lucien was the result of a one-night stand, a rare lapse in judgment from a young Ian Blackhollow before he became the cold, calculating man everyone would come to know.

Damien, though? He was planned. The perfect son, born to Ian's wife and true love. The heir to the Blackhollow throne. The chosen one. And while I don't know what that's left Lucien with, I can't imagine it's anything good. I couldn't find any connection to Blackhollow Industries. If Lucien plays a role in the company, it's not one they advertise.

When I'd told Quinn about my witness interview, he'd been thrilled. Apparently, Lucien was already on Quinn's potential witness list, but was even more prickly than his brother and impossible to pin down. Quinn had been trying for days to reach Lucien but hadn't had luck.

Of course, I didn't tell Quinn it was all thanks to Damien.

Something tells me Quinn wouldn't be too happy about how much time I've been spending with Damien. Eventually, I'll have to fess up, but for right now, I want to ride this wave and see where it takes me. I'll have to ask Quinn for forgiveness later.

Bennett makes a sharp turn through grand, fortress-like gates, and a sprawling estate emerges from the thick New England woodlands. I can't help but gawk. Blackthorn Manor is absolutely breathtaking.

Ancient oaks and towering maples line the driveway, their branches arching overhead. Sprawling, meticulously groomed gardens extend in all directions, filled with beds of beautiful orange-hued roses and lavender. A gardener pruning rose bushes waves at the car as we pass by. On the left, a private tennis court comes into view, its white lines sharp and freshly painted, a stark contrast to the ancient feel of the estate. On the right, I spot a large, well-maintained horse stable with open pastures. Thoroughbred horses with shiny coats and manes frolic in the grass.

Then we're at the main house—a massive, centuries-old

mansion, rising up from the earth like something plucked from the pages of a gothic novel. Stone walls weathered by time and seasons, yet untouched by decay. Dark ivy wraps around the exterior, climbing all the way to the gabled rooftops and tall windows. Spires pierce the sky, casting shadows over the manicured lawns below.

"That's the West House, where Lucien stays," Damien says, pointing to a large, dark-bricked Georgian-style manor that flanks the main house. It's more modern but still massive in size.

"And there?" I gesture to another building that's as big as a country inn.

"That's the guest quarters."

"It looks like a hotel!" I exclaim. "Is that where you stay when you're in town?"

He snorts. "Of course not. The main house is mine," he says, like I'm being ridiculous. "Well, the entire estate is, actually. It was passed on to me after my father's death."

"Not your mother?"

"No. Blackthorn Manor always passes down the male line." He smirks, a flicker of amusement in his eyes. "She prefers the pied-à-terre in Newport anyway."

I don't even ask. Of course, his family also has a place in old-money, self-important Newport.

Bennett parks the car at the front of the main house, and it takes everything in my power not to gape like a fool. Everywhere I look are signs of old-world wealth, though it also seems to exude an air of mystery like most ancient things do, the sort of place where whispers from the past still cling to the walls and every corner holds untold secrets.

"You really live here?"

"I do." He nods. "Though I'm not home as much as I'd like to be."

"Oh my God." A startled laugh bursts out of me before I

can stop it. "I can't believe you have all this, and you're staying next door to me at the Cottage. You're actually insane, you know that, right?"

He grins. "Well, someone has to keep you out of trouble." Before I can say anything else, he's already stepping outside. "Bennett will take you to Lucien's."

"You're not coming with me?"

"Lucien and I—we don't get along very well, I'm afraid," he says, though he doesn't look too sad about it. "You'll have better luck if I'm not around." He exhales a short, knowing laugh. "Especially since my brother is a sucker for a pretty face."

A blush creeps across the back of my neck. Mentally, I'm aware this is improper and I shouldn't want compliments from a client, and certainly not a client like Damien, but my body seems to feel completely different about the matter.

"Be careful, James." Damien turns to me, his tone suddenly serious. "Lucien is… slippery. Get what you can, but I wouldn't trust everything he says." His hand hovers over the door handle. "I'll see you later. I have a few matters to take care of inside."

I arch a brow. "Oh? Super secret cult business?"

Damien smirks. "The All Hallows Gala is coming up, and I need to finalize a few last-minute details."

I blink at him, surprised. "You're not seriously thinking of going?" I ask, remembering my conversation with Katie. She'd warned me about the possibility of Damien attending, but I'd forgotten all about it with everything going on.

"Of course I am. I never miss it." He says it casually, like this is any other year and not one where he's the prime suspect in a major murder case.

I let out a groan. "This is a terrible idea. Have you cleared it with Quinn?"

"I think you keep forgetting something, Counselor." His

voice is smooth, droll. "You and Quinn work for me. Not the other way around," he says and disappears inside.

Bennett drops me off at Lucien's house next, where a housekeeper greets me and leads me inside.

The interior of the West House is like stepping into another century. Old, luxurious, and dripping with wealth and history. Dark wooden panels line the walls, and grand antique colonial chandeliers hang from the high ceilings. A grandfather clock ticks softly from the parlor as I walk past, its sound muffled by richly woven antique rugs that stretch across the hardwood floors, their burgundy and gold patterns faded gently by time. Without hesitation, the housekeeper ushers me into Lucien's office, saying he's been expecting me. She gestures to the large, imposing dark walnut desk at the center of the room, and I take a seat. The air is heavy, like it's been holding its breath for years.

I take out my laptop and pull up my witness interview outline, racing through the questions in my head once more. I feel ready. Prepared. And then Lucien Blackhollow walks in, and every thought falls right out of my head.

Tall, dark, and handsome, the man is every bit as good looking as his brother, but there's something about the older Blackhollow sibling that immediately sets my nerves on edge. Every muscle in my body tightens, as if my brain is now on high alert that a predator is in my midst. Although with *that* face, a small part of me wonders what it would feel like to be caught in his sights. If I might even enjoy it.

"Miss Woodsen," he says, his voice smooth as he crosses the room with a calculated grace. His gaze drags over me—not in the sleazy way some men look at women, but with the sharp, assessing interest of a man who enjoys pulling people apart just to see what makes them tick. "I've heard a lot about you."

"Only good things, I hope," I say, forcing a smile as I

extend my hand. His eyes shift downward, briefly, like he wasn't expecting me to be so forward. He avoids the contact and takes the seat across from me.

"Depends on who you ask," he says. "Let's begin, shall we? I have an appointment in thirty minutes."

"So soon?" I ask. "I was hoping we'd have more time."

"Unfortunately, my schedule is packed."

"Okay, I understand. Thank you for agreeing to meet with me." I glance up at my outline and begin taking notes on my laptop. "I want to start with the night your brother's fiancée, Ms. Van Buren, was murdered. You were in Boston, correct?"

Lucien leans back in his chair, his eyes narrowing slightly. The way he watches me reminds me of a cat with a bird. Curious, mildly entertained, but ultimately unimpressed.

"I was at the All Hallows Gala, yes."

"And did you happen to see Ms. Van Buren while you were in town that day?"

"I did not. I was... otherwise occupied."

"When was the last time you saw her—before the murder?"

"Earlier that week, probably. I saw Vivienne frequently. More than my brother did, if we're being honest." He says it like it's no big deal, but the way he glances at me makes it clear he's referring to the sordid nature of his relationship with Damien's fiancée.

"Are you referring to an affair with the victim?"

I keep my tone neutral, trying not to let my disgust show. I don't know Lucien or the victim, and I don't want to think ill of the dead, but after what my ex put me through, I'm not fond of cheaters.

"Damien has always had an eye for exquisitely beautiful women," he says, his gaze flicking to my face for just a moment too long before he continues. "Though their character? Well… that's another story. Let's just say Vivienne wasn't the innocent flower everyone thinks she was."

"And yet you were with her—your brother's fiancée," I say, watching carefully to see his reaction.

Lucien's arrogant smile fades. "I suppose some temptations are hard to resist," he says and gives me a knowing look. "Isn't that right, Miss Woodsen?"

A flicker of heat rises in my cheeks.

"I don't know what you're talking about."

"I'm sure you don't," he says silkily. "In any event, you're not here to judge me, Miss Woodsen. You're here to figure out who killed Vivienne."

"Okay, so, who do you think killed her? Do you think it was Damien?"

"Oh, Damien is capable of most anything. Murder? Definitely." He chuckles darkly, tapping his fingers against the desk. "But no, not her. Not Vivienne. I don't think he loved her enough to get his hands dirty."

"I'm sorry. I'm not following," I say, the bitterness in his voice catching me off guard. "What do you mean by that?"

"Enough about Damien." Lucien leans forward, his gaze piercing. "You really came here to ask about the Veil, didn't you?"

My pulse quickens.

"What can you tell me?"

"More than Damien has told you, I'm sure." Lucien smiles coldly. "He's always been secretive about our legacy."

He walks over to the bookshelf, pulling out an old, leather-bound book, and bringing it back to the desk. As he flips through it, I see the yellowed pages are covered in strange symbols, like the ones I saw in the murder scene photos.

"The Mark of the Veil," I whisper, recalling its name.

"Yes." He nods. "The Veil is about power, Miss Woodsen. Power through sacrifice. For generations, my family has maintained their wealth and influence through evoking the ancient Veil rituals. You see, each generation is required to perform a new series of sacrifices in order to maintain our family's status and place within the Veil."

"Sacrifices such as…?"

His gaze sharpens, dark amusement dancing at the edges. "Oh, Miss Woodsen. I think you know exactly what type of sacrifices I'm implying."

My blood curdles, my hands shaking on the keyboard as I type.

He's talking about killing people!

Not that this is entirely new information. Professor Hargrove had said as much, but it's a whole other thing to hear Damien's own brother practically confirm it.

"The Blackhollows have always been a prominent part of the organization's leadership," Lucien continues. "Grandfather Blackhollow was the rumored 'high priest' within. After him, our father took over and continued the traditions before his… *untimely*… death a few years ago." He straightens in his seat. "And now another Blackhollow must rise up and carry on the legacy."

"You're going to become the high priest?"

"Me? Oh no, Miss Woodsen." He laughs, a cold, mirthless sound that echoes throughout the large office. "I'm the bastard son," he says, eyes darkening, and I see a flash of resentment. "I don't get to lead."

"Then who?" I ask, though I already suspect the answer.

"The eldest true-born son—Damien, of course."

I swallow hard, trying to process what he's saying. Damien Blackhollow, the leader of a dangerous secret cult? It doesn't make sense.

"He didn't tell me that."

"Damien's been keeping quite a few things from you, I imagine." His gaze strays to my mouth for the briefest second before meeting my eyes again. Then he leans forward, his voice dropping to a whisper. "Has he told you about your father yet?"

My blood runs cold.

"What–what about my father?"

Lucien smiles, his teeth sharp and gleaming. There's something almost indulgent in the way he watches me react, like he's enjoying peeling back my layers, piece by piece.

"Your father was involved with the Veil," he says. "Your mother's death—there's more to the story than you've been told."

The ground shifts beneath me.

"No, my dad worked in IT at Blackhollow Industries, that's all," I say, shaking my head. My hands drop from the keyboard, and I push the laptop away. "Dad was a nobody, just a work grunt for the company. You're lying."

"How… interesting. Even after everything you've been through, you remain loyal to your father." Lucien tilts his head, appraising me with something that feels dangerously close to approval. "I can see why he likes you."

I stiffen. "Who?"

"Come now, Miss Woodsen. Let's not be coy." His smirk deepens. "You must've noticed my brother's… interest."

I flush, suddenly needing to escape—to get away from Lucien's poisonous presence. "I need to go," I mutter, standing and grabbing my belongings.

"Pity. I was enjoying our time together," Lucien says, leaning back, his eyes widening with amusement. He's enjoying this.

I force myself to keep my voice even and professional despite how unnerved I am.

"Thank you for your time. It's been… enlightening."

"Oh yes. A real pleasure," he mocks. "You run along now, but be sure to ask your father about the Veil. And while you're at it, ask yourself why Damien hasn't told you any of this himself."

His words slither around me as I turn for the door, gripping my bag so tightly, my knuckles ache.

"Good luck, Miss Woodsen," he calls after me, smirking. "Just remember—sometimes the truth is more dangerous than the lies."

CHAPTER 13

The car ride home is quiet. The air between Damien and me feels thick, like it's pressing down on my body, making it hard to breathe. I lean back in the seat of his sleek car, my gaze fixed out the window as the towering trees of Blackthorn Manor fade into the distance. Lucien's words echo in my head, feeling more than a bit sinister.

My conversation with Damien's brother didn't go at all like I'd expected. He'd been far more open about the Blackhollow family and their ties to the occult than I'd thought he'd be. I doubted Damien would be happy knowing everything Lucien had shared with me. And that last parting shot, the way Lucien's eyes had glinted when he'd asked me about my father and alluded to Damien keeping some dark secret from me. Though Damien had warned me to be careful, that Lucien could be manipulative, something tells me Lucien didn't just throw that out to mess with my head. It felt truthful. Real.

Lucien knows something about the Veil and my dad. I'm certain of it.

I press my forehead against the cool glass of the car window, trying to make sense of it all. How could my father be connected to this? He was only an employee at Blackhollow Industries. He wasn't even an executive—just an IT guy.

When I glance over at Damien, he's busy responding to emails on his phone. His jaw is set, dark eyes staring ahead, hands resting casually on his lap. He hasn't said much since we left Blackthorn Manor. He looks completely normal, like a man who has nothing to hide.

"James?" He notices me staring. "Everything okay?"

"Just thinking," I say.

"You were with my brother longer than I expected."

"It was less than an hour."

"That's a lifetime for Lucien. He's usually very abrupt with people." He lifts a brow. "You must've charmed him."

"Hardly."

"Just remember, Lucien is not someone you want to get involved with." Damien shifts in his seat, angling his body toward me. "Well, don't keep me in suspense. Learn anything interesting?"

I can tell by the look on his face he knows something's off, but I'm not ready to talk about what I've learned. Not yet anyway.

"Maybe."

"So I was thinking," he says after a moment, "as long as you're still here in Salem's Fall, we should grab lunch. There's this charming little place—"

"Thanks, but I need to work."

The words come out harsher than I mean them to. There's a pause, a stretch of silence that feels like it's going to snap any second. His body stiffens slightly, jaw clenching. I can tell he's not used to being turned down.

"You need to take care of yourself, James. You've been pushing too hard."

I study him, my eyes narrowing. "Is that concern for my well-being? Or your case?"

He holds my gaze. "Both."

I can feel him watching me, waiting for me to say something further, but I don't want to tell him what I've learned yet. I don't know who or what to trust.

The moment the car pulls up to the Cottage, I grab my bag and bolt. "See you later," I say over my shoulder, already rushing for the entrance.

"James, wait—" he calls after me, but I don't look back.

I spend the rest of the day in my room with Lucky and room service, watching old sitcoms on TV while drafting discovery motions for Quinn to review and updating my case memo with notes from my interview with Lucien. I leave out one important detail about our meeting—I don't include the part about my dad. Ethically, I'm crossing a line by not including it. The information pertains to our case, and it's my professional responsibility to disclose it, but my gut tells me this isn't something I should share yet with anyone. Not even Quinn.

If I'm being brutally honest, it's not just the impact this information could have on my family, but I'm also worried about the impact it could have on my career. If there's a real conflict here, Quinn will have to take me off the case. Maybe I didn't want to be on the case in the beginning when things looked bad, but after all the progress I've made, I'll be damned if anyone sidelines me now. What I need to do is get to the bottom of things with my father first. Then I can decide my next steps.

The very next morning, I begin the short drive to Massachusetts Correctional Institution—the medium-security prison where my dad is incarcerated, about twenty miles away. It goes by in a blur. Before I know it, I'm stepping inside the familiar prison walls where I've spent so much time these past few years, shivering, rubbing my hands together to warm myself up. It's always freezing here.

I square my shoulders as a guard leads me toward the visiting room, trying not to gag at the strong smell of disinfectant, sweat, and something stale. The walls around me are painted in a bland, institutional beige, designed to drain the life out of the place and the people inside. My footsteps echo down the hallway, each step a reminder of the reality I'm about to face—my father, behind glass, a man whose life was stolen from him years ago. He's been in this place for nine years now, almost a decade. His life reduced to four walls, a narrow bed, and whatever peace of mind he can carve out of this cold, dead environment.

As I step inside the visitor's area, my stomach churns with a mix of sorrow and a bit of anger. Rows of small plastic chairs line the wall in front of thick, bulletproof-glass partitions. Each station is its own isolated world. Behind those partitions sit men who have been locked away, some of them for good reason. Others, like my father, for reasons that are less clear.

I take a seat at the booth labeled "Thomas Woodsen." My fingers smooth the wrinkles in my blazer as I wait. The ticking of a clock on the far wall is too loud, too persistent, like it's counting down to something inevitable. Around the room, other visitors are talking to their loved ones through the glass, their voices muffled by the barrier. An elderly woman leans in close to the partition as she speaks to a man on the other side. Her expression is unmistakable—grief. Loss.

The door creaks open behind the glass, and my breath catches in my throat. Every time I see my dad, it's like being hit by a freight train all over again. Guilt rushes through me as I take in his salt-and-pepper hair, almost entirely gray now. He looks older than I remember.

I try to come as often as I can, but I've been so busy at work. His once-vibrant pale blue eyes are duller, wearier, though they light up when they see me. He's still in good shape, trim and muscular, but the hard lines on his face tell me prison life has taken a toll on him in ways I can't begin to comprehend.

"Hey, kiddo," he says, his voice warm. "It's great to see you." He smiles as he sits down, a sad, tired smile that doesn't quite reach his eyes. I notice the way his thumb rubs over the spot where his wedding ring used to be—a habit I've seen a million times before.

"Hi, Daddy," I say, my voice cracking.

"James?" His expression instantly tightens with concern. "Everything okay? Is it Madison? Are you in trouble at work again?"

Dad knows all about my last screwup at the office. I email him often using the prison's monitored email system, updating him on my life and job, even Maddie. My little sister refuses to talk to him herself. She still blames him for Mom's death, no matter how many times I've tried to tell her I know he's innocent.

"No, nothing like that. Everything's fine." I shake my head. "But I need to talk to you. It does involve work, I guess. It's… complicated."

He straightens a bit, his expression growing more serious. When my dad looks at me, I always know I'm getting his full attention, that nothing else matters in the world more than what I have to say. Dad has always been the best listener I know.

"Tell me everything, kiddo. What's going on?"

I swallow hard, my pulse quickening. How do I even start a conversation like this?

"I'm on a new case at work. A new client," I say. "It's Damien Blackhollow."

The name hangs between us like a loaded gun. I watch as his grip tightens on the edge of the table, his thumb stilling over the place where his wedding ring used to sit.

"I don't understand," he says, his voice suddenly suspicious. "You're brand new at the firm and Blackhollow—he's an important man. Why you?"

"I'm not sure, but Damien sort of asked for me specifically. Threatened to pull his business if I wasn't on the team." I pause. When I say it out loud, it does sound more than a little strange that Damien would care so much about having someone like me involved in his case. "Listen, Dad. The point is that Damien is accused of murdering his fiancée, and there are a lot of similarities between his case and yours. His fiancée was stabbed multiple times, like Mom. The knife used is similar. And there were strange symbols carved into the walls and, um, the body... like Mom." I clear my throat nervously. I've never asked many questions about Mom's murder before, but I have to now. "Dad, I need to know what really happened. I need to know the truth about Mom's murder."

He's quiet, his gaze locked on the glass between us. I can see the tension in his jaw, the way his fingers flex and tighten.

"The truth..." he echoes softly, talking to himself.

"Please, Dad. You have to tell me."

His eyes snap back to mine, and I see something raw and broken flash across his face. He blinks it away quickly, but I saw it, and he knows I saw it.

"I didn't kill her, James," he says, his voice low and filled with pain.

"I know," I whisper, but the words feel fragile, like they could shatter at any moment. "But I need to understand what happened. I need to know what you got involved with."

"You shouldn't be anywhere near that man—that family." He slumps back in his chair, rubbing his temples as if trying to fend off a headache. "I didn't want you to get dragged into this. I wanted to protect you."

"Protect me from what?"

His eyes meet mine again.

"The Order of the Veil."

My pulse hammers in my ears as the world shifts and reality drops away.

"What do you know about the Veil, Dad?"

He sighs, his voice barely above a whisper. "I first came across the Veil when I was working for Blackhollow Industries. You remember, I did IT for the company, right?"

I nod.

"I found some private files hidden away in a folder on Ian Blackhollow's email server," he continues. "I know I shouldn't have snooped, but what I saw… I couldn't stop myself once I started reading." He swallows hard, his skinny Adam's apple bobbing up and down. "It was so shocking. Documents detailing rituals, sacrifices, power… It sounded like nonsense at first, but the more I dug, the more I realized it wasn't. It was real. All of it."

His gaze falls to the floor, and he presses his palms flat against the table, like it's the only thing still tethering him to this world.

"I… I went to Mr. Blackhollow—to Ian."

My heart pounds in my chest. "Oh, Dad. What did you do?"

"I thought—God, I thought it would help," he says. "All I wanted was to give you and Madison and your mother the life you all deserved."

"What do you mean? We had a great life."

"We never had enough!" he snaps. "No matter how hard I worked or how much I tried to save, it was never enough! We were always living paycheck to paycheck. I wanted more for you."

The look on his face breaks my heart.

"Dad?"

"They called it the Blood Rite. A sacrifice to fulfill my end of the bargain." He closes his eyes, his shoulders slumping in defeat. "I was ready to die that night. I thought I was giving my life for you girls and your mom. But something went wrong. It wasn't working." His voice begins to shake. "The knife wouldn't let me. It just… wouldn't.

"And then your mother—" He grips the table, his knuckles going white. "She stepped forward. It was like she understood something I didn't. She told them she would be the sacrifice—"

A cold chill spreads through me. I feel like I'm going to be sick.

"Dad, no… How could you do that?"

"I didn't *do* anything!" he cries, shaking his head furiously. "I wouldn't do it, James! I wouldn't take her life!" His breath shudders, his shoulders sagging like the weight of that moment is still crushing him. "But the knife—the Veil—didn't care. I tried everything I could to stop it. But it was too late. They took her anyway."

The room spins, tilting dangerously, like the ground beneath me is no longer solid. A cold, sharp pressure clamps around my chest, and suddenly, I can't seem to pull in enough air. My mother is dead because of some twisted, fucked-up ritual my dad and Damien's father agreed to.

I blink at him, my voice raw. "Why didn't you tell me?"

"I didn't want you to know what I'd done," he says, his voice breaking. "I lost your mother and then your sister. Madison… she wouldn't even look at me after what happened. I couldn't bear it if I lost you too, James."

"But what about your attorney?" My pulse pounds in my ears, my vision narrowing. "Why didn't he bring this up at the trial? Why didn't he say anything about the Veil?"

He lets out a bitter laugh. "Say what? That the Blackhollows—the wealthiest, most powerful family in New England—are part of some secret evil cult? Practicing witchcraft and sacrificing your mother in some gory ritual gone awry?"

"You could've done something," I say, my voice wavering

between accusation and desperation. "You could've fought back, tried to expose them."

"Expose the *Blackhollow family*? They would have crushed me and then gone after you and your sister for revenge." He shakes his head, a resigned look in his eyes. "No, staying quiet was the only way to keep you safe."

I shake my head, tears blurring my vision. A mix of fury and sadness roils inside me.

"You should have told me. I deserved to know the truth."

"You're right," he says, his face etched with regret. "I'm so sorry. For all of it."

I stand, my legs trembling as his terrible confession sinks in. I can barely bring myself to look at him.

"I have to go."

"Kiddo, wait," he pleads, but I'm already backing away, my heart shattered.

Without another word, I turn and make my way out of the prison, the weight of my father's words hanging over me like a death sentence. For the first time in years, I feel completely lost. Everything I believed about my family, about my father, was a lie. And Damien…

Damien knew the truth this whole time.

CHAPTER 14

The streets of Salem's Fall are buzzing with energy as I return from the visit with my father. With Halloween quickly approaching, the streets are even more crowded than when I first arrived days ago. Everywhere I look, tourists are wandering through the maze of little shops, clutching hot apple cider and pumpkin lattes in their hands. The sound of children's laughter echoes through the street as kids chase each other in witch hats and cat ears, holding on to broomsticks and colorful gourds.

It's almost too festive. Too perfect.

For a moment, I wish I could lose myself in it too, but there's a darkness hanging over me now, something no amount of fall cheer can shake. It's not just the weight of what I've learned about my father—it's this entire case. The deeper I go, the more twisted everything gets.

As I walk up to the Cottage, I see Damien leaning against his sleek black car. He watches me approach, arms crossed, face set in a hard line. He smiles politely, but the air crackles with tension. I can feel the anger radiating from him even before I get close.

That's okay. I'm none too happy with him either.

"Where have you been all day?" His voice is a low growl.

I stop short.

"You may be my client, Damien, but I don't report to you on my every move."

"I asked you a question." He quickly closes the gap between us. "Where were you?"

I square my shoulders and lift my chin. I'm not about to be interrogated by anyone, not even Damien Blackhollow.

"I went to see my dad. Not that it's any of your business."

"I was worried." I see the flare of something—anger, fear, maybe both—cross Damien's face. He takes a step back, running a hand through his hair. "You shouldn't be wandering around alone. Not after everything that's happened."

"I didn't realize I needed your permission to visit my father," I snap.

"Don't act like this is some normal situation." His eyes narrow, and he steps closer, looming over me. "You keep putting yourself in danger. You have no idea what's at stake."

The condescension in his tone causes me to lose all semblance of self-control and professionalism, and I'm unable to hold back my fury. How dare this man sit here and lecture me about danger when he's been keeping the most dangerous secret of my life from me?

"You knew, didn't you?" My voice trembles with barely contained rage. "About my father's connection to the Veil and my mother's death? You knew this entire time, and you let me walk into this case blind?"

Damien's jaw goes slack with surprise.

"He told you?"

"He's my father, Damien! Of course he told me!"

"Yes, but why now?" He scratches at his chin, brows furrowed together, a frown on his face. "Why would he tell you the truth now after all these years of hiding it from you?"

"What does that matter? That's hardly the point!"

He lets out a sharp, guttural curse.

"Of course! Lucien. That backstabbing son of a bitch."

His eyes blaze with fury as he steps closer. "He told you, didn't he? At your little meeting yesterday. And naturally, you ran straight to your father at the prison."

"Forget Lucien! He's not important." A sharp gust of wind whips through the courtyard, but I barely feel it over the heat prickling at my skin. "The question is—why didn't *you* tell me?"

"Isn't it obvious by now?" He grabs my wrist, almost desperately, and for a moment, I feel a surge of panic. "I wanted to keep you safe. There are things about the Veil—about my family and yours too—that are best kept secret. Knowing these things puts you in even more danger."

"Is this why you insisted I stay on this case? You wanted to keep me close so you could make sure I wouldn't find out about my dad?" My voice rises with each word. "Or did you pick me because of some sick game? Laughing at me the whole time behind my back?"

"Don't be absurd," he says, his voice low and rough. "That's not why I chose you, James."

"Then why? Why am I on this case, Damien?"

He sighs loudly, taking a step away.

"I recognized you the moment I saw you at the courthouse—Thomas Woodsen's daughter, all grown up and assigned to my defense. I knew you were too close to the truth, but I thought if I kept you close, I could protect you. Control what you learned. Maybe even shield you from all of it. I felt I owed it to you, after everything your family's been through." He groans, frustrated, raking a hand through his dark hair. "But instead, you've been completely foolish and reckless. Running around town, chasing leads like this is just another case when it's anything but. You don't understand what you're up against."

"I understand more than you think." My hands ball into

fists at my sides, my breath sharp. "And I don't need your help!"

Something shifts in his expression, quick as a flick of a knife—cold, calculated, lethal.

"Careful, James."

He says it like a warning, and I remember then that Damien is a Blackhollow first and foremost. I've started to grow too comfortable around the man, but if his family is deadly and dangerous, he very well may be the most dangerous one of all. I have to remember that.

"You may think you don't need my help, but I'm the only one keeping you safe right now." His voice is clipped, sharp, and I can see the tension in his shoulders. "If you keep pushing, it's not just your career that's at risk–it's your life and everyone and everything you hold dear."

I stare at him, my pulse hammering in my ears. I can feel the ground shifting beneath me, like everything I thought I knew is unraveling right in front of my eyes.

"Is that a threat?"

"It's the truth you keep demanding," he says, his voice low, almost a whisper.

"I don't do well with people trying to control me and telling me what to do," I say, folding my arms across my chest. "I'm going back to see the professor. At least I can trust him to be honest with me."

"You think you can trust *him*?" Damien laughs, a cold, bitter sound. "You can't trust anyone, James. Not him, not me, not anyone." His face darkens. "Your professor has his own agenda, believe me. But go ahead, go run back to him—see what you find out."

There's something in his voice, something I know I should listen to, but I'm too angry, too hurt to care. I turn on my heel and shout back over my shoulder.

"Fine! I will!"

I rush away from Damien, racing up the steps to the Cottage. I don't know why I'm so upset; I knew it from the moment I met him. Damien Blackhollow is not a good guy, and he's definitely not to be trusted.

Lucky is at my side the moment I return to my room, weaving between my legs and nudging my hand, his purr steady and comforting. I scoop him up, and he settles against me, warm and grounding. His soft black fur presses into my chest like he knows exactly what I need. He's the one constant in my life who I know will never let me down.

I stand like that for what feels like forever, holding my cat, trying to catch my breath. Everything feels like it's spiraling out of control. The more I dig, the more I realize how deep this rabbit hole goes. And I'm not sure I want to know what's waiting at the bottom.

Eventually, I force myself to text the professor, making sure he's around this late on a weekend afternoon. He texts back right away, thrilled to hear from me. We agree to meet at his shop in twenty minutes. I feed Lucky dinner and head out for the night, a cream-colored turtleneck sweater over my knit dress to protect me from the evening chill.

After a short walk, I push open the door to the Wandering Raven, the bell chiming as I step inside. Something feels different this time. There's a creeping stillness in the air, as if the shop itself knows what I've just uncovered about my family. Flickering candlelight casts long, twisted shadows against the walls, almost ominously.

I walk past the shelves stacked with old books, a ripple of unease tightening in my chest as I notice something I missed the last time I was here. Over in the corner, tucked away, is a glass case with an ancient-looking dagger inside. Its silver blade gleams under the dim lighting, intricate designs etched into the hilt. My breath catches as I realize the design closely resembles the one used in the murder of Damien's fiancée—

and my mother. The same curving lines, the same twisted spirals.

I take a step closer to get a better look. There's a plaque underneath it, the following words handwritten in neat, calligraphic script: *17th Century Sacrificial Blade. Origin: Unknown.*

I turn away, trying to shake off the creeping dread, but everywhere I look, something else strange catches my eye: a row of vials filled with dark red liquid labeled "Vampire Blood"; bundles of dried plants and herbs with labels like "Nightshade," "Foxglove," and "Wolfsbane"; a rusted iron key on display called "The Key to the Underworld"; a pinboard of dried, dead moths.

A cold sweat forms at the base of my neck. Was this place always this creepy? Or am I now just more aware of it since learning about the Veil and what's really at stake?

"James! Welcome back!"

I turn to see Professor Hargrove stepping out from behind a velvet curtain, his face lighting up. His smile is wide and warm. He's even better looking than I remember with that casual, easy charm. Not a trace of the coldness or anger that I'd just dealt with from Damien.

"I'm glad you texted. I didn't expect to see you again so soon." He steps forward, his eyes locking onto mine with a mix of curiosity and something a bit hopeful. "Back for another history lesson?"

I smile. "You could say that."

"Well, I'm flattered." His eyes flicker with amusement. "Tell me—how did you find Strega's Hollow?"

I hesitate for a moment, unsure of how much to reveal, but I remind myself that Hargrove is my best shot at figuring this all out. Damien has been lying to me from the beginning, hiding things. If anyone can give me the truth, it's the professor.

So I tell him everything—about the Hollow, about Lucien,

about what I've uncovered so far. I put it all on the table, everything except for my father's connection to the Veil. I still want to keep that little bit of information to myself. For now, at least.

Hargrove listens intently, his face growing more serious with each passing moment. When I finish, there's a moment of silence before he lets out a slow breath, rubbing the back of his neck anxiously.

"Lucien Blackhollow," he murmurs. "Now, there's a name I didn't expect to hear. I'm shocked Damien allowed you anywhere near his brother, considering those two can hardly stand to be in the same room together."

"Why do they hate each other so much?" I ask, my curiosity piqued.

Hargrove leans against the counter, his expression thoughtful. "Lucien has always been a thorn in Damien's side," he explains. "They're half-brothers, sure, but Damien's perfect existence has always been a reminder of something Lucien's questioned his whole life—his place. Ian Blackhollow never wanted Lucien and certainly never raised him to inherit the family empire. But Damien? Damien was the golden child, the one Ian groomed for power from the very beginning."

"And Lucien resents that?"

Hargrove's mouth twitches into something that isn't quite a smile. "Lucien resents a lot of things. His family. His position. That no matter how hard he fights for control, he'll never be Damien." He tilts his head. "Lucien has been circling the Veil's leadership for years, waiting for an opportunity to take what he believes should be his. And with Damien set to take the reins, well… let's just say it's not hard to imagine Lucien having his own plans."

I swallow hard. "You think Lucien could be involved in Damien's fiancée's death?"

"It wouldn't be the first time a Blackhollow committed

murder." His gaze meets mine with an intensity that sends a shiver down my spine. "James, you seem like a good person, but you're stepping into something far darker than you realize. There are forces at play here that even the Blackhollows can't control. I wonder if it might be best for you to forget what you've learned and return to Boston. Let someone else handle this case."

"I don't have a choice, Nick. I can't just walk away." I clench my fists, a steely resolve settling over me. "It's not only about my career anymore—this is personal."

"Personal? How so?" His eyes narrow. "Please tell me you aren't… emotionally attached to Damien. Or, even worse, that sociopath Lucien?"

"Oh no, nothing like that," I say quickly and look down at the gorgeous ring on my finger, twisting it back and forth. *Damien's ring.*

Part of me wonders if I'm being honest. I haven't known Damien long, but there have been moments where I've felt something between us. Something more than simply professional feelings. I have to admit I wouldn't be so hurt and angry by this betrayal if I hadn't started to care about him, just a little. Still, Damien alone is not what's keeping me here in Salem's Fall, desperate for the truth. It goes much deeper than that.

I glance over at Hargrove again. Something about the way he's looking at me makes me feel safe, like maybe I can trust him, and I so desperately want someone to trust in this damn town.

"It's my family." I sigh. "My father… he has ties to the Veil that I didn't know about until recently." Hargrove's eyes widen slightly, but he says nothing, waiting for me to continue. "My mother was killed in connection with some sort of sacrifice for the Veil—the Blood Rite. I don't understand it all, yet. I'm still trying to figure everything out, but I need to know what these rituals are about. I have to know what really happened to my family."

Hargrove is silent for a moment, his face a mask of contemplation.

"All right, James." He sighs reluctantly and gives me a slow nod. "I'll tell you what I know, but you're not going to like it."

He straightens, his voice lowering. "I told you about the Veil's rituals during the witch trials and how they kept their members safe from persecution. And how I believe the rituals continue to this day and have gotten far worse." He swallows hard. "But what I haven't told you is that these present-day power rituals don't require just any sacrifice anymore, but the murder of a beloved innocent."

I swallow, the knot in my stomach tightening. "So both my mother and Damien's fiancée were killed in these rituals?"

"Yes and no," he says. "Most likely your mother was sacrificed during a Blood Rite, but Damien's fiancée was something different. I believe she was part of the Ascension Ritual." Hargrove's lips curl into a humorless smile. "Some rituals, like the Blood Rite, require only one victim to complete the offering. But Damien is the Blackhollow heir. If he is to take over the Veil as its new leader, he must complete the far more complex Ascension Ritual—a series of four sacrifices, one per year, each on Veil Night. The killings escalate in violence, each more gruesome than the last. I suspect his fiancée was the third. The final sacrifice—the most important—will happen this year."

My blood runs cold. "Veil Night? What's that?"

"It's the most sacred night of the year for the Veil. It's when the barrier between the worlds is at its thinnest, allowing dark forces to cross over." He gives me a thin smile. "Us regular folk call it Halloween."

"And this fourth sacrifice—this murder—you're certain it's going to happen on Halloween?"

"If it doesn't, Damien's ascension is at risk, and someone else could take his place. The Veil must have a new leader." Hargrove's eyes darken. "Either way, blood will be spilled."

"Do you know who the final sacrifice is?"

Hargrove's eyes lock onto mine, his voice dropping. "I don't know for sure, but there are whispers," he says. "It must be someone in Damien's orbit. An innocent. Someone he's close with, someone he cares about."

My heart pounds in my chest, the pieces slowly falling into place.

The final sacrifice.

Halloween. Veil Night.

Just a few short weeks away.

I don't know who the next victim will be, but I know one thing. I'm running out of time, and I'm in too deep to walk away now.

CHAPTER 15

I return to my room at the Cottage just before nightfall. I shrug off my jacket, letting it slip to the floor, and drop onto the bed, staring at the ceiling. The shocking events of the day play a constant loop in my head:

The visit with my father.

My fight with Damien.

Hargrove's startling revelation about Damien's Ascension Ritual.

Lucky jumps up on the bed, nuzzling into my side, his soft fur brushing against my skin. He's been sticking close ever since we arrived at Salem's Fall, more than usual. I stroke his head absentmindedly, feeling the tension in my shoulders start to ease, though it never completely fades. The cat looks at me, his wide eyes filled with concern. Even Lucky knows something is terribly wrong.

"Thank goodness I have you," I murmur, scratching behind his ears. But his presence, comforting as it is, can't drown out the gnawing feeling that I'm in way over my head.

I reach for my phone and scroll through my missed messages and calls. Maddie is asking for more money for food. Apparently, the casserole I made for her is gone, and she's already blown through the two hundred I left her just a few days ago. I suspect the request is really for alcohol and clothes, but I'm too tired to argue about it. Instead, I Venmo her a few hundred dollars to hold her over until I return, whenever that is.

Quinn's name also pops up. Repeatedly. His texts are terse and to the point:

> Get back to Boston. NOW!

He's called too, and Quinn rarely calls. That's how I know it's bad. His angry voicemails are more of the same. The client—Damien, I suppose—is furious. The firm is losing patience. They think I'm wasting time and money here in Salem's Fall, and I'm on "thin ice."

I thumb through more messages. Katie has texted me too, cryptic and worried. Her words land like ice in my veins:

> Been hearing things at the office. Blackhollow is dangerous. You need to come home!

It seems like everyone wants me to turn tail and run back to Boston. Am I a fool to stay here?

But no, I've come too far.

Going back to Boston now empty-handed would mean going back a failure, and after my last screwup, I'd be lucky to get off memo writing duty within the next decade.

If I even have a job to go back to.

The only option is to get to the bottom of things. If I can figure out what's really going on and it exonerates Damien, we can win this case. But even if I find out Damien is guilty—if he is responsible for his fiancée's death—it can still be a win. I'll have saved the firm and Quinn the embarrassment of losing such an important case. We could strike a plea deal, figure out something that keeps us from getting a losing verdict. I'll be a hero.

Besides, there's more at stake now than just this case and my career. I need to find out how the Veil is connected to my mother's death. If they killed her and I can prove it, I have a shot at freeing my dad too.

I'm so close to unraveling the truth. I can feel it, like a live wire buzzing under my skin.

The Veil.

My dad.

The Blackhollows.

It's all connected somehow. I just need to keep pulling at the threads until it comes undone.

A soft knock at the door startles me from my thoughts. Room service has arrived. I let the waiter inside and he puts the tray of food on the table by the window. I stare at my dinner ambivalently. I'm not really hungry but forced myself to order something. I'll need all my energy for what's ahead.

Lucky rubs up against my legs, purring, as I scoop kibble into his bowl to feed him first. After he's done, I sink into the chair and grab a slice of cauliflower crust pizza, barely tasting it as I stare out the window. The world outside looks so normal. People walking around, tourists snapping pictures in front of the landmarks, couples laughing as they pass by. But I know better. Everything is wrong.

Lucky nudges my hand with his head, demanding attention.

"I wish I could make sense of this, boy," I whisper as I scratch behind his ears.

I think back to Lucien and what he told me yesterday about Damien's role as the heir apparent to the Veil. Lucien had practically dripped with satisfaction when he revealed that nugget of information, enjoying my shock. It isn't just that Damien is involved in things; he's at the very heart of it all—their leader. He was born into this darkness, destined for it.

Three sacrifices already. Three innocent people dead.

Who will be the final sacrifice on Veil Night?

Even if Damien isn't responsible for these murders, there's no denying that being close to him is dangerous in and of itself. The professor had said as much: the last sacrifice of the Ascension Ritual must be someone Damien's close with. Every rational part of me screams I need to stay away from Damien, that nothing good can come from this attraction I've been trying so hard to ignore.

His charm, his power, that magnetic pull he has—these are the things that ruin people, that lead them down paths they can't escape from. And yet, every time I see him, it's like I forget that he's accused of killing his own fiancée. And not just her. If the professor is to be believed, there are at least two other victims. Maybe more. For all I know, Damien and his family may have even played a role in my mother's murder.

I close my eyes and shake my head, trying to fight off the cold weight settling in my chest. One thing is certain. Damien Blackhollow is not safe.

He's never been safe.

As I crawl into bed, I listen for sounds next door, but hear nothing through the thick walls. For someone who's unusually obsessed with control, it's a bit odd how radio silent Damien has gone. Despite everything, I feel the sting of disappointment. I sort of expected him to burst through my door the second I got back from the professor's shop, but there's been no sign of him. Yes, I was the one who told him to stay away, but some small, irrational part of me thought he'd try harder to earn my forgiveness.

At the very least, I really did think he cared about my safety, at least a tiny bit, even if it was just on a professional level as his lawyer. But he hasn't checked in at all, even after knowing I went to go see Hargrove, a man he clearly doesn't like or trust. For all Damien knows, Hargrove—or the Veil, even—could've slit my throat tonight, leaving me bloody and dead in the cobbled streets of Salem's Fall somewhere.

Doesn't he care at all?

I snort, anger bubbling up inside me. Damn Damien Blackhollow. He has the audacity to act like a possessive beast at times, ordering me around, acting like he's protecting me, when he obviously doesn't even care if I'm dead or alive.

I glance over to the wall separating my room from his. Before the clear-minded, rational part of my brain can talk myself out of it, I push back the covers and slide out of bed. I tell myself I'll just check real quick. Just to see if he's back.

I tiptoe to my door and ease it open, peeking out. The hallway is quiet. Damien's door is shut—but not fully. A thin sliver of light spills through the crack. I hesitate, one last moment of sanity begging to take over.

I shouldn't.

I *know* I shouldn't.

But for someone so obsessed with control, he really should learn to lock his damn door.

A rush of nerves rises in my chest as I dart forward and slip inside his room. The intoxicating scent hits me right away. Dark spice, rich cedar, something unmistakably Damien. It's almost all-consuming in the small, empty room.

Inside, the space is as controlled and precise as the man himself. Luggage all put away. Bed made. Desk organized with sharp, deliberate neatness.

I shouldn't be here.

This is a complete breach of everything professional and ethical that a good lawyer should be doing. But then, what about Damien? The man isn't exactly the model client either. He hasn't been forthcoming about anything, has he? All the secrecy and mystery has led me to this.

That last thought justifies my next step. And the next.

I arrive at the desk, my fingers brushing over the smooth wood, pulse quickening as I glance at the open drawer.

Then I see it.

A knife.

Not a normal kitchen knife, or a Swiss Army knife, or even a hunting knife, but a large, sleek, curved blade with an intricate hilt—ancient, ceremonial-looking. A knife that looks remarkably similar to the sacrificial blades used in Veil rituals, almost identical to the one I saw in Hargrove's display case at the shop.

A prickle of unease rolls down my spine, and I take a step back, my pulse hammering in my ears.

Okay… maybe this isn't that weird…?

Damien Blackhollow is a rich, powerful man, after all. He probably has to protect himself against security threats all the time that are normal for a man of his wealth and status. I bet the guy has a whole collection of expensive weapons. Knives, guns, that sort of thing. Now that I think about it, I haven't seen him with a bodyguard, so perhaps he handles his own security detail. That's not totally outside the realm of reasonable possibilities… right?

My gaze snags on the Louis Vuitton designer briefcase propped up beside the desk, and my fingers twitch at my sides.

No… That's crossing a line. The door and the drawer were at least open, mostly, but the briefcase…

Before I can stop myself, I'm flipping the clasps open and tearing inside. Neat file folders. Sleek Montblanc fountain pen. A hand-stitched Smythson leather notebook, the kind that costs more than my monthly groceries. I frown, spotting a small amber prescription bottle nestled at the bottom of the suitcase. As I read the label, my stomach tightens.

Xanax.

An anti-anxiety drug. Powerful. Sedative-like.

A flicker of unease stirs deep in my gut. What the hell is

Damien doing with Xanax? He doesn't seem like the kind of man who struggles with anxiety or panic attacks. He's too controlled. Too composed. Something about this discovery bothers me, but I can't quite put my finger on why.

Then—a noise. I whirl around, my breath catching as I eye the door. It sounds like someone's coming down the hallway.

Shit.

I slam the briefcase shut. My hands tremble as I bolt for the door, slipping through the gap and darting back into my room. The moment I'm inside, I press my back against the wood, heart racing. My breaths come sharp and uneven, but I force myself to steady them.

It's fine.

I'm fine.

That flicker of unease lingers, but I push it down.

It's not like anything I've found tonight is exactly new information. So what? So Damien has a creepy-looking knife and prescription drugs—for whatever purposes. Damien isn't Mr. Rogers, clearly, but I already knew that. Nothing has changed.

So why does it feel like I've only just scratched the dark surface of Damien Blackhollow?

CHAPTER 16

October 18 (Two Weeks Until Halloween)

The next morning, I wake feeling like a ten-ton weight is pressing down on my chest as a flash of memory from last night hits me: Damien's door, slightly ajar. My hands, rifling through his things. The knife. The pills. Heat rises to my face, and I groan, pressing my palms to my eyes.

Jesus, James. What were you thinking?

Breaking into a client's room in the middle of the night? Snooping through his things like some kind of unhinged stalker?

And for what? The things I found were a tad bizarre, sure—but ultimately, nothing. A rich, powerful man having a fancy-looking knife and a prescription for Xanax? Not exactly damning evidence of any wrongdoing.

My eyes flick over to Lucky, curled up next to me. He looks so peaceful, so oblivious to the constant chaos that has now become my life. I envy him.

I roll over and grab my phone from the nightstand, scanning. Nothing news breaking, just more missed texts from Katie and another voicemail from Quinn, wondering why I haven't called him back and demanding an update. Some part of my brain registers Quinn's calls are a problem, but I don't let it get to me. I have bigger things on my mind than Quinn's wrath—like how the hell I'm supposed to piece together this twisted puzzle and solve this case.

I glance toward my phone again, pulling up Maddie's number. I still need to tell her about my conversation with our father and what I found out yesterday. She deserves to know the truth too.

My call goes straight to voicemail.

I tell myself not to worry. It's early and she's probably still sleeping, hungover from whatever shenanigans she got herself into last night. I'll call again later.

I rub the sleep from my eyes and climb out of bed. There's no time to waste.

Hargrove said there were at least two other murders tied to the Ascension Ritual before Damien's fiancée was killed, and if that's true, I need to learn more about them. There may have been others back when Damien's father, Ian, rose to leadership of the Veil years ago, too. If I can find out more about the previous rituals and uncover commonalities and patterns in all these past killings—and my mother's death too—I might really have something to go on.

The best shot I have is starting with the more recent murders. Those are probably still open cases. I can try to get information about them at the local police station or the courthouse, if they occurred in Salem's Fall. The older, long-buried cases, the ones possibly tied to Damien's father, will be cold cases. That means painstaking hours of digging through dusty files and microfiche at the local library archives or old court records.

It's going to be a long day…

I head for the bathroom, pulling my long blonde hair back into a loose but neat ponytail. Today calls for a put-together look. I'll likely be charming police detectives, court clerks, and librarians.

I pull on a fitted blouse in a soft ballerina pink color, pairing it with high-waisted slacks that look more expensive than they are. Over it all, I slip into my favorite cream pea coat, tailored just right, with polished buttons and a flattering collar. It's warm enough for the chillier weather, but still feminine and stylish. A simple gold necklace and small studs finish the look.

After I give Lucky a quick breakfast and some ear scratches, I head downstairs to grab a much-needed cup of coffee before I start my day. The Cottage lobby is quiet as I walk in. The tourist crowd must all still be asleep. It's so still, so calm—like the moment right before a brewing storm hits.

The scent of fresh coffee draws me toward the food counter, but then I stop dead in my tracks. Sitting in one of the old-fashioned leather armchairs, legs crossed with a casual ease, is a Blackhollow—just not the one I was secretly hoping to see.

Lucien Blackhollow.

His presence slams into me like a chilling gust of wind, setting my nerves on edge. Cold, steely eyes lock onto mine, and for a second, I forget how to breathe. Though Lucien and Damien share the same gorgeous features—the dark hair, the aristocratic jawline, the powerful presence—Lucien's darkness is sharper, more menacing, like a deadly cobra snake. Damien's darkness is magnetic; it pulls you in. Lucien's makes you want to run.

"Good morning, Miss Woodsen."

Lucien stands and beckons me over with a slow, predatory smile, like he knows exactly what I was just thinking. I swallow hard, my pulse racing as I force myself to walk over to his table. Despite my fear, my curiosity is too great.

"Lucien? What are you doing here?"

"I thought we might have a chat," he says smoothly, his voice like silk dipped in venom.

"What kind of chat?"

"About my brother," he says, his eyes glinting with some emotion I can't quite place as he steps closer. His gaze sweeps over me, boldly assessing. There's something in the way he looks at me. It's like he's cataloging every reaction, every breath. A slow, deliberate study. Not unlike Damien, but different. Damien watches me like he's trying to understand me. Lucien watches me like he already does.

"Okay, but first, I want to know why you sent me to see my dad." I cross my arms, glaring at him. "You wanted me to find out about his connection to the Veil. Why?"

"I'm sorry. I'm sure that must have been very painful." Lucien sighs, almost regretfully, though I'm not sure I believe he really feels badly. "I wanted you to learn about the connection my brother has to your family's… tragedy. I thought if you knew, you'd understand how dangerous he is."

"Why do you care what I think about Damien?"

"You shouldn't be with him," he says. "It's not safe for you."

A surge of anger flares up inside me. Because, of course, this is what people always assume, and I'm so damn sick of it! The partners, the associates, the judges. They take one look at me and decide I must be sleeping my way to the top. That I can't possibly be where I am because I worked my ass off. That I can't be in the same room as a man like Damien Blackhollow without falling into his bed.

And now Lucien is doing it too.

It's infuriating.

"I'm not *with* your brother, Lucien! He's my client." I clench my fists, my frustration boiling over.

Okay, yes, Damien Blackhollow is hotter than sin and maybe there is some weird, annoying, undeniable attraction between us, but I'm a professional! Why does everyone just assume I'm some dumb, weak woman who can't resist Damien's charms?

"Oh, I know you're not with him—yet." He grins coldly. "But my brother always gets what he wants, and for once, he shouldn't."

I narrow my eyes. "What are you trying to say? You think Damien wants *me*?"

"Oh, I'm quite certain he does." His tone is mocking, but there's something sharp beneath it, something dangerously close to admiration. "Someone like you—smart, brave, beautiful—I think you could actually be the one to make him happy. I imagine you could make a lot of men happy."

His gaze flickers, heavy with suggestion, sending a wave of heat curling low in my stomach. It's the kind of reaction I don't want to have—don't want to acknowledge. I hate the way he watches me, like he knows exactly what he's doing. Like he enjoys knocking me off balance. He's toying with me, and the worst part? My own damn body is betraying me. Because, objectively, Lucien Blackhollow is as gorgeous as his brother. There's no denying it. And like his brother, he knows exactly how to use that sharp-edged charm to his advantage.

Seriously, what the hell is in the Blackhollow gene pool? Do they breed them to be this insufferable?

I grit my teeth, shoving down the spark rising in my chest. I refuse to play along with whatever messed up game this is.

"What's your point, Lucien?"

"My brother doesn't deserve to be happy." Lucien leans closer, and I instinctively take a step back. "Damien isn't what he seems. He's a cold-blooded killer."

His words hit me like a punch to the gut. I stumble back, grabbing the edge of a chair to steady myself.

"*What?*" I whisper. "Are you saying he killed his fiancée?"

Lucien tilts his head, considering me with those icy, cold eyes. "Damien is responsible. One way or the other."

"I don't understand."

"You don't have to. You just have to understand how dangerous he is." His voice drops, calm and deliberate. "And it's not just his fiancée. He's responsible for our father's death too."

"But I thought that was an accidental drowning?"

"Oh, it was no accident, I assure you." Lucien's eyes flicker with a strange satisfaction as he watches me process everything he's just said. "Don't let him play you, Miss Woodsen. Leave this place, while you still can. Go back to Boston where it's safe."

"No." I shake my head. "I'm not going anywhere. Not until I get to the bottom of this."

Lucien's gaze hardens, a flash of anger crossing his face, but it's gone just as quickly. His lips part, as if he's about to say something else. Something important. But then he only shrugs, seeming to change his mind.

"Suit yourself," he says. "But don't say I didn't warn you."

He turns on his heel and strides out of the lobby, leaving me standing there, reeling from everything he's just dropped on me. I exhale, my pulse erratic, skin still prickling from the intensity of his presence. Both Blackhollow brothers are terrifying but in very different ways. Damien's danger is fire—it consumes, burns, pulls you in with its warmth even as it threatens to destroy you. But Lucien? Lucien is a blade. Cold. Precise. Sharp enough to cut through bone.

I don't know which scares me more.

Our conversation still lingers in my mind as I step outside onto the streets of Salem's Fall, the cool morning air biting at my skin. It's one of those crisp fall mornings where the sky is heavy with clouds but there's no rain yet, just the promise of it. There's a certain energy in the air, a mixture of anticipation but also something darker than just simple holiday fun. Every day the town inches closer to Halloween, the energy seems to grow more intense. It's like a ticking time bomb is hanging over my head now, thanks to everything I've learned about Veil Night and the impending fourth sacrifice.

I don't know what Lucien's angle is, but the information he gave me is too important to ignore. If even half of what he said is true, Damien is far more dangerous than I'd feared. If Lucien is to be believed, Damien is somehow responsible for not only his fiancée's death but his father's, and who knows how many others.

After a short walk, the Salem's Fall Police Department appears before me. Its stark brick exterior, all business, stands in contrast against the cozy, whimsical small-town shops and restaurants surrounding it. I push open the heavy steel doors and step inside, leaving the kitschy charms of Salem's Fall behind for the cold gloom of the government building.

A middle-aged woman with short-cropped hair and a scowl sits at the front desk, barely looking up as I approach.

"Can I help you?" she asks.

I step forward, forcing a polite smile. "I'd like to speak to someone in homicide, please."

Her eyebrows lift, a bit rudely. "Do you have an appointment?"

I suppress an annoyed sigh, reminding myself to stay calm. "No, but this is about an ongoing investigation in Boston," I say and pull out my business card, sliding it underneath the plexiglass. "My name is James Woodsen, and I'm an attorney with Whitehall & Rowe. I need to speak with someone regarding some recent murders in Salem's Fall that may be connected to my case."

Quinn would lose his mind if he knew I was doing this, using the firm's good name and reputation to seek information without his sign-off. We usually follow formalities like filing discovery motions or subpoenaing records from law enforcement, or we hire a private investigator, but all that takes time. Time is one thing I don't have.

Halloween is in two weeks.

"An attorney, you say?" the woman asks, suspicious. "Shouldn't you be going through official channels for any active cases?"

"Of course, ma'am. We're already in contact with the Boston DA's office, but I'm looking for information on past homicide cases in Salem's Fall—ones that might have connections to our defense." I lower my voice, like I'm letting her in on a secret. "Actually, I'm representing Damien Blackhollow." I pause, watching for a reaction. "I was hoping you might be able to help me out."

I wait, hoping that dropping Damien's name will get me somewhere. Everyone in this town seems to be either in awe of the Blackhollows or terrified of them.

Her expression changes right away. She straightens, her demeanor softening. "Let me call Detective Harris's office. He handles most of the homicide cases around here," she says, and I can tell the mention of Blackhollow has done the trick.

She presses a button on her phone. "Detective Harris? There's someone here to see you—she says she's with Damien Blackhollow's legal team." A pause. "Uh-huh. Okay. I'll have her wait here for you."

A few minutes later, a tall Black man steps out from the back office, his good looks slightly undercut by exhaustion. He's middle-aged, with close-cropped salt-and-pepper hair and a five o'clock shadow that suggests too many late nights on the job. His suit is wrinkled but well-worn, like it was tailored years ago and has seen more stakeouts than press conferences.

"Ms. Woodsen?" he says, extending a hand. "Detective Harris. Come on back."

I follow him down the narrow hallway to his office. It's

small and cramped, papers stacked high on his desk. A corkboard on the wall behind him is covered in crime scene photos and notes. The space is chaotic, and I can tell just by looking that he's swamped. Maybe this will work in my favor. Busy detectives don't have time to waste.

"What can I do for you today?" he asks and gestures for me to sit.

"I'm here as part of Mr. Blackhollow's defense team," I say. "You may have heard about the charges brought against him in Boston?"

He gives a grim smile. "I'd have to be dead not to hear about that."

"Yes, well, I'm looking for information regarding any murders that may have taken place in your jurisdiction on or around Halloween in the last few years. We have reason to believe that at least two murders occurred here in Salem's Fall or very nearby, possibly similar in style to the murder of Blackhollow's fiancée."

He sits up, a muscle twitching in his jaw. "You think there's a pattern here? Like a serial killer?"

"We're investigating the possibility."

"That's... interesting." He steeples his hands below his scruffy chin. "I have to be honest with you, I try to avoid getting into Blackhollow business as much as possible. It's very, uh, difficult when that family is involved," he says, his voice low and weary. "But I'll try to help you if I can, within reason."

I open my laptop to take notes of our conversation.

"I appreciate that, Detective. Anything you can tell me would be very helpful."

He sighs and taps his fingers against the arm of his chair. "There was one murder here two years ago, like the type you're looking for. A woman named Carla Moretti. She worked at Blackthorn Manor—housekeeping staff. She was found deceased the day after Halloween. Multiple knife wounds. Very gruesome. Bloody." He clicks his pen against the desk, staring at me for a beat before speaking. "The case is still active, so I can't disclose anything beyond what's already public record. Sharing investigative details could jeopardize the case."

My frustration spikes.

"I understand that, Detective, but this is critical to my client's defense."

He sighs heavily. "Look, I wish I could help more, but it's standard policy. And if the Blackhollows are involved, there's even less room to maneuver." He leans forward. "If you want official records, you'll need to file a discovery motion. But I'll be straight with you—ongoing investigations are usually sealed. You're not getting much, if anything." He lets the words hang, then shrugs. "Maybe you should be asking your client instead. He might have answers I can't give you."

I repress my sigh. If only I had a client who was forthcoming about these sorts of things…

"Was it ritualistic? Was it connected to the Blackhollows?" I press, refusing to back down. I didn't expect much from the local police, but knowing I'm on the right track—and still hitting a wall—only sharpens my frustration.

"Ms. Woodsen, please—"

"Can't you tell me anything? Anything at all?"

He sighs and lowers his voice. "You might check the local papers," he says, rubbing at the back of his neck, clearly uncomfortable. "There may be articles still floating around from before the Blackhollows shut that all down. Most of it has been scrubbed from the Internet, but you might find something at the library archives."

"Thanks, I'll do that," I say. "What about older cases? Are there any cold cases you could share with me that may be similar in style to Ms. Moretti's death? Any murders from, say, two or three decades ago—on or near Halloween? Maybe with a connection to Damien's father, Ian Blackhollow?"

"I've only been in this position for the last few years. Any cases that far back would have been handled by Detective Murphy—he retired a few years ago." He frowns, tapping his fingers on the desk, thinking. "But I imagine you could probably find something in the library archives for those as well."

"You sure you haven't heard anything else you can share? Even rumors?"

He leans forward, lips tightening. "I don't know what you're hoping to find, but if it involves the Blackhollows... good luck." He holds my gaze, and I catch something flicker behind his eyes—something wary and afraid. "Everything tied to them has a way of disappearing. Records vanish. Stories change. Maybe you'll find something useful in the archives, but... don't hold your breath."

His words settle heavily in the room. This is exactly what I feared. Apparently, Damien's family controls everything here, including the criminal justice system. Whatever happened decades ago—and even two or three years ago—is likely locked up behind a wall of wealth and influence. I stand, knowing this is as much as I'm going to get from him.

"Thanks for your time, Detective."

"You're welcome," he says. "I really do hope you find what you're looking for."

I've already got my hand on the doorknob when he clears his throat. "Oh, Ms. Woodsen?"

I turn back.

"You might want to try searching nearby towns. Danvers. Peabody." There's something in his eyes—hesitation, a warning. "And... good luck." A beat passes before his voice drops, quieter this time. "You're going to need it."

CHAPTER 17

I try not to feel like a failure as I walk away from the police station and head farther down the street to the Salem's Fall Public Library. I had been hoping to get more out of my visit with the detective, but at least I now have the name of another potential victim—Carla Moretti. I try to stay positive. Perhaps the library will have more information for me.

The wind picks up as I arrive at the entrance. The Gothic architecture looms in front of me, the dark stone and pointed arches giving it an ancient, imposing feel. The library, like most everything else in Salem's Fall, is steeped in history, carrying with it the weight of the past.

I push open the heavy wooden doors and step inside. Dim lighting casts long shadows that flicker across rows and rows of old books. The librarian, a silver-haired woman with her hair pulled into a neat bun, sits behind the large circulation desk near the entrance. As I approach, she looks up, eyes squinting toward me, horn-rimmed glasses perched on the tip of her nose.

"Can I help you?"

"I hope so," I reply with what I hope is a friendly smile. "I'm looking for information on a few local murders. Specifically, ones that happened on Halloween, going back a few years. And some older cases too, a few decades ago."

"Halloween murders, you say?" She clicks her tongue thoughtfully. "You'll want to check the archives. I'll show you where they are," she says, standing up and motioning for me to follow her.

She leads me down a narrow staircase into the archives. The deeper we go into the stacks, the quieter it becomes, the soft whispers of pages turning and muted chatter fading into silence. The air here is musty, cooler than the rest of the library. The scent of old leather and brittle paper is thick, the smell of history itself.

She points to an old microfiche machine that sits beside a tall metal filing cabinet. "That's where you'll find old newspaper clippings and public records. We're a small town, so not everything makes it online—especially not the old stuff. Files are arranged by date," she explains, giving me a thin smile. "The machine still works—mostly. If it starts acting up, just give me a shout."

I head for the files and slide the first reel of microfilm into the machine. The screen flickers to life, the motor whirring as I begin scrolling through old November editions of *The Salem's Fall Gazette*. I figure November is as good a place to start as any. Anything occurring on Halloween is likely going to show up in the papers then.

I start with the most recent case first, the one Detective Harris mentioned—Carla Moretti. Though Detective Harris wasn't as forthcoming as I'd hoped, I'm grateful I at least have a name to search for.

I find what I'm looking for right away. It turns out Moretti was not just a housekeeper. She was Damien and Lucien's former nanny and helped raise them. The articles don't dive too deeply into her relationship with the family, but there are subtle hints. Neighbors claimed she was a "mother figure," fiercely protective of the boys even as they grew up into adult men. Her body was found on the grounds of

Blackthorn Manor, her throat slashed and surrounded by eerie symbols.

My pulse pounds as I read more. The symbols found around her body were like the ones in the photos of Damien's fiancée's and my mother's murders—the Mark of the Veil. The case is still open, authorities asking for any leads. I take notes and pictures on my phone, every small connection I find tightening the knot in my stomach. There's no mention of the Blackhollow family being involved—nothing beyond the fact that the murder happened on their estate—but I know better. This was no random act.

I get through at least three more years of *Gazette* November issues but, other than Moretti, there's no other murders in Salem's Fall on Halloween. I don't know if I should feel disappointed or relieved. But then I remember how the detective mentioned the nearby towns of Danvers and Peabody.

Unfortunately, the library archives don't appear to have newspaper files for anything outside Salem's Fall, but on a whim, I swivel toward the desktop library computer beside me and jump online to run a search for recent Halloween murders in those two towns. Nothing for Danvers, but Peabody gets a hit right away.

Bingo!

It seems Elise Hartsworth—a former girlfriend of Damien's, his college sweetheart—was killed three years ago, on Halloween, at a dinner party in Peabody packed with New England elite. Hartsworth, a well-known socialite, was discovered in a secluded part of the estate's garden, her body brutalized and surrounded by ominous symbols carved into the ground. She was posed in what the papers described as a "sacrificial position."

The article highlighted her many accomplishments. She'd served as chair of the New England Historical Society's annual Gala. President of the Peabody Garden Club. Sought-after member of the Rotary Club. But her most notable claim to fame was her past connection to Damien Blackhollow. No charges were ever filed, though Damien was questioned due to their prior relationship. Though they'd broken up years prior to her death, he'd been seen with her recently, perhaps rekindling their romance. He was ultimately cleared of any wrongdoing, though rumors swirled about his involvement.

My skin starts to itch with excitement. I've uncovered something *huge*. Van Buren and Hartsworth. Two women Damien was intimately involved with, both viciously slain on Halloween in ritualistic manners. Plus, the nanny. Same method of murder. Same symbols. Same Blackhollow connection. The pattern is undeniable.

I continue scrolling through the microfilm, this time going back further—two decades—looking for anything tied to Damien's father. Eagerly, I scan through the records, searching for something that will connect the dots. More hours fly by, and I worry the library will close before I find anything else helpful, but then I hit the jackpot. A rash of murders in 1991, 1992, 1993, and 1994, all in Salem's Fall, all on Halloween night.

The victims were all from prominent Salem's Fall families, all found brutally slaughtered, their deaths never solved. The articles all give the same sort of vague details, but one universal similarity about the slayings stands out. Each body had the same ritualistic markings either carved into the skin or the surrounding walls and floors, or both. The symbols match the same design: spirals, pentagrams, jagged lines radiating outward. The Mark of the Veil.

There are reports of court proceedings—a series of lawsuits involving the Blackhollows and the victims' families that were mysteriously dropped or settled. And then, just a few weeks after the fourth murder, something shocking jumps out at me. There's a major headline in the papers: "Blackhollow Industries' Resurgence."

According to the article, Ian Blackhollow had been on the brink of bankruptcy in the early '90s. The family business was crumbling until suddenly in late November 1994—after the last Halloween murder—Ian acquired a string of new investments and partnerships. Blackhollow Industries' wealth skyrocketed again seemingly overnight.

I pull the film from the machine and sit back in the chair, staring blankly at the screen. My head spins. The murders, and then the Blackhollows' meteoric rise to power again. It's a coincidence, that's all.

I don't believe in the supernatural…

My phone vibrates sharply in my pocket, making me jump. I stare down at the screen and let out a long sigh. It's Katie again, for the third time today. I've been dodging her calls. She clearly thinks I'm crazy for still staying in town, and I'm not in the mood to argue. Still, she's my best friend and I can't ignore her forever.

"James, finally!" Katie's voice comes out in a rush, a mix of exasperation and worry when I answer. "Why are you avoiding my calls? Where are you—and please tell me it isn't Salem's Fall!"

"I can't leave yet, Katie. Too much is happening," I say, whispering as I look around the archive room, but I'm all alone. Everyone else has gone home for the evening.

"I'm freaking out over here!" Katie screeches into my ear. "Are you really still working for Blackhollow even after everything we've been hearing? James—he's a killer!"

"I'm a criminal defense attorney, Katie," I say. "This is part of the job. I can't just walk away."

There's a pause on the other end of the line. When Katie speaks again, her voice is quieter, more careful.

"Look, I know how important this is to you—prestigious

law firm, big paycheck, partner track," she says. "But a successful career isn't the most important thing in life."

I grit my teeth. Of course, Katie can say this.

Her family didn't just follow the New England old-money playbook—they helped write it. Their name is literally etched into Harvard's law school, with a building on campus bearing the Tang family name, for crying out loud. Their influence stretches from the United States all the way to Asia. Her grandparents were Beijing powerbrokers, deeply tied to China's political elite; her father is the former U.S. Ambassador to China. And while it's not her fault she was born into privilege most people couldn't fathom; she can't possibly understand what it's like to be me. To feel like you have to earn your place in this world, every single step of the way.

"I'm fine, Katie," I say, forcing a level of calm into my voice that I don't feel.

"I'm just scared for you. Everything I'm hearing about Blackhollow... it's bad. *Really bad.*" I can hear the worry in her voice. "You know I can't tell you much, but from what I'm hearing, things are moving fast on the DA's side. It's looking worse for Blackhollow every day, and now they're saying there could be another murder tied to him. An ex-girlfriend or something—"

"Wait, other murders? What do you mean?" I interrupt, trying my best to sound naive, like I haven't spent the entire day researching this myself. But I want to hear what the DA knows while being careful not to give away anything myself.

"I don't know all the details," Katie says, choosing her words carefully. "But rumors are flying that there could be more murders connected to your client than just the dead fiancée. From what I hear, this could be just the tip of the iceberg."

I pause, processing. It sounds like the DA is sniffing

around, but they haven't put the pieces together yet. That means I may still have the upper hand.

But I can't tell Katie that.

Even if Katie is my best friend and I have my own suspicions about my client's innocence, I can't share any of this with her. Even if Damien Blackhollow is some sort of crazed serial killer, I still feel some messed up sense of loyalty toward him, not to mention an ethical responsibility to keep his confidence.

At least for now.

She lets out a frustrated sigh. "Come back to Boston, James. No job is worth your life."

"I need a little more time. I promise I'll be careful."

"You'd better be," she warns. "Oh yeah, and Quinn's been calling me. He's worried about you too. Maybe give the poor guy a call back before he has a heart attack."

The mention of Quinn makes my stomach churn. I feel terrible for how I've been ignoring him. And it's not just because he's my boss or my job is on the line. It's Quinn. I hate the idea of him being angry with me, but I don't know what to say to him. I know he wants me to come back too, and I can't do that just yet.

"Thanks for calling, Katie." My voice comes out tight, controlled. "I have to go now, but we'll talk later, okay?"

I end the call right as the library lights begin to dim. It's closing time. With a sigh, I gather my things and step into the cool night air. Tourists pass by, laughing and snapping pictures, playing make-believe in their witch hats and brooms, oblivious to the real darkness lurking beneath the surface. They have no idea what's really going on in this town.

Back at the Cottage, I stroll through the lobby and head for my room. Holding my breath, I glance around, half expecting to see Damien in front of me, waiting for me with that smoldering gaze, but there's no sign of him. No sexy dark figure lurking about.

I feel a pang of disappointment.

Though I'm the one who told him to leave me alone, I didn't actually expect him to listen. He doesn't seem like the type to listen to anyone. I sort of thought he was more... I don't know—invested in me? If not in me, at least in his own murder case.

Lucky hops up to greet me as I walk inside my room, curling against my side while I settle onto the bed with my laptop. My fingers hover over the keys as I try to force my thoughts into coherent sentences to finish Quinn's case memo, but my mind is everywhere but the screen. The events of the last few days are a tangled mess, a web of secrets and lies that I'm still trying to unravel. Lucky flicks his tail, sensing my unease, but doesn't leave my side. I should order dinner—room service, maybe—but I'm not hungry. It's like I have no appetite.

After I finish my memo, I check my inbox again and am a little surprised to see there's nothing new from Quinn. He hasn't called or texted in hours either. Last night and earlier today, he was bombarding me with messages, demanding I come back to Boston. But now... now the silence feels ominous.

What if something's happened to him? What if he's been attacked like Mark?

My stomach clenches with worry. Mark was an asshole, but Quinn—Quinn is different. He's more than just my partner and mentor. Quinn is special to me. Maybe more special than I've allowed myself to feel because he's my boss...

I shake my head.

No, Quinn is fine.

He's probably just waiting for my memo before launching into another round of "urgent" messages about me leaving

Salem's Fall. Despite the seriousness of it all, I can't help the tiny grin tugging at my lips as I attach the memo to an email and hit send.

Quinn is going to lose his mind when he reads all this—the Veil's presence in Salem's Fall, not simply a relic of the past but an ongoing force; my conversation with Detective Harris and the library archives confirming a pattern of ritual murders stretching back decades; and worst of all, Lucien's revelation that Damien isn't just entangled in this world, but destined to lead it.

A hard knock at the door snaps me out of my thoughts. For a second, I almost hope it's Damien. I shouldn't want to see him after everything that's happened, but I can't help it. I take a deep breath and open the door.

"*Quinn?*" I blink in surprise. "What are you doing here?"

Quinn rushes forward and sweeps me into a tight embrace. His arms wrap around me, strong and warm, pulling me against his muscular chest. It's so unexpected, so unlike the usually composed and professional man I know, that I freeze for a moment.

"God, Woodsen," he mutters against my hair. "I thought something happened to you. You haven't answered any of my calls or emails for days!"

I pull back slightly, trying to process the intensity in his voice. Quinn is not a man of grand gestures or emotions. Seeing him like this, so vulnerable, shocks me.

"I'm fine," I say. "It's just been crazy here. I've been so busy with this case."

He pulls back, though his hands remain on my shoulders, his eyes scanning my face.

"Busy?" His tone is sharp, frustrated. "You can't possibly be so busy you can't even check in. I was worried, Woodsen! You don't get to do that—not when you're working for me."

I step back, folding my arms across my chest. "I'm handling it. You don't have to worry about me."

He looks down and sighs, almost defeated.

"This is all my fault. I never should've gotten you involved in all this."

"You don't understand, Quinn," I say. "I want to be on this case—I *need* to be on it. There's so much more at play here than we thought."

"Then tell me." Quinn steps closer, his eyes searching mine. "Tell me what's going on, and we'll figure it out together. But you can't do this alone. It's not safe."

I hesitate, glancing at my cat, who's watching us from his spot on the bed, his eyes thoughtful, unblinking.

"I'm not alone. I've got Lucky," I say, only half joking.

"I'm being serious."

I hesitate, shifting uncomfortably. "Well… Damien's here too. He's staying next door."

Or at least he was…

His whole expression darkens. "He's *what?*"

"It's not a big deal."

"Not a big deal?" he asks, his voice tight. "What the hell is he doing here?"

I sigh, rubbing my temple. "I don't know, Quinn. He's Damien Blackhollow. He does whatever he wants."

A muscle pulses in his square jaw. For a moment, it looks like he's about to argue, but then he shakes his head, exasperated. "Of course he does," he says, his tone quieter now, but there's still a frustrated edge.

"Quinn, listen. This is so much more than just one murder," I say. "Damien, his family, the Order of the Veil… there's a pattern here that dates back decades—maybe centuries. I can't leave now. I'm too close to the truth."

"And what truth are you hoping to find? That Damien Blackhollow isn't the monster everyone thinks he is?" Quinn's face hardens. "Because I've been talking to the DA, and I'm starting to worry that he may be." He pauses, taking a deep breath. "Or are you just trying to prove something to yourself?"

I wince at his words. They hit closer to home than I'd like to admit.

For a moment, we stand in silence, the weight of everything pressing down between us. When he speaks again, his voice is softer, almost pleading.

"I can't stand the thought of you getting hurt. That *I'm* the one putting you in danger." He steps closer, reaching for my hand. "I care about you, James. More than I should."

His voice breaks with emotion, and I look up, meeting his gaze. There's something raw in his eyes, something that wasn't there before.

"Quinn, I—"

"No, let me finish," he continues, his words slow and deliberate. "I care for you in a way I probably shouldn't—for a whole lot of reasons—but I do. How can I not? You drive me crazy, Woodsen." He drags a hand through his hair, his jaw tightening like he's fighting against himself. When his gaze locks onto mine again, there's no hiding the raw intensity there. "I can't just stand by and watch you in trouble." He steps closer, voice lowering. "Let me protect you. Come back to Boston with me."

I stare at him, the room spinning as his confession hangs in the air, thick and heavy. I don't know how to react. Part of me is elated. This gorgeous, successful, brilliant man likes *me*?

Quinn Alexander Kensington is everything I should want in a partner. I should be bouncing off the walls knowing how he feels about me. And I've thought about him this way too. I admit it. Who could be around Quinn and not think of him like that, at least once in a while?

And yet…

Though my heart is racing, it's not in the same way it does whenever Damien is near. This is comfortable but not electrifying. Safe but not consuming.

"I don't know what to say…"

"Leave with me—now. Tonight." Quinn reaches for me again, grasping my hands in his. "I'll have someone get your car in the morning."

"Quinn, I can't," I say, pulling back. "This case… I–I need to see it through."

He nods. "Just think about it," he says, his voice filled with quiet hope. "We can talk more in the morning. I'm staying here. I'm not leaving you alone in Salem's Fall."

I nod slowly, still reeling from his words. "Okay. Tomorrow then."

Quinn's gaze lingers on me for a long moment before he sighs, tucking a strand of hair behind my ear. "Goodnight, Woodsen."

I close the door behind him and lean against it, my mind a whirlwind of emotions. Quinn wants to protect me, take care of me, take me away from all this madness. And maybe I should let him. The safe choice may be exactly what I need…

I'm just not sure it's what I want.

CHAPTER 18

I wake up with Lucky on my pillow, his little paws reaching forward before he curls back up with a low rumble. My head is still tangled with thoughts of Quinn's confession last night about his feelings for me. Not that I didn't suspect there could be something more than just a professional fondness there—I've felt it too for some time now—but that Quinn would give in to the feelings and want to give this a shot? That, I didn't see coming.

I try to imagine a life with him. A beautiful, stable life with the one person who's been there for me since my very first day at the firm, steady and trustworthy, the very definition of everything I should want. Reliable, intelligent, kind. Always respectful of boundaries. He's a good man. Someone to lean on. Someone who will always put me first. He'd be the kind of partner who'd never let me fall.

And then there's Damien.

The very thought of him sparks something deep inside me. What a terrible idea it would be to follow that flame, yet it flares within me all the same. I know I shouldn't be anywhere near Damien Blackhollow. The fact that I'm even entertaining the thought of him, no matter how remote, is a whole new level of recklessness.

Damien is dangerous. Ruthless. Quite possibly a brutal

serial killer who makes a game of targeting the women who love him—even his own fiancée. And yet, every time I'm around him, it's like gravity pulling me in, unlike anything I've ever felt before. It's borderline insanity, but there's a magnetic pull there I can't ignore.

My phone vibrates beside me on the nightstand, and I glance over to see a text from Quinn:

> Breakfast. Downstairs in 30.

It's a command, not a question.

My stomach tight with nerves, I swing my legs out of bed and rush to get ready. I feed Lucky first, his bowl clinking as he scarfs down his breakfast like it's the first meal he's had in years. He finishes and looks at me, then his empty bowl, and starts whining. I chuckle, leaning down to pet the top of his little head. One thing about Lucky, he's never satisfied with a single meal. If I let him, the cat would weigh one hundred pounds. It's one small certainty in my otherwise completely uncertain life.

When he realizes no more food is coming, he gives me a look somewhere between disappointment and disgust before jumping onto the windowsill to watch people and sulk. I roll my eyes and head for the bathroom to get ready to see Quinn.

Well, as ready as I can get for something like this.

Whatever awaits me at breakfast, at least I can look presentable. I brush my hair and put on a dark cerulean blue sweater that brings out the color of my eyes. Quinn always notices those things. Then I swipe on some mascara and a soft pink lip before giving myself a last look in the mirror. It's subtle but enough to show I care.

"Alright, be back soon, boy. Wish me luck," I murmur to Lucky on my way out the door. He ignores me, still pissed no second breakfast is coming.

I spot Quinn immediately as I walk into the dining area of the Cottage. He's seated by a window in a crisp gray shirt and tailored blazer. He stands the moment he sees me, his eyes softening. He's so handsome, all clean-cut lines and that understated confidence he wears so well. It's the total opposite of Damien and everything I've been caught up in these past few weeks.

"Good morning," he says, every bit the gentleman as he helps me into my seat. "You look nice."

"Thank you."

He nods at the server as she pours a steaming cup of coffee for each of us. He hands me mine first, no sweetener or milk. Always efficient, always thoughtful.

"So…" He lets the word hang in the air, his gaze intense as it searches mine. "I hope I didn't freak you out last night."

I shift a bit in my seat and take a slow sip of coffee.

"You did hit me with a lot…"

"I understand." He nods slowly, his eyes never leaving my face. "But I needed you to know how I feel. I came here because I think you're in serious danger. This case, this town —it's not worth risking your life, Woodsen."

There's something in his eyes I haven't seen before, and it unnerves me. He's frightened … for *me*.

"Quinn, I told you last night. I can't just walk away." I sigh. "There's more to this case. It could change everything for me."

"You think I don't understand ambition? Career moves?" He leans forward, his hands clasped tightly. "But this case is different. It's not safe, and honestly, I don't trust Blackhollow. He's not who you think. I've been hearing things—things that could ruin careers and far worse."

I feel a twinge of anger. I don't know why, but I feel oddly protective of Damien. Even if I suspect him of all the same sordid things Quinn probably does, I don't like to hear Quinn talk badly about him. We're Damien's attorneys. Even if no one else has Damien's back, we should.

"He's our client," I say. "It's our ethical responsibility to zealously advocate for him, no matter our personal feelings."

Quinn lets out a slow breath, leaning back in his chair. "Are you certain this is just about your feelings of professional responsibility? You sure there isn't more going on here?"

A beat of silence stretches between us as he watches me, his jaw tight.

"More? Like what?" I ask, even though both of us know exactly what he's hinting at.

"Like something… romantic… between you two?"

"He's a client, nothing more."

I force my tone to stay even, keeping the defensiveness and hurt out of my voice. Okay, yes—maybe there's some crazy, unspoken attraction between Damien and me. But the idea that I'd act on it is, frankly, insulting. For Quinn to suggest it, knowing firsthand how hard I've fought against those kinds of insinuations at the firm, stings even more.

"I'm sorry, but it is Damien Blackhollow. You wouldn't be the first beautiful woman to fall for his charms." Quinn's fingers press into the bridge of his nose like he's holding back something sharper. When he drops his hand, his expression is tight and controlled, but his eyes burn with irritation. "He wants you to attend the All Hallows Gala with him tonight."

"What?" I frown. "I told him not to go to that."

"Well, not only is he attending, but he's insisting you go with him," Quinn says with a sharp, disbelieving laugh, shaking his head. "Says it's crucial to the case that you're there —claims it's for recon. Layout, timeline. His alibi hinges on being at the Gala, remember?"

"You can't be serious." Heat rises to my face. "This is completely unprofessional. Of course I'm not going to some ridiculous ball."

Quinn watches me carefully, his expression guarded. "You sound awfully sure about that."

"Because I am."

Yet even as the words leave my lips, something uneasy coils inside me. It's not just unease, though. It's something else. Something I don't want to name.

Would I go... if I could?

I've never been to anything like the All Hallows Gala before. Growing up, my family had exactly zero ties to high society. No private school balls, no charity fundraisers, no glitzy social events where the elite sipped champagne and pretended the rest of us didn't exist. Even when I was with my law school ex, William—a guy who came from old money and knew this world inside and out—he never took me to events like the Gala.

I told myself it wasn't a big deal at the time. It wasn't my scene. But I'd be lying if I said it didn't sting a little when he always took his sister to the Gala every year with their family's tickets. He'd brushed it off as tradition. Nothing exciting. No fun anyway. I'd nodded. Smiled. Pretended not to notice how relieved he looked when I didn't push back.

Now, though...

I can almost picture it. A lavish ballroom. Sweeping music and glittering chandeliers. Decadent food and dancing until my feet ached. If I'm being honest with myself, and if I wasn't in the middle of the most high stakes case of my entire life, the All Hallows Gala is something I'd love to attend. And if he wasn't my client—if there weren't murder charges and a lethal secret society hanging over us—Damien Blackhollow might be exactly the sort of man I'd want to go with.

I can't help but smirk to myself. And William would absolutely *die* if he saw me at the Gala with someone like Damien. But then I shake my head, pushing the thoughts away before they can take root.

"I promise you, Quinn, it's strictly professional between Damien and me." I pause, hesitating. I'm not sure how much I should tell Quinn about my family, but it feels like something has changed between us since last night. Even if he is my boss, he really does care about me. I feel like I can trust him. "But you're right, there is something different about this case. Something... personal." I look down at my coffee cup, tracing the edge with my fingertip. "I've found out things that tie me to this case in ways I can't ignore. Connections to my family I can't walk away from."

His eyebrows knit together, expression turning cautious. "What sort of connections?"

"I think my dad may have somehow gotten tangled up with the Blackhollows and the Veil." My chest tightens, but I force the words out. "That maybe there's a link between all of this and my mom's murder."

I drop my gaze, my fingers curling into my lap. I feel exposed, vulnerable, even though Quinn already knows about my dad's conviction. The firm uncovered it during my background check, but we've never actually talked about it. Not out loud. I've always suspected my past is a big part of why Quinn took me under his wing. I think part of him felt bad for me, basically becoming an orphan at sixteen.

"Woodsen." Quinn's voice is steady, but there's an edge to it. "Your dad had a psychotic breakdown and murdered your mother. There's nothing in the files to indicate anyone else was involved."

I glance up, surprised. "You've seen my dad's case files?"

He nods. "I wanted to know about your family. To see if I could help you—help your father." He hesitates, rolling his shoulders like he's shaking off a weight. "I went through the case, searched for anything that could justify reopening it or filing an appeal. There's nothing." His voice hardens. "I'm telling you. You're chasing shadows."

I feel myself getting defensive.

"Well, I'm sorry, but I disagree. There's something here."

"Come back with me," he says. "You can work on other cases. Safer cases. This isn't the only path to success." His voice is gentle but resolute as he reaches for my hand. "We'll figure this out—*together*."

"Quinn, I can't... I can't just walk away." I pull away and his face shifts to something like disappointment.

"So that's it, then? You're saying no to us too?"

My heart twists as I see the hurt in his eyes, raw and unguarded.

"Quinn, this... us... it's complicated. What about my career? Everything I've worked for?" My voice wavers, the walls I've kept up against him cracking. "Even if I admit that, yes, there are feelings, what good does that do? If something happens between us, it changes how everyone at work sees me. Maybe you don't have to worry about that, but I do."

"I know it's complicated," he says, his gaze steady. "But life's messy, Woodsen. You can't always keep everything in neat, professional boxes."

I swallow hard, forcing myself to hold his stare. "I need more time to figure out what I feel, Quinn. But please—don't ask me to choose between you and this case."

He nods, his expression hardening as he leans back, distancing himself physically and emotionally.

"The firm's been asking questions, you know," he says, his voice low, measured. "The partners are worried. They don't like the way this looks—a young junior female associate still wet behind the ears, running around Salem's Fall, working outside the firm's oversight and getting tangled up in whatever the hell is going on here."

I freeze.

"What does that mean?"

Quinn hesitates. "It means they want you back in Boston.

If you stay, you could lose more than just this case—you could lose everything."

Anger flares in my chest. "So what, you're here to strong-arm me into leaving? Are you going to fire me if I refuse?"

"Of course not." Hurt flickers in his eyes. "You know I'll always have your back, no matter what you choose. If you won't leave with me, I'll go back alone and try to cover for you for a few more days… it just might not be enough."

I take a deep breath, feeling the weight of my decision settle over me. Quinn. Boston. Back to the city, to stability, to the career I've sacrificed so much for with a good man I know I can trust and rely on.

And yet, something is keeping me here. Maybe it's Damien, maybe it's the mystery, maybe it's the need to avenge my mother's death and my father's conviction. Whatever it is, I can't ignore it.

"I need to see this through, Quinn," I say. "If I walk away now, I'll never forgive myself."

"All right." He presses his lips together. "If that's your choice, I don't like it, but I'll do whatever I can to help you."

The disappointment and sadness in his voice stings more than I want to admit. It's almost enough to make me change my mind, but the resolve inside me hardens.

He stands, a heaviness in his posture as he straightens and pulls out his wallet to leave enough cash to cover our breakfast. I feel the words catch in my throat. *I don't want you to go*, I want to cry out.

But I don't.

I've made my choice to stay, and I've got to live by it, no matter how hard it might be.

"Take care of yourself, Woodsen," he says and hugs me lightly, as if he's afraid he may break me. It feels like a goodbye, and the weight of my decision crashes down on me. The feeling of being alone—utterly, wholly alone—hits me hard.

But then, a familiar figure slips into the corner of my vision. Leaning casually against the doorframe of the dining room is Damien. He watches Quinn and me with an expression that hovers between boredom and annoyance.

The sinking feeling in my stomach tightens into something sharper, prickling at the edges as he strolls over. His eyes flicker from Quinn's face to mine. There's a glimmer of amusement there, the kind that's impossible to miss.

"Lovers' quarrel?" he asks, a mocking lilt to his voice.

Quinn's body goes rigid beside me.

"Blackhollow."

Damien's smirk doesn't falter. "Kensington."

I arch a brow at Damien. "Nice of you to finally return."

Damien's gaze slides to me fully now, taking me in like he's assessing whether I'm pissed, hurt, or just being difficult for sport.

"Did you miss me, Counselor?"

I huff out a laugh, shaking my head. "Hardly."

"Mm." He doesn't sound convinced.

Quinn, radiating tension, cuts in sharply. "What can we do for you, Blackhollow?"

"Nothing needed on your end, Kensington, unless you can squeeze into a size 2 haute couture gown?" Damien grins smoothly, slipping his hands into his pockets. "Bennett's waiting outside with the car. I assume she's coming back with me to the Gala today like we discussed?"

Quinn stiffens beside me. "You really think I can just demand she attend?"

"If you care about this case, then yes," Damien says.

Quinn huffs a bitter laugh, shaking his head. "The firm doesn't own her, Blackhollow. I can't tell her where to go."

"And yet, you were just trying to do exactly that, weren't you?" Damien lifts a brow. "Or did I mishear? It sounded like you were quite determined to pull her back to Boston yourself."

Quinn's jaw tightens, his hands balling into fists. I've never seen Quinn look this angry before. For a second, I worry these two might actually go to real blows.

I glance between them, incredulous. "Um, hello? Standing right here," I say, feeling like a doll they're fighting over, a prop in some testosterone-fueled power struggle. "Maybe, I don't know, ask *me* what I want?"

They both turn to me.

Watching.

Waiting.

I let out a slow breath, my pulse thrumming. I should say no. This is insane.

"Well, for one thing, this is a terrible idea," I say. "And second, I don't have anything to wear."

Damien tilts his head. "Don't worry about that. It's all been taken care of."

"Excuse me?"

His lips curl toward me in a knowing smirk. "Do you really think I'd take you to a gala without making sure you have the perfect gown?" His voice drops, velvet smooth. "It's waiting for you back in Boston, along with a full glam team at your disposal."

Quinn watches me closely, almost desperately, his eyes searching mine for something—anything—that proves he still has control over what I do. But something defiant sparks in my chest. If my career—and possibly my life—are already hanging by a thread, I might as well enjoy one damn night of fun. I turn to Damien, flashing him my sweetest, most saccharine smile.

"I'd love to go to the Gala with you."

CHAPTER 19

Boston, Massachusetts

By the time I step inside my apartment, I know something is wrong.

For one, it smells.

Not in a dead-body-something's-decomposing-inside-these-walls way, but in a twenty-something-who-has-no-concept-of-household-maintenance kind of way. Stale takeout. Overflowing garbage. The faint, sour tang of abandoned dishes in the sink.

Maddie sits sprawled on the couch, still in her pajamas at 1 p.m., remote in one hand, a half-eaten bowl of cereal in the other. She blinks up at me, looking startled.

"Holy shit, Jamie! You're alive."

I sigh. "Yes, Mads. I didn't die in Salem's Fall—*yet*."

"Well, of course, I know that." She giggles. "It's just that you've been weirdly MIA, and you're never MIA. Always bugging me about something or another and—"

"I think there's a 'Hey James, good to see you, big sis' somewhere in there," I mumble sarcastically as I drop my bags down and let Lucky out of his carrier.

Maddie shoves her cereal aside and hops up, wrapping me

in a tight hug. "You know I missed you, big sis!" she cries, a sweet smile across her face. Too sweet. Suspiciously sweet.

I glance past her to the wreckage of our apartment. The garbage can is overflowing, pizza boxes stacked precariously on the counter. At least a dozen empty beer cans and some empty handles of vodka line up along the kitchen table, and the sink is a graveyard of dishes.

I narrow my eyes. "Just how many parties have you had since I've been gone?"

"Oh, I only had a friend or two over," she says. "Don't worry. I was just about to clean it all up."

"Uh-huh." I arch a brow. "And I'm about to be nominated to the U.S. Supreme Court."

She giggles, grabbing me in another hug. "Seriously, I'm really glad you're back."

I shake my head, laughing. Maddie is impossible to stay mad at.

"Sadly, I'm only in town for a few hours," I say, pulling out my phone and ordering Instacart delivery. While I'm here, I want to stock her up on all the essentials—things like water, bread, peanut butter, and sliced turkey for sandwiches. "I have to go back to Salem's Fall in the morning."

"Oh, okay. That sucks."

Shockingly, Maddie actually looks disappointed.

Huh.

Well, look at that. I guess the kid really did miss me. Or at least missed my wallet and cleaning skills.

I start picking up trash and sweeping around the place as Lucky hops onto the couch's armrest. He stretches out and gets comfy, fixing Maddie with his signature unimpressed feline stare. Maddie glares right back, clearly no love lost between them.

"Make sure you take the little menace with you when you go," she says, but then to my surprise, she smirks and scoops

Lucky up into her arms. "Alright, I admit it. I even missed you a bit too, you big bag of fleas." She laughs and presses a quick kiss to his furry head.

Lucky tolerates the indignity for exactly three seconds before flicking his tail and darting off to my bedroom.

"See how much he loves me?" She grins. "He's practically obsessed."

"You two are ridiculous."

As I finish loading the dishwasher, a sharp knock echoes through the apartment. Maddie and I exchange a look.

"Expecting visitors? Another rager?" I tease, wiping my hands on a dish towel.

"No," she says, then smiles broadly. "Not until tonight, at least."

"Ha ha. You better be kidding."

I open the door to find three impeccably dressed people standing in the hallway. Two women, one man. All sleek, fashionable, and exuding effortless style.

The woman in front with cobalt blue hair in sleek waves beams at me like she's found her next great project. In her hand, she holds a garment bag marked Dolce & Gabbana. Beside her, another woman stands with the most gorgeous earrings I've ever seen—delicate resin pieces encasing real pressed flowers. She cradles a massive box of Christian Louboutin shoes like it's the holy grail and surveys me with quiet amusement. The man, who looks like he just walked out of a Milan runway show, is balancing two enormous rolling makeup cases.

"Good evening, Ms. Woodsen. We're your glam team." The woman with blue hair steps forward and flashes me a bright, excited smile. "We're here to get Cinderella ready for the ball."

Maddie, still in her pajamas, looks between them and me.

"A ball? *My sister?*" she asks. "Let me tell you, you have your work cut out for you."

Then she bursts out laughing.

Two hours later, after the glam team has worked their fairy godmother magic, I glance at myself in the mirror and barely recognize the woman staring back at me. The dress Damien chose for me is a masterpiece. Soft, ethereal ice-blue chiffon, delicate as air, like something out of a dream. A structured bodice that cinches perfectly at my waist and a neckline just daring enough to make me feel dangerous. It hugs my curves before flowing down in soft, weightless waves at my feet.

And the shoes...

Swarovski-covered designer heels shimmer on my feet, so dazzling, they look like they're dipped in liquid diamonds. I shift, and my heels catch the light, sending tiny rainbows scattering across the floor.

But it's not just my outfit. My hair and makeup... I've never seen myself like this before.

Brushed gold strands, styled in soft, elegant waves, cascade over my shoulders. And my makeup is completely different from how I normally wear it. It's far more glamorous. Black kohl liner and fake lashes paired with a sexy, deep, wine-stained red. I don't even look like me.

Maddie squeals, clutching at her chest like she's about to faint.

"James, you—" She shakes her head, her eyes wide with awe. "Oh my gawd! I thought they were kidding at first, but you really do look like Cinderella."

A laugh bubbles out of me, half disbelief, half nerves. "Yeah, well, let's hope this Cinderella doesn't lose her damn shoe—because there's no way I can afford to replace whatever these cost," I say, wiggling my toes inside the glittering heels.

"No, but seriously, you are stunning. Like, I think I might cry."

Maddie circles me and blinks hard, her eyes suddenly glassy. Her voice drops to a whisper. "You look like Mom, Jamie," she says. "She would've loved to see this…"

A lump forms in my throat as I think about how much Mom used to love getting us ready for things like this. School dances. Birthday parties. Even silly dress-up days at school. She'd insist on doing our hair, fussing over us, making us twirl around the living room so she could admire her work. Our mom never got to see either of us go to our senior prom or graduation. She never got to see us grow up.

"Oh, Mads," I whisper and put an arm around her, pulling her in tight. I press a kiss against the top of her messy ponytail. "Thanks, kiddo."

I glance at my reflection one last time, a strange mix of pride and disbelief stirring in my chest. The dress. The shoes. Damien's black tourmaline ring on my finger. These are easily the most beautiful things I've ever worn, and it's all thanks to him. Even if tonight is a complete bust, I'm grateful for this moment with Maddie.

"Thank you so much," I say as the glam team gathers up their things. "I love it all."

"Enjoy your night, princess." The woman with cobalt blue hair winks back at me.

A knock sounds at the door, and I open it to find Bennett standing there, ever-patient, hands clasped in front of him.

"Miss Woodsen, Mr. Blackhollow is waiting for you at the Gala." He steps aside, holding the door open. "Shall we?"

I frown. "He's not picking me up?"

Not that I have a lot of experience at this whole fancy gala thing, but it seems a bit rude to send your chauffeur to pick up your date.

Why isn't Damien here himself?

Bennett offers a smooth smile. "Mr. Blackhollow apologizes, but he has a few last-minute matters to attend to. He'll meet you at the museum."

I should be annoyed. But honestly?

I'm standing in a custom couture gown, wearing diamonds on my feet, about to step into a private car and be whisked away to one of the most exclusive events in all of New England.

So I just shrug.

"Let's go."

CHAPTER 20

The moment I step into the New England Historical and Cultural Heritage Museum, it's like stepping into another world.

Elegant chandeliers cast a golden glow over the vast hall, illuminating plush black velvet lounges, while flickering candles and towering candelabras shimmer like scattered stardust, their flames swaying as if caught in an unseen spell. Sprawling black marble tables overflow with the finest food and champagne: seafood towers laden with lobster, stone crab, and oysters, a caviar bar, and prime rib carving stations.

Yet, amid all the opulence, there are playful touches too. Crystal pumpkins in every color. Rows of intricately decorated candy apples that look like fine art. A towering chocolate fountain surrounded by decadent Halloween-themed desserts. All these things a reminder that, despite the Gala's over-the-top luxury, this night is still full of tricks—and more than a few treats.

From a grand, gilded balcony, a ten-piece orchestra fills the space with sweeping melodies, the music swelling in perfect harmony with the shimmer of diamonds and silk on the dance floor below. Elegantly dressed guests twirl and sway in a mesmerizing blur of movement, their designer gowns fanning out in waves of chiffon and tulle, their tuxedos crisp and tailored.

Politicians. Socialites. Hedge fund moguls. Titans of industry. New England's most powerful and privileged move effortlessly through the gilded opulence of the night. I even spot a few celebrities, their presence only adding to the spectacle of it all.

I don't belong here. But for tonight, I'll pretend I do.

Then—

A warm hand brushes my shoulder. I turn, and my jaw drops.

Damien.

He's breathtaking in his sharp black tuxedo, the crisp white of his shirt stark against the inky fabric. The dark silk of his tie catches the light, and the way he wears it all is effortless, commanding. His presence pulls at me, magnetic and all-consuming. The heat between us builds instantly, curling around me like a whisper of danger.

"You clean up well, Counselor."

I find my voice, but it's weaker than I'd like.

"You're late."

He smirks. "For good reason." He lifts his hand, and that's when I notice the small red box. His voice softens, more intimate. "I wanted to get you something special for tonight."

I take the box carefully, popping it open—and gasp. Inside, resting against rich velvet, is a stunning diamond necklace. The chain is delicate but strong, the pendant a flawless, deep-cut black diamond, shimmering under the chandelier light.

I glance up at him. "Damien, I can't—"

"Relax. It's on loan. A favor from the museum," he cuts in smoothly. "Allow me."

He lifts the necklace and places it around my neck, his fingers grazing the hollow of my throat as he secures the clasp. His touch is slow. Lingering. It makes my skin tingle with awareness, sending a delicious shiver over every nerve. When I glance up again, I catch him looking down at my hand.

"You're still wearing my ring," he murmurs.

"Yes."

"Good."

Something dark flashes in his expression—something proud, almost possessive. He extends a hand.

"Dance with me."

I hesitate.

Not because I don't want to.

Because I do.

Very much. Maybe too much—he's my client, after all. A man accused of murder. A man who's been keeping secrets from me since the day we met.

But then I remind myself—this is just a silly society ball. A fantasy. So I place my hand in his, and Damien Blackhollow pulls me into his arms, twirling me across the floor like something out of a fairy tale.

If fairy tales had murder suspects for princes.

The music swells around us, strings rising in perfect harmony as Damien spins me across the floor. It's effortless, like we've done this a hundred times before. His grip is firm but not forceful, his movements smooth and controlled. His fingers flex slightly around my waist, like he's memorizing the shape of me. And his expression… the way he's looking at me while we dance—like I'm something rare, something *treasured*—sends a soft buzzing through my entire body.

Too soon, the song ends.

"I'm afraid I have to make my rounds for a bit, though I'd much rather stay here with you in my arms," Damien says, voice low. But instead of stepping back, he leans in—lips brushing the shell of my ear. "Don't dance with anyone else," he murmurs, almost like a command cloaked as a plea. "Not tonight. You're mine."

Then, with a last lingering glance, he pulls away and disappears into the crowd to do whatever powerful men like him do at events like these. Handshaking. Social maneuvering. Kissing babies, maybe. A king moving through his kingdom.

I drift away from the dance floor, slipping toward the edge of the room to quietly observe things while he attends to his business. Champagne glasses clinking in delicate hands. Laughter rising in polite, controlled bursts. I scan the crowd, my gaze searching before I fully realize what I'm looking for. But Quinn isn't here tonight, even though his father, the Senator, is one of the Gala chairs.

I tell myself I don't care, but a strange hollowness settles in my chest. With a steadying breath, I push the sad thoughts away. Tonight is for cutting loose and having a little fun. I don't want to dwell on my issues with Quinn or the firm right now. They'll still be here tomorrow.

"Well, well. Look who it is."

I turn, and my stomach twists, a wave of nausea rolling through me.

William Winthrop stands in front of me. My cheating ex from hell. Smug. Smirking. Every bit the perfect, polished prep-school-boy-turned-lawyer. Blond. Blue-eyed. Indistinguishable from every other trust-fund WASP in New England. And clinging to his arm, looking similarly smug? Jess. My equally awful ex-best friend. Redheaded, pale, and sharp-featured, with a nose just a pinch too large and beakish, like an overconfident hawk circling for a kill.

My jaw tightens, but I force my expression into something neutral. Indifferent. I refuse to give these two assholes the satisfaction of knowing they can still get to me.

"Will. Jess," I say, my tone flat and unimpressed. "Didn't expect to run into you two tonight."

William lets out a dry chuckle. "And why is that? Didn't think my family could still get tickets?" he asks. "I've heard the invite list is even more exclusive this year, but Mom is on the fundraising committee now."

"No, that's not why," I say coolly. "I was just hoping I'd see you first so I could avoid you."

Jess makes a sound that's almost a laugh, but it's breathy, fake. "Oh, James. You always did have a sharp tongue."

William grins, full of himself. "Her tongue is one of the things I liked best about her."

Another sickening twist coils in my gut.

Ugh, gross.

I can't believe he just said that, and in front of his new girlfriend too. I really don't know what I ever saw in the guy.

"So, how'd you get invited?" William asks, eyes sweeping over me with thinly veiled skepticism. "Doesn't seem like your scene."

I offer a small, cool smile. "People change, Will. And you don't really know me anymore."

His smirk falters for a split second, but he recovers quickly, glancing at Jess, who looks equally curious.

"How've you been, James?" she asks, her voice honeyed but patronizing. "We haven't seen you in ages. We miss you."

As if she didn't rip my heart out and stomp all over it.

As if they weren't the ones who betrayed me.

"I've been busy," I say.

"Oh, right. Still toiling away at Whitehall & Rowe, aren't you?" William asks, condescension dripping from his voice. "Congrats, James. Really. It's a nice little firm. Good pay. I know how hard you worked for that job—you've always been into that sort of thing." He flashes a self-important grin, chest puffing out. "Me? I'm more interested in public service. I want to serve the people."

I grip my clutch tighter, heat rising to my face, but I refuse to let him bait me. His family is loaded, he can afford to "serve the people." The rest of us have to work hard to put money in the bank.

"How nice for you, Will. Good luck with that."

Jess sighs, long and dramatic, like this entire conversation is some great burden on her. As if *she's* the wronged party.

"Look, James, we want you to know we're sorry. Truly." She rests a delicate hand on William's arm, throwing him a look before turning back to me with a saccharine smile. "But sometimes, you can't fight fate, you know? When something feels right, you have to follow your heart."

Oh, I want to slug her. I really do. She's practically begging for it…

"Yeah, no hard feelings, right?" William adds, his smirk deepening. "You'll understand one day, when you find someone of your own."

That's it. I can't listen to this crap any longer. I open my mouth to respond, ready to verbally eviscerate them both—

But I don't have to.

"Oh, she's already found someone," Damien says, coming up behind me. His hand rests lightly at the small of my back, possessive, grounding.

Jess's eyes go wide, her breath hitching as she takes in the man now standing beside me, like she can't quite believe what she's seeing. Next to her, William stiffens, his bravado slipping, his face going pale.

"You're… you're Damien Blackhollow, aren't you?" William asks, his voice losing its usual arrogance.

Damien tilts his head, studying William like he's something stuck to the bottom of his expensive shoe. "And you must be the idiot ex-boyfriend."

William bristles.

"Excuse me?"

Damien's smirk is pure sin. "Can't say I'm impressed. I expected someone… better."

William goes rigid, his hands curling into fists. "Hey, now. Listen here—"

"No, you listen." Damien steps closer, towering over my ex. "You had your chance with her. I don't know what she was thinking back then, but she's clearly smartened up." His grip tightens on my back, his smile slow and deliberate.

William's mouth opens, then snaps shut. He looks like he can't decide whether to argue or run away. For a brief moment, I almost feel bad for him—almost. But even if this is a lie, even if Damien and I aren't even remotely together, watching William squirm? Watching his face turn red, his confidence crumble? God, it feels good. Maybe it's silly and petty, but after everything he's done, I'll take it.

Without another word, William turns on his heel and stalks off, fists clenched.

Jess, ever the social climber, lingers a beat. She casts me a lingering look before flashing Damien a too-bright, nervous smile. "Well, it was nice seeing you, James! We should catch up sometime!" she calls out, wiggling her fingers in an awkward wave before scurrying after William.

Damien watches them go, his smile only deepening.

"That was unnecessary," I say, though I can't help but laugh at my ex-boyfriend scampering off with his tail between his legs. "Sure was fun, though."

"I aim to please."

I hesitate, then murmur, "He's right, though, you know."

"Really?" Damien snorts, unimpressed. "I can't think of a single thing that poor son of a bitch could be right about."

"My job. Whitehall & Rowe. Succeeding at the firm is all I've ever wanted." I brush my fingers over the stunning black diamond at my throat, glancing around at the opulence of the Gala—the sparkling gowns, the extravagant feast, the endless flow of glittering drinks. "Tonight has been lovely. And… thank you. But I need to get back to reality now."

This evening was supposed to be about recon—layout, timeline, Damien's alibi. But somewhere between the diamonds and the dancing and Damien's charm, I let myself forget. Just for a little while, I stopped acting like a lawyer.

Damien's easy smile falters.

"What do you mean? The night's still young." His voice is light, teasing, but there's something else beneath it—something real. He's enjoying this. Enjoying me.

"Not for me, it isn't."

Halloween. Veil Night. It's all coming to a head, fast.

The Gala was a fun distraction, but I'm not going to find any answers here. They're in Salem's Fall. I have to find Professor Hargrove and tell him everything I uncovered at the police station and the library. If anyone can help me make sense of it, it's him.

Damien's jaw tightens, like he already knows he's not going to like what I say next. "James—"

"I'm sorry. I have to go," I say and unclasp the necklace, pressing it into his palm. I'm already shifting back into reality as I turn toward the exit, the lingering haze of indulgence and luxury fading into urgency.

"Right now?" Damien's voice is laced with disbelief. "James, slow down. I thought we were having a good time."

I hesitate, just for a second. "I need to get back to Salem's Fall to see Nick. There's new evidence in your case I want to discuss with him."

The shift is instant. His expression hardens, curdling into something darker.

"Hargrove again?" His voice is strained now, carrying an edge. "You sure don't waste time adding new admirers to your collection, do you? First Quinn. Now Hargrove. And let's not forget how you somehow sweet-talked my brother into spilling our family secrets." His head tilts, as if mock thoughtful. "Who's next—the mayor of Salem's Fall?"

I shoot back, "Good thing you're immune to my charms, then. Right?"

Damien's eyes glint with challenge.

"Am I?"

For a moment, the world narrows to just him. The tension between us coils tight, hot, electric. I swallow hard, tearing my gaze away and stepping into the cool night air, leaving him behind before I can make another mistake. Before I say something I can't take back.

But I still feel him, long after I've left the museum.

His gaze. His presence. His heat.

And despite everything—despite Damien Blackhollow being dangerous, manipulative, and entirely too smug—my traitorous heart still races. Because for a few fleeting hours, real or not, he was mine.

CHAPTER 21

Salem's Fall, Massachusetts

The sky hangs overcast as I walk toward Professor Hargrove's shop the next morning. The damp chill of Salem's Fall settles into my bones as I try Maddie's phone—again—but it just goes straight to voicemail. I let out an annoyed groan, shoving my cell into my coat pocket. Frustration curls in my chest.

Maddie wasn't home when I returned to the apartment late last night to grab Lucky. Probably out partying, as usual. That wasn't surprising. But I'd been hoping my irresponsible little sister would at least answer one of my dozens of calls and texts by now. Maddie might not be the poster child for responsibility, but she's never been this bad. Surely, she's seen my messages, right?

Worry gnaws at the edges of my thoughts, but I tell myself she's still out, crashed on a friend's couch somewhere. She's fine. I saw her less than twenty-four hours ago, and from the looks of my poor apartment, the girl was having the time of her life.

I turn the corner and the professor's shop appears, the chime echoing hollowly as I step inside the Wandering Raven. The store is empty, the light low and flickering, casting strange, shifting shadows over the shelves. The smell hits me first. Old wood and herbs, like before, but now with something sharper beneath, a metallic tang that lingers in the air. Immediately, I feel it—a creeping sense of wrongness. The air feels thick, as if something is… off.

My instincts tell me to back away, to leave this place, but I steel myself and walk deeper inside. I shake away the bad thoughts, dismissing them as just a culmination of all the crazy shit I've learned these past few weeks. It's only natural that all the creepiness would catch up with me, making me paranoid and jittery.

As I walk toward the counter, the now-familiar rows of strange artifacts and occult souvenirs seem more menacing. The glass-eyed voodoo dolls watch me, their vacant stares more unsettling. The old leather-bound books look sinister, their cracked and frayed spines whispering of horror stories best left forgotten. Noticeably, the ceremonial dagger that usually sits in the glass case tucked in the corner—the type of knife used in the Veil's ritual murders—is gone.

That's strange.

My mind scrambles for a reasonable explanation. Did someone buy it? Did Hargrove take it out for cleaning or… something?

I don't know why, but the missing knife unnerves me more than anything else I've seen so far in the shop. My gut screams another warning, and this time, I seriously contemplate turning around and leaving. But then I see it—a new artifact in the store. A mask, prominently displayed on the wall, tilted slightly, as if it'd been placed in a hurry. My breath stutters, and I take a slow, hesitant step closer.

I *know* that mask.

Silver-plated metal, polished to a mirror-like shine. Empty, vacant eyes. Strange symbols etched along the edges. It's the same mask my attacker wore my first night in Salem's Fall. My gaze flickers to the small plaque beneath it.

Veil Ritual Mask: Worn by high-ranking members of New England occult secret society, the Order of the Veil.

A sick feeling coils deep in my stomach as I realize the man who attacked me on my first night in Salem's Fall wasn't some random mugger. He was part of something bigger, something connected to Damien and the Veil. But who? For what purpose?

My mind reels, grasping for explanations, for logic, for anything that could explain this. Had it been a warning? A staged scare? Or something else entirely? Had someone meant to really hurt me that night? Maybe even kill me…?

"James?"

I jerk back from the mask as Hargrove emerges from the back of the shop, his face brightening with a warm, welcoming smile.

"What a lovely surprise!" he says, clapping his hands with delight. The scent of cloves and incense grow stronger as he approaches. "I'm so glad to see you again."

His friendly hug is comforting, and I shake off my wariness. I notice he looks rather dashing today, dressed in a dark tweed suit that seems a bit overdressed for a normal day at work in the shop.

"You look nice. Are you going somewhere?" I ask.

"Me? No." He gives me a little wink. "You look nice too."

"Thanks." I grin. "So, I think I found out something important about the Veil and the Ascension Rituals you mentioned." My voice is eager, almost breathless. "I need to talk to you about it."

He stills, his gaze flicking toward the back of the store. Quick, uncertain. Like he's checking for something—or someone.

"Right now?"

I take a step back, worrying I'm interrupting something. "Oh. Are you busy?"

"No, no. Now is fine." His voice is steady, but something feels off—a tension just beneath the surface. He takes me by the elbow and leads me to the small wooden table where we've sat before.

I spill everything—how Ian Blackhollow used the Veil's rituals to transform his bankrupt business into a kingdom of wealth, how Damien seems to be moving along the same dark path, with three sacrifices already in his wake: the Blackhollow nanny, his college sweetheart, and, of course, his most recent fiancée.

Hargrove listens with rapt attention, his eyes never leaving mine. His smile widens larger with every revelation. He's eager, almost a bit too much, as he drinks in the details. Rather than the horror I felt upon uncovering all this, he seems excited by the gruesome information.

"And you're absolutely certain Ian Blackhollow's business turned around after the fourth sacrifice?"

I nod. "Yeah, that's what the article said, at least."

His eyes gleam with something I can't quite read. "You're telling me these rituals actually work? There's real proof?"

There's an almost hungry edge to his words.

"I don't know if you can say that exactly." I shrug, trying to downplay it. "I don't believe in the supernatural or anything like that." Then I hesitate, remembering who I'm talking to. He *does* believe, and I don't want to insult him. "I mean, don't you think it's all just a coincidence?"

My excitement over what I've uncovered dims. He's not reacting at all how I expected. Instead of focusing on the real-world implications—that the Blackhollows could be a family of killers—he seems more interested in the rituals themselves. In whether they actually work.

His hand caresses the open book in front of him absentmindedly. My gaze shifts to its faded pages, and I spot the Mark of the Veil. That same oddly familiar, dark, twisted design I've now come to know.

"This is a unique piece," he says, following my gaze. "*The Book of Eternal Rites*. It's from a much older collection of the Veil's artifacts. It's kind of a manual, so to speak."

"A manual for what?"

He ignores my question. "Have you told Damien or his brother about what you've discovered?" he asks, shutting the book with a loud thud and pushing it aside. Some blood stains dotting the cuff of his white sleeve catch my attention.

"Did you cut yourself, Nick?"

I watch as blood slowly drips down the tips of his slender fingers and onto his clothes and the surface of the old wooden table. Something about it puts me on edge. He looks down, his eyes widening in surprise as he notices it too.

"Oh, I'm fine," he says, wiping his hand on his pants and rolling up his sleeve.

"Right…" I drag my focus back to what matters. "I guess what I don't understand is what happened with my family. My dad said he had the knife, that he was ready to go through with the Blood Rite ritual. But if these rituals are real—if they actually *do* something like you say—then why didn't it work?" My hands go cold in my lap, heart pounding. "Whatever that ritual was supposed to do… it failed for him."

Hargrove's face changes. His brows draw together in concentration, his lips thinning thoughtfully as though he's calculating something important.

"Of course… I see it now. Your father's ritual must have failed because it was missing a Tether—someone bound to the Veil by blood, oath, or love," he murmurs, a spark of something intense flaring behind his eyes. "*The Book of Eternal Rites* makes reference to this. It's clear the person sacrificed can't be random; it has to be a Tether. Your parents probably lacked any true connection to the Veil. Without that bond, the ritual is meaningless. It's just theatrics."

"I'm not sure I understand…"

"It's better if I show you." Hargrove straightens and stands. "I think you're finally ready to see for yourself."

He starts toward a door behind us and motions for me to follow. A jolt of unease makes me hesitate for an instant. The rational part of my brain tells me I have no reason to fear Hargrove—he's a respected professor and has been nothing but friendly and helpful in every encounter—and yet, I can't ignore that something today feels wrong.

He's too intense. Too eager. It's a bit unsettling, though I don't know why exactly.

But then I remember all the unanswered questions, the mysteries half-revealed. My career is on the line. My family. And I have to admit, even though I shouldn't be so invested, I'm dying to know the truth about Damien too. I have to understand what's really going on.

So I follow Hargrove through a narrow, shadowed corridor and into the tiny backroom. The air is colder here, heavy and still. A single hanging light bulb swings from the ceiling, casting strange shadows. The sickening scent of something coppery like blood has grown so strong it almost overpowers my senses. In the center of the room is an altar, cluttered with candles, herbs, and things that look ominously ceremonial. Symbols—the Mark of the Veil—are carved into the floor beneath.

A faint, muffled whimper cuts through the stillness.

I whip around, my stomach lurching as my gaze lands on a bound figure in the corner. A woman, eyes wide with terror, gagged and tied. Her wrists and ankles are raw and bleeding, the ropes biting into her skin. Her blood…

That must be what I saw on Hargrove's sleeve…

"*Professor,*" I breathe, my stomach clenched with terror.

The reality of the situation seeps into my bones, a sense of betrayal flooding over me. "What is this? What's going on?"

"Please understand, James," he says, locking the door behind us, trapping me inside. "They took everything from me. I should've been the most renowned occult studies professor in the country, but because of the Blackhollows, I was dismissed. Humiliated. Forced to work in a tiny little curiosity shop, begging for scraps. They made me into a joke!" His eyes narrow, fury radiating off him. "But now"—a dark, twisted smile spreads across his face—"I finally get it all back. Even better, the Veil is going to give it to me."

"I... I don't understand."

"I needed proof and now I have it," he says. "You've told me the rituals are real, that they work. I can have what they have."

I back away slowly, chest tightening with fear as I realize exactly what he intends to do. He's going to kill this poor woman right in front of me.

"But you can't," I whisper, my voice trembling. "It won't work like this. It takes four sacrifices—each on Halloween—on Veil Night. You told me that."

He chuckles, though his gaze is cold and resolute.

"Oh no, James. I see you haven't been fully paying attention." His hands clutch the book from earlier, *The Book of Eternal Rites*, and I see he brought it in here with us. "That's for the Ascension Ritual—to lead the Veil, remember? For my purposes, a single, precise offering at any time will suffice."

"Please, you can't do this," I plead. "You can't kill her. This isn't right."

The woman in the corner whimpers louder, fighting desperately against her bonds as if she's just realized how much danger she's in. Hargrove barely looks at her. It's like she's little more than an object, a component for his crazy experiment. Then his gaze shifts back to me, a terrifying glint of excitement there.

"You're absolutely right, James. It isn't right. Not when the better sacrifice—a Tether—stands before me." He smiles as he says the words, slow and deliberate, like he's savoring the moment. *"You."*

A cold, sickening dread crashes over me as I realize this man doesn't just have an unhealthy fascination with the Blackhollows and the Veil—he's obsessed. Unhinged. Professor Hargrove is totally and utterly bat-shit crazy.

His hand shoots out, locking around my arm like a vise.

Panic surges through me.

"Please! Don't!" I gasp, struggling against him. *"Let me go!"*

My hand brushes against something cold on a nearby table. Without thinking, I grab it—a small vial of some strange liquid—and smash it against his face. He stumbles back, growling in pain, his face now bloody and gashed from the broken glass. I rush for the door, but I can't get past him, can't reach it.

And then he's coming toward me, blade in hand. That's when I realize where the ritual knife from the glass case went. It's been down here all along, waiting to be used for this very moment.

"Don't fight me!" he cries, his eyes filled with a fevered light. "You're going to be part of something meaningful. Something beautiful. I'll never forget your sacrifice for me."

My heart races, a wild, erratic beat that fills my ears as the realization sinks in. This is the end for me. I'm going to die here in this shitty hidden room inside the Wandering Raven, and no one will ever even know what happened to me.

Maddie and Lucky will be all alone.

I won't be able to save my father.

I thought I'd have more time. But as Hargrove's eyes

gleam with terrifying satisfaction, I know there's no escaping my death.

The room closes in around me, the walls pressing tighter, the air growing heavier. My mind scrambles with panicked thoughts: I'll never see my family or friends again, never have a life beyond this room, beyond this moment. All the things I fought for, all my hard work... and for what?

For this?

Suddenly, Hargrove lunges forward, the dagger glinting as it catches the dim light. I throw my hands up, and pain explodes down my arm as the blade grazes my skin. I scream as a sharp, burning sting rips through my body. My muscles shake, every nerve and fiber tensing, bracing for the final death blow. I want to fight, but there's nowhere to go, no one to help me.

But then—a strange red light fills the room. Hargrove pauses, his eyes widening in horror as the symbols on the altar floor begin to glow. His hand wavers, the knife trembling as if held by an unseen force.

"No!" he whispers, backing away. "What's happening? Why isn't it working?"

The knife seems to move of its own accord, turning slowly until the blade points toward the center of Hargrove's chest. He fights against it, his hand shaking with terror as he tries to force the blade away, but the knife inches closer, unstoppable, as if guided by a power he can't control.

"Help me!" he screams, his voice high-pitched with desperation. His face twists in terror toward me. "James! Please!"

I'm paralyzed as the horror unfolds before me, and the blade plunges into his chest with a sickening crunch—again and again, vicious and relentless. Each strike lands harder than the last, the sound of tearing flesh and cracking bone filling the tiny room.

Blood oozes from his body, splattering, pooling beneath him, dark and sticky, thickening in the dim light. He seizes as he collapses to the floor, flopping around like a fish on a hook, gasping for its last few breaths of air. Then he goes limp. His lifeless eyes fix on the ceiling, his mouth frozen in a scream.

My chest heaves as I fight for air, my mind caught in a spinning web of shock and horror. I can't stop seeing the terrified look in his eyes. The knife savagely plunging into his chest over and over.

No! This isn't real!

My gaze drifts back to Hargrove's face again, twisted into something monstrous in death.

I don't understand. It looked like the knife turned on him by some unseen force, but inanimate objects don't just turn on people. They don't move on their own, right?

A strangled sound—a whimper, soft but desperate— echoes in the room and I remember the woman.

"It's okay. I've got you," I say, forcing myself to turn away from the professor's bloody corpse to help her. My hands tremble as I fumble with the knotted cloth covering her mouth.

"Thank you," she rasps, taking in greedy gulps of air.

I focus next on the binds around her wrists, my hands sticky and clumsy with blood. Eventually, the knot loosens and she's free. She lunges for the key on Hargrove's lifeless body, fumbling only for a second before unlocking the deadbolt. The door flies open, and she tears through it, disappearing without so much as a backward glance.

A chill seeps through my bones, holding me in place. My entire body feels numb as my mind attempts to catch up to what just happened. It seems like ages pass before my legs finally move again on their own, carrying me toward the exit, through the darkened shop and then outside into the street.

Somehow, hours have passed since I stepped inside the

occult shop. The sun is gone, night all around me. As I pull out my phone, I notice my hands are still covered in blood. It smears everywhere as I attempt to call the police, only to realize my phone battery is dead. I let out a hollow, empty laugh. That's just great. Of all the days to forget to charge my phone.

My mind scrambles, and I remember the police station isn't too far. I can walk there. The police… they'll know what to do.

It's eerily quiet as I head down the street, silence pressing down on me, amplifying the hollow echo of my footsteps. I can't shake the sensation of eyes watching, of something sinister lurking just beyond sight. I scan the empty streets with growing unease and quicken my pace.

A sudden flicker of movement catches my attention. At first, I think I'm imagining things—just my frayed nerves playing tricks—but then I see him. A figure, half-shrouded in shadows, lurking. Dread pools in my stomach as I take in the now-familiar Veil Ritual Mask. The silver-plated face gleaming beneath the streetlights. The contoured, expressionless metal.

My attacker has returned.

I try to run, but he moves impossibly fast, quickly cutting off my escape. He lunges, grabbing my arm with a force that sends shockwaves through my body, and slams me onto the cobblestones.

I struggle—twisting, kicking—but he's too strong, his grip unyielding. His fist connects with the side of my face and pain sears through me, stars exploding behind my eyes. My vision fades. The last thing I see is the masked man, looming over me, and then…

Darkness.

CHAPTER 22

October 24 (One Week Until Halloween)

I wake slowly, my mind pulling through layers of thick fog. My head throbs in rhythm with my heartbeat, the pain dull but persistent, settling like a weight on my temples. For a disorienting moment, I can't remember anything. But then memory floods back.

Hargrove's death.

The figure in the mask, chasing me.

And then... nothing.

I blink groggily, my vision swimming as I take in my unfamiliar—but undeniably opulent—surroundings. An imposing four-poster bed looms around me, draped in impossibly soft bedding, its heavy canopy falling like a shroud. Soft candlelight from crystal sconces flicker around the room, casting shifting shadows across dark hardwood floors. A plush, intricate tapestry rug stretches beneath me, while deep burgundy velvet curtains hang heavy over the windows, sealing out daylight. It's all so beautiful and grand, but with a sinister edge, like something straight out of a Gothic horror novel.

"You're awake... Finally."

My heart skips as I whirl around to find Damien Blackhollow sitting in a leather chair on the other side of the room.

Arms crossed over his muscular chest. Dark, piercing eyes fixed on me. His face holds a look that's both anxious and... relieved?

But then my attention shifts, and I blink again, certain I'm hallucinating because Lucky is nestled in Damien's lap. The cat who hates pretty much everyone but me seems completely at ease, eyes closed in utter contentment, purring as Damien scratches behind his ears. At the foot of the bed, I notice my bags from the Cottage, neatly stacked in a row.

"Where... where am I?" I ask, my throat raw as if it hasn't been used in weeks.

"Blackthorn Manor, of course," he answers simply, like that explains everything.

A mix of emotions swirls inside me. Confusion. Alarm. Worry.

"How did I get here?" I cough, my chest achy and rattling. I'm sore all over, like I've been hit by a Mack truck. My right arm throbs, and I glance down to see someone has bandaged it where Hargrove's knife cut me. "And Lucky? My luggage?"

Damien leans back, one eyebrow arching with a hint of smugness. "Oh, you mean how did I retrieve a cat and a few bags from the B&B? Not exactly hard when you're a Blackhollow. Let's just say nobody raised an objection."

He gently sets Lucky down on the floor and advances a few feet toward the bed, stopping just short. A spark of anger simmers just beneath his controlled exterior, his voice hardening.

"You were *attacked*, James—again! Do you have any idea what would've happened if I hadn't shown up when I did?"

I blink, startled. "You... you saved me?"

A muscle twitches in his jaw, dark eyes flashing. "Yes," he snaps. "I saved you. And it seems like I'm constantly having to save you, doesn't it? Because you're too damn foolish and stubborn to listen." He closes the distance between us, his voice rising now. "I *warned* you to be careful in Salem's Fall. I told you not to go to the professor. But you—" His jaw flexes. "You never listen."

I push myself upright, a hot spike of anger surging through me.

"Wait—you think this is my fault? You think I wanted this to happen?"

"No, of course not, but your stubbornness has nearly gotten you killed. *Twice!*" His voice is rough, but something else flickers behind his anger, something I wasn't expecting. Fear. "Damn it, James! Why couldn't you just listen to me?"

I stiffen, my hands curling into fists in the sheets as I think back to the Wandering Raven and the mask hanging on the wall, displayed like some kind of sick trophy. The mask my attacker wore my first night in Salem's Fall—and the night I was attacked at Hargrove's shop. The same mask connected to the Veil. I still don't have all the answers, but I think I'm finally starting to put some of the pieces together.

"I don't listen, because all you keep doing is lying to me!" My voice shakes with emotion. "That mugging my first night in Salem's Fall was the Veil, wasn't it?"

Damien's entire body tenses and I see it—hesitation. Guilt. It's barely there, just a flicker before he schools his expression, but I catch it. And it's all the confirmation I need.

"I don't know what you're talking about—"

"Don't." My voice drops, low and accusing. "That man… he was wearing the Veil Ritual Mask, wasn't he? I know it's all connected somehow."

"James—" A muscle feathers in his jaw, his shoulders slumping slightly. "Let me explain."

I fold my arms across my chest.

"Please do."

"That first night… yes, that was me. Or rather, Bennett." His voice is clipped, reluctant. "I told him to make sure you understood how dangerous this place is. That you didn't belong here."

A cold, bitter laugh escapes me.

"You set me up."

"No." He shakes his head. "I wanted to scare some sense into you. That's all."

"And the last attack?" I scoff. "Your plan got a little out of control, then, huh?"

He stiffens, a flicker of hurt flashing across his face. "You can't really believe I had anything to do with that. I have no idea who that was." His voice drops, steady but urgent. "I would never hurt you."

And just like that, the fight goes out of me. My anger dissipates, turning off like a fire hose, replaced by fear as I remember how close I almost came to dying. I suck in a shaky breath, forcing the words out.

"Nick… he… he tried to sacrifice me."

"He *what*?" Damien's expression darkens, fury igniting in his eyes. Before I can react, he swipes a hand across the dresser, sending a crystal vase crashing to the floor, shattering on impact. Water and crushed petals spill onto the hardwood into a soggy, wet mess. "I'll kill that bastard!"

"Too late. He's already dead," I say, oddly touched by the strength of Damien's reaction.

I guess he does care if I live or die, after all…

"Tell me what happened," he orders.

The memory of Hargrove's last moments alive makes my stomach twist. I start to shake under the sheets. "He took me into some secret hidden room in the shop," I whisper. "He wanted to sacrifice me for some twisted Veil ritual, but the knife turned on him, killing him instead. I barely escaped…" I swallow hard, my hands clammy against my sides. "Did you know what he was planning?"

"If I'd known what he was capable of, he wouldn't have

lived long enough to touch you," he says, his voice a low growl. There's a possessiveness there, a dangerous edge to his words that makes my pulse race wildly.

As much as I want to believe this beautiful, powerful man standing in front of me, I've learned the hard way to trust no one and nothing in Salem's Fall. If nothing else, Hargrove made sure to teach me that lesson. It's not one I'll forget anytime soon.

Damien may be telling the truth when he says he saved me from yet another attack, and maybe he's not actively trying to hurt me right now, but that doesn't mean his intentions are pure. Even if he did rescue me, what am I doing here—*in his house*? Shouldn't I be in a hospital somewhere?

Hell, if he really wanted me safe, wouldn't he have sent me back to Boston—to Maddie or even Quinn? Somewhere far from all of this?

"Why am I really here?" I narrow my eyes, studying him, uncertainty coiling uneasily in my stomach. "And don't pretend this was some noble act of rescue."

Shadows flicker across his sharp, perfect features, softening them just enough to make him look almost vulnerable, a rare glimpse of uncertainty breaking through his usual steely armor.

"You want the truth?"

"No, I want you to keep lying to me," I say sarcastically.

He paces toward me, raking a shaky hand through his dark hair. "I'm falling for you, James. God help me, but I am." He takes a shuddering breath, his fingers brushing against my skin in a way that sends a traitorous heat through my body. His touch lingers, tracing a slow, deliberate path along my jaw.

"And I don't fall for anyone," he murmurs, almost to himself. "Not like this. Not ever." His gaze drops to my mouth, hungry and haunted all at once. "It's against every instinct, every damn shred of control and self-preservation I have, but I can't seem to stop myself when it comes to you."

I stare up at him, heart pounding against my ribs.

"I—I don't understand…"

I wasn't ready for this confession of feelings, not from him, not from a man who's the living embodiment of everything I've been taught to run from. The anger has vanished from his eyes and there's something else lurking there now, something softer, something I don't dare name.

"Neither do I, believe me." He laughs, roughly, almost mockingly. "Do you think I wanted to feel this way about someone who's clearly here only because of obligation? Someone who only sees me as the next steppingstone in her career?"

The words sting, and a part of me recoils at how little he must think of me if he really believes I'm only here because of my ambition. Yes, my job is part of the reason, but it's not the only thing still keeping me in Salem's Fall.

Not even close.

I sigh, torn between the rational part of me that knows I shouldn't feel anything for this man—that this could all be a trick—and the reckless, dangerous part that clings to every word.

"Even if you're telling the truth. Even if you do have… feelings… for me, that doesn't mean I can trust you." I meet his gaze, searching for something—anything—that makes this make sense. "You could be lying. You could be behind everything. The murders. The sacrifices. Hell, for all I know, Professor Hargrove and the masked men work for you. How am I supposed to believe a word you say?"

Damien's eyes darken. He steps back, his expression shuttering like a door slamming shut, a wall rising between us.

"Of course you can't trust me," he says, a bitter smile tugging at his lips. "I've been raised in a family that's built its legacy on manipulation, on secrets and witchcraft and blood sacrifices. Despite what I feel for you, I'm not the good guy in this story. I never will be."

I cross my arms, defiance hardening my resolve.

"You're right. You're not."

I can't allow myself to fall for this man, no matter how much he makes my heart race. I'm not the kind of woman that believes in fairy tales and happy endings, not after everything I've seen in my life. A love confession from a man like Damien Blackhollow? And just a few days before he's meant to sacrifice a fourth victim—a Tether, a woman like me—in order to ascend the Veil ranks? It all feels just a little too coincidental…

"Take me back to the Cottage," I demand.

"No," he says, shaking his head. "You're not going anywhere. Not until this is over."

"You don't get to make that decision for me."

"Believe me, I wish I didn't have to, but if it means keeping you alive, I'll do whatever it takes." His gaze sharpens, his voice now dropping to a dangerous whisper. "The Veil has something planned for you. It's not safe for you out there. Not with Veil Night just a few days away."

"A few days? How long have I been here?"

"Almost a week."

My jaw drops.

"A week?"

"You've been in and out of it for days. Gave me quite the scare, but my doctors said it looked worse than it really was. That you just needed rest. But if you think for one second that I'm going to let anyone else try to harm you—" He stops himself, inhaling deeply, as if grappling with the intensity of his own feelings. "I won't let anyone hurt you again."

"Oh, is that why I'm your prisoner? For my own protection?" I let out a sharp, disbelieving snort. "How convenient—locking me up just days before Veil Night."

"Convenient is the last thing you are," he mocks, his laugh bitter and low. "You're reckless. Headstrong. The most infuriating woman I've ever met." He takes a step forward, gaze burning into mine. "And yet, no matter what I do—no matter how hard I try—I can't get you out of my fucking head."

His hand comes up—slow, deliberate—and curls around the side of my throat, thumb resting just below my jaw. Not tight. Just enough to make me feel owned. He pulls me in until our faces are inches apart, his eyes dark and unreadable. For a beat, he just stares at me, like he's trying to capture every detail. Like he's at war with himself.

The air crackles, the magnetic pull between us undeniable. It's not safe. None of this is safe. He's dangerous, I know that. A man capable of things I can barely comprehend. But I can't look away. A dark, twisted force draws me closer and closer even when I know I should run.

This isn't some sweet, soft fairy tale. It's messier. Twisted.

And God help me, I want it anyway.

My breath catches as his lips graze mine, a fleeting touch that sends a surge of warmth and fear spiraling through me. My hands find his chest, but instead of pushing him away like I know I should, I cling to him, pulling him in, letting myself get lost in the thrill of feeling his body against mine.

Before I know what's happening, his hands tangle in my hair and his mouth crashes into mine in a fierce, searing kiss. A groan escapes him—low, guttural, like he's been holding back for far too long and can't anymore. His body presses against mine, all heat and tension and need, like he's trying to memorize the way I fit against him.

For a brief, reckless moment, I forget everything but the feel of him. Lips touching. Tongues meeting deliciously. Breath tangling. My entire body explodes like I've been struck by lightning, like I'm on fire and am going to die, but it will be the most exquisite death anyone's ever had. Never in my life have I been kissed the way this man is kissing me.

But just before I tumble completely off the cliff—past the point of no return—a sliver of reason cuts through the fog of my desire.

"No, we can't..." I murmur against his mouth, breathless. "This is wrong..."

He jerks back slightly, eyes darkening—confused.

"James?"

"You... you're dangerous, Damien." I shake my head, my breath coming in shaky bursts. "You can't just kiss me and expect me to ignore what I know about you."

"Maybe I am dangerous," he admits. "But I'm the only one who can keep you safe."

"Safe? From what—*from you*? No, you're as bad as Nick," I say, my voice trembling. The words taste bitter on my tongue, but I've known this all along. Nothing about Damien is safe. "You're just another man who will stop at nothing to get what he wants."

"Yes." He doesn't flinch, doesn't look away. "I will."

A cold chill slithers down my spine. His admission is a reminder of the darkness lurking within him, a darkness that no amount of chemistry and attraction or professed feelings can erase. He's everything I should fear, everything I should run from. A man who bends morality to suit his needs, who doesn't hesitate to do whatever it takes to reach his end goal—no matter how wrong.

A memory flickers in my mind—faint, but persistent.

The fancy restaurant. The wine. The overwhelming exhaustion that hit me out of nowhere. I'd been drinking, sure, but not enough to feel like that.

I look up at him sharply. "That night at dinner, you drugged me, didn't you? I wouldn't listen about the Hollow, so you made me listen." The pieces snap together as I finally understand just how far this man will go to control me. "The Xanax," I whisper, remembering the prescription bottle I found in his briefcase at the Cottage. "That's how you did it, isn't it?"

His expression darkens. "How do you know about the Xanax?"

"It doesn't matter!" I snap, my pulse pounding in my ears. "How could you do that to me?"

His eyes lock onto mine, a storm brewing beneath their surface.

"I did it for your own damn good. I needed to keep you safe."

"You drugged me—against my will—to keep me *safe*?" I let out a sharp, bitter laugh. "Do you have any idea how messed up that sounds?"

He doesn't answer immediately. A muscle in his jaw clenches, and for the briefest moment, something like regret flickers across his face. But then it's gone, buried beneath that familiar cold resolve.

"Maybe so. But it worked."

Anger curls hot in my stomach, but it's not enough. I'm not nearly angry enough for what he did. I swallow hard, feeling off-balance and confused at my own emotions. I should be furious at the sheer violation of him taking my autonomy —my choices—away. I should be looking at him with nothing but loathing, demanding he let me go, threatening to make him pay.

But I'm not.

Because I can't ignore the truth in what he's saying. I would have gone that night to the Hollow. Like with Hargrove, I probably would have walked straight into something I wasn't prepared for, and I don't know if I would have made it back alive. I hate that he's right, but even more I hate that some part of me—some sick, twisted part—doesn't hate him nearly as much as I should. Beneath my anger, something unexpected slithers. Something unsettling. Something like... gratitude.

And I don't like it. Not one bit.

Damien Blackhollow is far more dangerous than I ever suspected. He can control me, manipulate even my very emotions, bend my reality until I can't tell right from wrong anymore. A man like this... what else has he done? What else is he capable of?

"You did it, didn't you?" The words slip out before I can stop them. "You killed those women—Carla, Elise, Vivienne. I'm sure they also believed your lies when you told them how much you cared for them."

Something cracks in his expression—a flash of pain, raw and unguarded. His hands clench at his sides like he has to physically restrain himself. "You have no idea what you're talking about!" His voice is sharp, almost desperate. "I *never* hurt those women."

"I don't believe you."

"Believe what you want." His lips press into a hard line. He looks almost... wounded, like he can't quite believe I think so little of him. But then, just as quickly, his expression steels over, his voice turning cold. "But remember this—I'm the only one keeping you from becoming the Veil's next sacrifice."

"So that's it? You're really doing this?" I ask, my voice unsteady, like I'm still waiting for him to take it all back. "You're just going to keep me here against my will?"

"Now you're getting it, Counselor." He smirks, but there's no humor in it. "You'll find all the doors and windows in this house are locked to you. Otherwise, you're free to roam within these walls however you like. All this"—he gestures around the room—"all that's mine is now yours too, to do with as you wish. If you need anything, just ask, and I'll make sure you have it," he says. "But you won't be leaving Blackthorn Manor until I say so."

A sharp pulse of panic shoots through me as I realize just how screwed I am. Trapped in this fortress of a house, away from all my family and friends, solely at the mercy of Damien Blackhollow—a man who could be my savior or my doom.

"You can't just keep me here! You're—you're a monster!"

"Maybe I am," he says, my heart hammering as he leans in and presses a soft kiss to my temple, catching me off guard. "But it's a role I'm willing to play if it means keeping you safe. Because if I let you leave, you won't live to see November."

Then he strides to the door and slams it shut. The sound echoes through the room, final and unyielding, sealing my fate inside this gilded cage.

CHAPTER 23

Damien doesn't visit me again, though I can still feel his presence lingering in the walls, in the silence of the room around me. Though he said I could have free rein of his home, I sulk in my bedroom instead. He's effectively cut me off from the rest of the world, taking my cell phone and my laptop and keeping them who knows where. The shifting light outside my window, fading from morning brightness to the deep hues of dusk, is my only measure of time.

All that being what it is, if I wasn't so frustrated about being trapped against my will—with a case that urgently needs my attention—I might actually enjoy my time at Blackthorn Manor. There's no shortage of delicious gourmet meals and expensive wines. Damien has them sent to me multiple times a day. And he attempts to alleviate my boredom with the stacks upon stacks of books dropped off at my door daily. Romance. Horror. Thrillers. Fantasy. He leaves me a bit of everything. Under any other circumstance, the amount of good food and books he showers upon me daily would be the perfect little escape.

I can't help feeling conflicted.

On the one hand, I'm furious. How dare he lock me up like I'm some helpless damsel? But part of me, the part I don't want to admit out loud, not even to myself, can't help but feel a bit flattered that he's gone to such lengths to protect me and keep me pampered at the same time.

Not to mention that love confession.

I'm still reeling from his admission of feelings for me. I can't deny there's something thrilling about being wanted like that—by a man like him. And then there was that kiss…

Just thinking about it sets my body on fire all over again. The way he pulled me close, his lips so commanding and possessive. It was like he reached right into my soul and ignited something I didn't know I had. I can still feel the heat of him lingering on my lips, a slow-burning ember that refuses to go out. Like a moth to his flame, I'm drawn to him against all reason. But that's the thing about moths and flames.

That pretty fire kills.

I let out a long sigh, feeling Lucky shift against my leg in the bed. Despite the cat's company, the room feels vast and empty. It's like a vacuum of beautiful darkness pressing down on me. My eyes catch the single orange rose in a slender vase on the nightstand, its petals curling like a burnished flame. No note, but unmistakably from Damien. He hasn't returned—not that I've seen—but every morning, there's another rose, slipped in while I sleep.

Eventually, my curiosity gets the better of me, and I decide to check out the rest of the house. I slide out from under the covers and give Lucky a quick scratch behind his ears before standing. He follows my every move, his eyes mirroring my own uncertainty as I steel myself and push open the bedroom door, stepping outside.

I make my way down the winding staircase, my fingers trailing along the dark mahogany banister. The halls are dimly lit, the walls a rich burgundy with intricate molding running along the top. The air smells faintly of wood polish and something darker, muskier. In the heavy silence, every step I take echoes, Lucky's little paws pitter-pattering behind me.

The main foyer stretches out below, its wood floors polished and shining. Sunlight slants through tall, arched windows, casting a hazy glow that feels almost intrusive in Blackthorn Manor's cool, shadowed interior. A wrought-iron chandelier hangs above, its dozens of flickering lights casting shifting patterns across the walls.

As I walk past the library, my gaze drifts over an enormous stone fireplace, strange symbols carved into its surface. Antique trinkets sit carefully arranged on the mantel, each one probably worth a small fortune. Massive oil paintings hang in thick frames and towering bookshelves stretch to the ceiling—a dream library filled with books of every shape and size.

I can't deny the allure of Blackthorn Manor. The place reeks of old money, every corner dripping with an air of power and opulence. If I weren't effectively a prisoner here, I might actually be able to appreciate its beauty.

A loud, demanding growl from my stomach reminds me I haven't yet eaten. I turn down a hallway in search of food, the polished floors giving way to sleek, checkered tiles of the kitchen. I nearly jump when I find someone already standing there. An older gentleman in formal attire watches me with quiet amusement, as if he's been expecting me. He's dressed in a vintage black suit with coattails, complete with a bow tie, like someone who just stepped out of an old movie.

"You must be Miss Woodsen," he says, bowing slightly, hands clasped in front of him.

I blink, caught off guard. "Uh, yes. And you are?"

"My name is Edward Jottingsworth, Miss. I'm Mr. Blackhollow's butler," he explains. "I'm here to be of assistance should you require anything during your stay."

I try not to smirk. Of course Damien has a butler.

For a fleeting second, the instinct to beg for help sparks in my mind, but I push it down just as quickly. This man works for Damien. Whatever kindness he might offer, it won't extend to letting me walk out the front door. And it's not like I'm being tortured—I'm just... stuck.

"Oh, um... thank you," I say, offering a polite smile. He looks nice enough, and it's not his fault Damien has me trapped here like a prized possession. "I was just looking for something to eat."

"I'd be more than happy to prepare something for you," he says, leading me into a large, gleaming kitchen outfitted with every modern appliance imaginable.

He gestures for me to sit at a small breakfast nook tucked away in the corner. Lucky curls at my feet as I sit and watch Edward move with an almost unsettling efficiency, retrieving ingredients and setting them out on the counter with practiced ease.

"What would you prefer for brunch, Miss?" His voice is soft, but there's an underlying precision to it. It's clear he's hosted many guests here at Blackthorn Manor.

"Oh, anything's fine. Just something simple."

He nods and sets to work with an almost hypnotic grace. I feel slightly overwhelmed. The absurdity of it all—a prisoner being served breakfast by a butler in a grand gothic mansion—doesn't escape me.

"The meals at Blackthorn Manor are prepared daily by outside chefs and delivered," he explains, plating my meal. "Mr. Blackhollow prefers to keep in-house staff at a minimum, within a select circle of trusted employees—especially this time of year."

Goosebumps rise along my arms as I'm reminded again of how close we are to Halloween and Veil Night and whatever that may bring.

Moments later, Edward places a plate before me arranged so meticulously, it looks like it belongs in a five-star restaurant: a mouthwatering crêpe with eggs, turkey bacon, and a fancy French cheese; crisped fingerling potatoes with truffles; fresh fruit and berries with chantilly cream. The aroma is intoxicating.

"If you'd prefer, I can arrange for your meal to be served in the dining room, Miss," he says.

"Sure, that sounds... nice."

He nods approvingly and leads Lucky and me through an elaborately decorated corridor, his steps quick and purposeful as he guides me into a formal dining room as grand as the rest of the place. An antique ebony table stretches the length of the room, its dark surface polished to a soft sheen beneath a towering crystal chandelier. On the far wall hangs a massive gilded mirror, reflecting flickering candlelight from the wall sconces, adding to the room's quiet, opulent grandeur. Through the floor-to-ceiling windows is a stunning view of the grounds, trees shedding their autumn leaves in a beautiful cascade of orange and gold.

"I do hope you enjoy your stay with us at Blackthorn Manor, Miss Woodsen. Even if the circumstances are... less than ideal," Edward says, something in his eyes—understanding, maybe even sympathy—as he leads me to the dining room table.

But then something stops me cold in my tracks. At the other end of the table, cloaked partially in the shadows, is Lucien. His expression, half amusement and half something darker, freezes the breath in my lungs.

"Hello, Miss Woodsen," he says, his voice dripping with that predatory charm I've come to expect from him. He leans back, gesturing for me to take the chair across from him. "Please, have a seat. Join me."

My pulse quickens as I debate whether to sit or flee. Lucky stiffens next to me, teeth showing, ears flat against his head.

"Um, hi..." I mumble, reluctantly walking over and sliding into the oversized velvet chair. Lucky stays in the corner, far away from Lucien, studying him suspiciously as

Edward gracefully places my breakfast plate down and leaves the room.

"I trust you're enjoying your stay at Blackthorn Manor?" Lucien asks with a slight smirk, steepling his fingers underneath that perfect chiseled chin.

"Enjoying isn't exactly the word I'd use."

"Ah, well, in any event, it seems my brother has got you right where he wants you—and just in time for Veil Night tonight."

My pulse speeds up.

"Wait—what day is it?"

His smile widens, devoid of any real warmth. "October 31st, of course."

I can't believe it. How is it already Halloween?

And if I'm still here tucked away in Blackthorn Manor, then what does that mean? Am I safe?

Or is there still plenty of time for something horrible to happen to me?

"Are you suggesting Damien has me trapped here for the ritual?" My fork shakes in my hand, but I steel my voice. Lucien is always playing games, always trying to get the upper hand. Maybe I should be afraid of whatever Damien has planned for me, but I refuse to give Lucien the satisfaction. "To be honest, I find this all incredibly confusing." I sigh, taking a bite of my potatoes. "If your brother really wants me dead, he didn't need to go to all these lengths to save me from a masked killer and pamper me with gourmet meals and gifts, just to kill me himself."

Lucien leans forward, his eyes gleaming with something dark and unsettling. "Who says it's you he's after?"

Okay, now I really *am* confused.

I set my fork down, my fingers tightening around the edge of my plate. "Isn't that what you were implying? That your brother trapped me here to be the Veil Night sacrifice?" I glance at Lucien, searching his face for any hint of a tell. "I thought... the Veil... I thought it's supposed to be someone tied to Damien, a 'Tether'—someone like me."

He gives a slow sigh, swirling his glass with deliberate calm. "Of course, that's what Damien wants you to think, so you'll stay out of the way. He's all too happy to let you play the fool in this little horror show," he says, voice almost mocking. "Tell me, Miss Woodsen, how is your sister?"

His question sends a jolt through me.

"Maddie? What does she have to do with any of this?"

"Had any... trouble... reaching her lately?"

His tone is casual, but the words tighten like a vise around my chest. My mind races back to my recent attempts to reach Maddie right before the professor's death, and I realize the last time I spoke with her was the night of the Gala. That's been, what—six? Seven days ago?

More?

"What do you mean?" I ask, a prickling unease snaking through me. "Are you saying Damien is after my sister?"

"Damien? I don't know." Lucien shrugs. "The Veil, most certainly. They tend to stay consistent with their methods. Female. Innocent. Tethered." His eyes narrow, as if doing some sort of calculation in his head. "Well, tethered enough to Damien through you, that is. You were right about that—you're the connection."

A tremor runs through me, and I swallow hard, a cold weight settling in my stomach, heavy and full of dread. Lucien watches me, his gaze unyielding and almost... pitying.

"You see it now, don't you?" His voice is soft, almost gentle. "All along, you've been focusing on the wrong things, worrying about your own life. But the Veil... they're always one step ahead."

"You're lying. Damien would have told me if something bad was happening to Maddie."

"Why? Because he *cares* for you? Is that what he told you?" Lucien laughs, a hollow sound that fills the cavernous room. "My brother has always been a master at manipulating those around him." He leans forward, his voice dropping as if sharing a secret. "Truthfully, I think he really may have… feelings… for you, but someone has to die for the Ascension. So he locks you in here in this beautiful cage, keeps you distracted, feeds you lies—all for your own protection, of course. All while your poor sister is out there in the Veil's clutches, awaiting her death while Damien secures his future reign."

"If you're convinced your brother is so evil, why are you telling me this? Why not let him win his little game?"

Lucien's gaze shifts, a hint of some deep emotion quickly buried. "Because this isn't just Damien's game. It's mine too," he says. "And I refuse to let my brother have everything he's ever wanted without facing any consequence."

"I don't believe you…"

"You should," he says matter-of-factly. "Because the truth is, Damien is exactly who you feared he might be."

The room feels like it's closing in, the walls pushing against me, as I try to piece everything together. Every word Damien has ever said. Every look. Every unexplained moment. Could he really have been keeping this from me, using me as some pawn while my sister is in trouble?

Maddie—she's just a kid. He couldn't really mean to harm her, could he?

My breath hitches, the full horror of my situation sinking in. I'm trapped in Blackthorn Manor, locked away while Maddie is out there, in unimaginable danger, and there's not a damn thing I can do about it. I have no phone, no means of escape, and every second I spend here, helpless, is a second wasted.

My hands tremble as I shove my chair back and bolt out

of my seat. I need to get out of here somehow. She's my little sister, my responsibility. I have to find Madison.

"What's wrong, Miss Woodsen?" Lucien watches my reaction, his gaze sharp and penetrating. "Suddenly not feeling so safe under Damien's *protection*?"

I glare at him, fury boiling under the surface, mixing with the fear churning in my gut. Because if Lucien is telling the truth, then he's just as bad as Damien for sitting by idly while my sister's life is in peril. I realize I'm caught between two men, both powerful, both dangerous, each with motives as twisted as the other.

"My sister... I need to get to her." I step toward Lucien, my last hope—a hope that fades with every second of his cool, impenetrable gaze. "Please, tell me where she is," I say, my voice cracking. "I have to help her."

He watches me with a detached curiosity, his expression mocking, but there's a hint of something almost empathetic too. For a moment, he seems to consider my words, and something almost human flickers behind his cold exterior.

But then, he gives a small, dismissive shrug.

"It's out of my hands, unfortunately." He sighs, giving me a hollow smile. "Even if I wanted to, I can't just walk into the Veil's inner sanctum and demand they return their sacrificial lamb. The wheels are already in motion, I'm afraid."

"Please, Lucien." My hands tremble at my sides. "There has to be a way. Tell me where she is..." I beg.

"I'm sorry. Truly, I am. But I can't help you," he says. "Although... you don't need me to. You already know the answer." He watches me intently, his gaze unnervingly sharp. "Ask yourself—where would they take someone meant for sacrifice?" His voice dips into a coaxing whisper. "You've come across it before, buried in the history you've been so meticulously digging up."

Panic grips me, my thoughts spinning, the truth just out of

reach. Fragments of places, whispers, hints—they swirl in a fog of madness I can't quite unravel. I take a shuddering breath, forcing myself to sort through the chaos, to find what fits.

Then it clicks. Old places tied to dark rituals, where power lingers in the air, places like—

"Strega's Hollow!"

Lucien slow claps, a smug smile spreading across his face. "Well done," he drawls. "Shame you're trapped in Blackthorn Manor, locked behind these doors and windows. However will you escape to save your poor sister?"

"You can get me out, can't you?" I meet his gaze, desperately searching for any sign of mercy, any crack in his cold mask.

"It's not a matter of what I can do. It's what I'm willing to do—and I don't risk myself for lost causes. No matter how pretty they may be." He leans forward, his expression unyielding as he raises his glass in a mock toast. "Enjoy the rest of your meal, Miss Woodsen," he says. "I must be on my way. I've got somewhere special to be."

I barely see him through the fog of despair that overtakes me as he turns to leave. The finality in his goodbye is a death sentence that fills me with a dark, horrific realization. No one at Blackthorn Manor will help me. No one will save Maddie.

My sister is going to die, and there's nothing I can do to stop it.

CHAPTER 24

After Lucien leaves, Lucky and I are alone in the cavernous, cold dining room of Blackthorn Manor.

Utterly and completely alone.

My hands lie uselessly on the table as I stare down at the untouched silver and crystal, each glittering facet mocking me. Lucky moves from the corner of the room to my side, perching quietly on the chair beside me. His eyes fix on me with an intensity—silent, unwavering—as if he understands just how horrible things are.

How did this happen?

How could I have been so blind?

I've been so wrapped up in my own ambition, my need to prove myself, that I missed the real danger staring me in the face. I'd been so stupid to think I could outsmart the Veil. Now my little sister is somewhere out there, alone, facing horrors I can barely comprehend.

A wave of nausea rises in my throat.

Halloween—Veil Night—is tonight, and if Lucien is right, then Maddie doesn't have much time. Meanwhile, I'm trapped here in Blackthorn Manor, in the beautiful prison Damien designed to "protect" me, but in reality, it's just another web I've been caught in.

A shaky breath leaves me as tears prick at my eyes. All I

can think about is Maddie. Her bright, laughing face. That tiny gap between her front teeth she's always been self-conscious about. The way she dramatically squeals and acts like she's about to faint whenever she gets excited. How she nudges me at dinner when I'm being too serious, or pouts into the phone to get her way, always knowing exactly what to say to wear me down. And now she's out there, all alone.

I can't lose my sister.

Not like this.

Lucky shifts, leaping from the chair to my lap, curling against me with a low purr. I scratch behind his ears, lost in my feelings of anger and helplessness, until he head-butts my hand sharply, startling me.

"Lucky? What is it?"

He stares up at me, eyes gleaming with an intensity I've never seen, before jumping down from my lap and trotting toward the doorway. He pauses, looking back at me expectantly.

"I don't understand. You want me to follow you?" I ask, feeling ridiculous talking to my cat, but something in his steady, knowing gaze spurs me to my feet.

I walk over and he takes off again, tail shaking purposefully as he slinks around the corner. Every time I catch up to him, he runs farther away, making me chase him all through the manor's labyrinthine hallways. I have no idea what Lucky is doing, or why, but for some strange reason I can't explain, I feel compelled to follow.

Eventually, he leads me down a quiet, dim corridor and stops beside a small door. He scratches at the wood, letting out an insistent meow.

"Um... you want me to open this?" I ask, still feeling foolish as I turn the handle.

The door swings open to reveal a narrow, spiraling staircase. I take a slow, hesitant step downward, and then Lucky bolts past me, a sleek shadow slipping between my legs. He races down the stairs, his paws barely making a sound, tail flicking once before he vanishes into the darkness. I follow after him, clinging to the rickety banister for support as the air turns cooler and mustier.

At the bottom, I'm met with an old, damp stone corridor. The place is dimly lit by torches that flicker like they've been burning for ages. It's almost like I'm no longer in Blackthorn Manor but have wound up in another world entirely.

"What is this place?" I murmur, my voice echoing eerily in the silence.

Lucky keeps going, his little paws padding softly on the stone floor as he winds through the corridor with purpose. Finally, we reach a small, hidden room at the far end and Lucky leads me inside.

I gasp, a jolt of shock racing through me. Sitting on top of an old dresser, plugged into the wall, are my cell phone and laptop. Damien must have stashed them here, somewhere he assumed I'd never find them.

"How did… how did you know?" I ask Lucky, but the cat just curls around my ankles and stares at me with that mysterious twinkle in his bright eyes.

I lunge for the phone and turn it on. Over a dozen missed calls. Each notification blinks back at me. Most from Katie and Quinn… and one from the Massachusetts Correctional Institution.

Dad.

I stare at the screen, my breath catching. My father rarely calls, not unless it's important.

My fingers shake as I click into the voicemail and the automated message plays: "You have a call from Massachusetts Correctional Institution. An inmate, Thomas Woodsen, attempted to contact you. To receive future calls, please ensure…"

The voice drones on, but I stop listening. My grip tightens on the phone as my gnawing sense of dread grows.

Why would my dad be calling today of all days?

Halloween and he's reaching out from his prison cell?

The timing chills me to the bone, like he knows something I don't. But what? I thought he'd told me everything about the Veil and the Blackhollows the last time I saw him.

Then something else catches my eye. A small robin's egg blue Tiffany box sits on the dresser beside my laptop, the kind used for expensive rings. I don't want to open it, but I know I have to, even if I already have a very bad feeling about what's inside. With numb fingers, I reach out, open the lid—

Vivienne Van Buren's missing engagement ring.

A sharp breath hitches in my throat as I stare at the missing ring, the one the police believed was stolen from the murder scene when they were still chasing the botched robbery theory. Why is it here? In Blackthorn Manor, hidden away in Damien's secret little underground room?

I rifle through the dresser shelves and drawers, frantically searching, because if Damien hid his fiancée's ring here, then what else is he hiding? There has to be something.

I find old documents, yellowed with age. Stacks of photographs. Nothing that means anything. Until—

A familiar-looking white plastic access card, edged in silver, peeks out from beneath the papers. Mark's Whitehall & Rowe building ID. The same card every Whitehall & Rowe attorney carries to get in and out of the firm's building. The same one that should've been in Mark's wallet the night he died.

My pulse thrums so loudly, it drowns out everything else.

What the hell is going on?

Lucky brushes against my leg again, snapping me out of my spiraling thoughts, before darting through another winding corridor at the back of the room. I glance once more at the unsettling collection of items—Mark's access card, Vivienne's ring, my stolen phone and laptop. All of it adds up to something that doesn't look good for Damien, but I don't have time to unpack it all now. Maddie needs me.

I rush after Lucky, clutching my phone to my chest as I follow him through the dark passageway. Seconds later, we spill out of a heavy steel door and into the open air behind the manor. A black sports car sits idle on the driveway. I run to it, heart exploding as I peer through the window and spot the keys sitting right there in the cup holder like the best Christmas gift ever. It's as if they were left there on purpose, waiting for me.

As I glance back at Lucky, his yellow eyes lock on mine with an expression that almost feels knowing. It's as if he understands exactly what's happening, like he anticipated this all along.

"You... you led me to this, didn't you?" I whisper, the realization making my skin prickle.

Lucky tilts his head and gives a soft, reassuring meow, weaving between my ankles like a silent blessing. Hope surges through me. I finally have a way to get to Maddie. I reach down to scoop him up, ready to place him in the car—but he slips away, darting into the dense woods behind Blackthorn Manor.

"Lucky! No—get back here!"

I scan the dark trees, but he's already gone, swallowed up by the shadows. Panic twists in my chest as I call after the cat and take a shaky step forward, torn between chasing after him and the urgency of saving my sister. Every instinct screams at me to run after Lucky, to make sure he's safe. He's not just a cat—he's family. My rock. My constant, faithful companion.

But then I see Maddie's face again in my head and am filled with the desperate urgency to get to her. I don't know how much time she has left.

"Lucky!"

My voice cracks, the hollow silence that fills the space he left behind already feeling heavy, chilling. Tears sting my eyes as I hover by the car, desperately glancing back at the woods one last time. I don't want to leave him—but something tells me he'll be okay. Lucky found me once, all those years ago, slipping out of the shadows in the alley behind my school when I needed him most. Almost like magic. He'll come back to me again.

And then, as if the universe itself answers, a rustle in the distance—the faintest flicker of movement—almost like Lucky is telling me to go. Somehow I know that whatever lies ahead, I have to face it alone.

"You know where to find me, Lucky," I whisper fiercely and slam the car door shut, clutching the wheel. There's no more time to waste. Maddie needs me, and whatever's ahead, I'm all she has left.

The car rumbles to life as I start the engine and make my way out of Blackthorn Manor, driving as fast as I can through the winding roads. I tell myself that whatever happens next, I can handle it, but the truth is I'm more terrified than I've ever been in my life. Veil Night is here, and somewhere out in that vast, dark unknown, Maddie is in trouble, her life hanging in the balance. It all feels like a bad dream, one I can't wake up from.

I fumble for my cell phone as I race toward Strega's Hollow, my fingers hovering over the keypad. The most logical thing would be to alert the authorities that Maddie has been kidnapped, but can I really trust the Salem's Fall police? Everyone in this damn town either seems afraid of the Blackhollows or tangled up in their web.

But what other choice do I have? A bloodthirsty, dangerous cult has kidnapped my sister. I can't do this alone, and isn't this exactly what the police are supposed to handle? Protecting innocent people from monsters like the Veil?

I press the phone to my ear as the line rings, and a gruff voice answers on the other end.

"Salem's Fall Police Department, Officer Wickerson speaking."

I clear my throat. "This is James—James Woodsen. I met with Detective Harris a few days ago," I say, my words coming out in a jumbled rush. "I need to speak with him. It's an emergency."

"Sorry, Detective Harris isn't here," the officer replies, already sounding disinterested. "Something I can help you with?"

"Please, listen to me. I have to speak with Detective Harris," I say, my voice rising with desperation. "My sister's been kidnapped. She's at Strega's Hollow. The Blackhollows took her and, uh, a group called the Veil. They're planning to hurt her. They've done it before and—"

"Ma'am," he cuts in, clearly annoyed. "Is this some kind of Halloween prank?"

"No, it's not a prank! My sister's in real danger, and if you don't help her, she's going to die!"

The officer sighs audibly.

"Look, Miss, we get a lot of calls this time of year about spooky nonsense. Strega's Hollow is off-limits tonight, and any trespassers will be prosecuted to the full extent of the law," he says with frustrating calm, like he's reading from some kind of script. "Now I suggest you go home and celebrate Halloween like everyone else."

"No! Please, wait—!" I yell, but he's already hung up on me.

My hands shake with frustration as I clutch the phone to my chest. Clearly, the police aren't an option. My thoughts reel as I try to think about anyone else who might help, and then I remember my dad's voicemail from the prison.

Maybe he's not the man I always hoped he was, but still, he's my father. He's dealt with the Veil before. He could have advice for me.

I dial the prison and wait.

"Massachusetts Correctional Institution. How can I direct your call?"

"It's James Woodsen," I say, my voice strained. "I need to speak to my father, Thomas Woodsen."

"Sorry, Miss, no personal calls after three p.m. Try again tomorrow during regular hours."

"But it's an emergency!" I clutch the phone tighter, desperation clawing up my throat. "Please, I'm begging you. It's life or death!"

There's silence, a beat too long, and then, "Hold on. I'll see what I can do."

I press my lips together, listening to the dead air for what feels like forever, and then I hear his voice.

"James?"

"Daddy," I say, the ache in my chest making my voice crack.

"James, listen to me," he says, his voice filled with urgency. "You shouldn't be anywhere near Salem's Fall tonight. I've been digging in more, researching things from over here. There's something about today… about Halloween. It's too dangerous—"

"Yes, I know, it's called Veil Night. But, Dad, I can't leave." I blink back the tears burning at the edges of my eyes. "It's Maddie… she's been taken. The Veil is going to sacrifice her!"

There's a sharp intake of breath on the other end.

"They have Madison? *Oh God, no…*" His voice trembles, guilt spilling through every word. "This is all my fault. If only I hadn't—"

"Dad, stop!" I shout, fighting to keep my emotions under control. "That's in the past. I need you right now. Please, there's got to be something you can tell me that'll help. We have to get her back!"

I can almost feel him through the phone, struggling with his own thoughts.

"One thing I know, don't trust anyone connected to the Veil. They'll do anything to keep their secrets. It doesn't matter what they tell you, not even if you think they're on your side," he says, his voice raw. "Not even Damien Blackhollow—especially not him."

"I figured that part out already, trust me," I say through gritted teeth.

"There's more," he says, his tone shifting, uncertain, like he's working through something in real time. "There's something I missed about these rituals. A piece I still don't understand…"

The line falls silent again, and I can almost hear his mind working. My dad's always been good at puzzles, at piecing things together. It's why he excelled at his IT job—finding hidden patterns, spotting errors in the code.

"The ritual… the knife wouldn't take my life, but why did it take your mother? We were both willing to die for our family. So why her, not me?" His breath shakes as he swallows hard. "I missed something, James. There must be more to the ritual. Something we don't yet know." He pauses. "If they have Madison, it's for a reason. But I don't think it's for what you fear. I don't think it's Madison they're truly after…"

A static-like tension hums between us.

"I'm so sorry. I wish I was there with you—that I could do more." His breath shudders through the line, his voice cracking. I can feel his guilt like a weight in the air between us. "If I could take it all back, I would. I'm a terrible father, but please know, I only ever wanted what was best for our family."

"Dad"—my voice shakes—"I forgive you, okay? I need you to know that."

"I don't deserve it, but thank you, James," he says. "I love you."

The call ends, leaving only silence and the cold weight of our conversation settling over me. A chill snakes down my spine as I put the car in park and look up.

I've arrived at Strega's Hollow.

CHAPTER 25

Strega's Hollow looms ahead, ancient and ominous. Skeletal trees claw at the sky like twisted hands, and shadows stretch across the mist-cloaked ground. The air feels thicker here, charged with a malevolent energy that prickles across my skin.

The once-popular tourist attraction is deserted. Even the chilly fall breeze has stilled, and with it, any sense of normalcy. It feels like the Hollow is holding its breath, like I've stepped into another universe where dark things lurk in the shadows, waiting to consume anyone foolish enough to enter. A shiver of apprehension runs through me, but I can't turn back now. Not when Maddie's running out of time.

My fingers tremble as I pull out my phone, sending a final message to the two people who will take it the hardest if I don't make it out of this.

To Quinn, I write:

> I don't know if I'll make it through tonight. Please, if anything happens to me, make them PAY. And know I care about you too. So much.

And to Katie, a softer message:

> I love you, Katie. If I don't make it back to Boston and Maddie does, please be there for her and Lucky too. Take care of them for me.

I stare at the words, at the simplicity and finality of them. Then, with a last, resolute breath, I slip the phone into my pocket.

"Okay, Maddie," I whisper. "I'm coming for you."

My breath hitches as I approach the locked gates. They look impossibly high, but I have no other choice to get inside the Hollow, so I grab hold of the cold iron and drag myself up. The metal scrapes against my palms as I go higher, and my legs tremble with the effort. By the time I get all the way to the top, every muscle in my body aches. I swing one leg over, my pants catching on the edge, tearing as I scramble down to the other side, and then land with a rough thud on the damp earth.

Ahead of me now lies the main building, looming against the black night sky. There's no moonlight, just a strange, oppressive darkness that feels like it's sinking into me. Though I've been here before, the place feels completely foreign at night. Any charm the Hollow had in the daytime is gone, replaced by an ominous and chilling emptiness.

I have no idea where to look for Maddie. She could be anywhere, in one of the buildings on the property or somewhere outdoors on the massive grounds within the gates. I use the flashlight of my phone and try to find my bearings, thinking back to the layout from when I visited weeks ago. But now every corner seems warped, like it's been rearranged just to throw me off.

With each step, my heartbeat quickens, thudding in my chest. My hands tremble as I push through overgrown bushes, looking for signs of Maddie or the Veil and Damien. It hits me then how utterly alone I am; I have no idea what I'm doing and no one to turn to or guide me. Not even Lucky is with me now. It's all on me.

Somehow, I find my way back to the stone slab from the tour weeks ago. *The sacrifice slab.* It looks just like I remembered. There's no Maddie tied to it about to be sacrificed or anything like that. There's no one around at all.

But then, a faint sound reaches my ears. It's a low, rhythmic chanting that drifts toward me as if through the trees themselves. Dread curls in my gut as I follow the noise, moving away from the stone slab toward the dense underbrush a few yards away. The chanting grows louder with each step I take, a deep murmur rising up from somewhere beneath the earth.

It doesn't sound like any language I know. Latin maybe? Or something even older, something twisted and primordial. It has an almost hypnotic, magical feeling to it. It pulls me toward an old, gnarled tree, bigger than all the rest. There, half-hidden by tangled roots and dirt, I spot a small, rusted door set into the ground.

I kneel down, my fingers brushing against the corroded metal to clear away debris until I notice the symbols etched into its surface, faint but unmistakable. Symbols like the ones in Mark's notes and the books in Hargrove's shop. Like the ones at Damien's fiancée's murder scene and the ones at my mother's. Symbols that speak of blood and sacrifice.

The Mark of the Veil.

Taking a deep breath, I grab hold of the handle and tug upward. The door swings open, releasing a gust of cold, stale air from below. My stomach tightens as I peer down into the darkness, a set of stone steps descending into shadows.

I hesitate, the weight of the moment crashing over me. I'm about to step into something ancient and terrible, something no amount of preparation could ever make me ready for. Once I cross this threshold, there's no turning back. But if

Maddie is down there—if she needs me—hesitation isn't an option.

I take my first step, the chill of the stone seeping into my bones. The chanting swells as I descend, wrapping around me, vibrating in my chest. Each step pulls me further from safety, deeper into the earth's dark heart.

Eventually, the stairs give way to a narrow corridor lined with rough stone walls. Torches are mounted along the sides, their flames flickering, casting shadows that dance and twist along the passage. The air here is thick and damp, tinged with the faint metallic scent of blood. I fight against every instinct in my body that begs me to turn back, to run.

At the end of the corridor, I finally glimpse it—a large chamber, the glow of more torchlight spilling out from within. I press myself against the wall, inching forward until I can peer inside.

Hooded figures are everywhere, wearing that creepy, expressionless mask I've come to know—the Veil Ritual Mask. There must be dozens of them in their floor-length black robes, all chanting in that same haunting language. They stand arranged in a wide circle around an altar at the center of the room, surrounded by blood-red candles. Carved into the floor beneath the altar are more symbols. Some I recognize, like the Mark of the Veil, but many others I don't. The markings glow with a strange phosphorescence, writhing in the flickering light, almost as if they're alive. And then, at the very foot of the altar, bound and gagged, is my sister.

Anger flares hot and fierce as I take in the sight of her. Maddie stands barefoot in a long white shift dress I've never seen before, her hair tangled, mascara streaking down her cheeks. Her wide, terrified eyes dart between the masked figures moving around the room, her body trembling. Beside her, at the head of the altar, is Lucien. Hood down, mask off, his presence as commanding and chilling as ever. His hand settles on Maddie's shoulder, a gesture that's almost casual—almost possessive. And then, from the shadows, Damien emerges.

He looks different somehow, taller and more imposing, his face illuminated by the torchlight. His features are sharper, eyes dark and intense, filled with a strange energy that makes him seem almost otherworldly. In his hand is a ritual knife—the same kind used in the Veil's sacrifices—its silver blade gleaming, sharp and deadly. Despite everything I've learned about him, I've never truly been afraid of Damien before—until now.

He begins to speak in that strange, guttural language, his voice low and resonant, curling through the chamber like a dark melody. The words are foreign, incomprehensible, but the urgency in his tone is unmistakable. All around him, the hooded figures lift their voices to join him, their chanting rising in a fevered pitch.

Every muscle in my body tenses as he approaches the altar, his gaze fixed on Maddie as he raises the knife. A wave of terror crashes over me, suffocating, paralyzing. I can't believe this is happening. He's really going to do it. He's really going to kill my sister!

Without any thought for my own safety, I step out from my hiding place.

"Let her go, Damien!" I scream, my voice ripping through the chanting like a gunshot.

The room plunges into shocked silence as every head turns toward me, every pair of eyes locking onto me. Damien freezes, his gaze snapping to mine, his expression flickering with something I can't read. Shock, maybe? Anger, definitely. But there's something else there, something raw and vulnerable that I hadn't expected to see—panic.

"What the hell are you doing here?" His voice shakes with fury, but there's a tremor beneath it.

"What am *I* doing?" I can feel the weight of the hooded figures' eyes on me, dozens of dark shapes watching my every move, but I refuse to look at them. All my focus is on Damien. "What are *you* doing? You have my sister tied to a fucking altar! You're going to kill her, Damien!"

"You fool!" His jaw tightens, gaze flickering with something I can't quite place. "You don't understand—"

"Silence, Blackhollow!" One of the Veil members leaves the circle, approaching Damien. Tall and broad-shouldered, definitely male, but with his hood and mask covering his face, I can't make any details out. "Remember your oath."

"I'll do whatever I damn well please!" Damien raises his knife and the man quickly shrinks away. Then he turns back to me. "I would never hurt your sister. This was never about her."

"But you need a sacrifice!" I can barely keep my voice steady, the fury and betrayal boiling over. "Stop lying to me. I know all about the Ascension."

"The Veil demands a sacrifice, yes, but it's not Maddie they want." His voice is rough, strained as he turns his dark, pained eyes on me.

"What are you talking about…"

"Hell, James! Why couldn't you have just trusted me?" Damien's expression tightens and something flickers across his face dangerously close to despair. "They brought your sister here to lure you out. I was keeping you safe," he says, his voice rough, almost bitter. "You had to come here tonight of your own volition; those are the rules. She was the trap—and you walked right into it!"

The words hit me like a punch. My breath stutters and I stumble back, struggling to stay upright as it all comes together.

"You knew they were after me all along, and you didn't say anything?" My voice trembles. "How could you—"

"I wasn't *allowed* to tell you! I did everything I could to stop this. I didn't bring your sister here, and I sure as hell didn't bring you!" His gaze shifts, his expression hardening into cold, sharp fury as he whirls on his brother. "How did she get out of Blackthorn Manor, Lucien? That place was sealed up tighter than Fort Knox."

Lucien's smirk is infuriatingly calm. "I may have laid some bait, something about her poor little sister needing saving. Left a car and some keys." He shrugs. "A little nudge in the right direction, brother. That's all it took." He pauses, eyes gleaming with satisfaction. "She's a bit of a hellion, if you hadn't noticed. Or is that what you like best about her?"

"You sick bastard!" Damien growls. He lunges for Lucien, but several of the Veil members step in, holding him back. "This was your plan all along, wasn't it?"

"Perhaps." Lucien looks unfazed. "But I've only done what you couldn't. I've ensured that the ritual will be completed, and the Blackhollow family will maintain its leadership of the Veil." He turns to me, a twisted smile stretching across his face. "Sorry, it's nothing personal. You're just the key to unlocking the prize."

My stomach churns as I glance between the two brothers. "I still don't understand. If it's me you're after, why is Maddie here?"

Lucien chuckles darkly, clearly savoring every second of this. "It's not just about killing the Tether. The sacrifice must be voluntary," he says. "The ritual has always been about choice."

I stare at him, struggling to make sense of what he's saying. "But my father's ritual... both my parents were willing to die, so why didn't it work? The professor said there wasn't a Tether but—"

"Poor Daddy Dearest didn't understand the rules, did he?" Lucien tilts his head, mock sympathy in his expression. "Neither did that fool Hargrove, from what I hear." He snorts, stepping closer. "That's why they both failed. They didn't know what the knife demands. It's not just the Tether requirement; both ends of the sacrifice must be voluntary. Giving isn't enough. The ritual also requires someone to *take*."

A cold dread pools in my stomach. His words echo in my mind, and suddenly, I can't breathe.

"Your mother figured it out first," he continues. "Smart lady, apparently. Offered herself to save your family. But your father?" He clicks his tongue. "Whether he didn't understand or just couldn't bring himself to do it, he refused to take her life. And without that final act, the ritual stalled."

"But… my mom—she still died."

"Yes, I'm afraid she did," Lucien continues. "The ritual should have fallen apart, but the knife… well… it doesn't like unfinished business. So it took her instead—like it took Hargrove when his ritual failed."

I step back in horror, wetness forming in the corners of my eyes as Maddie begins crying hysterically, her sobs tearing through the gag. A hollow ache spreads through my body.

My mother… she chose to die for us, but her death was meaningless. An incomplete sacrifice. A senseless, empty tragedy.

I squeeze my eyes shut, fists clenched at my sides. It was all for nothing.

"Enough with the story time," a masked Veil member grumbles from the far side of the circle. "Let's get on with this already. I'm going to be late for my wife's Halloween party."

Another man sighs impatiently, nodding his hooded head. "Yes, finish the ritual and let's go, Blackhollow," he snaps, like my impending doom is just some trivial matter standing in the way of their evening plans.

I want to kill him.

I want to *kill* them all.

"Silence!" Damien shouts, moving closer, blocking me from the masked men. He turns to me, his expression pained. He looks almost as broken as I feel. "I was trying to keep you away from all this, to make sure you'd never have to face this choice."

Lucien laughs, a sharp, mocking sound that echoes throughout the chamber.

"My little brother. Always so noble," he says before turning to me, a cruel glint in his eyes. "It's a simple decision you have to make, Miss Woodsen. You willingly give your life for your sister's—let Damien sacrifice you—and he ascends to lead the Veil. Or you walk away, and the knife takes your sister instead." He sighs. "The latter is a bit of a waste, if you ask me. Someone still dies; it just means no throne for poor Damien. Either way, the Veil will get a life tonight."

Maddie shakes her head, tears streaking her face. "James!" she cries, her words muffled through the gag. "No!"

Terror runs through me as I look down at my little sister, bound like a sacrificial lamb at the altar. It feels as if my heart is breaking in two.

I turn back to Damien, trembling. "You're really going to let this happen? You're going to let one of us die?"

"To be fair, my brother doesn't have a choice. You saw to that when you showed up here on Veil Night," Lucien says, advancing on me, his voice a mocking whisper. His smile widens as he gestures to my sister. "It's your call, Miss Woodsen. So what's it going to be?"

I clench my hands together to try and stop my body's shaking as I reach for Maddie. I gently stroke her cheek, wiping away her tears. There is no choice. I know what I have to do.

My whole life, I thought ambition made me worthy. That if I chased power hard enough, I'd finally matter. That winning was the only way to survive. But now I see it clearly—

Love is what makes me whole.

Love is what makes me brave enough to do what needs to be done.

"It's going to be okay, Maddie," I say softly and lean over to kiss her cheek. "You're going to be just fine." Then I turn to Lucien, and I'm proud how my voice comes out steady and firm, despite the fear clawing at me. "I'll do it. I'll give my life for hers."

A choked sob escapes Maddie's throat, muffled by the gag, but the terror in her eyes says everything. She thrashes against her restraints, shaking her head so hard it looks like she might snap something. I see her mouth form one desperate word over and over—

No. No. No.

"Excellent." Lucien's eyes gleam with triumph. "Let's begin, shall we?"

He gestures to a few of the Veil members, and they come forward. One of the impatient men, the one complaining about his spoiled party plans for the evening, grabs my hands roughly and jerks them behind my back. I grimace as pain shoots up my arms, but do my best to ignore it.

What does a little pain matter now anyway? Not when I know what's about to happen next.

Instead, I look over at my sister and lock eyes with her, trying to pour every ounce of strength and love I have left into that gaze. Her shoulders shake with silent sobs, her whole body trembling in fear.

"I love you, Mads," I whisper, my voice breaking. "More than anything in this world." I lean in and press a kiss to her cheek, lingering there for a heartbeat. "You're going to have a long, beautiful, amazing life. You're going to do everything we ever dreamed of," I promise, even as my throat tightens. "The hardest thing isn't dying. It's living—and you're going to have to do it for the both of us now."

"How touching," Lucien murmurs. "Beautiful, really."

"Just get this over with." I glare at him as he takes his place beside me at the altar.

"Stop! Get away from her," Damien growls, his voice cutting through the madness. His face is twisted with a mix of rage and desperation as he grabs me from the man holding my arms and pulls me into his side. "No one touches her."

A few Veil members move forward to stop Damien, but he shoves them all away with a strength that almost seems supernatural.

Lucien's face fills with shock as he turns to his brother. "You don't mean to—"

"I'll do it," Damien says, his voice grim but determined. "I'll take her place."

CHAPTER 26

A stunned murmur ripples through the masked Veil members, the sound echoing off the stone walls as Damien's declaration hangs in the air. Some of them shift uneasily, others stiffen. My mind reels, struggling to process what he just said. Take my place? What is he talking about?

What the hell does that mean?

A sharp, clipped voice breaks through the noise. "No!" one of the men hisses. "You can't!"

Another man surges out of the circle, his voice filled with barely restrained anger. "This isn't how it works, Blackhollow. The ritual requires her!"

Lucien holds up a hand, silencing the men. "Relax, gentlemen. We should let my dear brother make his foolish little choice," he says, an ecstatic gleam in his eyes. "And you understand the consequences? You'd renounce your ascension and stop the last sacrifice… for her?"

Damien's gaze softens as he looks at me, his face resolute.

"I would."

A low muttering rises up all around me from the Veil members, one that builds into a rolling, taunting laughter.

"Wait, what?" I stammer, barely able to comprehend what's happening, still half-expecting to wake up from this nightmare I've somehow gotten trapped in. "You can do that? Give up your place as Veil leader?"

"Not just Veil leader, sweetheart," Lucien says. "I'm afraid the rules also call for him to forfeit his life." His look is mocking, triumphant, the kind of expression a predator wears when its prey finally surrenders. He's savoring this, every twisted second of Damien's downfall.

Shock, then horror, runs through me.

"Damien, no…"

"I have to. It's the only way to keep you and your sister safe," he says, his eyes locked on mine, as if we're the only two people in this horrible place.

My heart pounds in my chest, a frantic, raw beat. I can't believe what he's saying. Damien is planning to die for me? To give up everything, even his very life, for mine?

Lucien laughs, low and vicious, his satisfaction barely restrained. "Well, isn't this touching?" he drawls, his face lit with cruel delight. "The heir to the Blackhollow family, sacrificing everything for a girl. Really, Damien, I didn't think you had it in you."

My hands curl into fists at my sides as I stare at Lucien, horror and fury twisting inside me. "You planned this! You set him up, using us as bait so you could force him into this!"

Lucien's eyes narrow slightly. "Let's not pretend my brother is some tragic hero," he says in that infuriatingly detached, uncaring voice. "Until you came along, Damien had no problem fulfilling the necessary rituals of the Veil, trust me. If he's no longer strong enough to do what needs to be done, then that's on him."

"Call me weak if you want, brother, but I'll do whatever it takes to save her," Damien says, a silent fury emanating from him as he locks eyes with Lucien. His fists clench, voice low and steady. "And if giving up everything is what it takes, then I'll do it."

Lucien scoffs, shaking his head. "Always so melodramatic, aren't you? Right until the very end."

"Damien, you can't..." I say, my voice trembling. "There must be another way."

Damien's shoulders drop, a quiet acceptance settling over him. He gently squeezes my hand—brief, fleeting, like a silent apology.

"There isn't, I'm afraid," he says.

I shake my head at Lucien, my body burning with anger and disbelief. "Is this really what you want? You want your brother to *die*—just so you can take what he has?"

"He doesn't deserve to lead." Lucien's gaze flickers to Damien, his eyes loaded with disdain. "He's too willing to throw everything away. He lacks the ruthlessness, the vision. Look at how he'd rather die for you than claim his rightful place," he says. "Pathetic."

"Better to die for something than to live for nothing, like you, brother," Damien replies.

Restless murmurs ripple through the masked figures as they shift behind the brothers, exchanging impatient glances. "Finish the damn ritual," one growls. "We're running out of time."

Lucien waves them off with a flick of his wrist. "Patience, patience. You'll get your blood soon enough," he says to them. Something dark flashes in his eyes as he glares at his brother. "Don't pretend you're better than me. We both know you've done just as much, if not worse," he sneers. "Don't act like your hands are clean."

"I've *never* betrayed those I cared about."

"Oh, is that so?" Lucien's tone is mocking as he gestures to me. "If you truly cared to keep her safe, she never would've set foot in this place. But no—you let her get drawn in, knowing exactly what was at stake."

"That's not true." Damien's face tightens. "I tried to make

her leave, and when I couldn't, I protected her as best I could."

"You may tell yourself that, but we both know the truth." Lucien's laugh is a harsh, hollow sound. "She's here because you couldn't stay away. And now, dear brother, you're going to pay for all you've done."

Lucien steps closer to Damien, a manic intensity radiating from him. The tension between the brothers is so thick, it nearly chokes me.

All around us, the murmurs grow louder as members of the Veil exchange wary glances, watching intently, waiting to see which brother will emerge the victor in this battle for control. I realize then that this isn't just about Damien and Lucien; it's a turning point for the entire Veil.

"You're just like him, you know," Damien says, his eyes burning as he holds Lucien's gaze. "Father was a cold-hearted, manipulative bastard who would stop at nothing to get what he wanted. One day, it's going to be your undoing, like it was his."

"Oh, is that why you killed him?"

Lucien's words ripple through the underground chamber like a shockwave. A stir moves through the masked figures, uneasy and shifting as they glance at one another. A few take an instinctive step back from the circle, as if the very accusation taints the air.

Damien stiffens, eyes narrowing. "What are you talking about?"

"The pool, Damien. He *drowned!*" Lucien practically spits the word. "Water always was one of your strongest elements. That death had your mark all over it. You always wanted to be in charge, always been obsessed with ruling, just like him."

"You can't possibly think I killed our father." Damien's voice is sharp, but the flash of pain across his face—genuine, raw—makes my heart lurch. "He was an evil man, and he deserved to die, but that wasn't me. I never wanted his life." His jaw tightens, hands flexing at his sides. "No, if anyone was desperate enough to end his rule, it was you."

Lucien's expression darkens. "Don't lie to me!" he snaps, his voice laced with bitter resentment. "I know you killed him—and Vivienne too! You killed the one person I truly cared about in your rush to the top. She may have been promised to you, but I loved her, and now she's dead." His breathing turns uneven. "And Elise. And Carla, who practically raised us. You sacrificed them all!"

Damien's eyes widen. "*Me?* I thought you were the one who killed them."

"You never loved Viv, not like I did." Lucien lets out a short, humorless laugh. "To you, she was just a toy—a plaything."

"I didn't love her, that's true. But I didn't want her dead," Damien says, low and grim. "I didn't want any of them to die."

A tense silence stretches between them. For the first time, Lucien hesitates, and I see the raw vulnerability on his face, like he's trying to take this all in and process it. His shoulders slacken slightly, and for a moment—just a moment—I see something almost like regret. But then, just as quickly, it vanishes, his features smoothing into something cold, impenetrable.

"So what, then? You expect me to believe you're some innocent bystander?" His voice is laced with contempt. "That all this carnage just happened around you?"

"Yes! That's exactly what you should believe, because it's the truth!" Damien's dark brow furrows like a new thought is now occurring to him. "Lucien, take a minute here and *think*. There's something we're not seeing. Isn't it strange that these deaths line up so perfectly with the Ascension Ritual, yet neither of us admit to having a hand in them?"

The room falls deathly silent.

For the first time, I'm absolutely certain Damien had nothing to do with the murder of his fiancée or any of the other women. He's so close to death now, he has no reason to lie. But if it wasn't him, and if, for once, Lucien is telling the truth—a rare possibility, but not impossible—then who *is* responsible? Who is capable of something like this?

And why?

I look around the chamber at the masked men surrounding us. It has to be someone in the Veil, right? Someone here right now in the room?

Both Blackhollow brothers seem so powerful, more powerful than any person I've ever known, the idea that someone else may have been pulling the strings all along shakes me, leaving a cold, hollow feeling in my chest. If even the Blackhollows aren't in control, then who is?

"Nice try. You always find a way to twist things so you look like the noble one, the savior. But not this time." Lucien seizes the ritual knife from Damien but pauses, his gaze flicking to me. His eyes glitter with something dark and mad as he holds the blade out toward me. "Why don't you do the honors, Miss Woodsen? You'd be doing everyone here a favor."

The room spins, and for a second, I can't breathe.

"What? No!"

"You've been craving power your whole life, haven't you? The prestige, the ambition, the opportunity to become someone important." He places the knife in my hand. "Well, here's your opportunity—join me."

"Join you?" I ask, not sure I understand. "You mean become part of the Veil?"

"Why not?" he asks, gripping my wrist and angling it toward Damien's chest. "All you have to do is make the right choice."

Maddie shakes her head beside me, a muffled cry slipping

through her gag. "No!" she manages, her voice hoarse with horror. *"James, don't!"*

"Enough," the Veil member closest to Maddie snaps, tightening the ropes with a sharp pull.

I'm fully aware this is more of Lucien's twisted game, to turn me into something monstrous, just like him. And yet, as I stare at the knife, my fingers gripping tighter around its handle, I can't help but wonder what it might feel like to use it.

An image flashes in my head, and for a moment, I can see the life I've always dreamed of. Success. Power. I would no longer need to prove myself to Quinn. To the firm. I would never have to prove myself to anyone ever again. I can have a life without want. Without fear. Everything I've ever dreamed of is within my grasp.

I know it's wrong to think like this, but isn't Damien a lost cause anyway? Even if it's not by my hand, won't Lucien or the Veil take him? Or the knife even?

The image of Professor Hargrove ripping the blade through his chest, killing himself against his own will, comes back to me in a horrible rush. The knife must have its victim, right? If this is all inevitable, why not take what's mine?

Why let it all go to waste?

"He's right," Damien says quietly, a heaviness in his voice. "Do it. It's what you want."

Our eyes meet, and I see Damien's quiet strength, the way he's willing to give up everything in order to keep me safe, to give me what I want in life. He would sacrifice everything for me, let me kill him, and take all that the Veil offers.

But all the power in the world is worth nothing if I have to lose my humanity to achieve it.

"No, Lucien," I say, my voice shaky but resolute. "I won't become a monster like you just to satisfy my ambition."

Lucien's smile falters. "Shame," he says, a flicker of something almost like surprise—or maybe grudging respect—

passing over his face before it hardens back into that mask of cold resolve. "You had such promise."

A cruel smile twists his lips as he rips the knife from me and lifts the blade, turning to face the rest of the Veil. A ripple of excitement moves through the room as several members step forward, lifting their hands toward Lucien in silent reverence. The others begin to sway in unison, their chanting beginning again, louder, more feverish. The sound vibrates through the cold stone walls, echoing through the chamber. Even if I still can't understand the language, I'm certain of the purpose now.

They're death chants.

A select few men step forward, lighting red candles on the altar. The flames flicker oddly at first, as if resisting, shadows rippling over Lucien's face, carving it into something terrifying. With each new candle lit, the energy in the room thickens, coiling like a snake ready to strike. Lucien raises his hands, and the chanting softens, falling to a near whisper as his voice rises, powerful and commanding.

"To the East," he says, his voice reverberating off the stone walls, "I call upon the Watchtower of Air. Bring forth your winds, your clarity, your vision."

A gust of wind sweeps through the chamber, icy and piercing. It cuts right through me, chilling me to the bone as I feel it coil around my limbs like invisible chains.

Lucien pivots to face the other direction. He lifts his arms higher, his voice deepening. "To the West, I call upon the Watchtower of Water. Bring forth your wisdom, your healing, your depths."

A dampness fills the chamber, and from the corners of the stone ceiling, water begins to drip, darkening the ground in small, growing puddles. The smell of earth and wet stone fills my lungs. It feels as though I'm underwater for an instant, drowning in the weight of whatever dark forces Lucien is unleashing.

"To the North," he continues. "I call upon the Watchtower of Earth. Bring forth your strength, your endurance, your guardianship."

A rumble echoes beneath my feet, a deep, pulsing tremor like an earthquake, that makes the ground shift and crack beneath us. Dust rains down from the ceiling as the stone floor quivers, the walls seeming to close in, more solid and impenetrable than ever.

Lucien closes his eyes, and a note of finality enters his voice. "To the South, I call upon the Watchtower of Fire. Bring forth your fury, your courage, your transformation," he says and the temperature in the chamber spikes, a sudden, oppressive heat filling the air. Sweat beads along my brow, a suffocating heat pressing down on us, as though the walls themselves have caught fire.

Lucien turns back toward the altar, his eyes gleaming. One by one, each blood-red candle flares up almost to the ceiling, a violent burst of light that seems to reach for something unseen.

I blink, struggling to adjust to the dim red glow that now fills the room. The Veil members hardly flinch, keeping their focus on the ritual, but their faces are tense, eyes darting as the atmosphere tightens with an eerie tension.

"Bring forth the sacrifice," Lucien orders.

Two masked men step forward from the shadows and grip Damien by the shoulders, dragging him toward the center of the altar. He doesn't resist, but there's a defiance in his gaze as he locks eyes with me. The calm resolve in his face sends a wave of nausea through me. He's accepted this, accepted his death, all for me.

His eyes don't leave mine. "If things were different... if we had more time..." he says softly, his voice barely audible over the chanting. "I would've given you the world."

I can't bear it. I bite my lip so hard I taste blood, my heart thudding while I reach for Maddie. She whimpers in my arms, and I watch, barely able to breathe, as the dark masked figures sway in unison, hands lifted toward the altar. The air fills with an unnatural energy that skates along my skin like a static charge.

Panic claws at me, wild and suffocating, as I watch Damien at the altar. He doesn't fight, doesn't struggle—he just lets them press him against the cold stone. The masked figures hold his arms tight at his sides as Lucien steps forward, eyes gleaming with triumph. Slowly, deliberately, he lifts the knife high, the polished blade catching the crimson candlelight.

"No—please!" I scream. *"Stop!"*

Lucien's gaze shifts to me, and I see an almost imperceptible smile playing at his lips.

Then, all at once, the flames erupt.

CHAPTER 27

The underground chamber plunges into chaos as the candles at the altar flare dangerously, flames shooting up in a torrent of fire like the wicks have been doused in gasoline. The heat is sudden, blistering. The entire place erupts into screams as the flames climb the walls and race along the floor, licking the stone like a ravenous creature unleashed, igniting robes and hoods of the masked Veil men standing all around me. All hell breaks loose as the men shove and trip over one another, desperate to escape the sudden blaze.

I watch in horror as one man behind me is engulfed in flames and stumbles forward, his hands clawing at his face, writhing in agony as the fire consumes him. He collapses to the ground, his screams echoing, piercing and guttural. Skin blackens then blisters under the relentless heat before he finally collapses in a smoldering heap, his body charred and lifeless. The acrid smell of burning flesh and fabric invades my senses, turning my stomach.

I pull Maddie close, shielding her from the sight, but I can't unsee it—the twisted, blackened remains of what was once a person.

Thick, acrid haze fills the air, burning my throat as I struggle to see through the frenzy. Amid the shifting smoke, I spot Lucien. His face is illuminated by the raging fire, twisted in something close to satisfaction. His arms lift dramatically, his voice booming as he calls for order, demanding the Veil members calm down, but the gleam in his eyes betrays him. He's reveling in this. He wanted this destruction.

And then, suddenly, he's beside me.

A flash of silver—a blade raised high above Maddie. Fear slams into me, sharp and paralyzing, and I cry out. For a terrible second, I think he's going to strike her down. But then, with a flick of his wrist, the knife slices through her bindings. He grabs me and shoves me roughly toward Damien.

"Get them out of here!" he orders his brother.

Damien hesitates, his brows furrowing. "But the knife—"

Lucien doesn't even pause. He seizes a masked man at random—one scrambling to escape the flames—and, with ruthless precision, plunges the blade straight into his heart. The man gasps, a wet, choked sound, eyes wide with shock. Lucien yanks the knife free and shoves the dying man into the fire.

"It's done." His voice is eerily calm as he drags the blade across the sole of his shoe, smearing away the blood in one deliberate stroke. "The Veil has its sacrifice. Now go."

I hesitate, disoriented, heart hammering, mind racing. This has to be a trick. Lucien doesn't save people. He doesn't do mercy. But Damien wastes no time. His arm hooks around my waist, anchoring me to his side.

"Thank you," he whispers to his brother.

For a fleeting moment, something shifts in Lucien's expression. A crack in his cold indifference, a flicker of something almost like regret. But it's gone in a breath, his mask snapping back into place. "Leave," he hisses, his words barely audible over the roar of the flames. "Before I change my mind."

Lucien waves us toward the shadowy doorway I entered earlier, his presence still crackling with danger, even as he grants us our escape.

Damien takes off, gripping my hand tightly as I reach back and pull Maddie with the other, her hand clammy and trembling in mine. We weave through the frantic crowd, dodging bodies as the fire blazes around us. Heat scorches my skin and I cough, eyes streaming, as we slip back into the cold, shadowy tunnel. Behind me, I can still hear Lucien barking commands, trying to control the madness, but his words are lost in the sea of screams.

The smell of earth and stone fills my lungs, blissfully replacing the choking smoke from the chamber. The dampness inside chills me to the bone, pressing in from all sides, amplifying every sound and every heartbeat that pounds against my ribs. Damien's hand tightens around mine, grounding me, steadying me in the dark, twisting tunnel. Maddie clings to me, her breathing fast and shallow beside me.

The tunnel stretches longer than I remember, each twist and turn identical to the last. A part of me fears we're only going deeper, that this endless maze will swallow us whole, but Damien's steps are confident, purposeful. I force myself to trust him and focus only on the warmth of his hand, on the rhythmic squeeze of his fingers. Finally, a faint sliver of light appears up ahead.

Damien quickens his pace, leading us through the narrow passage and into the cool night. I gasp, the fresh air filling my lungs in sharp relief as we emerge into a secluded clearing near the edge of Strega's Hollow. Nearby, a sleek black Lamborghini sports car waits by the fence line. Damien unlocks the doors with a flick of his wrist, gesturing for Maddie to take the back seat. She scrambles in, exhausted but alive, and I slide in next to her.

"I knew you'd come for me, Jamie!" She lets out a sob, shaking in my arms as Damien fires up the engine. "No matter how scared I got, I just… I knew it."

"I'll always come for you." I hold her tight against me. "It's going to be okay now, Mads. I promise."

Damien is silent as we speed through the gates and down the narrow, winding road. Trees blur. Every twist of the road tightens the grip of fear in my chest. I imagine each passing shadow is one of the Veil, still after us, unwilling to let us go free.

"Where are we going?" I glance at Damien, still trying to catch my breath.

"Blackthorn Manor," he says, his gaze focused on the road ahead as we weave through the darkened streets.

I stare at him, incredulous. He can't be serious.

"We need to get out of Salem's Fall," I say. "We have to get as far away as possible, somewhere they can never find us."

"Trust me." A hint of that familiar, infuriating cockiness returns in the curve of his mouth. "Blackthorn Manor's the safest place we can be right now."

"You keep asking me to trust you, but how am I supposed to do that when you're always hiding things from me?" I owe him my life—again—but that doesn't erase the fact that he's still keeping secrets.

"Not now," Damien says tightly.

"Now is the only time we have," I shoot back. "Because once we're there, who knows what you'll say—or hide—next." I fix my eyes on him. "I found Mark's access card at Blackthorn Manor. And Vivienne's missing engagement ring. Why do you have them?"

His jaw tightens. "You shouldn't be going through my things."

I let out a sharp laugh. "I wasn't snooping!" I snap. "I just—found them." My frustration boils over as I remember exactly where they were. He's the one who hid my things in the first place. And now he's mad at me? "They were right next to my cell phone and laptop. You know, the ones you took and hid from me?"

For a long moment, he says nothing. His grip on the wheel tightens, knuckles flexing, but his face remains maddeningly calm.

"James, I'm not always going to do things I can explain—or want to," he says. "Either you trust me and how I feel about you, or you don't."

I lean back, tension still thrumming beneath my skin. As frustrating as it is to be kept from the full truth, especially for someone like me, there's something in his tone—an unwavering certainty, a quiet force—that makes me second guess myself and my need to always know everything. Besides, haven't I learned my lesson tonight?

I almost died. Maddie too. And Damien... he threw himself into the fire—literally—for us. It was so close. Too close. If I'd just listened to him, none of this would've happened.

I know he's not innocent. There was the staged attack my first night in Salem's Fall. Not to mention the whole drugging-my-wine-at-dinner and Mark's stolen access card. After finding that card, I feel certain Damien knows far more about Mark's "accidental" death than he's let on. And there's Vivienne's missing ring too. And a thousand other unanswered questions, all adding up to something I'm not sure I really want to know.

But... I do believe Damien about one thing.

Whatever he's guilty of, it isn't killing the women he loves. And as twisted and morally gray as his actions have been, I know it was only meant to protect me.

The exhaustion of the night presses down on me, draining any remaining argument. Maybe, just this once, I don't have to fight him. If he says Blackthorn Manor is safe, perhaps I should listen. At the very least, it's safer than being out in the open.

As we pull onto the winding driveway of the compound and the towering gates close behind us, a strange sense of calm settles over me that I can't explain. There's an unspoken power surrounding this place, something ancient and steady that feels almost protective. It's like stepping into a protective bubble, sealed off from the chaos and fear that has chased us all night. For the first time this evening, my pulse slows, my breathing evening out as we near the main house.

And then, I spot Lucky.

He sits on the front doorsteps, his golden eyes catching the light as he watches us pull up. His black lips tilt up, almost like a smile.

A rush of emotion surges through me, warm and overwhelming, and I race over to the cat as soon as Damien puts the car in park. "Lucky!" I murmur, bending down to scoop him up into my arms.

He presses his furry little head against my chin, purring loudly, a steady vibration that seems to echo my own relief. It's as if he's been watching over me all along, guiding me to this very moment, and now—finally—he's returned to let me know I'm safe again. I hug him tighter, savoring the warmth of his small body against my chest.

Maddie slips out of the car behind me, her face pale and exhausted. Before she can say a word, Lucky jumps out of my arms and darts toward her, stopping just short of her feet. His tail flicks, ears flattening like he's debating whether or not he actually cares. But then, after a long pause, he lets out a soft, rumbling purr. Maddie lets loose a shaky laugh, blinking down at him in surprise before gathering him into her arms.

"Ugh, you little menace," she mutters, pressing her face into his fur. "I swear if I had died, you wouldn't even notice."

Lucky tolerates the affection for exactly three seconds before letting out an indignant meow and squirming free. He lands gracefully, giving her shin a single approving headbutt, then struts off like the whole thing never happened.

The butler from earlier—Edward—appears at the front door then, his expression calm and composed. It's almost jarring to see someone so serene after everything that's happened in the past few hours.

"If you'll follow me, Miss Madison, I'll escort you to your room," he says to my sister in that smooth, courteous tone, as if he's been expecting her.

Who knows, maybe he has?

This was probably Damien's plan from the start—to bring Maddie home safe and sound tonight. If only I hadn't shown up and ruined everything.

Maddie hesitates, glancing at me, searching my face for reassurance that it's okay to go inside the house with this strange new man. I step closer, brushing a few stray strands of hair from her face, my chest tightening at how small and fragile she looks.

"It's alright, Mads," I tell her. "We'll be safe here."

Her lower lip wobbles, and before I can react, she flings her arms around me, squeezing so tight, it knocks the breath out of me. "I was so afraid, Jamie," she says. "I thought—I thought I was gonna die."

I swallow hard, pressing a kiss to the top of her head. "Not a chance. You're stuck with me for the long haul, kiddo."

She sniffles, then pulls back just enough to look at me, her brows knitting together. "Are you okay? You're shaking."

"I'm fine. I was just really worried about you."

"I love you, big sis."

"Right back at ya," I murmur, a little choked up. "Now go get some rest, okay? I'll check on you soon."

"How about some fresh clothes and a nice warm meal, Miss Madison?" Edward asks Maddie, escorting her inside.

Maddie perks up with almost comical enthusiasm, like

someone just flipped a switch. "Do you have cheeseburgers here?" she asks brightly. "And fries! Oh, and a chocolate milkshake!"

A laugh bubbles out of me despite everything, warmth settling in my chest. Yep. That's my Maddie.

"Whatever you desire, Miss Madison." Edward's lips twitch like he's trying to hide a smile. He turns to my cat next, addressing him as if he's a human. "And we've got fresh salmon in today for Mr. Lucky as well."

Lucky darts to Edward's side, his tail flicking like he understands every word. And honestly, after everything I've seen these past few weeks, I wouldn't be surprised if he does.

I laugh as I watch my sister and my cat vanish into Blackthorn Manor, both following Edward and his promises of delicious food like he's the Pied Piper, and they're powerless to resist.

And then, it's just me and Damien.

He watches me with an intensity that sends a thrill down my spine. There's a softness in his eyes, something vulnerable and longing, that I haven't seen before.

"You know I meant what I said back there, right? That I'd die for you," he says, stepping closer, his gaze holding mine. "There's nothing I wouldn't do for you. I would've bled for you. Burned for you. Without you, I'm already dead."

He looks down, his composure cracking for just a moment. "Believe me, I know how that sounds. I know we haven't known each other that long, and I never thought I'd feel this way about someone so fast. But it's true."

His hand lingers on my cheek, warm and steady. Everything else fades. The Veil. The danger. The darkness lurking just beyond these walls. All I can feel is him, his presence wrapping around me like a promise, binding us in a way that feels deeper, older, than anything I've known.

His arms wrap around me, pulling me close, and for a split

second, we just hover there, caught in the space between hesitation and surrender. Then his lips find mine.

The first touch is soft, almost careful, but there's a fire beneath it—something restrained, aching, waiting. And then, all at once, the restraint snaps. His fingers tangle in my hair, his grip tightening around my waist as he deepens the kiss, pouring into it everything we've left unsaid. It's desperate and consuming, a kiss that feels like a confession, like an unraveling of everything we've been holding back for so long.

The world blurs at the edges, melting away into nothing. There is no danger, no Veil, no past, no future. Only this.

Only us.

When we finally break apart, my breath is uneven, my heart racing. His forehead rests against mine for a lingering moment, like he's grounding himself, like neither of us are quite ready to let go.

"Um, I should probably… lie down." I gulp, my legs wobbly, my brain all fuzzy from that kiss and struggling to catch up. "Maybe sleep. Like Maddie. That sounds… smart."

There's a heat in his eyes that makes me feel breathless.

"Sleep? No, I don't think so."

He takes my hand, leading me up the stairs and through the grand hallways, their twists and turns like a maze, until we reach a heavy door at the corridor's end. He turns the knob and steers me toward the threshold, but it's not the bedroom I stayed in when I was last here at Blackthorn Manor.

It's *his*.

A sharp, dizzying heat rushes through me as he ushers me inside, every nerve in my body on fire. The scent of cedar and woodsmoke lingers in the air, wrapping around me like something tangible, something inescapable.

The room is enormous, its sheer scale making me feel small. Tall, arched windows let in slivers of starlight, casting long silver shadows across the dark wood floors. Heavy bookcases line the walls, their shelves filled with worn leather volumes, artifacts, and things I can't quite make sense of in the dim glow. And at the center of it all—his bed.

It's the biggest bed I've ever seen, draped in dark, decadent fabrics that look soft enough to float away on. I turn to face him, my heart pounding. There's a vulnerability in his expression that makes my chest ache, a softness that I didn't think he was capable of. He reaches out, his fingers brushing my chin, tilting my face up to meet his gaze.

"You don't have to be afraid anymore, James," he whispers. "You're mine now. And I don't let anyone touch what's mine."

His mouth claims mine in another kiss, this one deep, possessive, and fierce—like he's branding me, sealing something unspoken and unbreakable between us. One hand fists in my hair, the other wrapping firmly around my waist as he draws me against him, bodies aligning like a puzzle only we can solve.

He walks me backward, slowly, deliberately, until the backs of my knees hit the edge of the bed. His mouth never leaves mine—hungry, reverent, like he's trying to memorize the taste of me. He lifts me without warning, his hands gripping the backs of my thighs as he hoists me up against him. I gasp, arms circling his shoulders, legs instinctively wrapping around his waist. His strength is effortless, commanding—and for one breathless second, I feel completely and utterly possessed.

Then he tosses me onto the bed, not rough, but with a dark sort of hunger, his body following mine a heartbeat later. His mouth finds mine again, deeper this time, and the weight of him above me steals every thought but one—him. All of him.

The world outside fades, swallowed by the shadows of Blackthorn Manor, until there is nothing left but him.

Us.

In this moment, I don't care if the Veil still lingers in the dark, waiting. I don't care what Lucien wants or what unfinished dangers may still hunt us. I don't even care about Damien's secrets, no matter how deep, how dark, how terrible they may be.

Because whatever comes next, whatever horrors still lie ahead, I know I won't be facing them alone anymore.

EPILOGUE

Boston, Massachusetts
December 1 (Eleven Months Until Halloween)

The quiet, comfortable hum inside the walls of Whitehall & Rowe feels almost surreal, the thick glass windows of the building holding back the roar of the Boston streets below like a barrier between the rest of the world and me. I never thought I'd be so relieved to be back in my office, the smell of old, dusty files and printer ink surrounding me. Outside, people are just beginning their Saturday mornings, walking dogs and going on coffee runs. I got in early today to get some work done, but I won't be staying late.

Not like I used to.

One thing I've realized these past few weeks is that there are other things more important than my career. Like friends. Like family. I've promised myself a night out on the town tonight and plan to meet Katie and Maddie for "girls' night" at Maddie's favorite restaurant. I don't feel guilty about it anymore, like I used to, or like I should be doing anything else with my time.

Lucky curls himself underneath my desk, his soft, rhythmic purring echoing in the quiet office. I smile and reach down to scratch him behind the ears. He's been super dramatic with separation anxiety ever since we got back from Salem's Fall. He's like my little shadow, following me around the house and even sneaking into my work bag in the hopes I'll take him to the office with me. Today, I gave in, knowing we'll be out of here well before any of the partners show up later.

The letter to the District Attorney I've been working on sits on my laptop screen, almost finished. My hand trembles as my fingers hover over the keys. It's a formal statement of "new evidence," presenting what we've uncovered in Damien's case, tying the Veil to the murder of Damien's fiancée, and clearing him of all charges. If all goes well, I'll be working on my father's appeal next, representing him pro bono to get him released from prison based on what I've uncovered about the Veil's illegal activities and involvement in my mother's death. Quinn and the firm have already given me their full blessing.

Each word I type feels charged. The weight of everything I've uncovered these past few weeks presses down on me like a layer of fog. It turns out that Damien and Lucien were both telling the truth. Neither of them had played a role in the prior sacrifices of Damien's fiancée or the other murdered women, nor were they responsible for the death of their father, Ian Blackhollow. It had been the Veil all along—at least, a small faction of it—pulling the strings. I'm optimistic that once the DA's office looks into things, they'll be able to put the pieces together and release Damien of all charges. He'll be a free man any day now.

Free, but not innocent.

I'm not a fool. I know it's entirely possible he has Mark's blood on his hands—in some manner—and who knows how many others I'll never know about. Then again, Damien never claimed to be a good man, just not a man that hurts the people he truly cares about. He's still dangerous. Possibly a killer, and who knows what else…

I know I should move on, but try as I might, my complicated feelings for Damien Blackhollow won't go away no matter how much distance I put between us. When I close my eyes, I can still see him. His face half-cast in shadows. His touch lingering like a ghost. The haunting way he looked at me when I told him I had to leave Salem's Fall and didn't know if I would—or could—ever see him again.

After our escape on Veil Night, Maddie, Lucky, and I stayed with Damien at Blackthorn Manor. At first, it was like a fantasy. I was surrounded by every luxury, with people catering to my every need, wrapped up in Damien's attention and protection.

But eventually, Lucien returned. Late at night, I would hear the brothers whispering their secret plans to one another. Lucien was now the rightful leader of the Veil, and Damien would be pardoned and able to rejoin again, if he wanted to. Lucien sought revenge on the Veil members responsible for all the recent murders and claimed to want to take the Veil in a different direction—though I wasn't sure if that was a good thing or a bad thing. Lucien even promised my safety, and Maddie's too, swearing we'd be under his protection if we stayed at Blackthorn Manor.

My thoughts about Damien's brother are frustratingly complex, the lines between ally and enemy blurring whenever I think of Lucien. I didn't see it coming, that he would be the one to save us all. I still don't know how, but I'm certain he was the one that created the chaos that allowed us to escape Veil Night. I remember reading during my research that fire was one of the four elements sacred to the Veil, a calling to ancient sacrifices from Salem's Fall's darkest days, the days of witchcraft. Lucien must have used that link to fire to his advantage, I just don't know why or how.

Why would he risk everything for us?

Whatever his reasons, I wasn't sure we could trust him. I knew it was time for Maddie and me to leave Salem's Fall.

Besides, Maddie and I had to get back to our real lives. Even if Damien—and Lucien, *if* he was to be believed—were willing to protect us from the Veil, they still had their hands full with their own problems without worrying about us. Damien was still a Blackhollow. Still about to become a Veil member again. Even if I could somehow figure out how to safely be with a man like him, I didn't know if it was fair to expose Maddie to that world. Whatever world it really was…

I still don't know what was real and what wasn't. I don't trust the things I'd seen with my own eyes—supernatural things that should never be possible, like a knife claiming lives, and fires starting spontaneously with the sweep of one's hand. I've tried to convince myself it was all a figment of my imagination, and for the most part, I've succeeded. The mind has a way of erasing, of washing out the horror and the unbelievable, turning it into logical fragments so they're easier to live with.

Damien didn't take my leaving Blackthorn Manor well, but he let us go, reluctantly promising to give me space. Since then, he's vanished without a word. Even though it's what I asked for, I'm not sure how I feel about it. Perhaps what we had was always meant to stay hidden in Salem's Fall.

A text alert jolts me back to reality.

> See you at six! Can't wait—and DO NOT be late!

Maddie's message flashes across the screen, and warmth blooms through me.

> P.S. And yes, I'm wearing a dress. No, I'm not bringing a coat. Fashion over function, Jamie!

I muffle a laugh and shake my head, already picturing my sister shivering in one of her tiny little outfits in the December cold. All the while insisting she's fine, before somehow talking me into giving her my coat. I type out a reply with a blue freezing-face emoji:

> At least wear tights, you terror. 🥶

Another beep.

> P.P.S. Ew! No, grandma!

I grin as my screen floods with an over-the-top avalanche of snowflake emojis. Classic Maddie. Some things never change.

With a smile still lingering on my lips, I turn back to my computer screen and my DA letter. The firm is thrilled with how things have turned out and are eager to have a win this huge in their column. Damien's exoneration will make every paper in the metro area, maybe even the nation. And thanks to Quinn's high praise, I'm also back in good standing. The partners are already talking about putting my name up on the senior associate board for next year.

I'm genuinely appreciative, but there's a dullness in the excitement that would have once been bright and all-consuming. An emptiness I can't shake. I don't know if it's from everything I've seen or if I've simply changed too much, but my job is no longer the end all be all it once was.

I still haven't decided about Quinn either.

Since I've returned to Boston, he's made it very clear that he's willing to do whatever it takes to be with me, even leave the firm. Quinn is everything I should want. He's stable, smart, handsome, and wealthy by anyone's standards. I try to focus on how wonderful he is, on how much he's been there for me. Quinn could be the one who makes everything right, who pulls me back from the shadows I've waded through.

It's *almost* perfect.

A few moments later, I finish my letter. It's succinct, each word sharp and clear. After I attach it to an email and hit send, I check my inbox and find a new case assignment is already waiting for me. A pang of doubt gnaws at the edges of my mind.

Is this really what I want? To bury myself in cases, in wins, climbing the corporate ladder, all while pretending the past month didn't happen? Can I truly be happy going back to the promise of a "normal life" and a future with someone like Quinn, perfect as he may be? It's what I always thought I wanted, yet here I am, feeling like a stranger in my own office with the realization that maybe I don't want this after all.

But then... *what* do I want?

I'm still thinking about it all as I step outside my apartment building later that evening and onto the busy Boston streets to meet Maddie and Katie for dinner. The crisp December air hits me, carrying the unmistakable scents of roasted chestnuts and pine needles and the faintest hint of cinnamon from a nearby café.

The holidays are in full bloom now, the entire city sparkling as if it's been dusted in stardust. No more pumpkins and spooky decorations. They've all been replaced by garlands strung across shop windows and twinkling lights winding up lampposts. The street ahead is lined with Christmas trees decorated with colorful ornaments. Couples stroll by hand in hand, bundled up in scarves and wool hats, their laughter and warmth adding to the holiday buzz. Halloween's darkness is long gone, replaced by the promises of a new season.

As I walk, my fingers absently find the locket now at my neck—my mother's. I'd searched for it for years, heartbroken when it disappeared not long after she died. I thought it was gone forever.

Then, the day I returned from Salem's Fall, it turned up—tucked behind an old velvet tray in my jewelry box, half-buried beneath a brooch I haven't worn in forever. I must've somehow missed it before. I've been wearing it ever since.

The holiday lights around me flicker—green, then red. A red just a little too deep, too sharp. Almost like a warning. Something on the back of the locket glints, and an engraving I swear wasn't there before catches my eye.

Forever Tethered.

I pause, heart skipping once. There's a part of me that wants to believe it's from her—a message I never saw, never needed until now. A quiet reminder that I'm not alone. That I never was. That I'm always tied to my mother, even if she's no longer physically here.

But another part of me knows better. The words don't feel like hers. And the locket… maybe it didn't just come back on its own.

I let my fingers fall from the cool metal, suddenly aware of the way the air has shifted around me, subtly at first, then more insistently. It's a prickling awareness that slides down the back of my neck. I pause, glancing over my shoulder. The light around me flickers again—and then I see him.

Damien.

He stands across the street, half-hidden in the shadows, a ghost of a smile playing at his lips. For a moment, I can't move, caught in the intensity of his gaze. He's as gorgeous and impossibly magnetic as ever, his presence charging the air around me like an approaching storm.

A gust of wind sweeps through me, cold and unnatural, and I pull my winter coat tighter. The Christmas lights on the nearby trees pulse, as though they're bending under his influence as he walks toward me. Every step is measured. Powerful. Smooth as a panther stalking his prey.

I find myself rooted to the spot as Damien stops directly in front of me. His eyes scan my face. The knowing smile that curves his lips is both thrilling and unnerving, a reminder that no matter how far I go, how much I try to convince myself I'm better off without him, he's always there, woven into my life in ways I can't escape.

"Hello, Counselor," he says, his voice low, as if meant only for me.

My breath catches, heart hammering. "What are you doing here?"

He doesn't answer right away, just tilts his head, watching me with that calm intensity that makes me feel like I'm the only person in his world.

"You didn't really think I'd stay away for long, did you?" His eyes glint with amusement. "Someone has to make sure you're staying out of trouble."

"I'm safe now. You don't have to worry about me," I say, glancing around, hyper-aware of the holiday cheer surrounding us. It feels so at odds with his presence, the quiet threat he and the Veil bring just by existing.

He edges closer. "You think it's all over because you left Salem's Fall? You're smarter than that, James."

The holiday lights overhead cast his features in strange patterns, like he's shifting between two realities—the wealthy, respectable businessman most of the world knows and the other Damien, someone darker, someone still dangerous.

"I left Blackthorn Manor to get space." I swallow hard. "I need you to respect that."

His gaze is searing, as if he knows exactly how torn I am.

"I *let* you leave Blackthorn Manor because I wanted you to see what life would be like without me." He leans in so close, I can feel his cool breath against my cheek. "But now that you've had some time, you have a choice to make. I'm not going to wait around forever."

My chest tightens, a war raging inside me. Damien's words settle over me, threading through every doubt, every unspoken desire I've tried to bury. He's giving me a choice, yes, but the weight of it feels crushing.

I think of the firm, of Quinn, of the life I fought so hard to protect. Quinn is the right choice. He's the *safe* choice—the one that means dinners at home, predictability, a life of certainty, a steady world not just for me, but for Maddie too.

I tell myself to make the smart decision, that I'm done with Salem's Fall, with rituals and secrets and shadows. Damien is a mirror, a reminder of my own thirst for power and ambition, my own relentless pull toward darkness. Choosing Damien would mean surrendering to a life of secrets and shadows.

"Damien, I'm sorry. I can't follow you into that world," I whisper, even if the pull I feel toward him is undeniable. Even if, deep down, something in my heart whispers that I'll never truly feel alive again without him by my side.

He searches my face, and I see the flicker of understanding in his eyes as I come to my decision. Then he nods, the barest movement, like he was expecting this answer.

"I know," he says. "I wouldn't have picked this life myself either if I'd been given the choice."

"You wouldn't?"

"No." A small, almost amused smile tugs at the corner of his mouth. "That's why I'm leaving it behind."

"You're *what?*" I stare at him, open-mouthed. "Damien… you're a Blackhollow. How can you leave?"

He steps closer, his voice quieter, intimate in a way that sends a shiver through me.

"I'll still run Blackhollow Industries, of course. But the Veil—Lucien can have it. He always wanted it more than I did. I only stayed because it was expected of me, it was my legacy. But you…" He shakes his head slightly, like I've somehow unraveled him. "You make me want something different. Something more. A new legacy." His fingers trail down my arm before catching my hand, his grip warm and grounding. "I don't want control. I don't want power. I just want *you*."

The wind howls around us, sending holiday lights swaying above. It feels like the world is shifting beneath my feet, like something ancient and immovable is finally breaking apart.

I should question this, make sure he's not lying again, not manipulating me. Because there's still so much I don't know. All the unanswered questions. All the gray and blurred lines between us. Can I really trust him?

But then I look up and see the way his eyes soften as he watches me. I feel the way his touch steadies me, and I realize none of it matters. I know one thing with absolute certainty. This. Us. It's undeniable.

His hand extends toward me, palm open, waiting.

"So, what's it going to be, Counselor?"

The lights around us flicker again, and the ground seems to hum beneath my feet. For a split second, I see a shadow move in the reflection of his eyes—a glimpse of something otherworldly. But I blink again, and it's gone. With fingers trembling, I reach for him, knowing that this choice will change everything.

Then he kisses me.

It's not gentle. It's not careful. It's fierce and consuming, a collision of fire and frost. His grip tightens as if daring me to pull away, but I don't this time. I couldn't even if I wanted to.

The world disappears, lost to the press of his mouth, the heat of his body, the way he steals my breath and gives me his in return, sealing my fate to his.

Forever.

When we finally break apart, I'm dizzy, my heart pounding against his. The way he looks at me—like I belong to him, like I always have—makes it impossible to imagine ever walking away again. The city lights blur around us, but the shadows don't reach us anymore.

This time, we step into the light.

Together.

Want more of the dangerously powerful Blackhollow billionaire brothers? Find out what happens when Lucien Blackhollow—the coldhearted new ruler of the Veil—finally meets the one woman who can undo him. And she's the last person anyone saw coming...

Click here to read this exclusive bonus story!

Before Fall… there was Summer! Don't miss *SUMMER RENTAL*, the unputdownable bestselling book in the Dark Seasons Thriller Series.

Available now!

EXCERPT FROM SUMMER RENTAL

CHAPTER 1
DAY 1: Thursday—Three days before July Fourth

It isn't supposed to rain in paradise.

At least, that's what the sign said when we turned off the highway and onto the rickety, two-lane bridge moments ago. It was painted a bright tropical yellow and read, *"Palm Key Island: it's always sunny here!"* Naturally, the "i" was dotted with an orange.

As I watch the rain fall from my cramped middle seat in the back of the SUV—the absolute worst spot in the car, of course—I tell myself it's just one of those quick summer showers we get in Florida. It won't last long. They never do. But when we pull up to the driveway of our rental home for the weekend and the rain still hasn't stopped, I start to worry.

We all hop out of the car and I eye the dark, ominous clouds with growing concern. The five of us hold jackets and sweatshirts over our heads and rush to grab luggage from the cargo area of Cam and Val's brand-new Range Rover. It's just one of the lavish gifts the twins received from their parents at graduation a few weeks ago.

"Just a little rain, everybody," Cam says next to me, overly cheery as usual. She runs a hand through her dark sleek bob, pushing glossy hair off her face and behind pearl-studded ears. "It'll clear up any minute."

"You sure?" I ask, dodging raindrops.

"Yes, Riley. I'm sure," she says, laughing as she elbows me lightly in the ribs. She surveys the rental house with a pleased expression on her pretty face. "Look! It's perfect—just like I said it'd be!"

Other than the pesky drizzle, I have to admit she's right. It looks way better than I expected. For starters, the two-story house is much larger in person than it was in the photos. Elegant and charming, it even has a big wraparound veranda and two dreamy, towering columns that make it seem like something off the cover of a romance novel. A row of palm trees on either side of us catches the late afternoon breeze, green leafy fronds gently blowing back and forth. The unmistakable salty scent of the ocean wafts in my direction.

When Cam first told me about the summer rental, I'd been suspicious. We were still dressed in our orange and blue Bishop Lake Preparatory High School graduation gowns when she pulled out the rental agreement from her shiny white Gucci tote. Another graduation gift. Val got one too, although hers was fire-engine red, her "signature" color.

Right away, I thought the posting was fishy. No way a house directly on the sand in ritzy Palm Key Island was only a few hundred bucks during the busy July Fourth holiday weekend. Something had to be wrong. My money was on a broken air conditioner, or maybe a gross, putrid smell like rotten eggs the owners couldn't get rid of. Not that I could be picky. The only reason we were getting a rental in the first place was because I couldn't afford a room at the fancy hotel where everyone else from school was staying. Somehow, Cam convinced her snobby twin sister Val and our other two best friends, Blake and Nia, to join us.

"I can't wait to see the inside!" Cam races toward the house, rolling her designer luggage behind her. Her initials "CGR"—for Camila Gisele Ramirez—are custom-painted in pale pink along the trim.

Her twin sister sprints after her. Val's colorful, vibrant dress billows behind her and catches the wind. Full and plush lips, painted her usual bold shade of red, are set in a pout as her stiletto Louboutins click along the pavement. Val bought the shoes yesterday even though she already has dozens, just like them, in her closet back home. What Valentina Lorraine Ramirez wants, she gets.

"I get first dibs!" Val yells as Cam opens the lockbox hanging on the front doorknob.

The rest of us watch from a safe distance by the car as the twins fight over the key. Val attempts to claim the biggest room in the house, even though she did none of the work to book our trip.

"What a brat," Nia mutters next to me, rolling her eyes. Nia has the most gorgeous eyes. Fox-shaped and the color of liquid onyx with lashes so long and thick you'd think they were extensions like Val has, but Nia's just lucky to be naturally stunning.

"Typical Val," Blake says. "Fifty bucks says Cam caves and gives her the master. She's such a pushover."

"Cam's just a people pleaser," I say, defensive of my best friend, even if I sort of agree. We all know Cam lets her twin get away with murder. "Besides, I'm sure all the rooms are nice."

"Whatever." Blake grabs her surfboard and throws it over one tan, muscular shoulder. Beautiful, beachy blonde hair bounces down her shapely backside. "Let's just unpack and change. I wanna hit the beach."

Nia gives me her suitcase to bring inside and pulls her iPhone out of her pocket to film her arrival for her social media followers. She smiles and waves at her "Nia-maniacs," as she likes to call them, her toothy grin even brighter than usual against her flawless dark skin. Nia just landed a brand deal with a toothpaste whitener, and they gave her a year's supply of product.

Just like Cam predicted, the rain stops, and the sun appears as Blake helps me unload the car. We go fast, hoping to have time to lay out before the sun goes down.

The six-hour drive from Bishop Lake took far longer than expected.

First, Val made us late by insisting on bringing two enormous suitcases, even though we didn't have room. Cam's begging didn't work; it wasn't until Blake threatened to throw Val's suitcases into the lake in front of the twins' house that Val recanted. Blake could do it, too. She was our state champion in both shot put and discus throw and has a full ride to Stanford in the fall.

Then, after waiting for Val to repack—and listening to her complain the whole time—we missed not one, but two, of the highway turnoffs. Combining that with Nia's demands we make multiple bathroom stops on account of the new flat-tummy tea she was drinking for an Instagram collab, it's a miracle we made it before nightfall.

"Jesus, Cam. What'd you put in here—bricks?" I ask, entering the foyer like a pack mule with Cam's massive nylon duffle slung over my shoulder and dragging Nia's bulging suitcase and my roller bag behind me. I drop Cam's bag down and wince, rubbing at my aching muscles.

"Sorry." She grins. "I didn't know what we'd need, so I packed everything. Beach towels. Sunscreen. Paddle ball," she says and then gestures around the place. "So what do you think? Cute, right?"

"Totally." I suppress a groan. Only my friends would call this place "cute."

The rental is huge. The apartment my mom and I share back home could fit in the foyer alone. The dark wooden floors are freshly mopped, and the rich cream walls, though bare, are crisp and bright, as if newly painted. Cool air blows from the vents above my head, so I know my fears of a broken air conditioner were unfounded. Best of all, no bad smells. If anything, it smells strongly of bleach, as if recently cleaned and scrubbed from top to bottom.

I take a few steps down the hall to find a formal dining room. Past that, the hallway opens up to reveal a gorgeous spiral staircase and spacious living room amply furnished with two overstuffed leather couches and matching recliners. On the other end of the house is a kitchen that butts up against floor-to-ceiling glass patio doors. A big deck and screened-in pool is out back. I can even see the beach from here.

Blake rushes into the living room and stands in front of the enormous fifty-five-inch flat screen TV. She grabs an iPad off one of the couches and starts pushing buttons until Lady Gaga comes on, and upbeat dance music plays from the wireless speakers overhead. Blake grins over at us and turns the volume up super high, singing along and shaking her booty to the beat.

Val inches toward the stairs. "So, I'm just gonna head up and unpack and—"

"I already told you," Cam says. "You can't take the master bedroom, Val. We're drawing numbers."

A strangled whine erupts from Val. "And I told you, *Camila*. I need the biggest room for all my clothes and makeup."

"It's fine with me," I say to make things easy for Cam. She's always caught in the middle, trying to appease Val's over-inflated sense of entitlement while not pissing off the rest of our friends.

"Me too. I don't even wear makeup," Nia says, coming up behind me. If I didn't know better, I might believe she's being sincere. She really doesn't need makeup. "Besides," she adds with a mean little smirk, "you're gonna need all the help you can get with that nasty little breakout on your chin."

Val pulls down her oversized designer sunglasses. "Very funny," she says, curling her freshly painted nails into a fist. "Keep it up and you're gonna need help for a black eye."

Val and Nia don't exactly get along. Cam told me they

used to be tight, but that all changed last year. Before then, the wide consensus was that Valentina Ramirez was by far the most beautiful girl at school. That all changed, seemingly overnight, after Nia's braces came off and her boobs grew in. Now they're rivals. I guess it also doesn't help that Nia just started dating Val's latest ex-boyfriend, Tyler Singh.

"Great, so we all agree Val can have the master," I say in my peppiest voice, trying to diffuse the tension. "Put me anywhere. I'm just happy to be here."

Blake frowns at me and I know what she's thinking—that I'm a pushover, too, just like Cam.

She's not wrong.

"I still can't believe your mom wouldn't give you enough money for the hotel," Val says. "The Seasider looked so lux, and the spa has those special hydro-facials from Sweden, and—"

"Val," Cam warns.

Val shrugs. "I mean, I guess this is fine, too."

"I'm really sorry. She's the worst," I say, shoving my hands into the pockets of my cut-off jean shorts and doing my best to ignore the winces of guilt. I don't like lying, but it's necessary. I've worked too hard building up a certain image for myself, and I'm not going to jeopardize that now. I know people say real friends should like you for the "real you," but those people don't hang out in the same circles I do.

My friends would never understand the truth. Their families are all *rich* rich. Nia's dad is a former professional basketball player, and Blake's parents own a real estate business, building homes all around the state. And the Ramirez family, well, they're one of the wealthiest families in the South. The twins' grandparents started the largest American-Spanish language television network in the country.

I used to be like them. My dad was a well-respected financial adviser in Miami. We had it all. The six-thousand square foot house. Luxury cars. Ski trips to Aspen in the winter and beach trips to Saint-Tropez in summer. Everything was perfect until Dad's firm got caught embezzling client funds. He went to prison, Mom filed for divorce, and we changed our last names and moved to central Florida. The only thing we had left was Dad's old 'Benz and enough money for a shitty, low-income housing apartment to start over.

I was lucky to get into Bishop Prep for senior year. My academic scholarship paid for school, but I had to get an afterschool job for everything else. Working at the Mouse Trap, a cheesy restaurant near Disney, gave me money to help Mom with bills and just enough left over to afford the right clothes and makeup so I could fit in. If it wasn't for Mr. Ramirez's black Am Ex helping with my share of the already cheap rental, there's no way I'd even be on this trip.

"I'll take this room," Blake says and plops her surfboard in front of the downstairs bedroom closest to the pool. I know from the pictures it has an insane ocean view. Blake might not go head-to-head with the twins, but she's not going to take scraps, either.

"I'll take whatever's left. I don't plan on sleeping here, anyway." Nia digs into her suitcase and pulls out a skimpy neon green bikini. "I'm gonna freshen up and meet the guys."

"Guys?" Val asks, her voice tight. "What guys?"

Nia struts toward the guest bathroom and closes the door without answering.

"That little *puta*!" Val turns to the rest of us, angry red blotches forming on her tanned, over-contoured cheeks.

"She's talking about Ty, isn't she?"

"Relax," Cam says. "It'll be fine."

"But I told you. I don't want to see that asshole!" Val hisses.

"What's the big deal?" Blake asks. "I thought you dumped Ty. And Nia likes him."

"Nia likes to piss me off—that's what Nia likes," Val grumbles.

"She's been like this ever since second grade. Remember when I won the Miss Orange Blossom Pageant instead of her? She always wants what I have. It's pathetic." A flash of panic flickers across her face and she turns, grabbing me by the elbow. "You don't think Ty really likes her, do you? I mean, she's not even that pretty."

"Oh no." I hold my hands up and back away. "I'm not getting in the middle of this."

"Ugh, you're so spineless, Riley," Val says and turns hopefully to Blake.

"You're joking, right?" Blake asks. "Nia's smoking hot."

She starts changing out of her tracksuit right there in the hallway and puts on a sexy one-piece that runs so high up her backside it might as well be a thong. Blake has an amazing body from sports. She's not afraid to show it off, either. To boys. To girls. She doesn't discriminate.

"Oh, never mind." Val makes a dismissive face at her.

"You'd screw anyone."

"Forget Ty, would you?" Blake proceeds to throw sunscreen, towels, and a football into her beach bag. "This place is gonna be crawling with hotties. You don't bring sand to the beach."

Val seems to consider this for a moment, licking at her bottom lip thoughtfully.

"You know what? You're absolutely right," she says. "And at least if that dirtball is here, that means Seb's coming." She lets out a dreamy moan. "He's soooooo sexy."

My chest flutters at his name. Sebastian Ramos is easily the best-looking guy in school: dark green eyes that turn colors with his mood, six-one inches of muscled, ripped body that just won't quit, and a Colombian accent so hot he could melt ice. The boy is charisma incarnate.

Unfortunately, he's off limits. Val's been in love with him for years.

"Hate to break it to you, babe, but that's never gonna happen," Blake says.

Val crosses her arms over her chest. "You don't know that."

"Yeah, I do. You've been trying to get back with Seb ever since he dumped your ass in ninth grade," Blake says. "If it was gonna happen, it would've happened by now."

"That's not—"

"It's okay," Blake says, cutting Val off with a knowing grin. "He doesn't like me either, and trust me, I've tried many, many times. Such a shame. I bet he's a great kisser. And other things." Cam and I giggle as Blake pretends to hump her surfboard. "Sadly, Seb's a sucker for those nice, quiet, do-gooder types. Like our little Ri Ri over here…"

"Oh no. Seb and I are just friends," I say, my cheeks heating. Sebastian doesn't like me like that. He's made that painfully obvious, which is probably a good thing. Val would lose her mind if Sebastian and I ever got together.

We'd been close all year, it's true. Sitting next to each other in class and studying in the library. I went to as many of his soccer games as I could. Sebastian was the star of our school's team with a full ride to Princeton. Of course, I had a huge crush on him—like everyone else in school.

There was a time I thought he might have feelings for me too, right after he kissed me at Nia's graduation party, but the next day he acted like nothing happened. He's avoided me ever since. I had no idea he was coming this weekend. I wonder if—

"Forget Sebastian Ramos." Cam gives me a sympathetic look. She's the only one I told about the kiss. "I've got someone way better and—good news—he just texted he's here."

"Who?" I ask, my chest tightening. I'm pretty sure I know the answer, and I'm not nearly as excited as she is.

"Jonathan?"

"Yes!" she shrieks.

Cam has been trying to set me up with Jonathan Chang all year, always trying to get us together every time he's home from college on break. He's a year older than us and cute enough, but… I don't know. He's so awkward. Always getting too close and trying to touch me. Always staring at me for too long or when he thinks I don't see. He's never crossed the line or anything, it's just… Something about him creeps me out a bit. The girls used to be tight with his younger sister, Jordyn.

She died last summer.

Want more?

Mean Girls meets Scream in this heart-pounding psychological thriller filled with danger, twists, and shocking betrayals where nothing is as it seems. Don't miss this bestselling book in the Dark Seasons Thriller Series—perfect for fans of '90s horror movies and books by Holly Jackson, Frieda McFadden, and Natasha Preston!

GET SUMMER RENTAL NOW!

CONNECT MORE WITH REKTOK

I hope you loved *Salem's Fall*, and if so, I would be very grateful if you could write a review. I'd love to hear what you think, and reviews online make such a big difference in helping new readers discover one of my books for the very first time.

If you'd like to keep up to date with me and be the first to know about any new releases, bookish news, and giveaways, please sign up at the link below. I'll never share your email address, and you can unsubscribe at any time.

Sign up here >>> www.RektokRoss.com

Please know I also adore hearing from readers. You can contact me anytime at my email at RektokRoss@gmail.com or through any of my social media channels (@RektokRoss, everywhere). And if you like readalongs and talking all things bookish, you can join my Facebook reader group *The Book Nook by Rektok Ross*.

Thanks so much for all your support, and I hope to hear from you soon!

Rektok Ross

AUTHOR'S NOTE TO THE READER

Dear Reader,

First and foremost, thank you for reading *Salem's Fall*. I know your time is precious, and there are a million other books you could be reading, so it means the world to me that you chose this one. If you've been with me since my debut thriller *Ski Weekend*, I want to give an especially huge thank you for sticking with me through all four "Seasons Series" books. What a wild ride it's been—and how fitting to close things out with my favorite season of all: fall. From Halloween to haunted houses, pumpkins to sweater weather, fall has always held a special place in my heart. It only made sense to wrap up this four-book thriller journey (*Ski Weekend*, *Summer Rental*, *Spring Harvest*, and now *Salem's Fall*) with a story full of moody New England vibes, cult secrets, and gothic chills.

But *Salem's Fall* is more than just spooky atmosphere. For this book, I wanted to return to my roots as a trial attorney. Though I practiced commercial litigation and IP law (not criminal law like James), it was fun—and a little surreal—revisiting life as a young associate. It reminded me just how tough it was being a young woman in a field that was predominantly older and male. There was always the unspoken pressure to be perfect, to work harder, to prove I belonged. I burned the candle at both ends for years—at the cost of friendships, life experiences, and even my health. In *Salem's Fall*, I wanted to explore not only the external obstacles women experience in high-powered, male-dominated industries, but also the internal ones so many of us face in the business world, regardless of gender. The perfectionism, the guilt, the constant need to achieve. What does success really mean, and at what cost does it come?

As for the plot? Confession time: I've always been a little

obsessed with dark romance—even before I knew what that term meant. I grew up crushing on the Goblin King in *Labyrinth*, swooning over Damon Salvatore in *The Vampire Diaries*, and secretly shipping Clarice and Hannibal in *Silence of the Lambs*. I remember watching that movie and thinking: What if Lecter was terrifying and hot? What would that story look like? *Salem's Fall* is my answer to that question. And, of course, as a forever fan of *The Craft*, *The Skulls*, and *The Secret Circle* books, I couldn't resist adding witches, secret societies, and spooky cult vibes to the mix.

So pour yourself a pumpkin spice latte, curl up under a flannel blanket, and enjoy the ride. And if you walk away from this book with chills, questions, or an intense desire to Google New England cults at 3 a.m.—well, my job here is done. :)

All my best,

Rektok Ross

ACKNOWLEDGMENTS

As always, thank you first and foremost to my readers. You are everything, and I truly appreciate every single review, post, share, DM, TikTok/Reel, and email from you. Connecting with you and building my reader community is the greatest joy. Special thanks to my Street Team—you guys are the best! —and also to all the "Book Nookers" in my Facebook book club and reader group *"The Book Nook by Rektok Ross."* (We're always looking for new members! Come join us—I've got links to join on all my socials, and you can always email or DM me too!)

Huge thanks to my editorial team: the fabulous Amy Tipton, Beth Lynne, Crystal Blanton, and Tandy Boese. Couldn't do this without you.

Continued thanks go out to all my friends in the publishing and entertainment industries for your support of my work. Thank you always to the incredible booksellers, librarians, educators, and media who continue to champion my books. I see you and appreciate you. Special thank you, as always, to all the dear friends who are so supportive of me and this journey—you know who you are (because I've named most of you already in prior books, lol!)

Finally, a huge thanks goes to my family. To my mom, as always, the one who made me a reader and fangirl first. Dad, Lance, and L, for all the pep talks and love, and all the DeCesares—thank you for always cheering me on. Derek, Dani, and Ro—love you guys so much! To Michael, the one who makes this all possible and has become the first reader of all my books now. (Whether he likes it or not.) And last, but certainly not least, to my furry writing buddies—Ghost and Blair.

ABOUT THE AUTHOR

Author photo © Agency Moanalani Jeffrey

Liani Kotcher (writing as Rektok Ross) is a trial attorney turned award-winning and bestselling author, screenwriter, and producer. An avid reader since childhood, Liani writes exactly the kind of books she loves to escape into herself: exciting thrillers with strong female leads, swoonworthy love interests, and life-changing moments. She graduated from the University of Florida and obtained her juris doctorate at the University of Miami School of Law. Originally from South Florida, she currently splits her time between San Francisco, Los Angeles, and Las Vegas with her husband and her dogs. She is the recipient of several awards, including the American Fiction Awards, IAN Book of the Year Awards, and the Chanticleer Dante Rossetti Book Awards. You can find her online at @RektokRoss and her website, www.RektokRoss.com.

Join her Readers Group:
www.facebook.com/groups/thebooknookbyrektokross/

Made in the USA
Middletown, DE
21 September 2025